Seraph of the End
—VAMPIRE REIGN—

8

STORY BY **Takaya Kagami**
ART BY **Yamato Yamamoto**
STORYBOARDS BY **Daisuke Furuya**

CHARACTERS

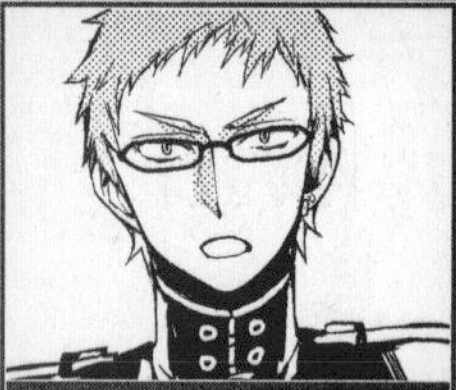

SHIHO KIMIZUKI

Yuichiro's friend. Smart but abrasive. His Cursed Gear is Kiseki-o, twin blades.

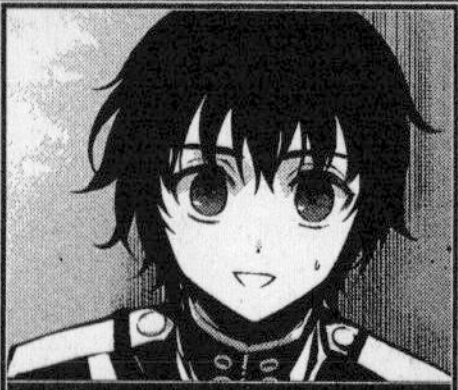

YOICHI SAOTOME

Yuichiro's friend. His sister was killed by a vampire. His Cursed Gear is Gekkouin, a bow.

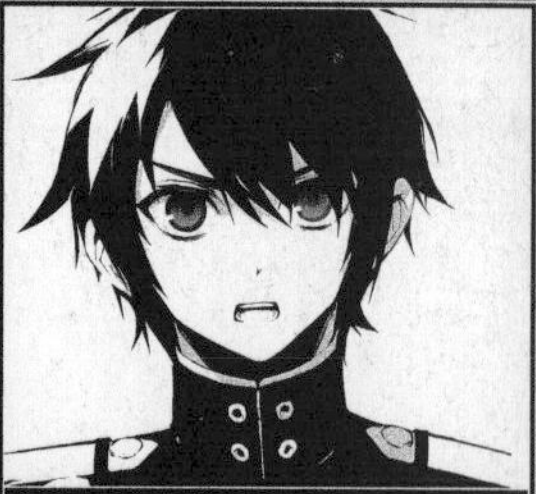

YUICHIRO HYAKUYA

A boy who escaped from the vampire capital, he has both great kindness and a great desire for revenge. Lone wolf. His Cursed Gear is Asuramaru, a katana.

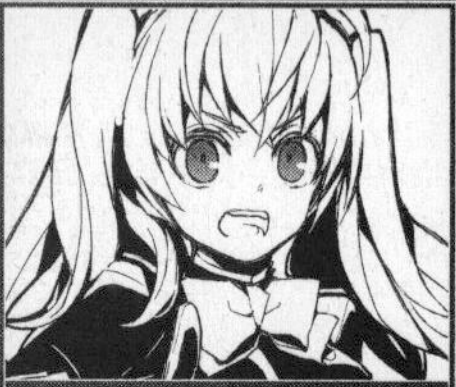

MITSUBA SANGU

An elite soldier who has been part of the Moon Demon Company since age 13. Bossy. Her Cursed Gear is Tenjiryu, a giant axe.

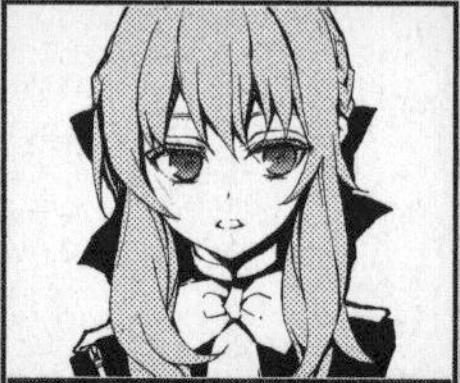

SHINOA HIRAGI

Guren's subordinate and Yuichiro's surveillance officer. Member of the illustrious Hiragi family. Her Cursed Gear is Shikama Doji, a scythe.

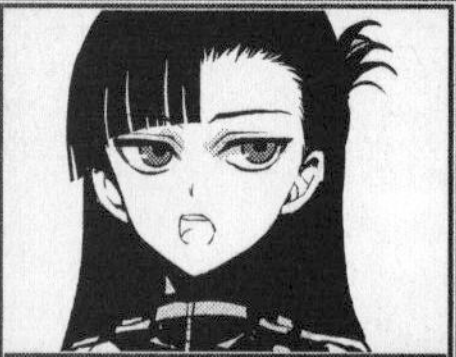

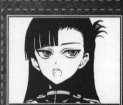

SHIGURE YUKIMI

A 2nd Lieutenant and Guren's subordinate along with Sayuri. Very calm and collected.

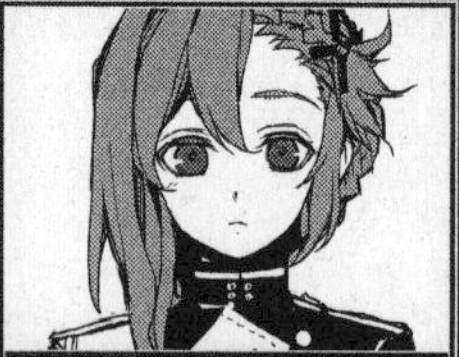

SAYURI HANAYORI

A 2nd Lieutenant and Guren's subordinate. She's devoted to Guren.

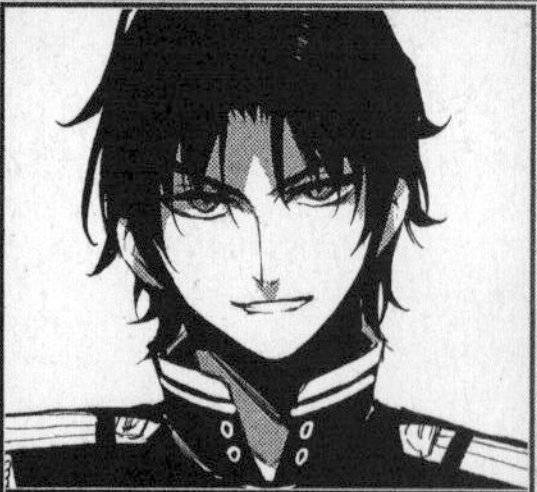

GUREN ICHINOSE

Lieutenant Colonel of the Moon Demon Company, a Vampire Extermination Unit. He recruited Yuichiro into the Japanese Imperial Demon Army. His Cursed Gear is Mahiru-no-yo, a katana.

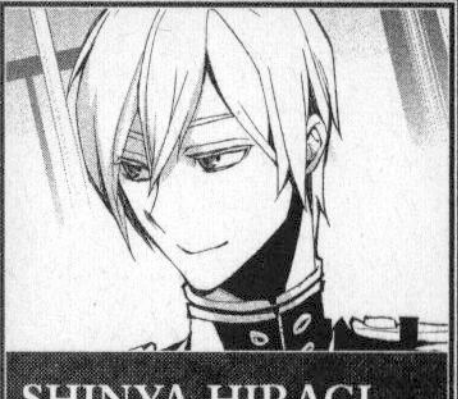

SHINYA HIRAGI

A Major General and an adopted member of the Hiragi Family. He was Mahiru Hiragi's fiancé.

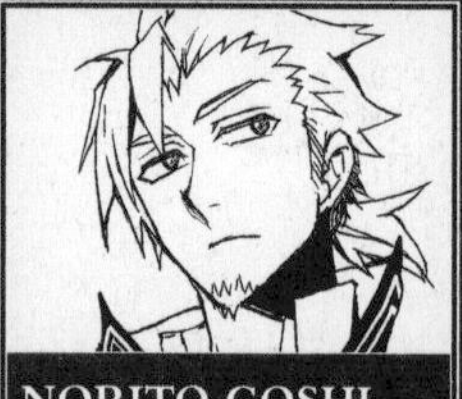

NORITO GOSHI

A Colonel and a member of the illustrious Goshi family. He has been friends with Guren since high school.

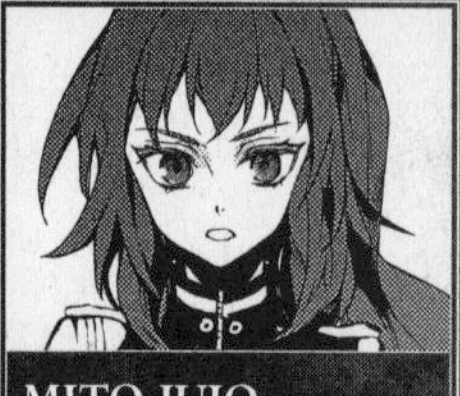

MITO JUJO

A Colonel and a member of the illustrious Jujo family. She has been friends with Guren since high school.

KRUL TEPES
Queen of the Vampires and a Third Progenitor.

MIKAELA HYAKUYA
Yuichiro's best friend. He was supposedly killed but has come back to life as a vampire.

LUCAL WESKER
A Fifteenth Progenitor vampire who rules a section of Nagoya.

CROWLEY EUSFORD
A Thirteenth Progenitor vampire.

FERID BATHORY
A Seventh Progenitor vampire, he killed Mikaela.

STORY

A mysterious virus decimates the human population, and vampires claim dominion over the world. Yuichiro and his adopted family of orphans are kept as vampire fodder in an underground city until the day Mikaela, Yuichiro's best friend, plots an ill-fated escape for the orphans. Only Yuichiro survives and reaches the surface.

Four years later, Yuichiro enters into the Moon Demon Company, a Vampire Extermination Unit in the Japanese Imperial Demon Army, to enact his revenge. There he gains Asuramaru, a demon-possessed weapon capable of killing vampires. Along with his agreement Yoichi, Shinoa, Kimizuki and Mitsuba, Yuichiro deploys to Shinjuku with orders to thwart a vampire attack.

In battle against the vampires, Yuichiro discovers that not only is his friend Mikaela alive, but he has also been turned into a vampire. After, Yuichiro undergoes further training and not only grows stronger as a fighter, but also becomes much closer to his squad mates.

Now, the war between vampires and humans grows ever closer. Yuichiro and his friends head to Nagoya to rendezvous with Guren to launch an attack on the vampire nobles who reside there. Yuichiro and his squad must now eliminate their target, Fifteenth Progenitor Lucal Wesker. Can they manage to work together and fulfill their orders?

Seraph of the End
VAMPIRE REIGN

Seraph of the End
—VAMPIRE REIGN—

8

CONTENTS

CHAPTER 28
Livestock Revolt 005

CHAPTER 29
Who's Pulling the Strings? 051

CHAPTER 30
Sword of Justice 097

CHAPTER 31
Shinya and Guren 143

Chapter 28 Livestock Revolt

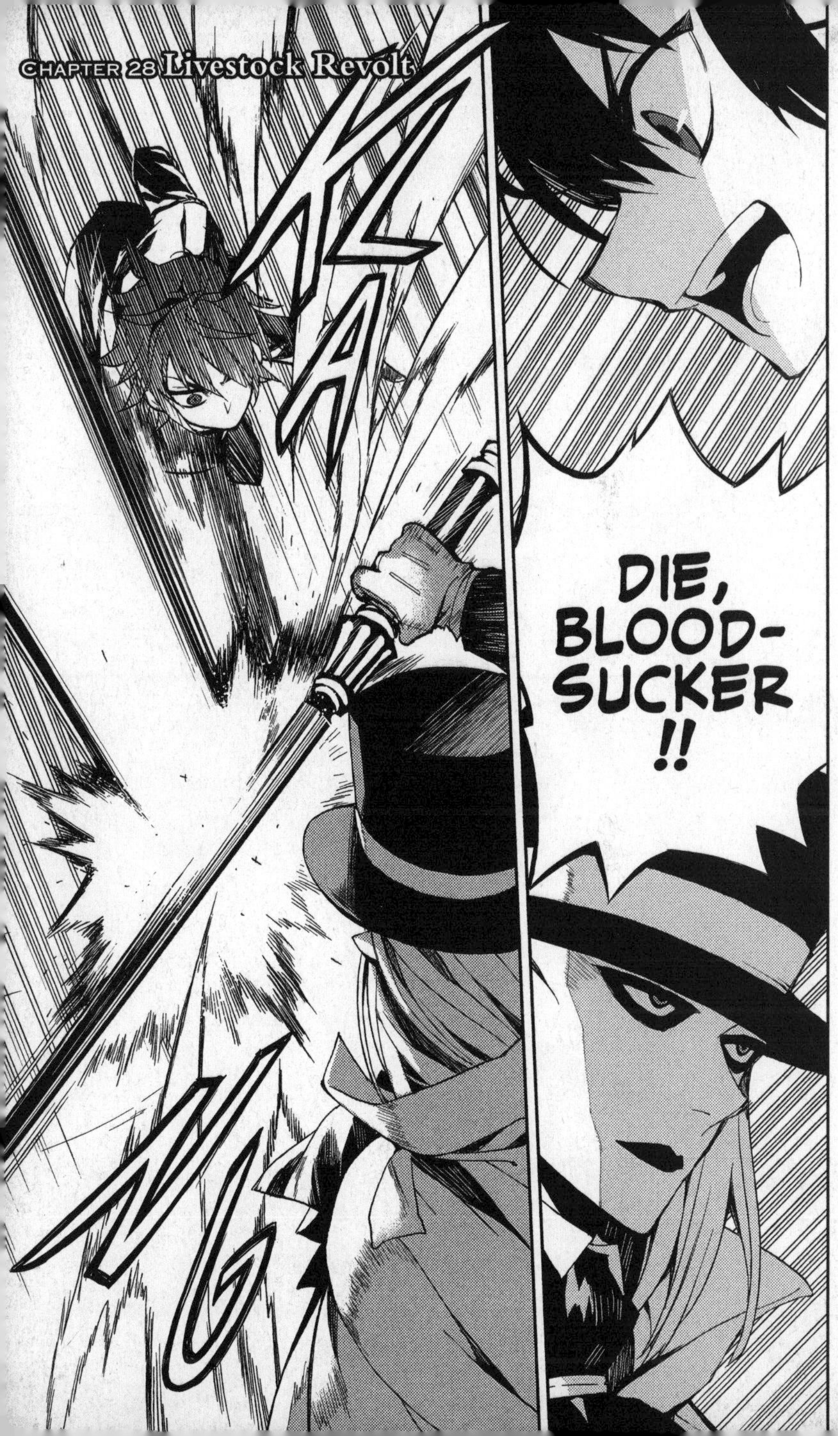
DIE, BLOOD-SUCKER!!
KLA
NG

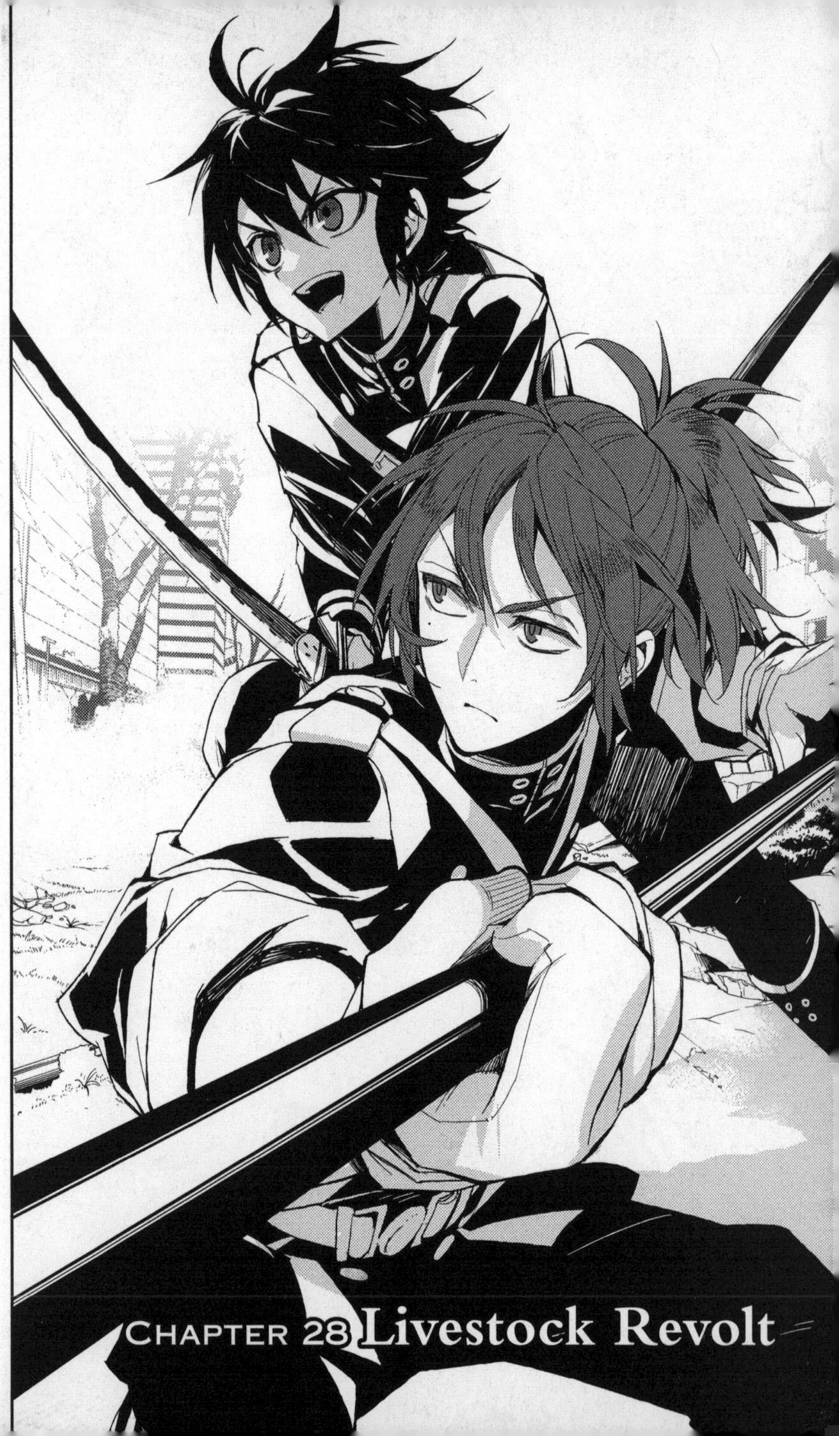

Chapter 28 Livestock Revolt

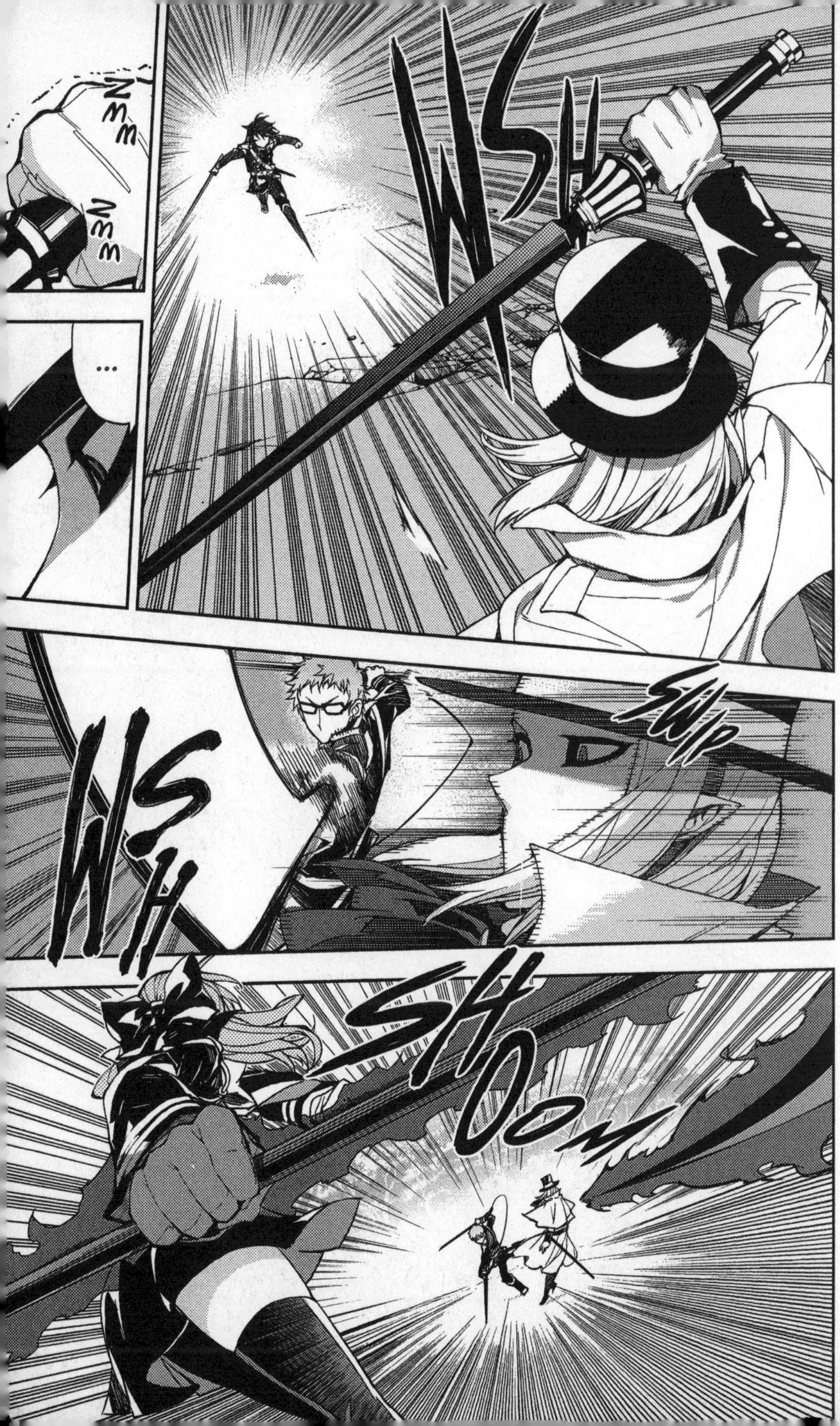
WSH
ZMM
ZMM
...
SWIP
WSH
SHOOM

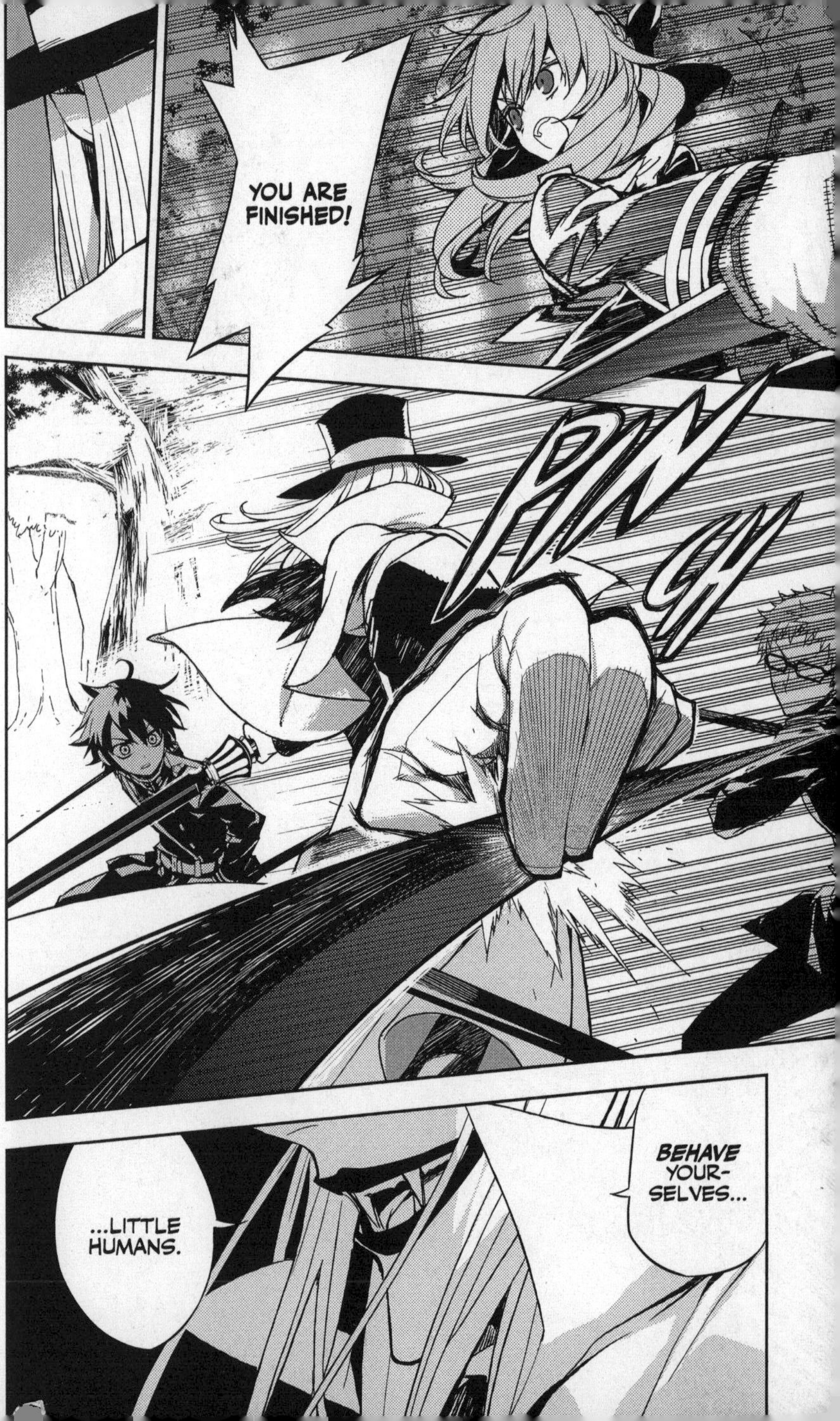
YOU ARE FINISHED!
PINCH
BEHAVE YOUR-SELVES...
...LITTLE HUMANS.

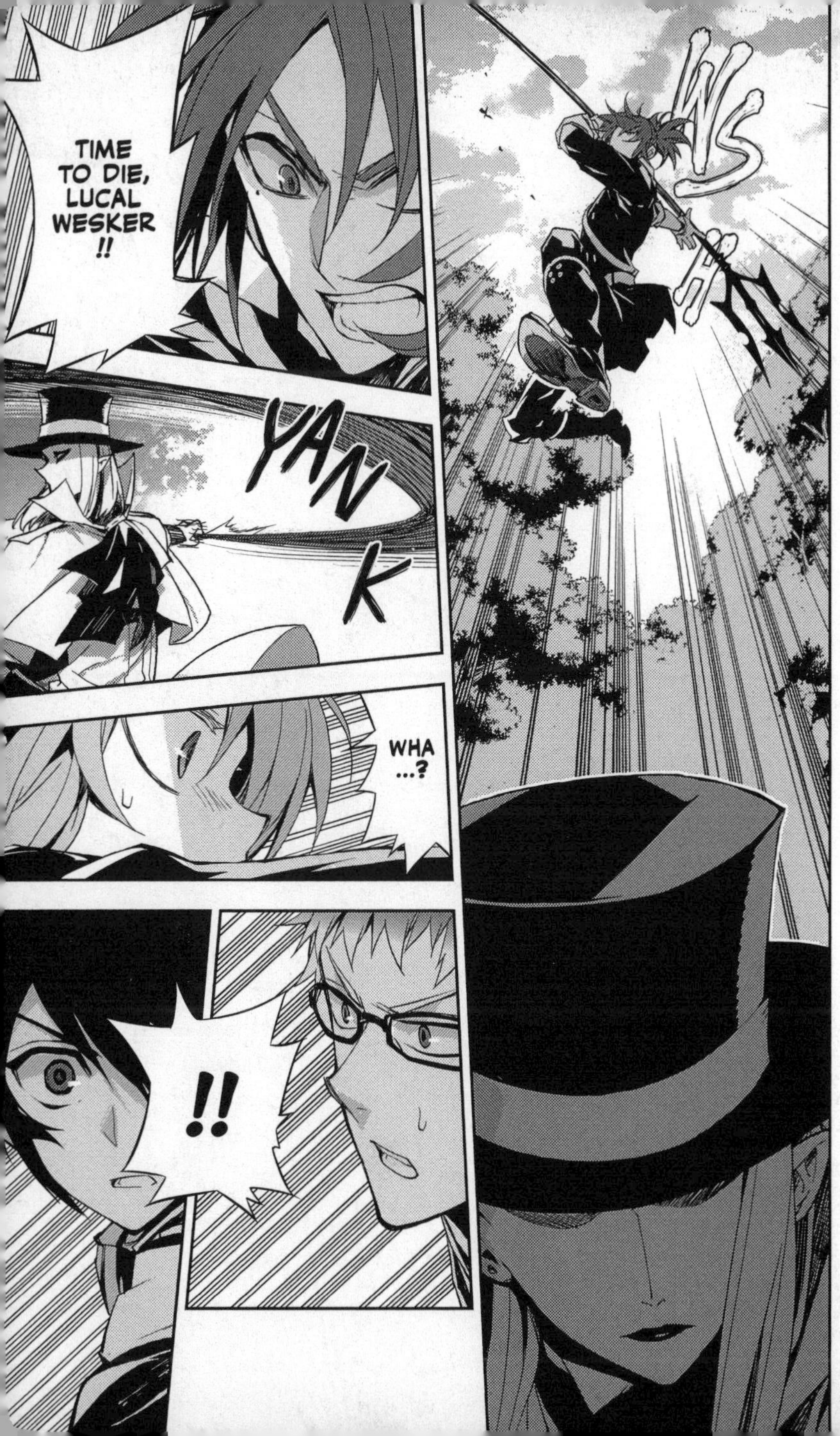
TIME TO DIE, LUCAL WESKER!!
YANK
WHA...?
!!

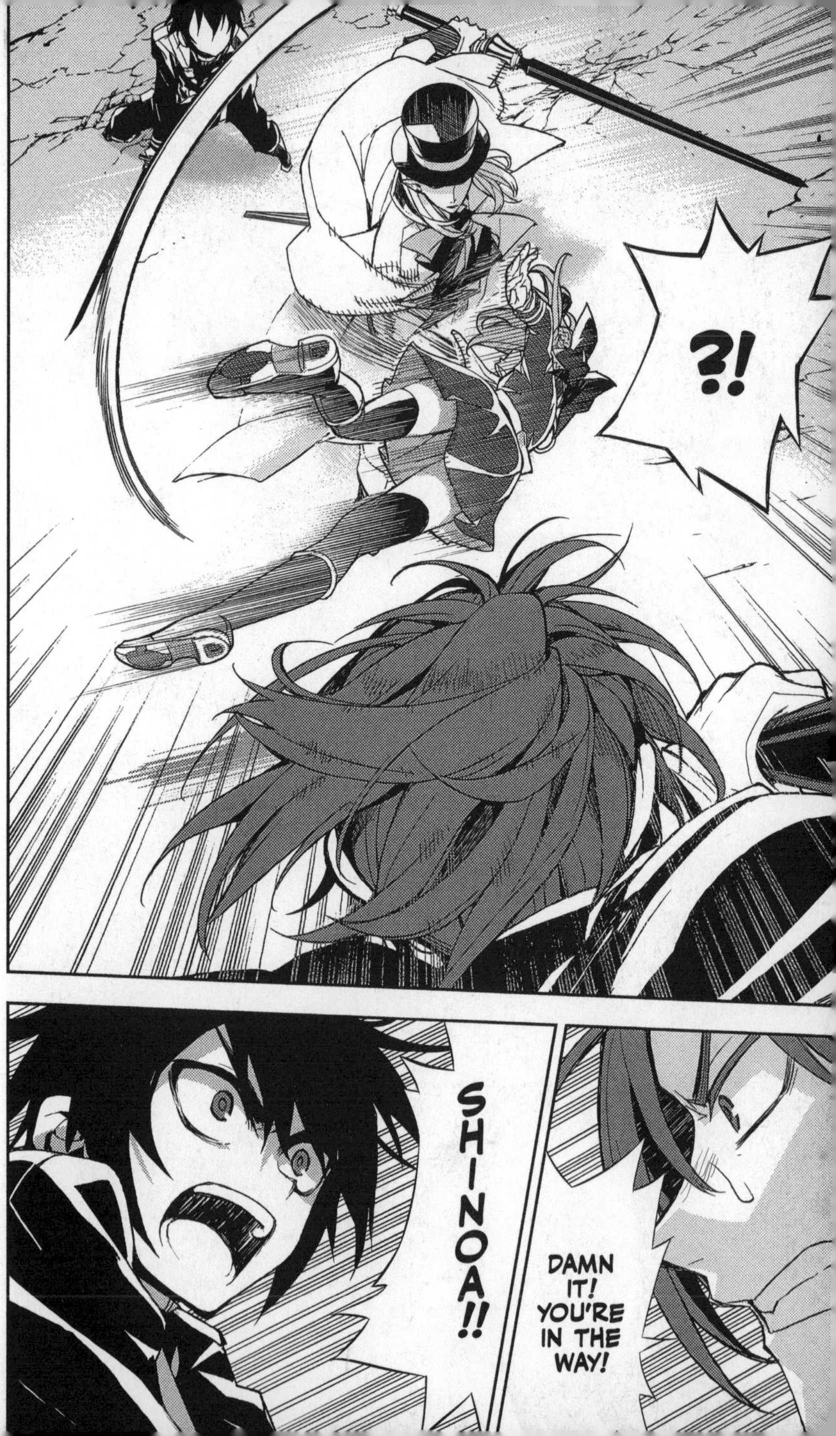
?!
DAMN IT! YOU'RE IN THE WAY!
SHINOA!!

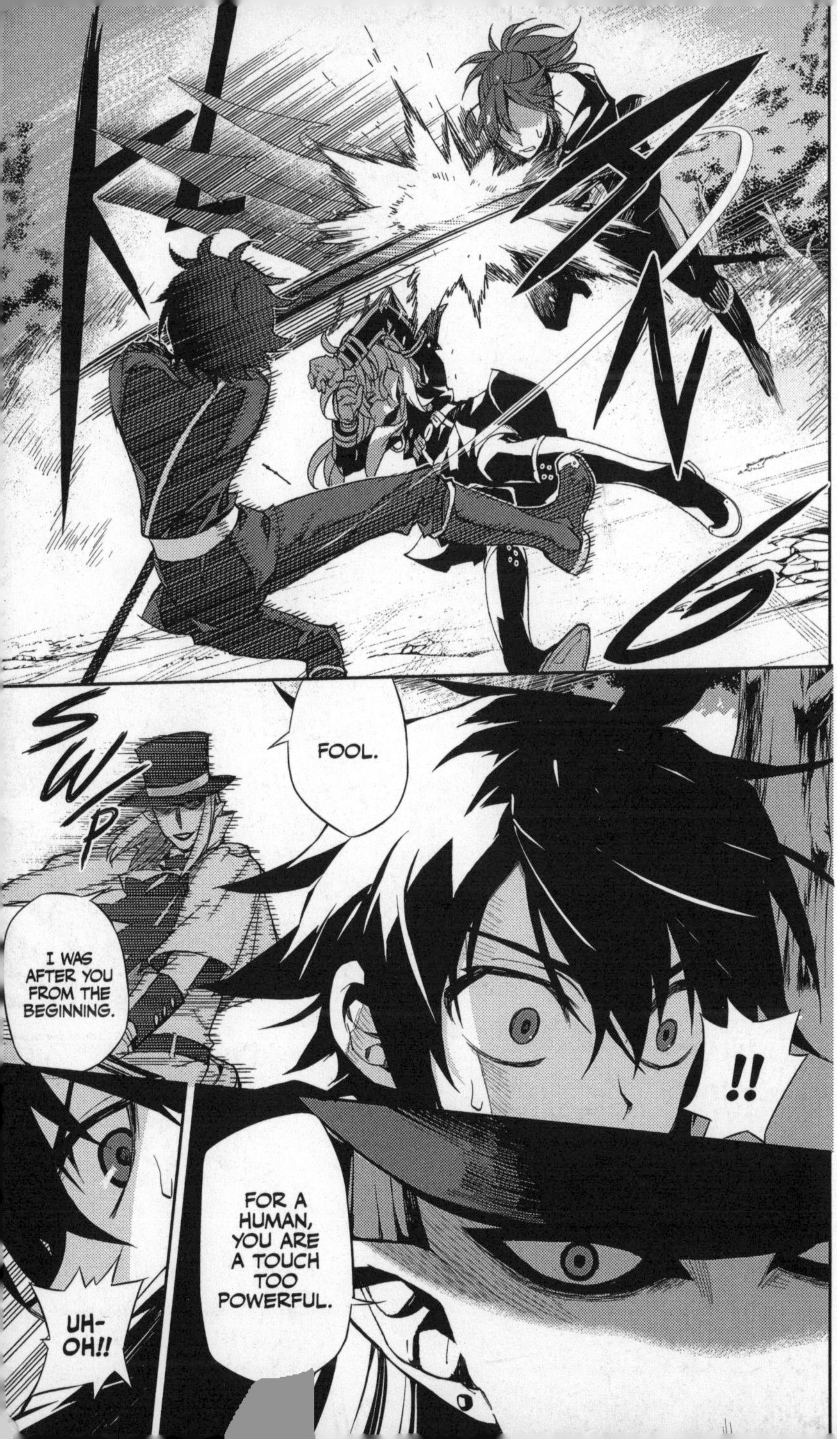
FOOL.
SWIP
I WAS AFTER YOU FROM THE BEGINNING.
!!
FOR A HUMAN, YOU ARE A TOUCH TOO POWERFUL.
UH-OH!!

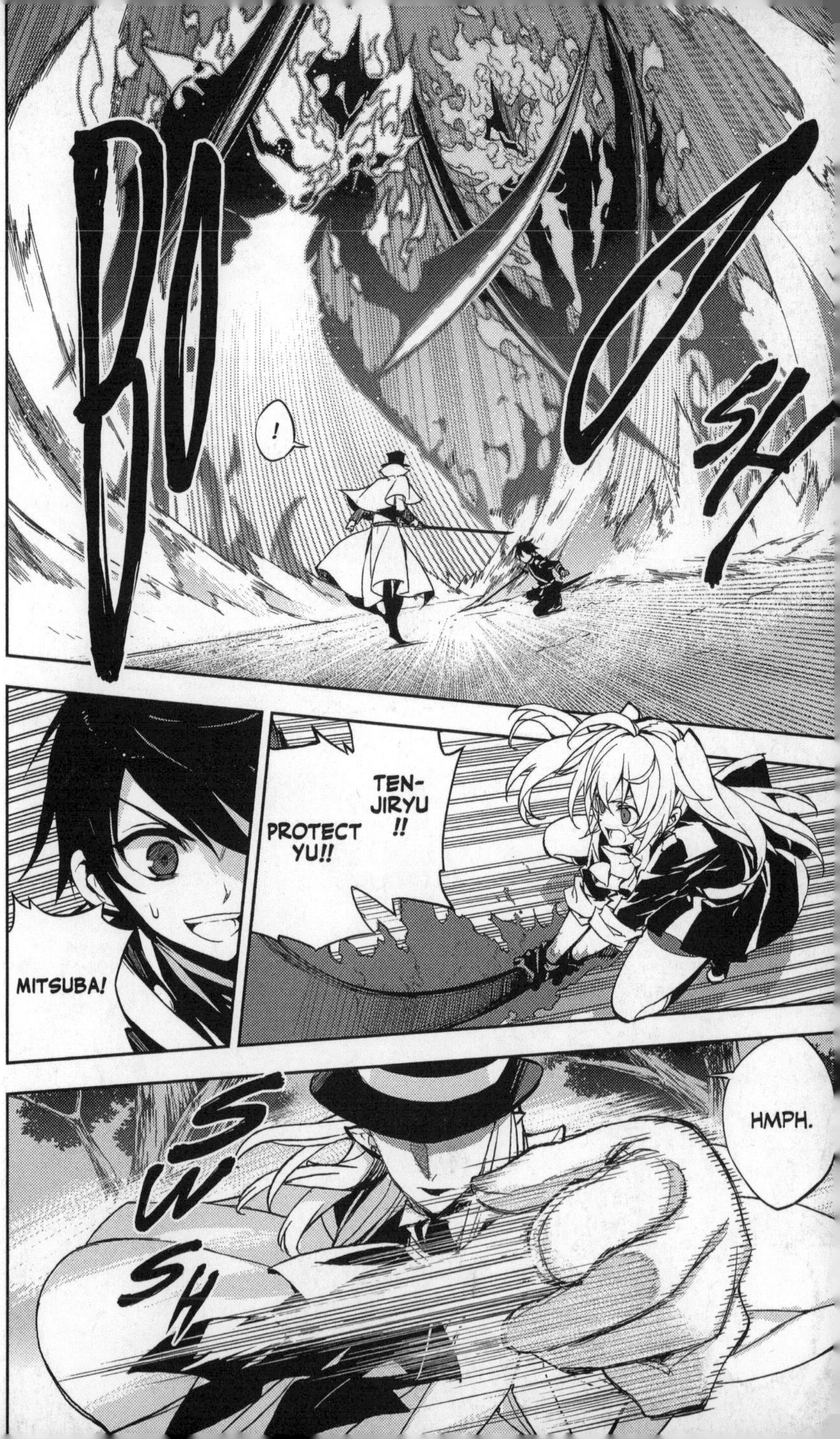
BOOSH
!
TEN-JIRYU!!
PROTECT YU!!
MITSUBA!
HMPH.
SWSH

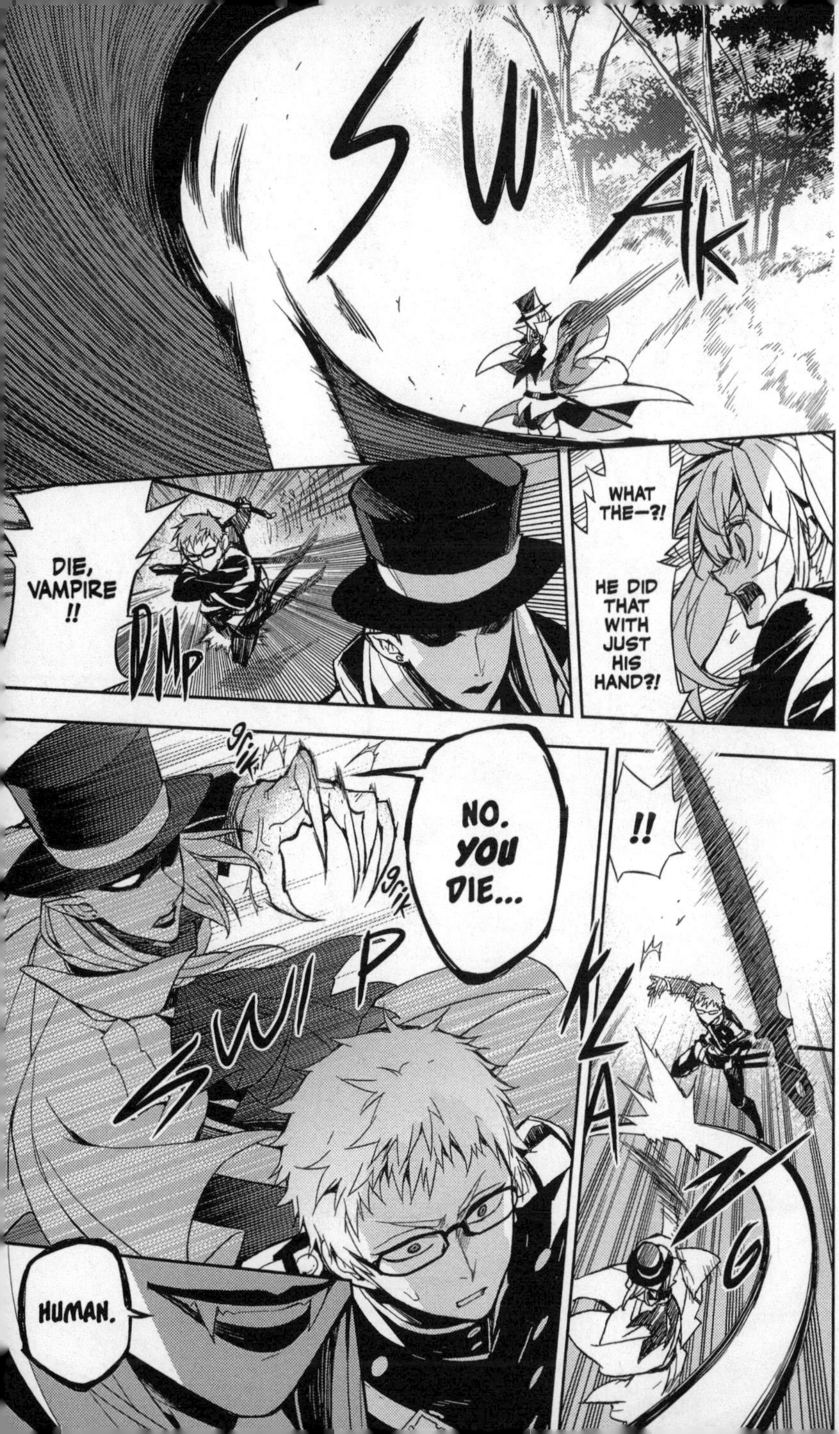
SWAK
WHAT THE—?!
HE DID THAT WITH JUST HIS HAND?!
DIE, VAMPIRE!!
DMP
!!
KLANG
grik
NO. YOU DIE...
grik
SWIP
HUMAN.

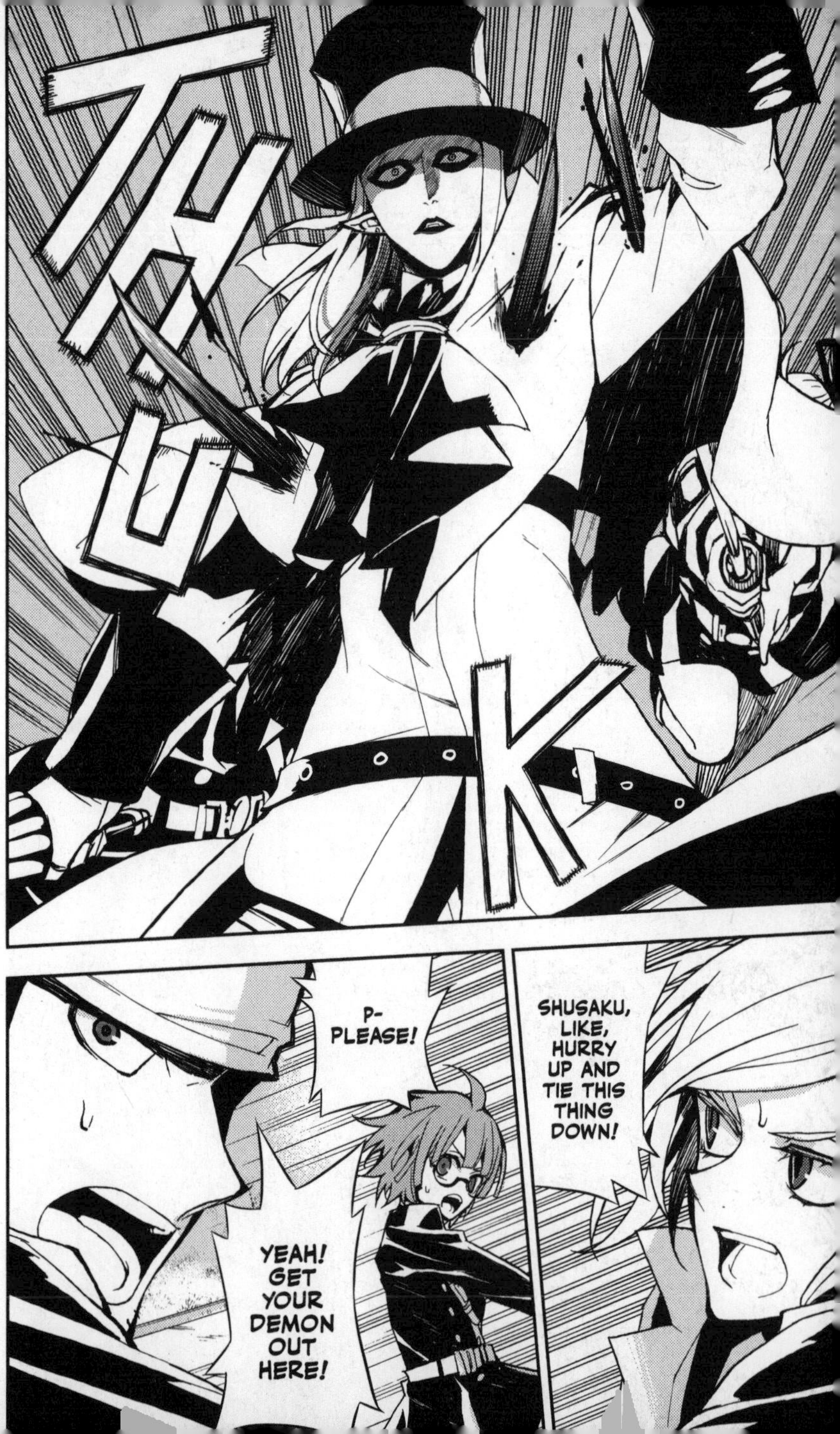
THUK
SHUSAKU, LIKE, HURRY UP AND TIE THIS THING DOWN!
P-PLEASE!
YEAH! GET YOUR DEMON OUT HERE!

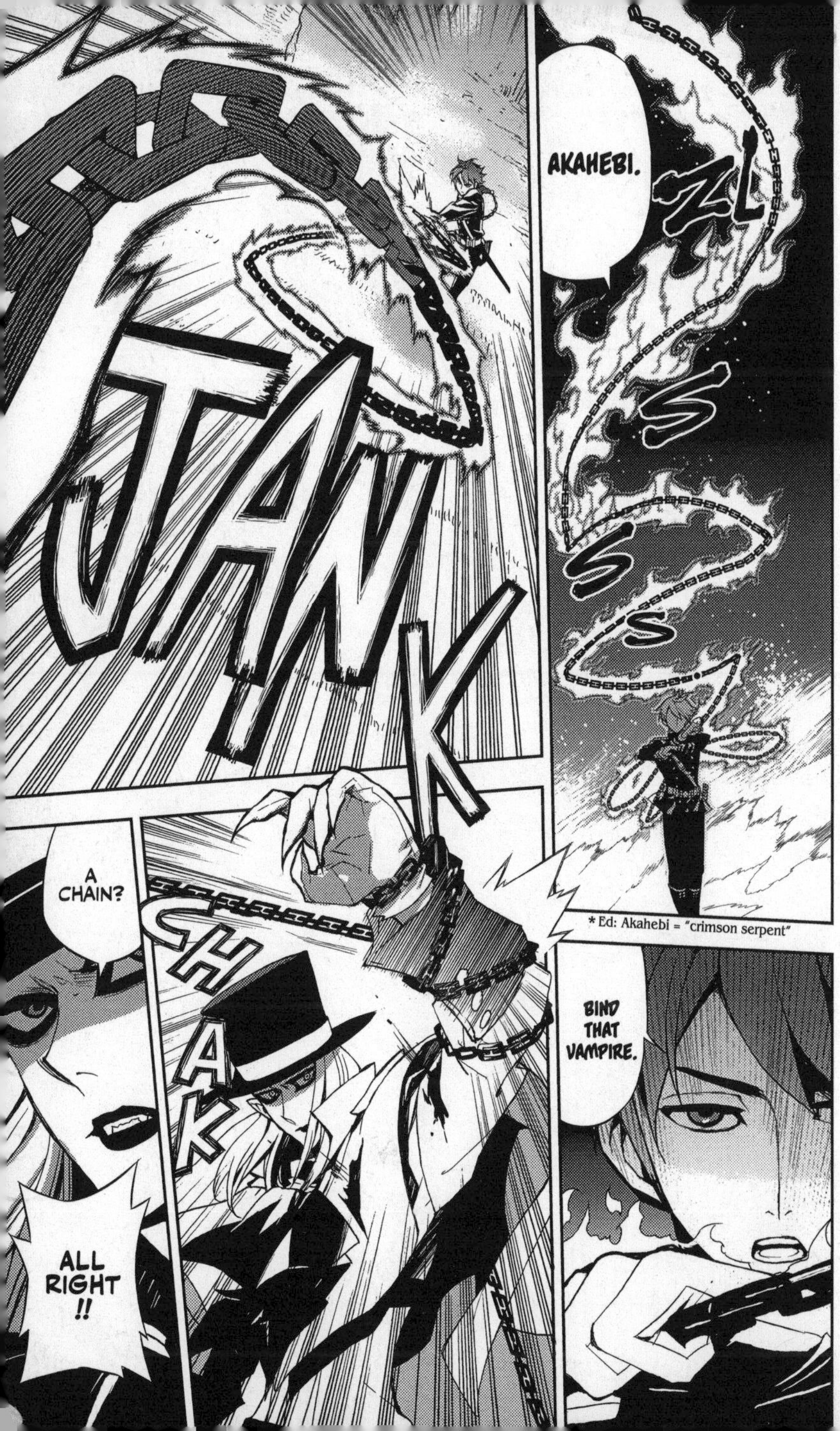
AKAHEBI.
ZL
SSSS
JANK
BIND THAT VAMPIRE.
CHAK
A CHAIN?
ALL RIGHT!!
* Ed: Akahebi = "crimson serpent"

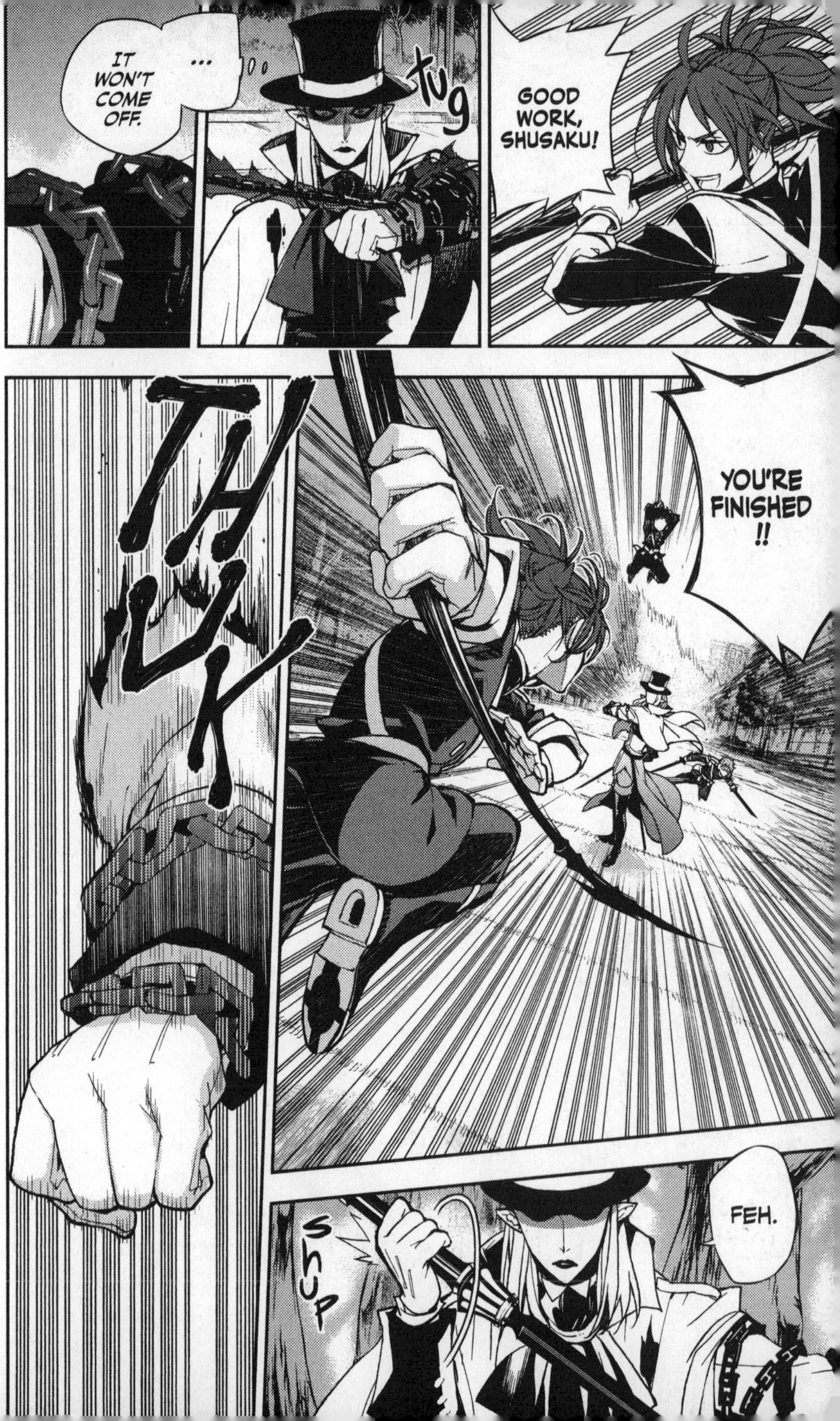
GOOD WORK, SHUSAKU!
tug
...
IT WON'T COME OFF.
YOU'RE FINISHED!!
THUK
FEH.
SHUP

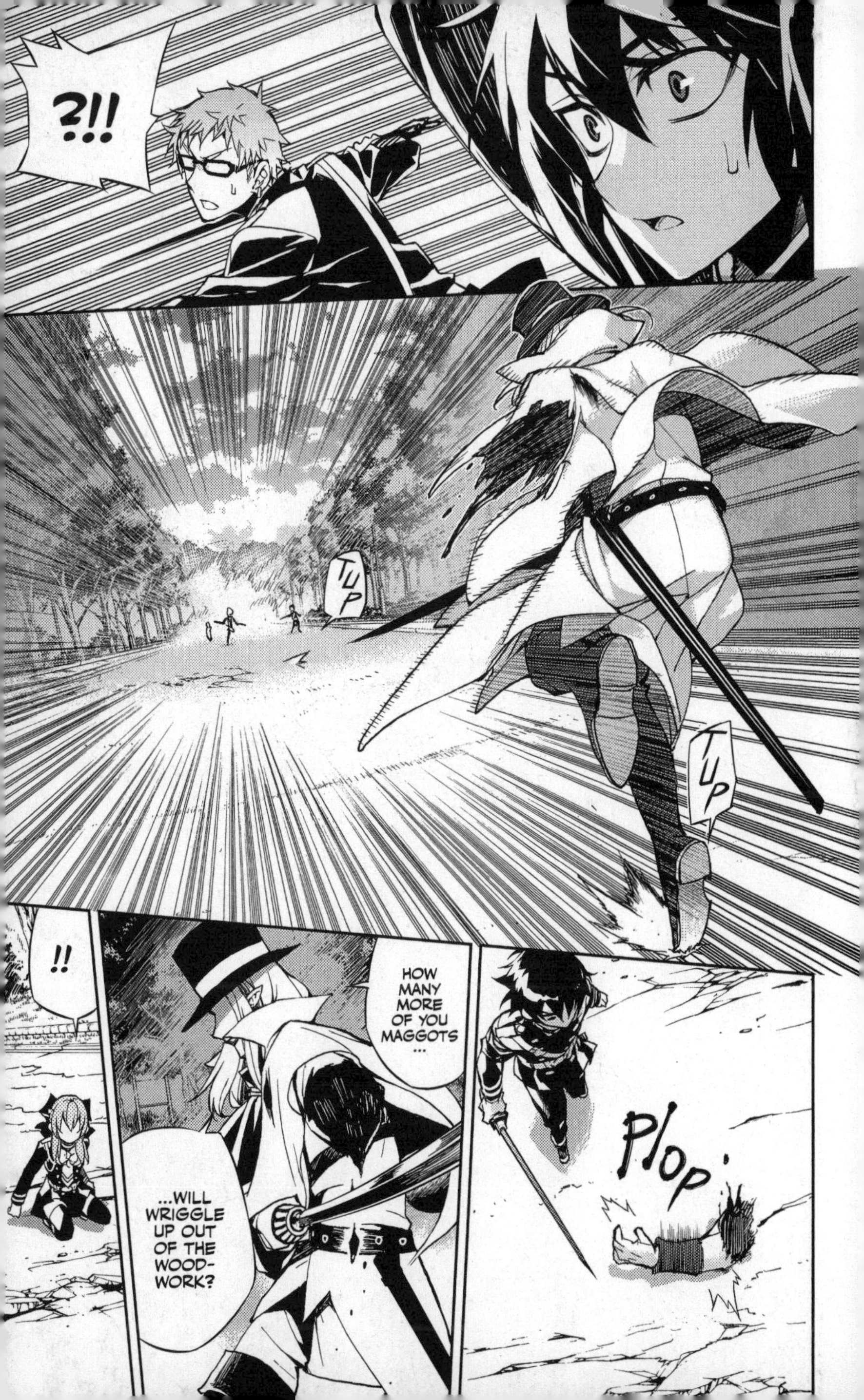
?!!
TUP
TUP
PLOP
HOW MANY MORE OF YOU MAGGOTS...
...WILL WRIGGLE UP OUT OF THE WOOD-WORK?
!!

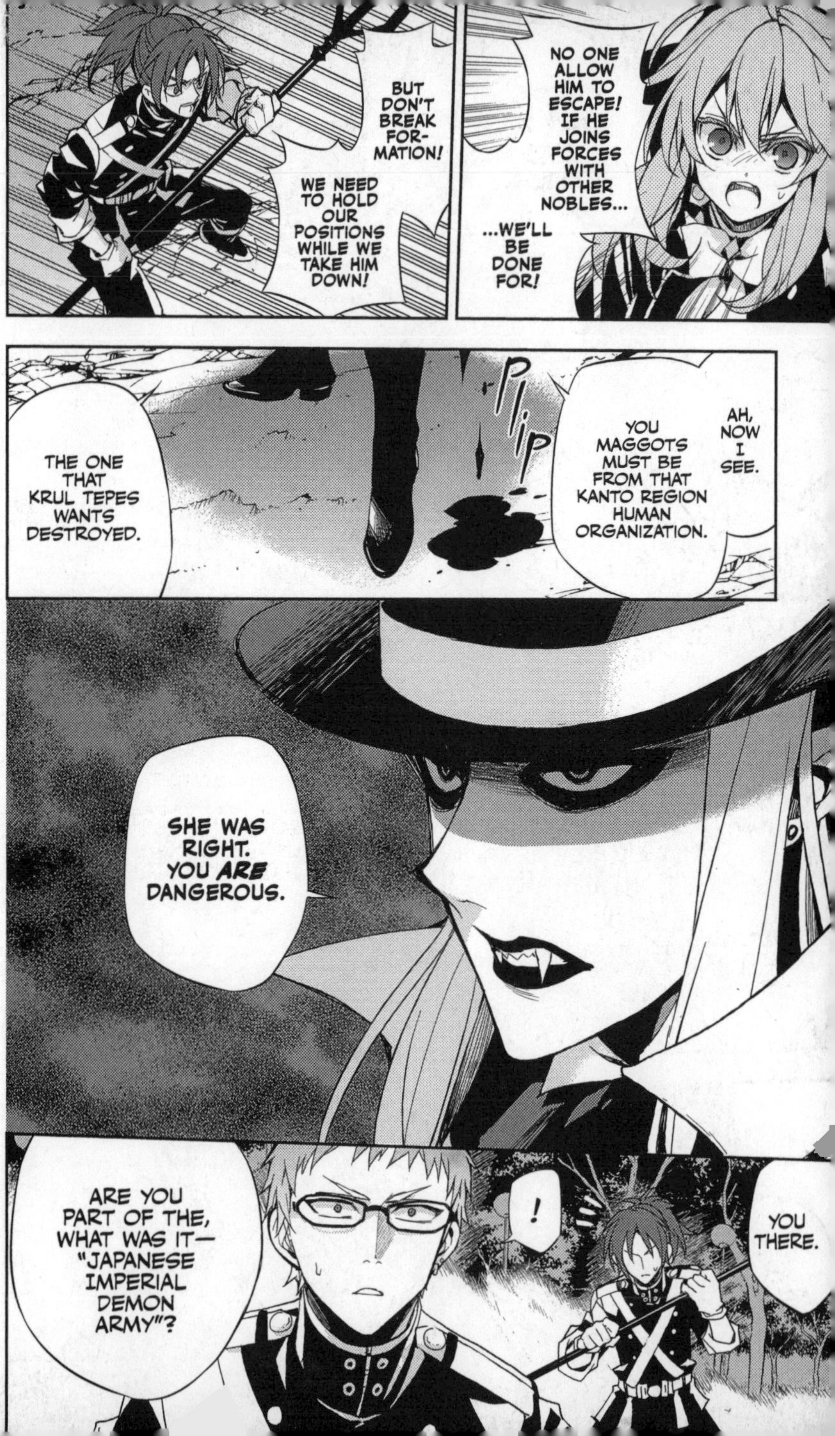
NO ONE ALLOW HIM TO ESCAPE! IF HE JOINS FORCES WITH OTHER NOBLES...
...WE'LL BE DONE FOR!
BUT DON'T BREAK FOR-MATION!
WE NEED TO HOLD OUR POSITIONS WHILE WE TAKE HIM DOWN!
AH, NOW I SEE.
YOU MAGGOTS MUST BE FROM THAT KANTO REGION HUMAN ORGANIZATION.
PLIP
THE ONE THAT KRUL TEPES WANTS DESTROYED.
SHE WAS RIGHT. YOU *ARE* DANGEROUS.
YOU THERE.
!
ARE YOU PART OF THE, WHAT WAS IT— "JAPANESE IMPERIAL DEMON ARMY"?

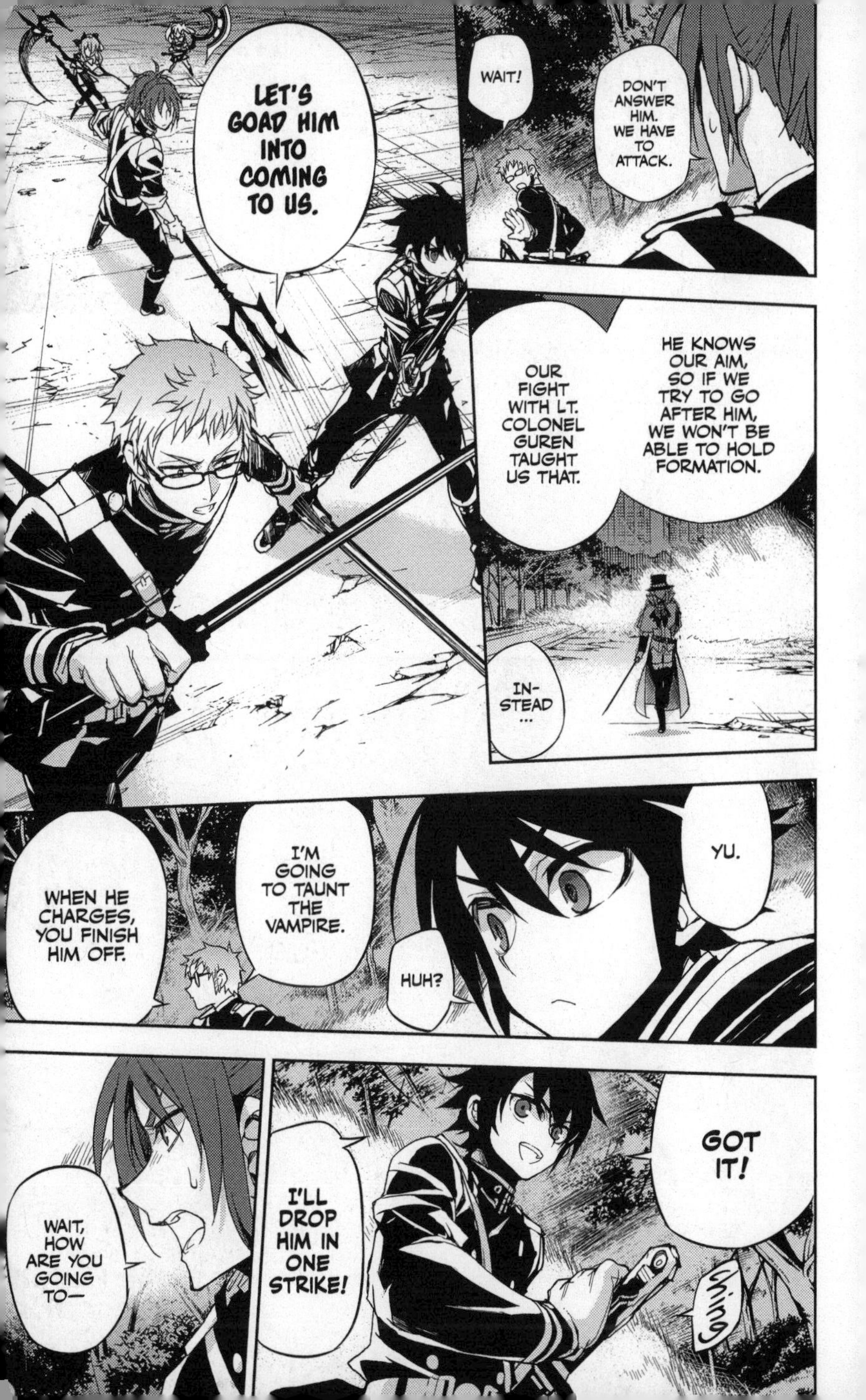
DON'T ANSWER HIM. WE HAVE TO ATTACK.
WAIT!
HE KNOWS OUR AIM, SO IF WE TRY TO GO AFTER HIM, WE WON'T BE ABLE TO HOLD FORMATION.
OUR FIGHT WITH LT. COLONEL GUREN TAUGHT US THAT.
IN-STEAD...
LET'S GOAD HIM INTO COMING TO US.
YU.
HUH?
I'M GOING TO TAUNT THE VAMPIRE.
WHEN HE CHARGES, YOU FINISH HIM OFF.
GOT IT!
I'LL DROP HIM IN ONE STRIKE!
Chiing
WAIT, HOW ARE YOU GOING TO—

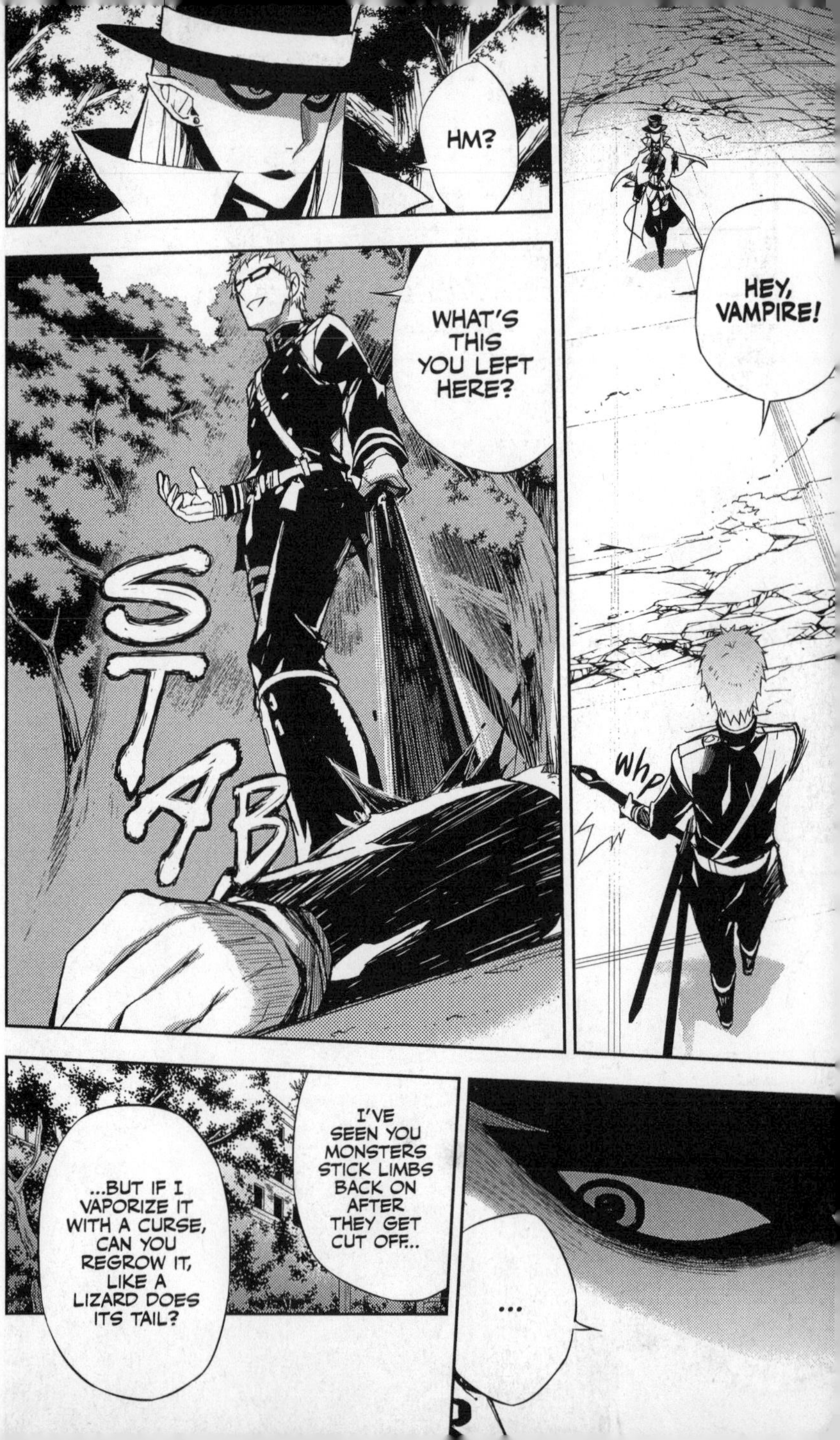
HEY, VAMPIRE!
whp
HM?
WHAT'S THIS YOU LEFT HERE?
STAB
...
I'VE SEEN YOU MONSTERS STICK LIMBS BACK ON AFTER THEY GET CUT OFF...
...BUT IF I VAPORIZE IT WITH A CURSE, CAN YOU REGROW IT, LIKE A LIZARD DOES ITS TAIL?

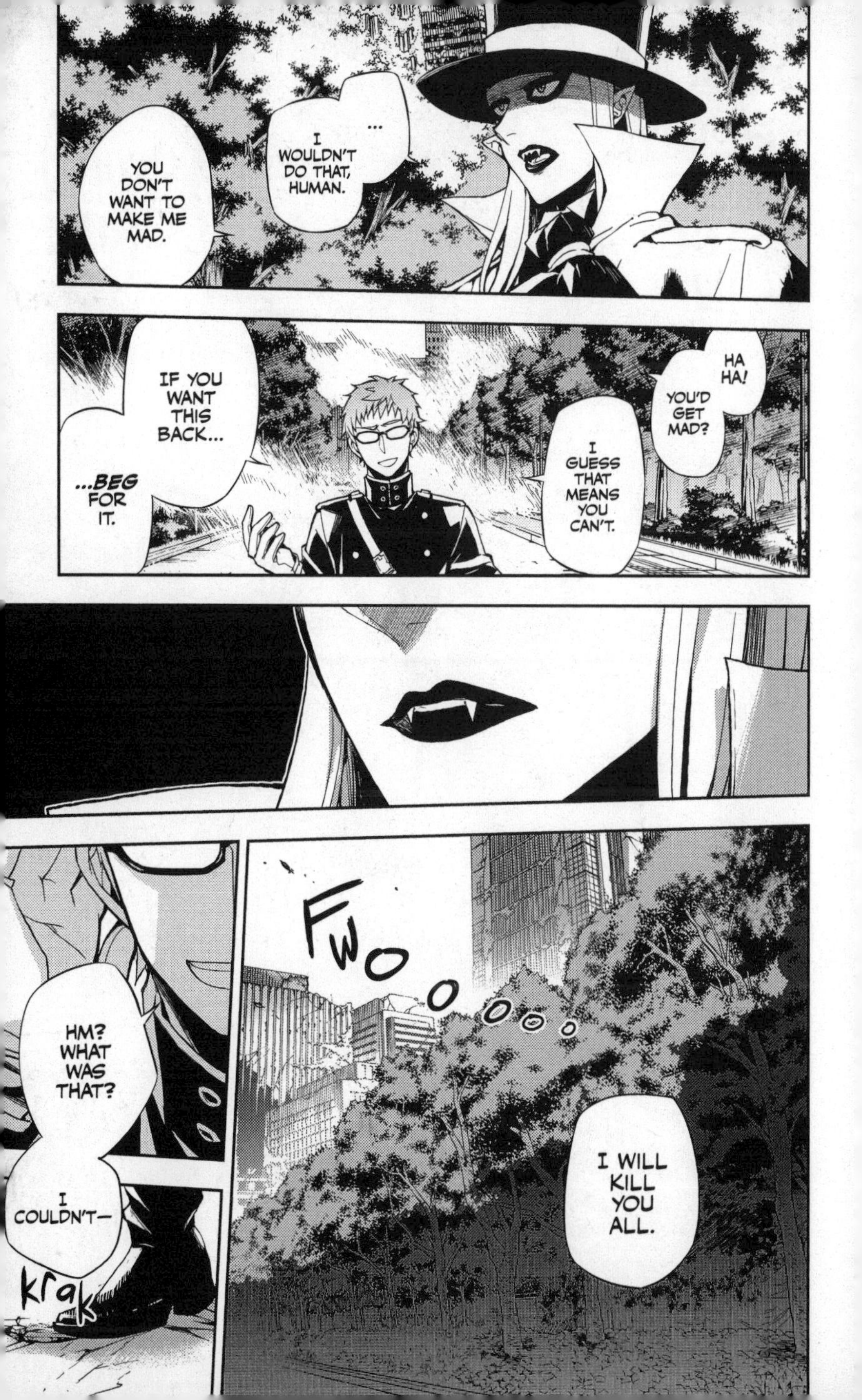
...
I WOULDN'T DO THAT, HUMAN.
YOU DON'T WANT TO MAKE ME MAD.
HA HA!
YOU'D GET MAD?
I GUESS THAT MEANS YOU CAN'T.
IF YOU WANT THIS BACK...
...BEG FOR IT.
FWOOOOOO
I WILL KILL YOU ALL.
HM? WHAT WAS THAT?
I COULDN'T—
krak

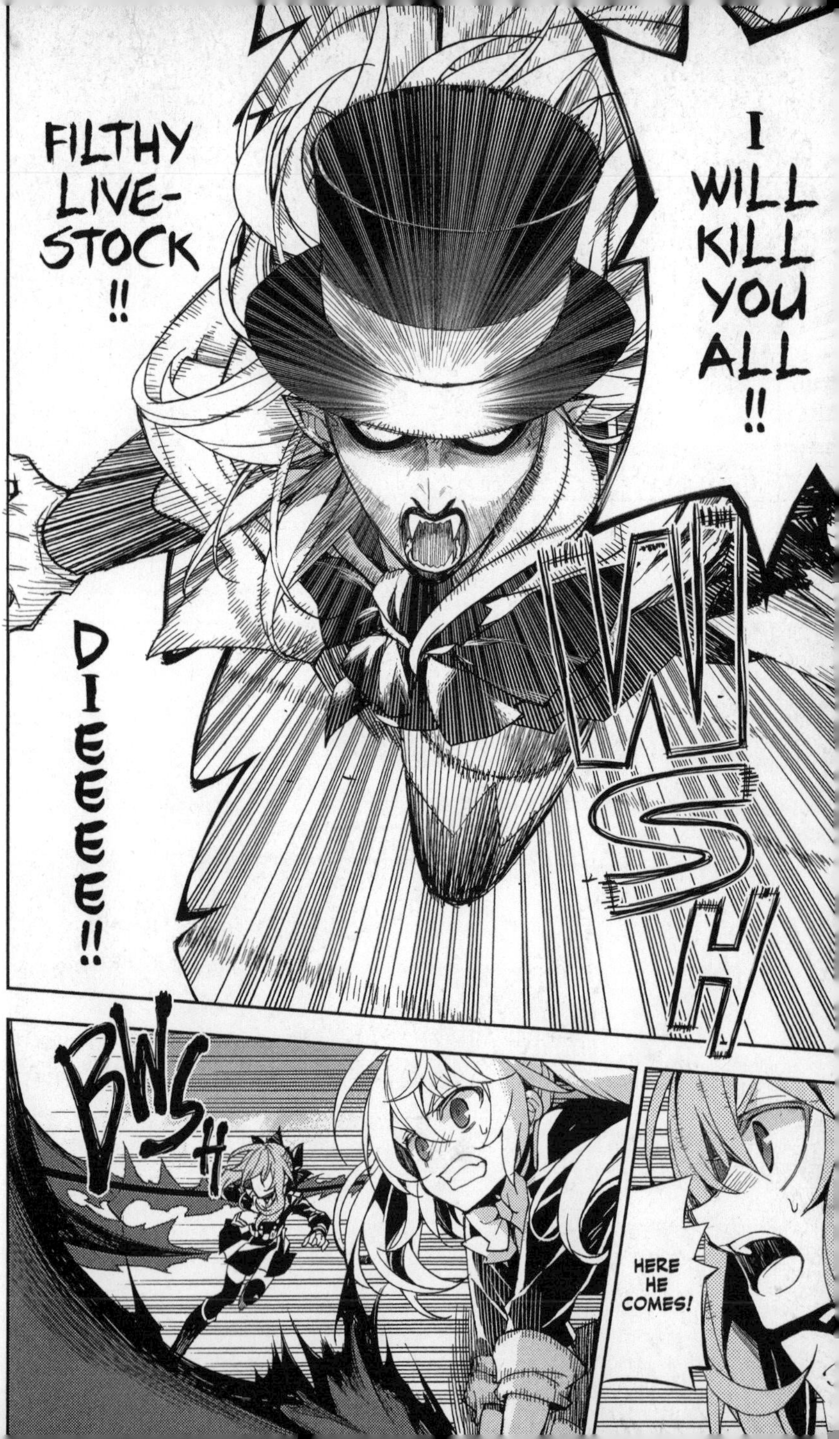
I WILL KILL YOU ALL!!
FILTHY LIVE-STOCK!!
DIEEEEE!!
WSH
HERE HE COMES!
BWSH

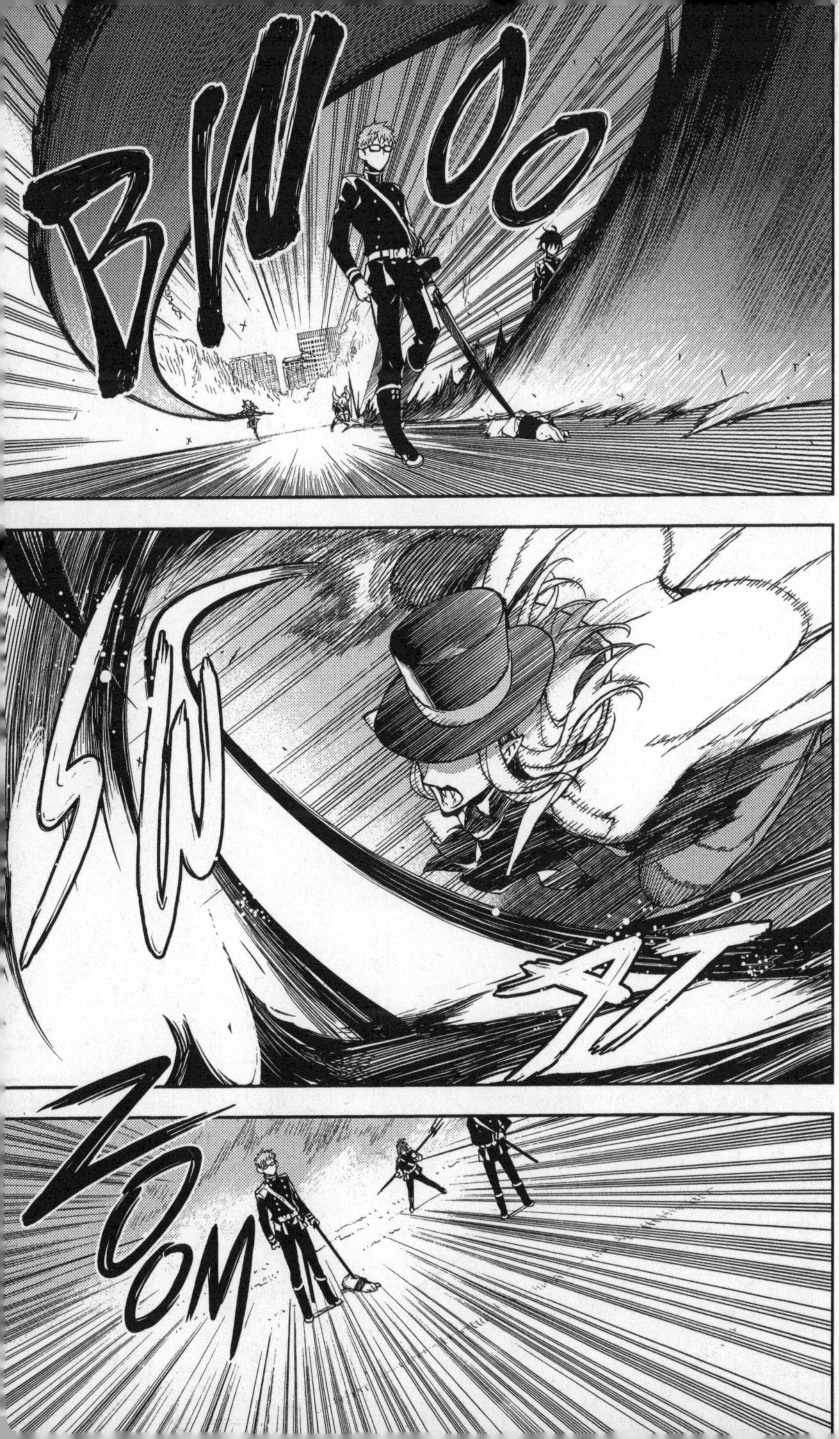
BWOOO
SWAT
ZOOM

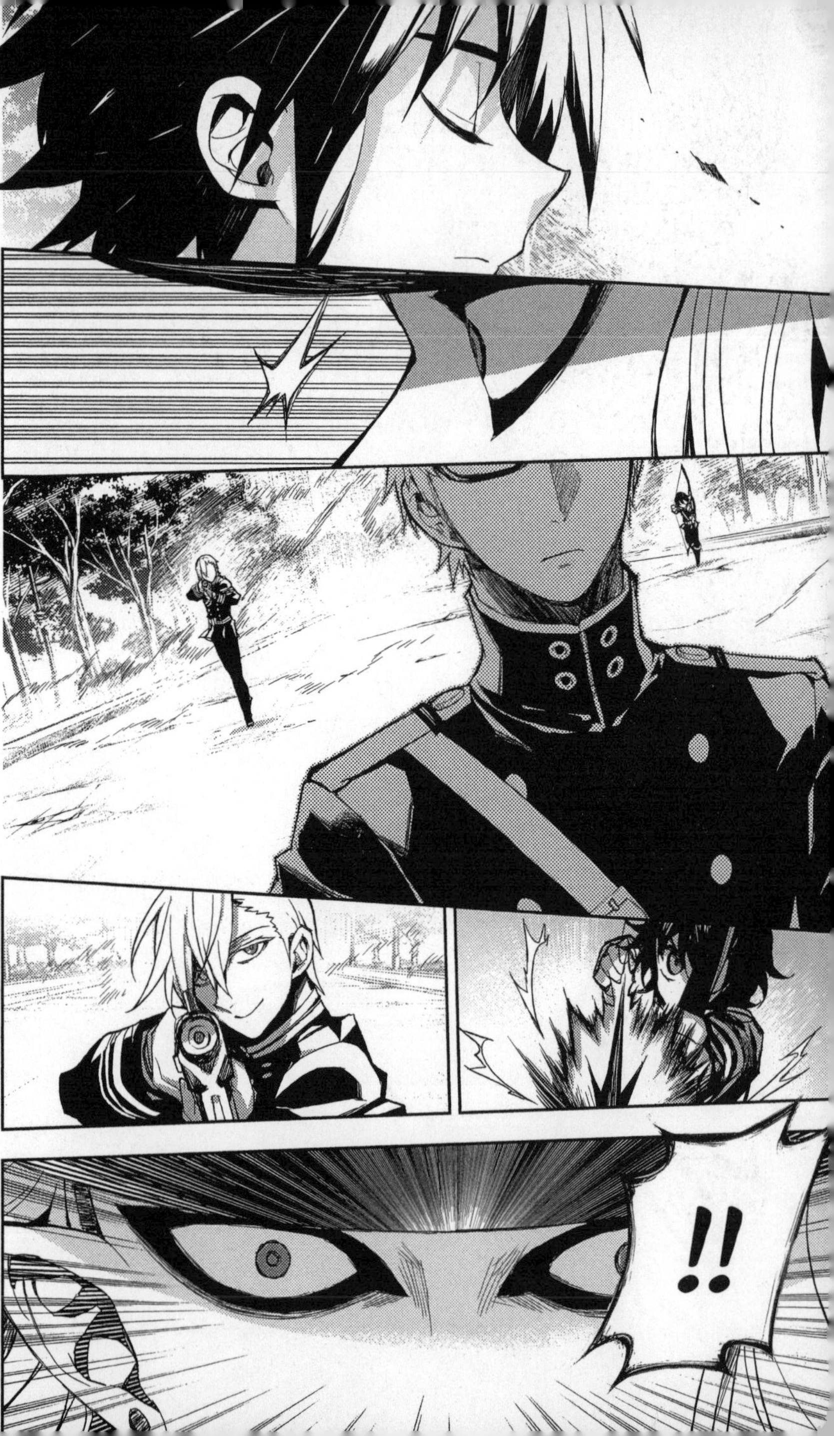
!!

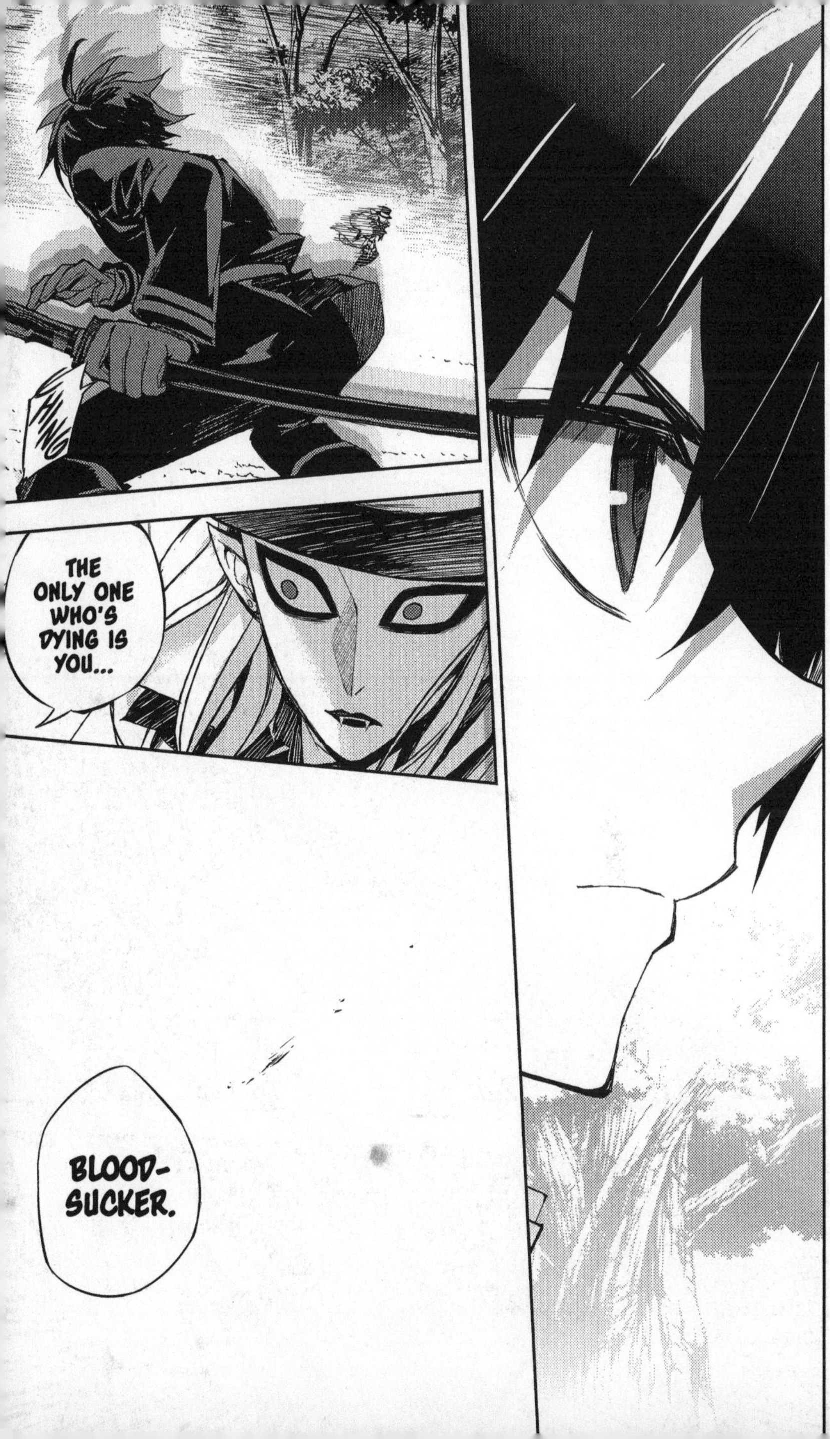
CHING
THE ONLY ONE WHO'S DYING IS YOU...
BLOOD-SUCKER.

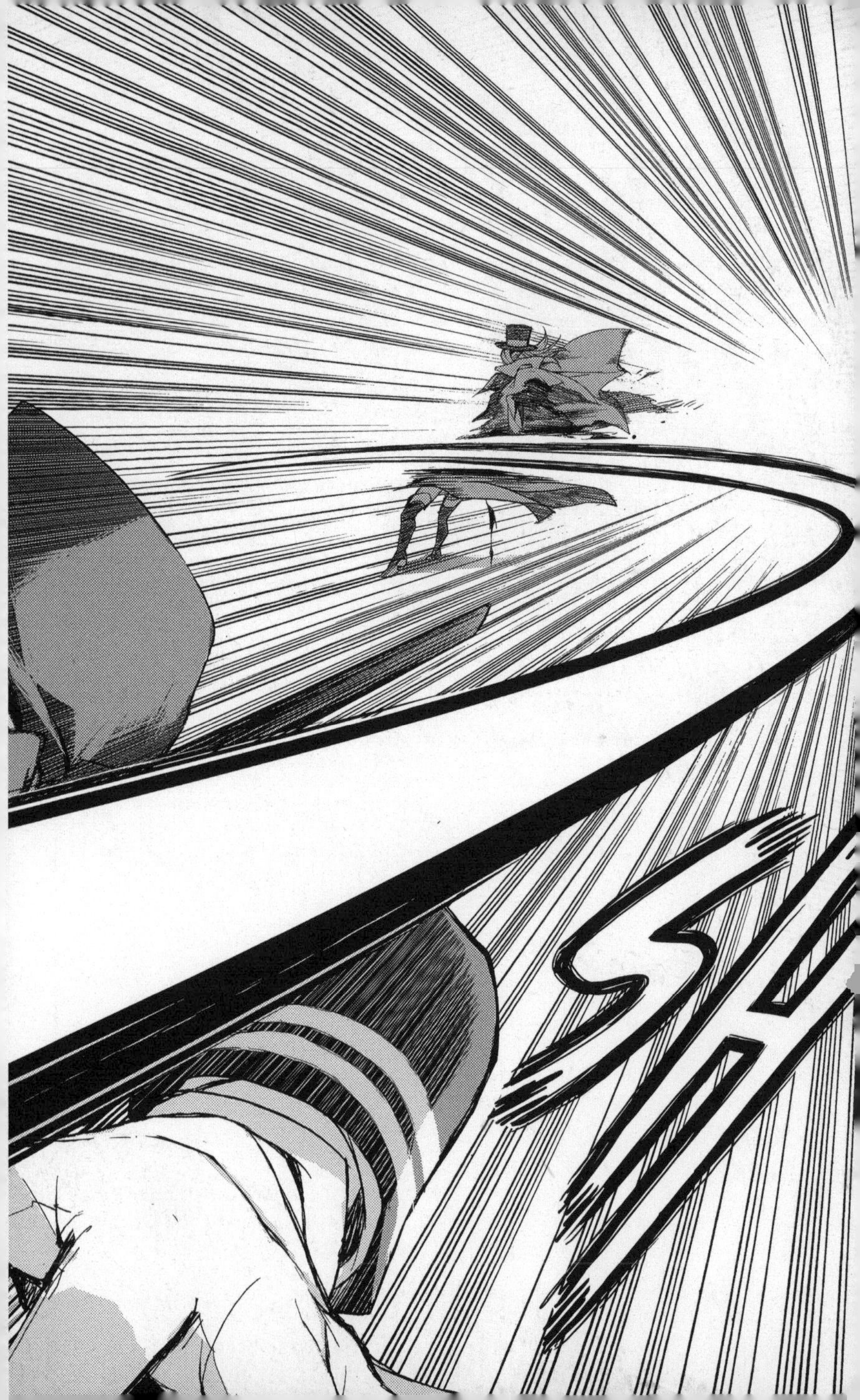

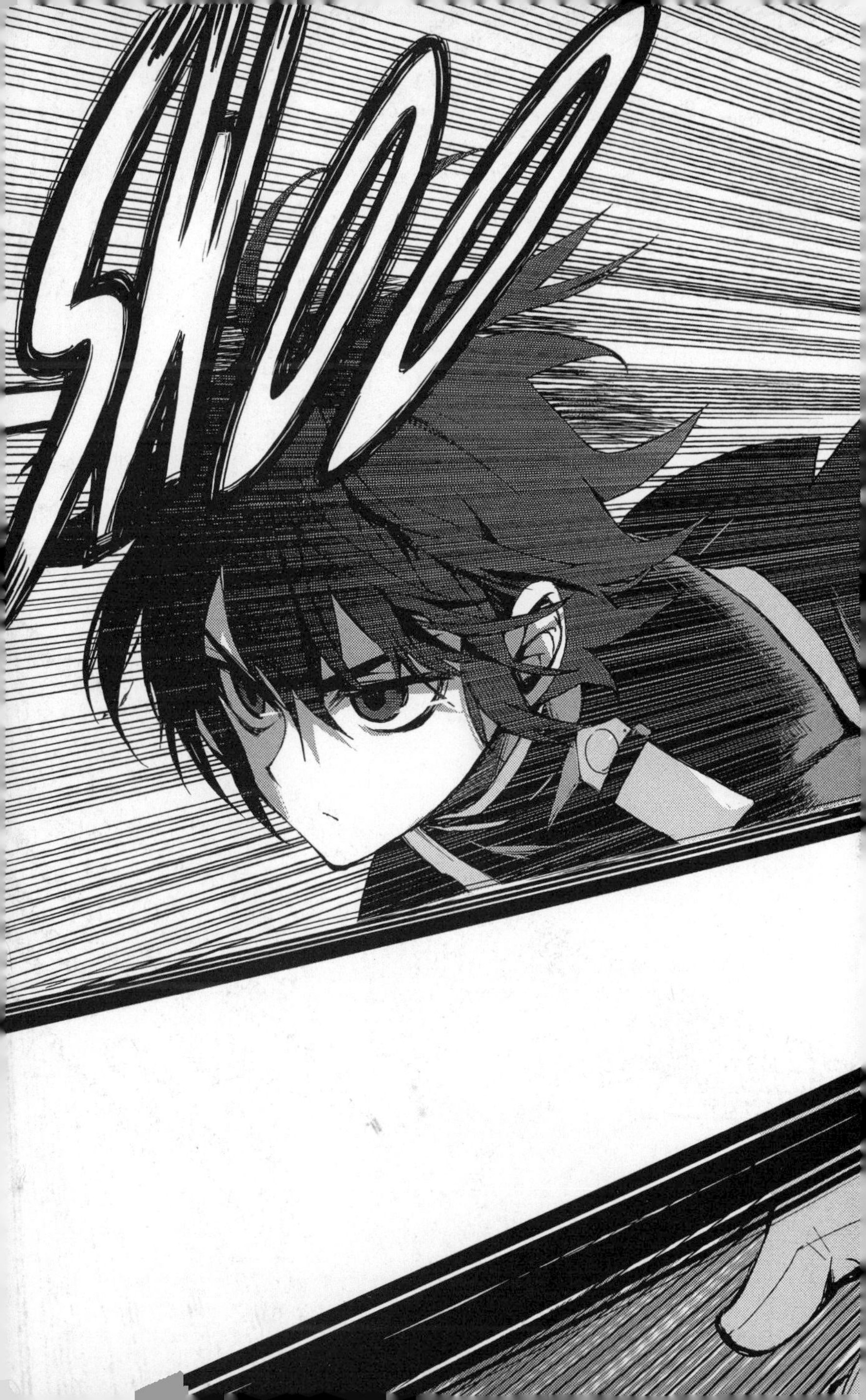
SHOO

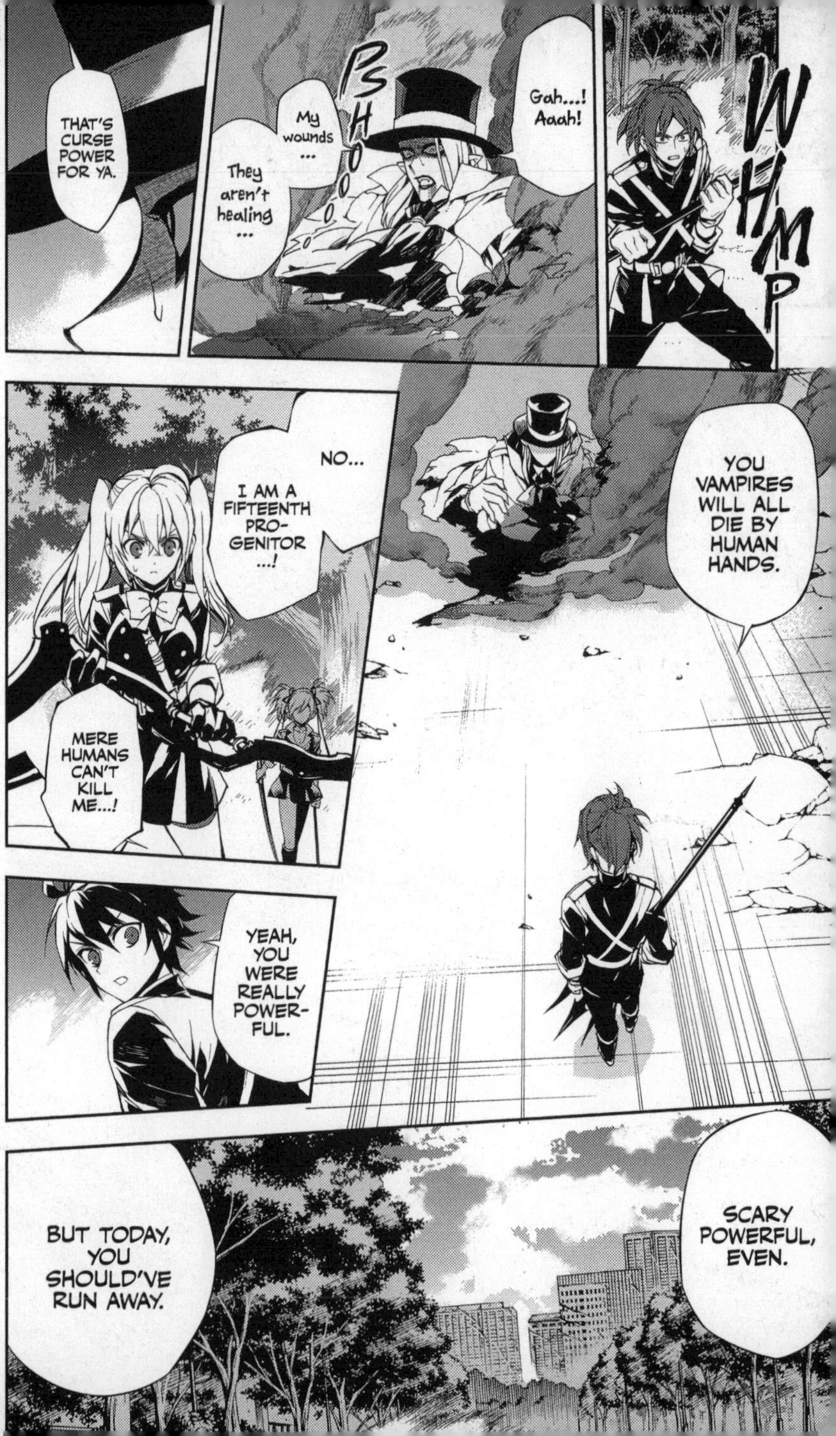
WHMP
...
Gah...! Aaah!
PSHOOO
My wounds ...
They aren't healing ...
THAT'S CURSE POWER FOR YA.
YOU VAMPIRES WILL ALL DIE BY HUMAN HANDS.
NO...
I AM A FIFTEENTH PRO-GENITOR ...!
MERE HUMANS CAN'T KILL ME...!
YEAH, YOU WERE REALLY POWER-FUL.
SCARY POWERFUL, EVEN.
BUT TODAY, YOU SHOULD'VE RUN AWAY.

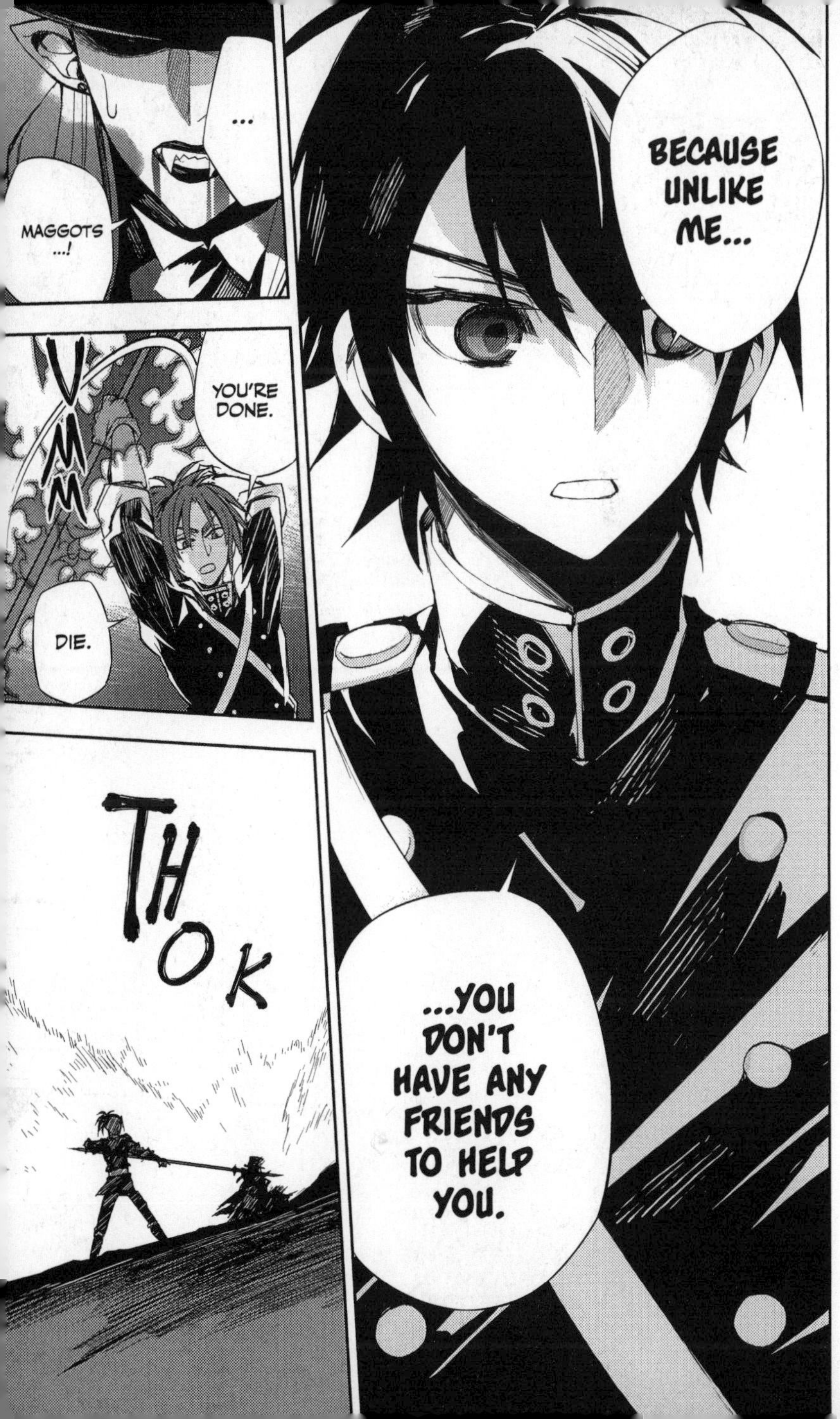
BECAUSE UNLIKE ME...
...YOU DON'T HAVE ANY FRIENDS TO HELP YOU.
...
MAGGOTS ...!
YOU'RE DONE.
VMM
DIE.
THOK

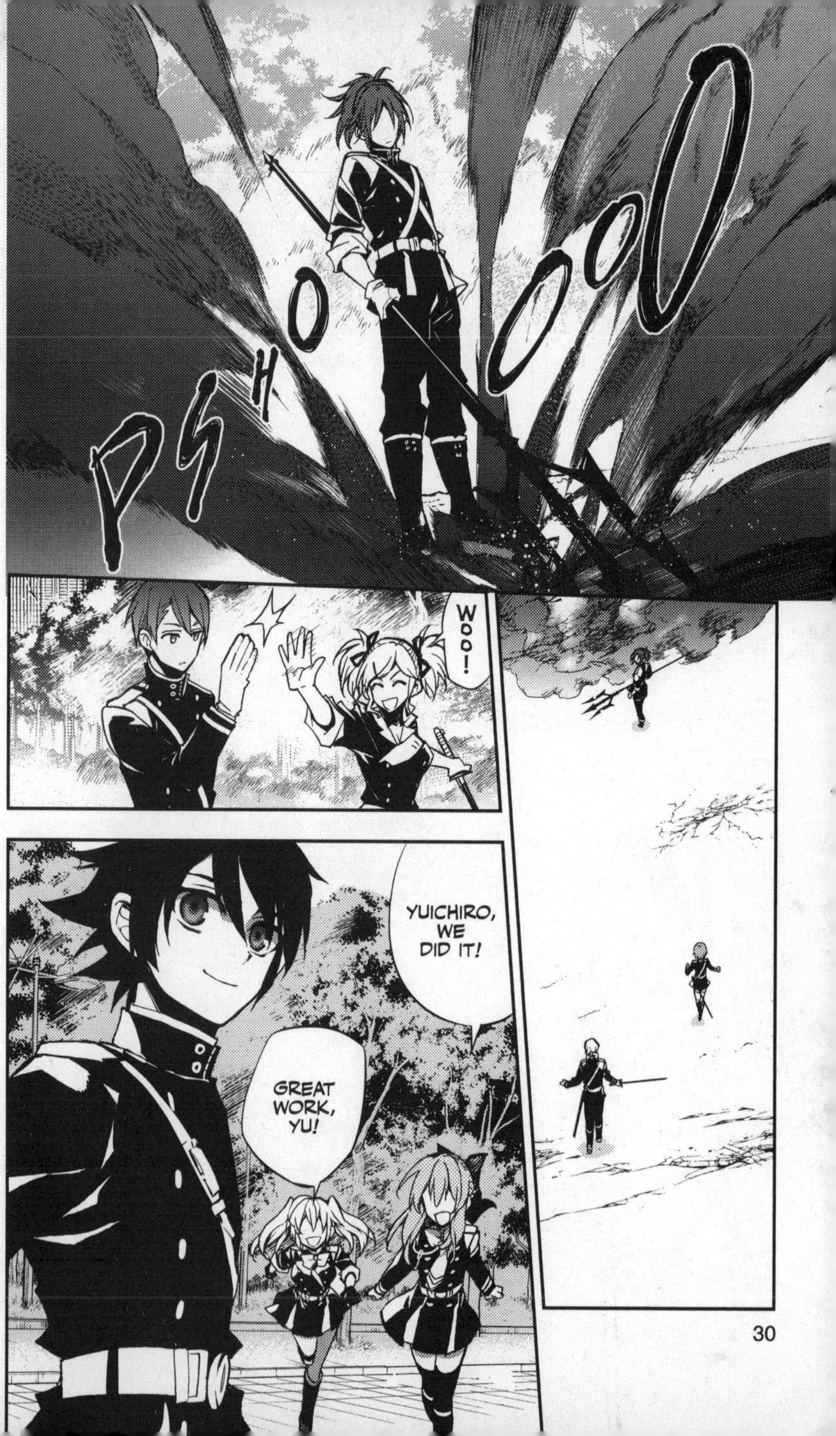
DSHOOOOO
WOO!
YUICHIRO, WE DID IT!
GREAT WORK, YU!

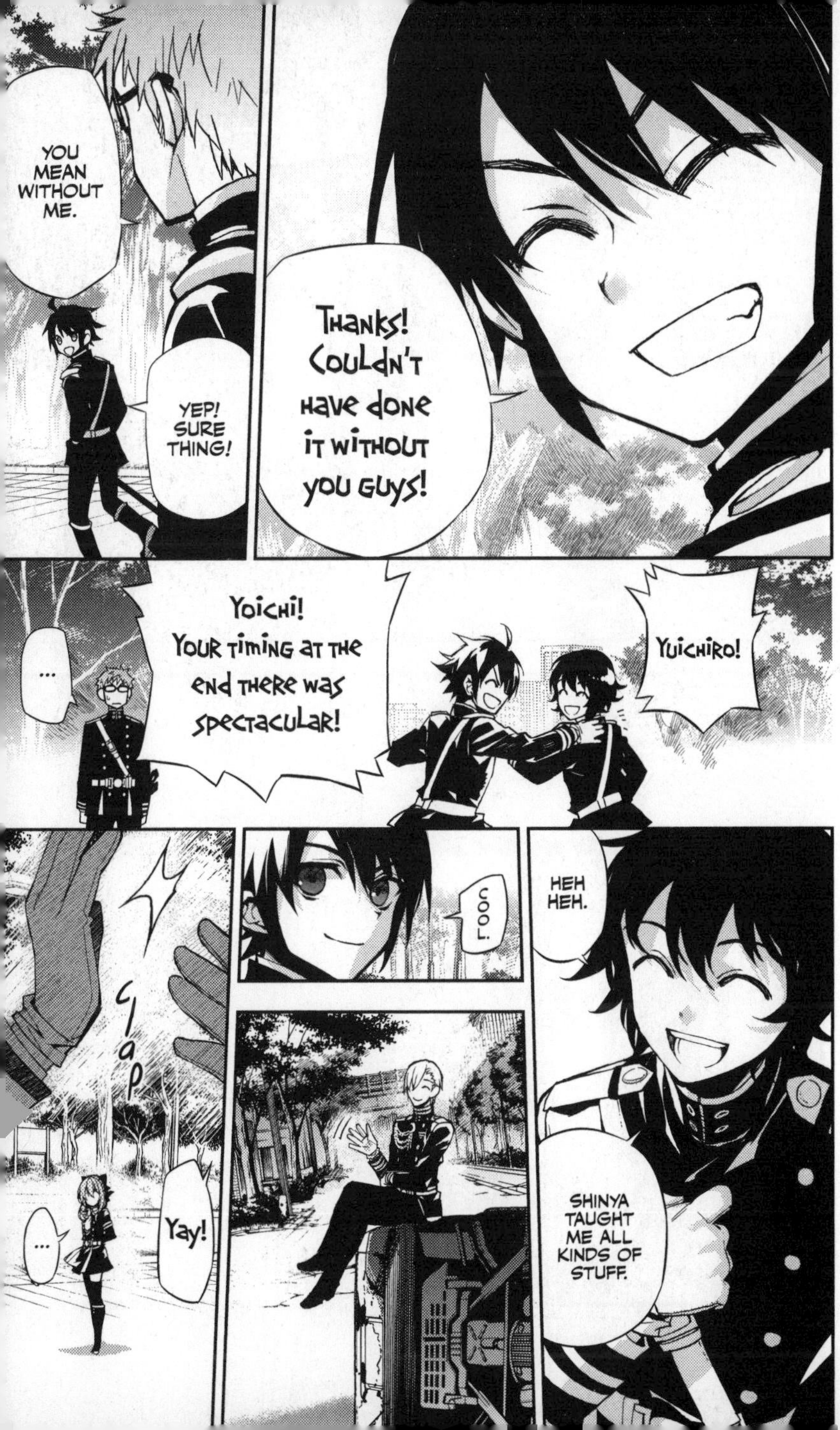
Thanks! Couldn't have done it without you guys!
Yep! Sure thing!
You mean without me.
Yuichiro!
Yoichi! Your timing at the end there was spectacular!
...
Heh heh.
Shinya taught me all kinds of stuff.
Cool.
Clap
Yay!
...

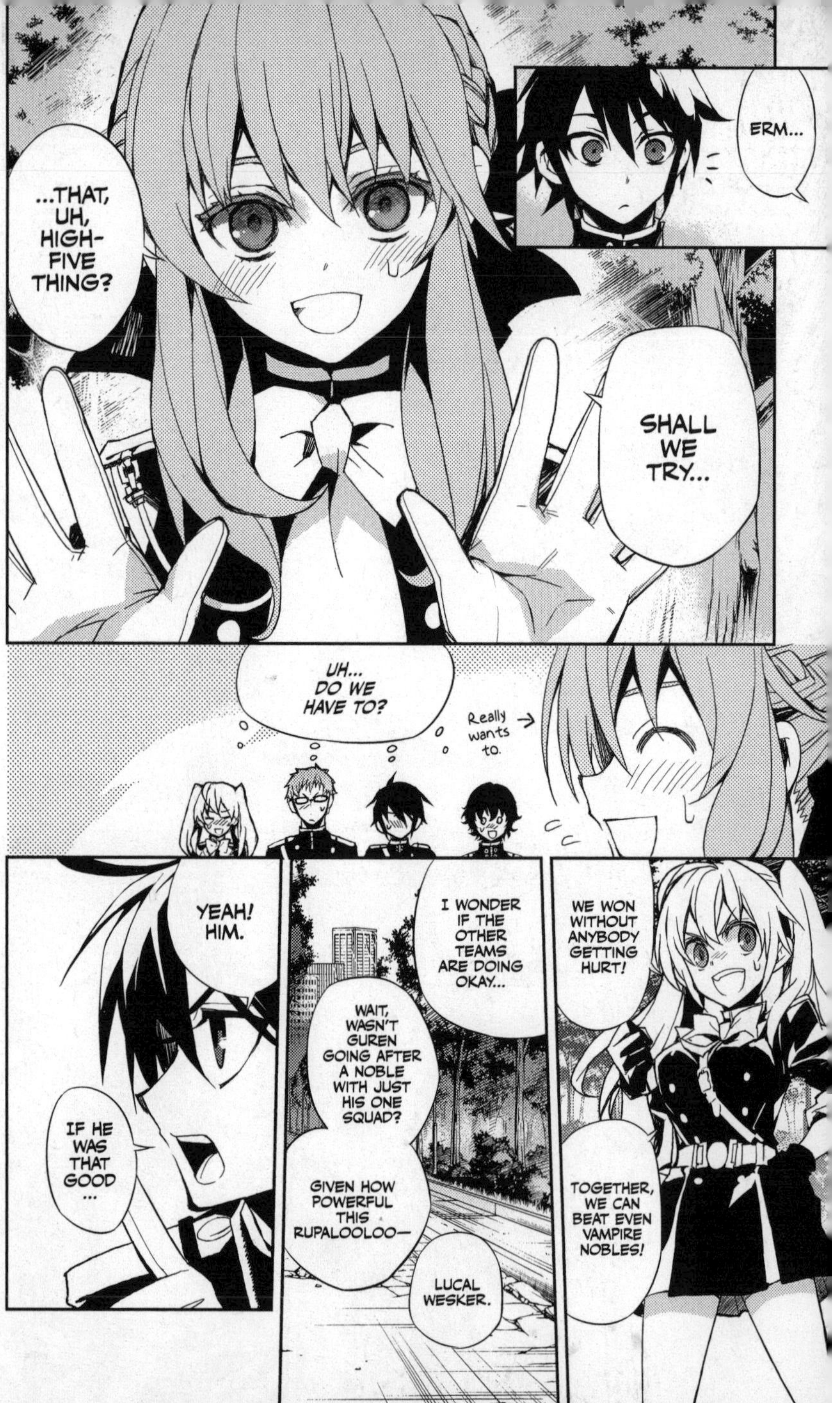
ERM...
SHALL WE TRY...
...THAT, UH, HIGH-FIVE THING?
Really wants to.
UH... DO WE HAVE TO?
WE WON WITHOUT ANYBODY GETTING HURT!
TOGETHER, WE CAN BEAT EVEN VAMPIRE NOBLES!
I WONDER IF THE OTHER TEAMS ARE DOING OKAY...
WAIT, WASN'T GUREN GOING AFTER A NOBLE WITH JUST HIS ONE SQUAD?
GIVEN HOW POWERFUL THIS RUPALOOLOO—
LUCAL WESKER.
YEAH! HIM.
IF HE WAS THAT GOOD ...

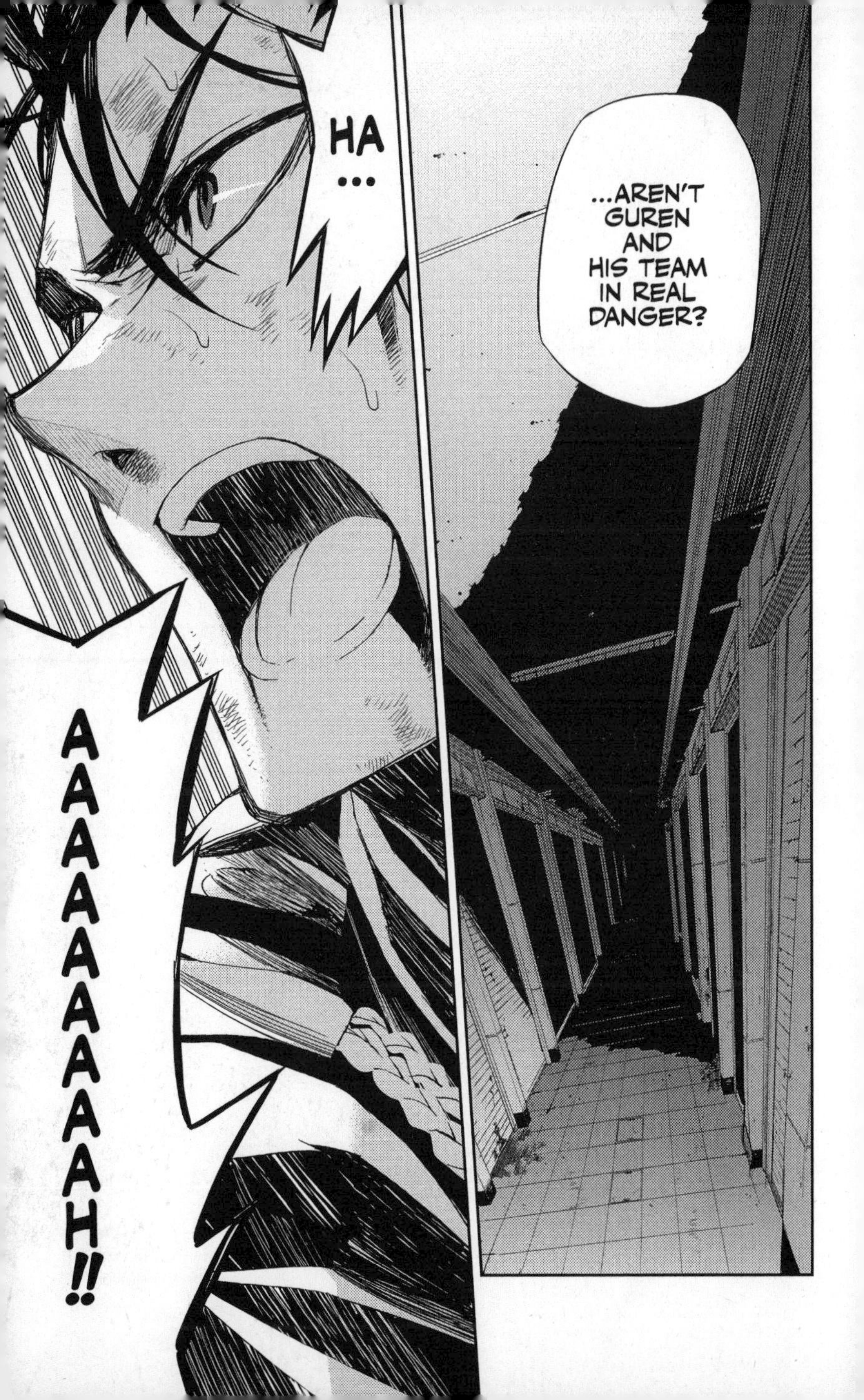
...AREN'T GUREN AND HIS TEAM IN REAL DANGER?
HA...
AAAAAAAAAH!!

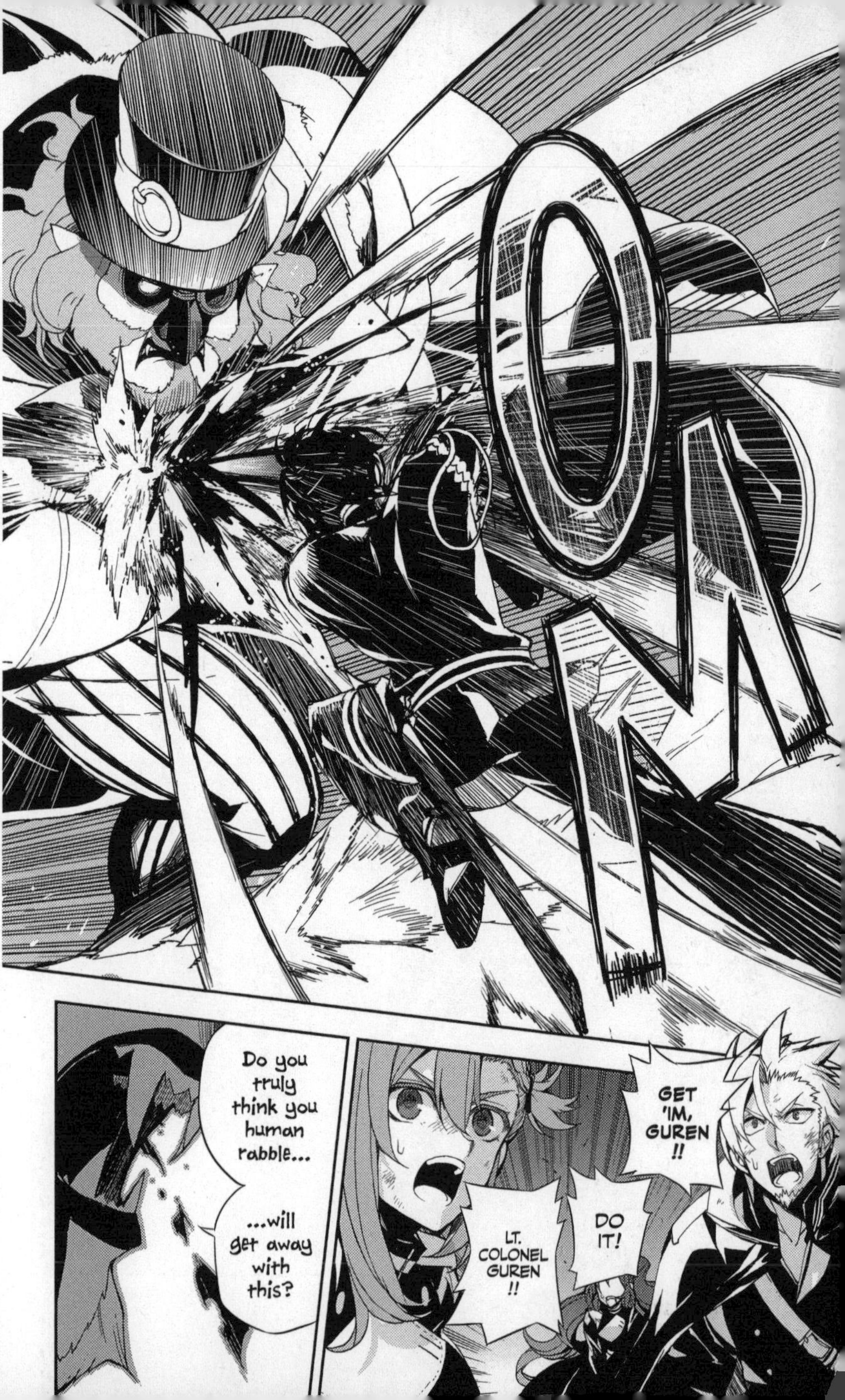
GET 'IM, GUREN!!
DO IT!
LT. COLONEL GUREN!!
Do you truly think you human rabble...
...will get away with this?

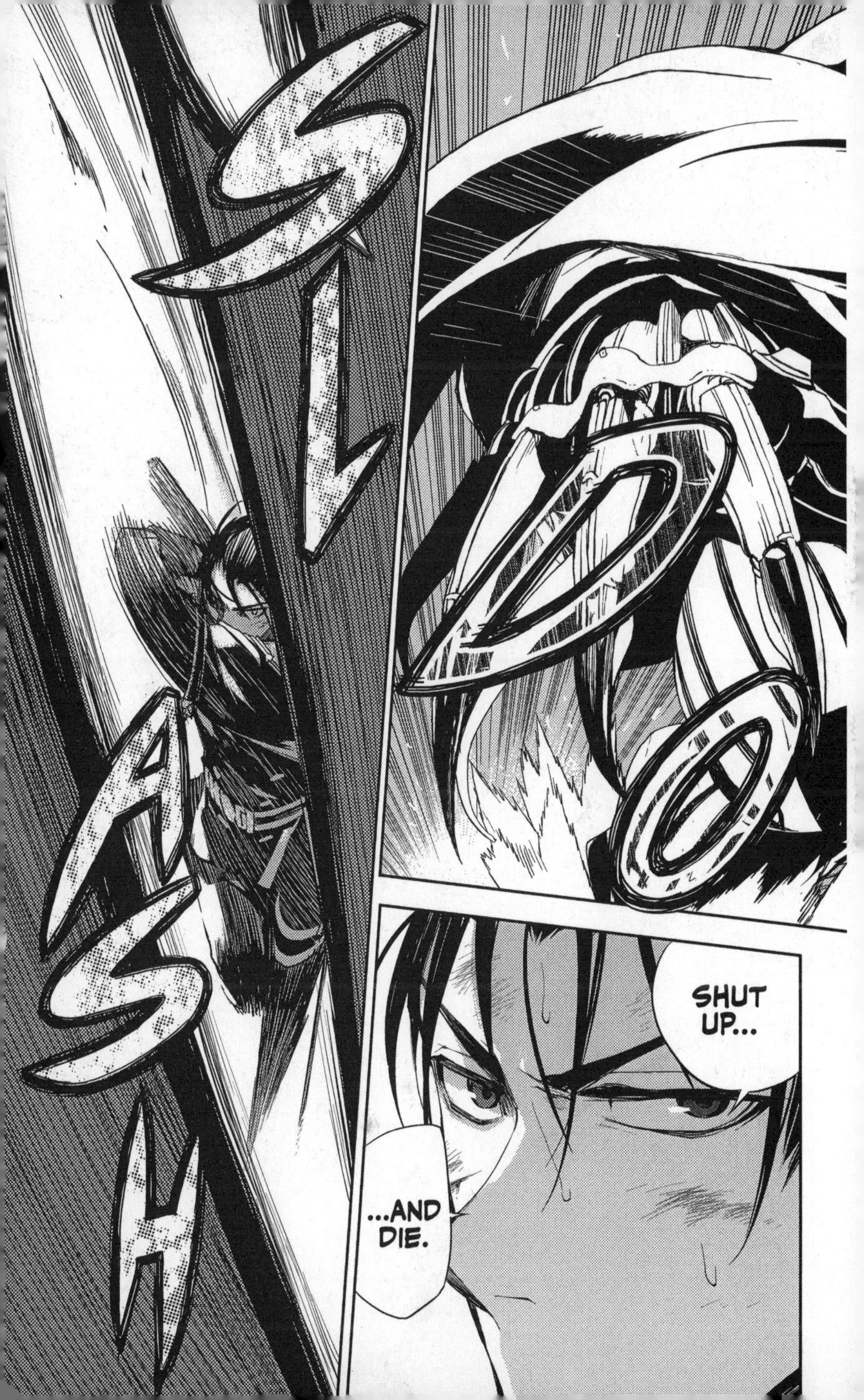
SHUT UP...
...AND DIE.
SLASH

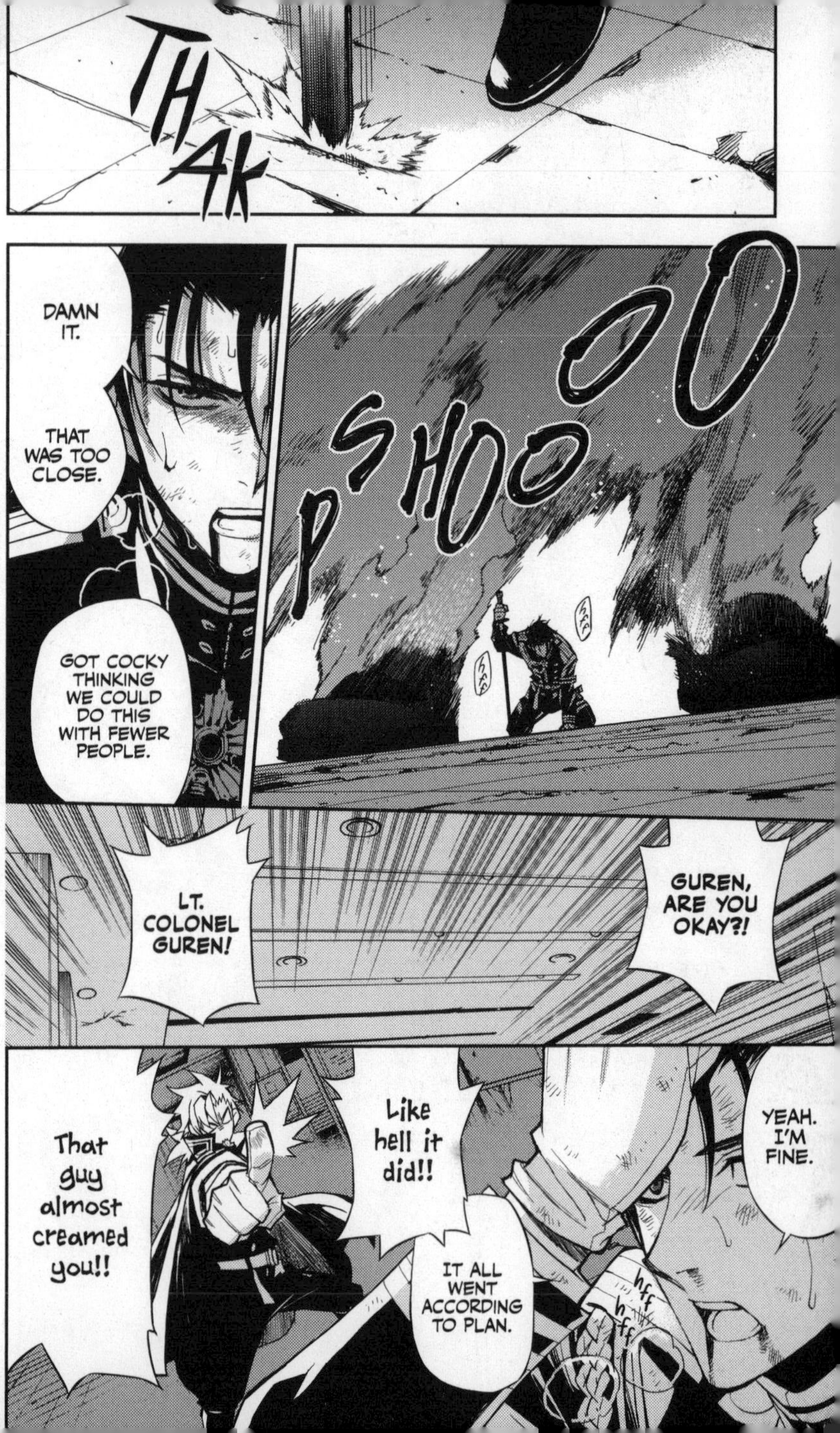
THAK
PSHOOOO
hff
hff
DAMN IT.
THAT WAS TOO CLOSE.
GOT COCKY THINKING WE COULD DO THIS WITH FEWER PEOPLE.
GUREN, ARE YOU OKAY?!
LT. COLONEL GUREN!
YEAH. I'M FINE.
hff
hff
IT ALL WENT ACCORDING TO PLAN.
Like hell it did!!
That guy almost creamed you!!

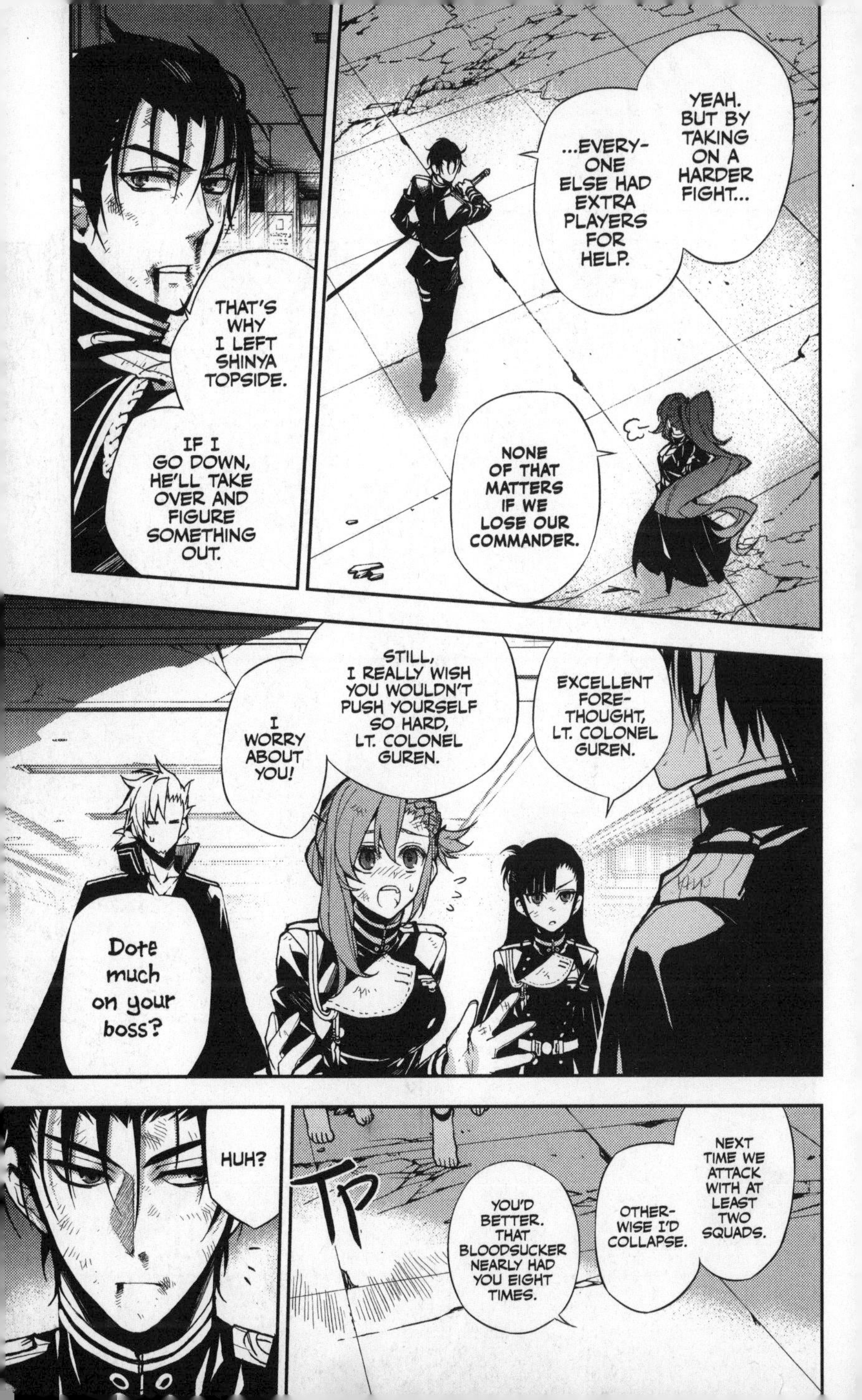
YEAH. BUT BY TAKING ON A HARDER FIGHT...
...EVERY-ONE ELSE HAD EXTRA PLAYERS FOR HELP.
NONE OF THAT MATTERS IF WE LOSE OUR COMMANDER.
THAT'S WHY I LEFT SHINYA TOPSIDE.
IF I GO DOWN, HE'LL TAKE OVER AND FIGURE SOMETHING OUT.
EXCELLENT FORE-THOUGHT, LT. COLONEL GUREN.
STILL, I REALLY WISH YOU WOULDN'T PUSH YOURSELF SO HARD, LT. COLONEL GUREN.
I WORRY ABOUT YOU!
Dote much on your boss?
NEXT TIME WE ATTACK WITH AT LEAST TWO SQUADS.
OTHER-WISE I'D COLLAPSE.
YOU'D BETTER. THAT BLOODSUCKER NEARLY HAD YOU EIGHT TIMES.
HUH?

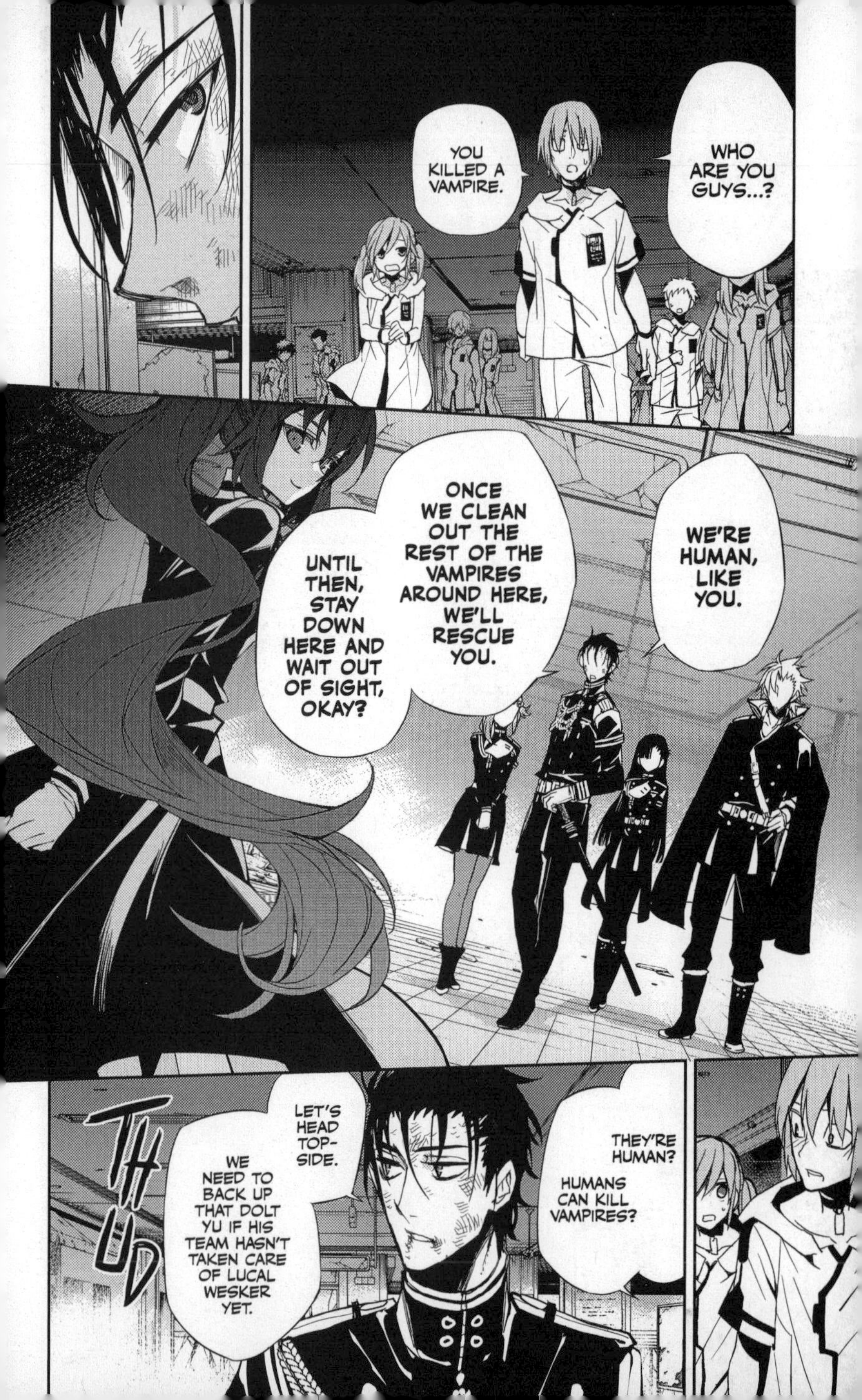
WHO ARE YOU GUYS...?
YOU KILLED A VAMPIRE.
WE'RE HUMAN, LIKE YOU.
ONCE WE CLEAN OUT THE REST OF THE VAMPIRES AROUND HERE, WE'LL RESCUE YOU.
UNTIL THEN, STAY DOWN HERE AND WAIT OUT OF SIGHT, OKAY?
THEY'RE HUMAN?
HUMANS CAN KILL VAMPIRES?
LET'S HEAD TOP-SIDE.
WE NEED TO BACK UP THAT DOLT YU IF HIS TEAM HASN'T TAKEN CARE OF LUCAL WESKER YET.
THUD

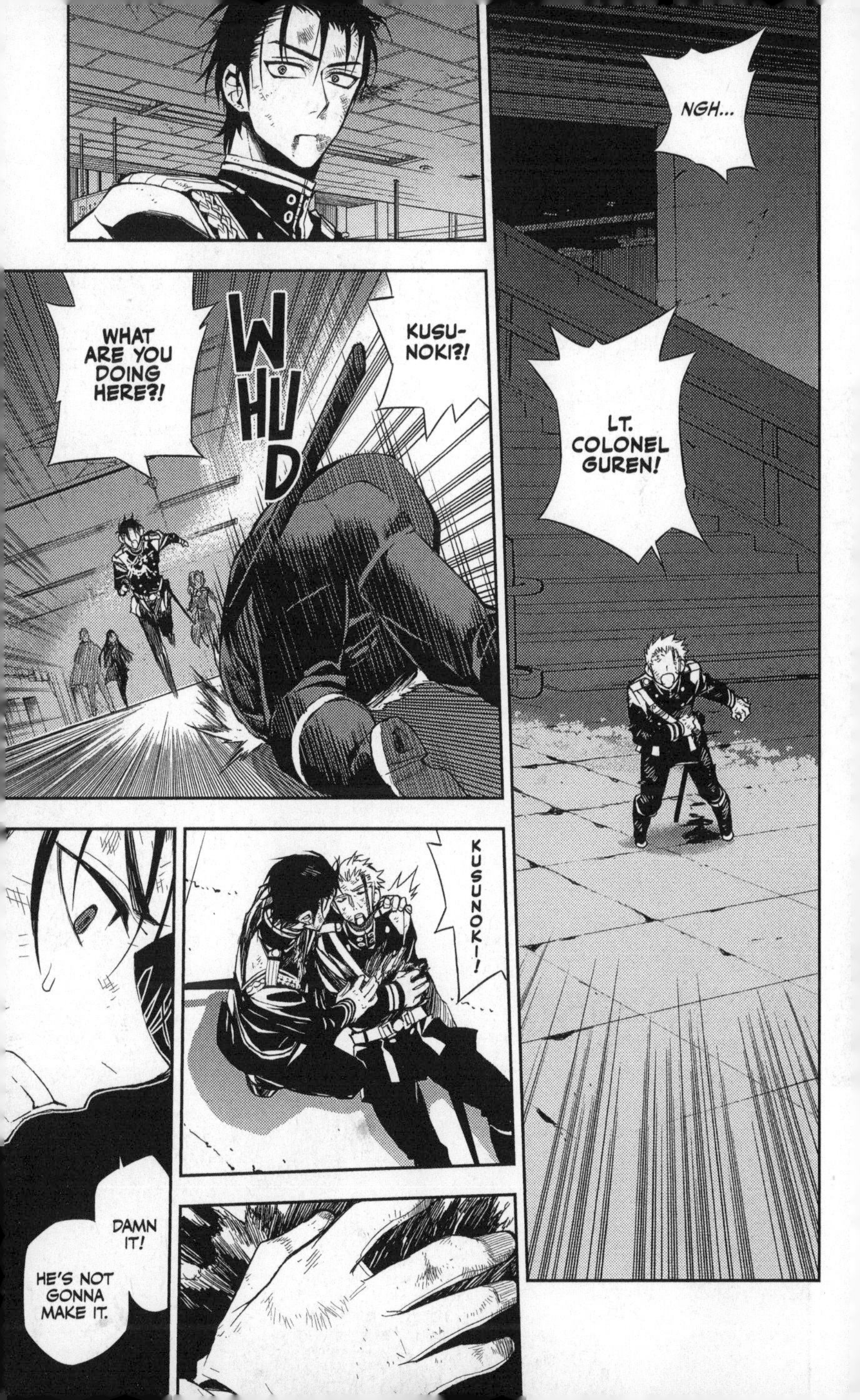
NGH...
LT. COLONEL GUREN!
KUSUNOKI?!
WHUD
WHAT ARE YOU DOING HERE?!
KUSUNOKI!
DAMN IT!
HE'S NOT GONNA MAKE IT.

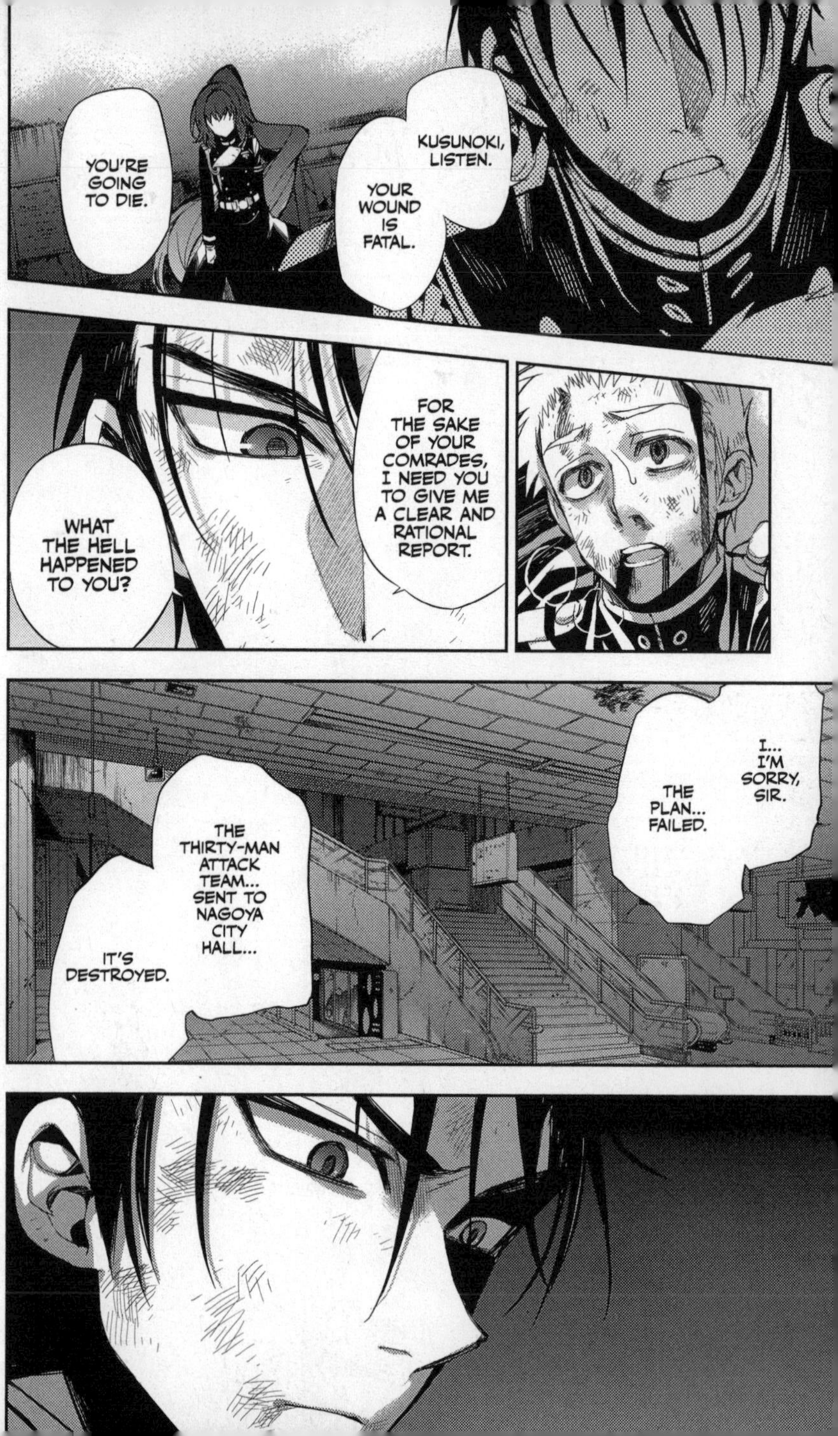
KUSUNOKI, LISTEN.
YOUR WOUND IS FATAL.
YOU'RE GOING TO DIE.
FOR THE SAKE OF YOUR COMRADES, I NEED YOU TO GIVE ME A CLEAR AND RATIONAL REPORT.
WHAT THE HELL HAPPENED TO YOU?
I... I'M SORRY, SIR.
THE PLAN... FAILED.
THE THIRTY-MAN ATTACK TEAM... SENT TO NAGOYA CITY HALL...
IT'S DESTROYED.

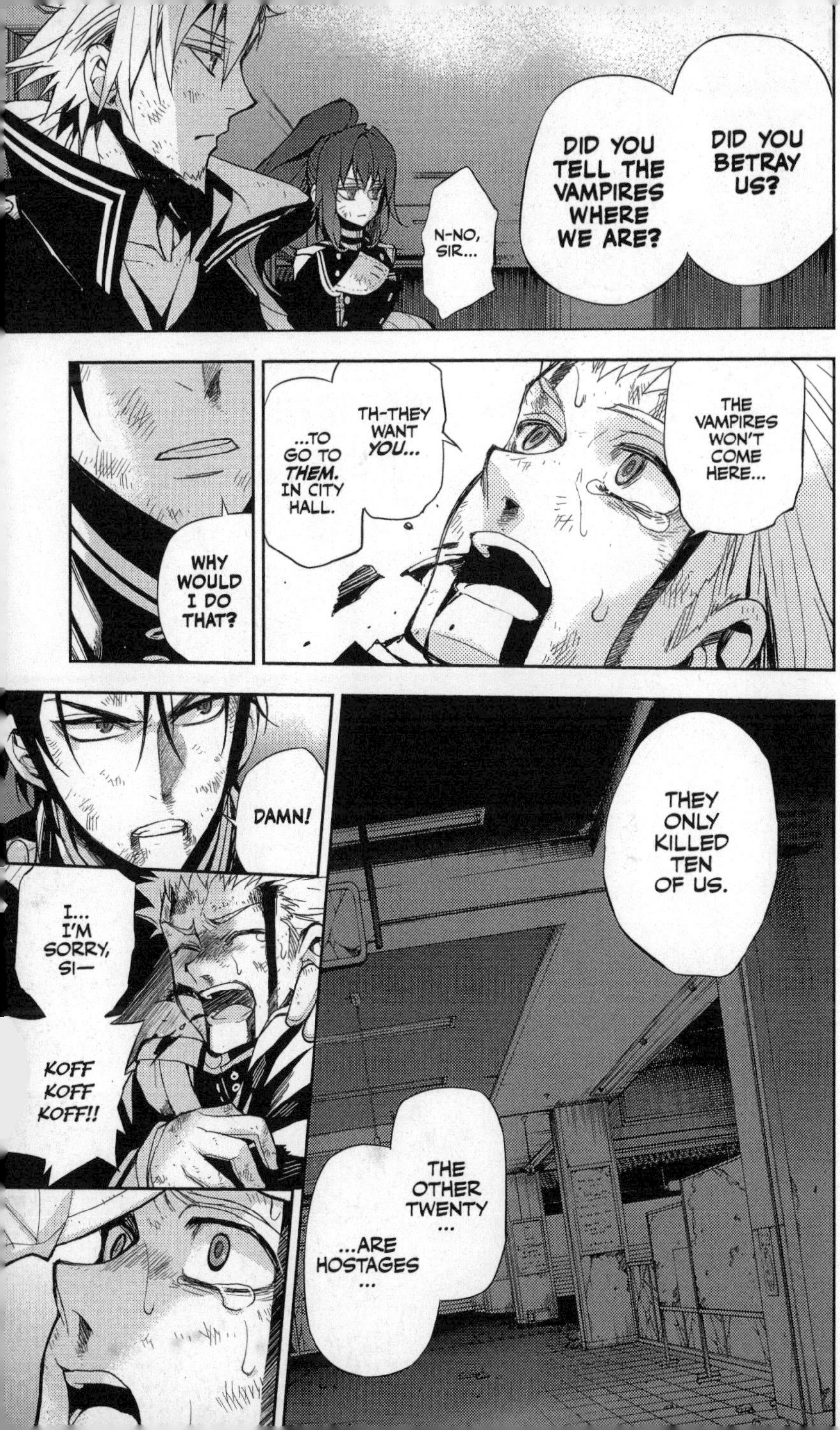
DID YOU BETRAY US?
DID YOU TELL THE VAMPIRES WHERE WE ARE?
N-NO, SIR...
THE VAMPIRES WON'T COME HERE...
TH-THEY WANT *YOU*...
...TO GO TO *THEM*. IN CITY HALL.
WHY WOULD I DO THAT?
THEY ONLY KILLED TEN OF US.
THE OTHER TWENTY...
...ARE HOSTAGES...
DAMN!
I... I'M SORRY, SI—
KOFF KOFF KOFF!!

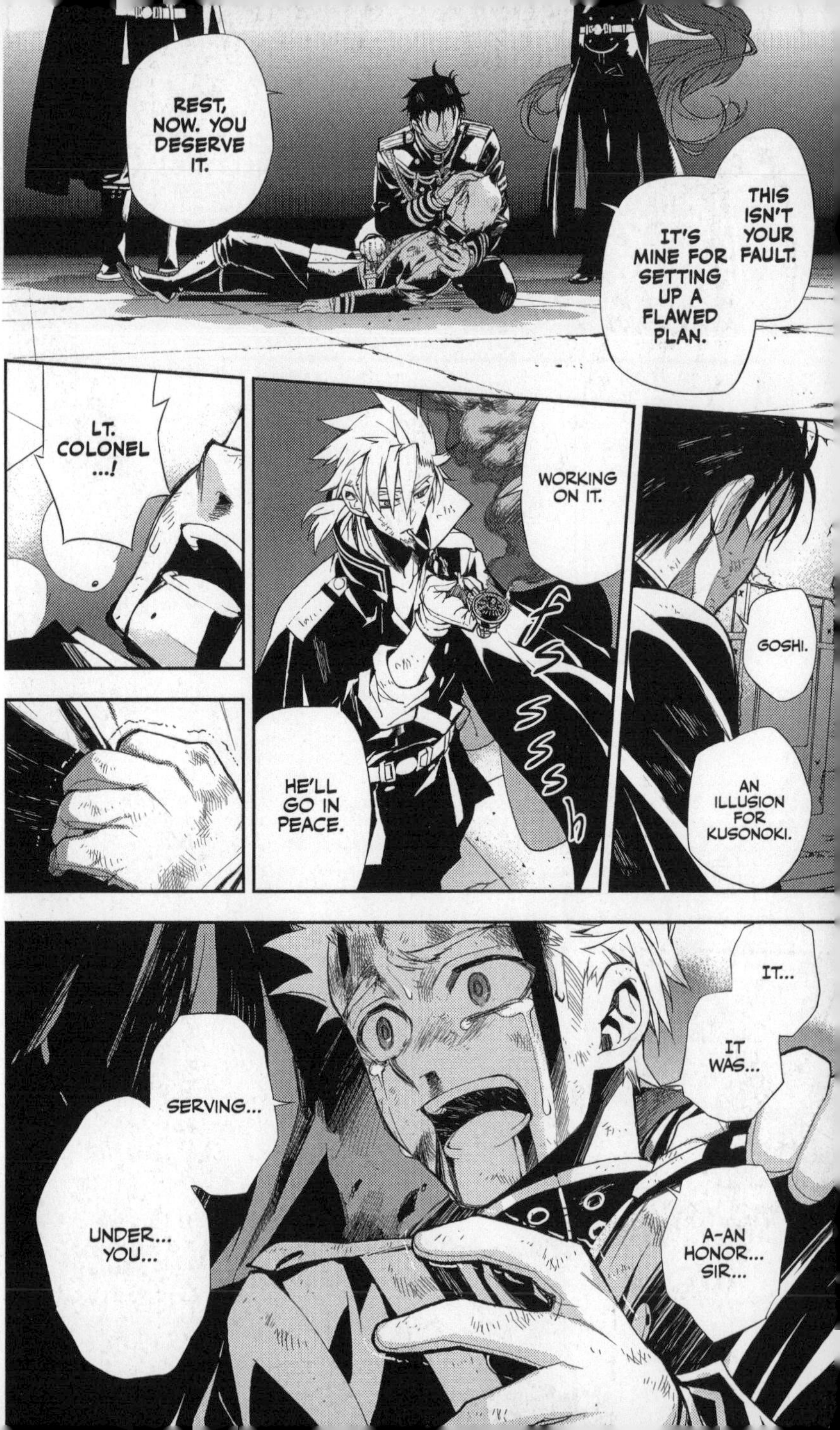
THIS ISN'T YOUR FAULT.
IT'S MINE FOR SETTING UP A FLAWED PLAN.
REST, NOW. YOU DESERVE IT.
GOSHI.
AN ILLUSION FOR KUSONOKI.
WORKING ON IT.
fsssh
HE'LL GO IN PEACE.
LT. COLONEL ...!
IT...
IT WAS...
SERVING...
UNDER... YOU...
A-AN HONOR... SIR...

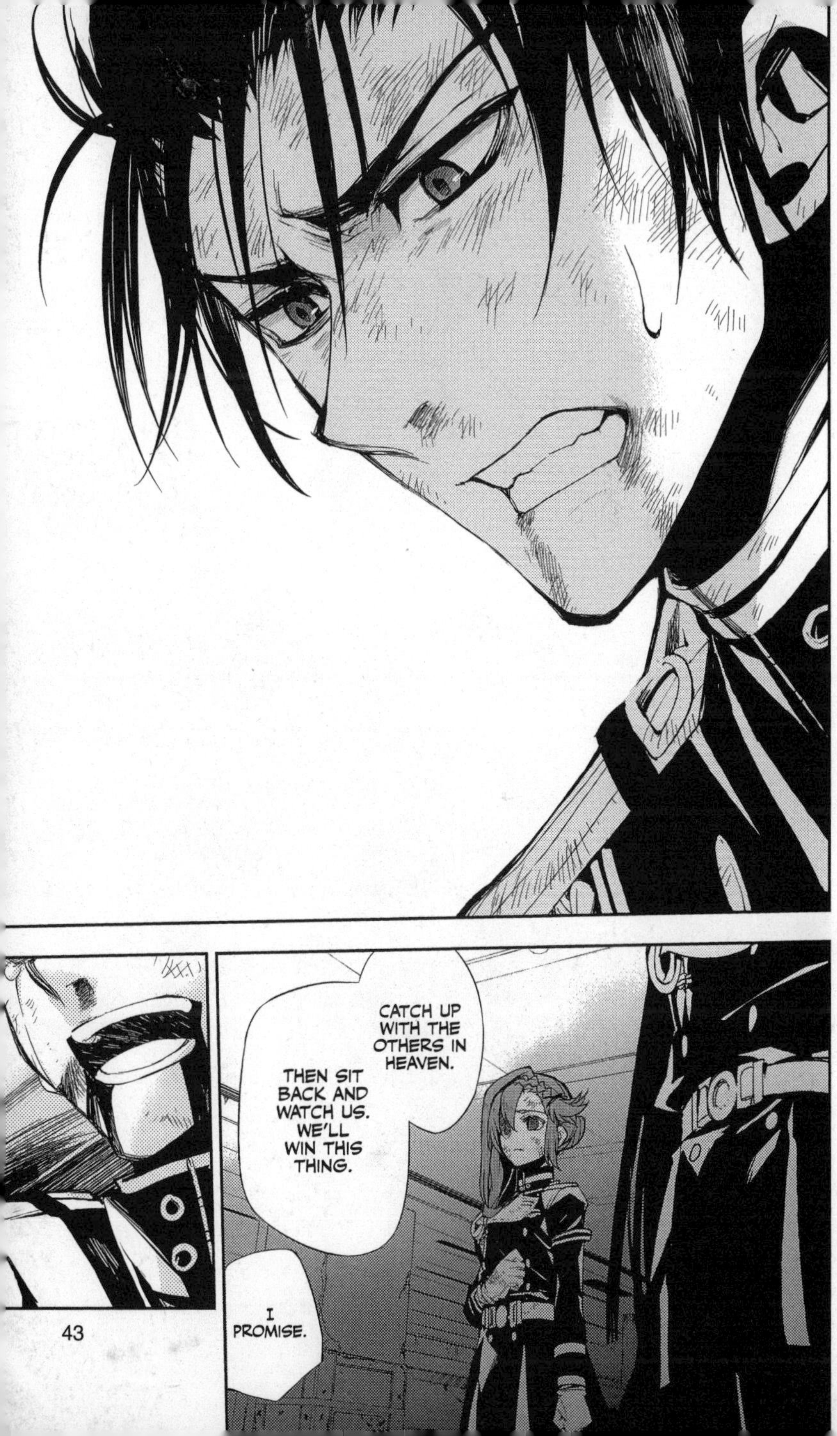
CATCH UP WITH THE OTHERS IN HEAVEN.
THEN SIT BACK AND WATCH US. WE'LL WIN THIS THING.
I PROMISE.

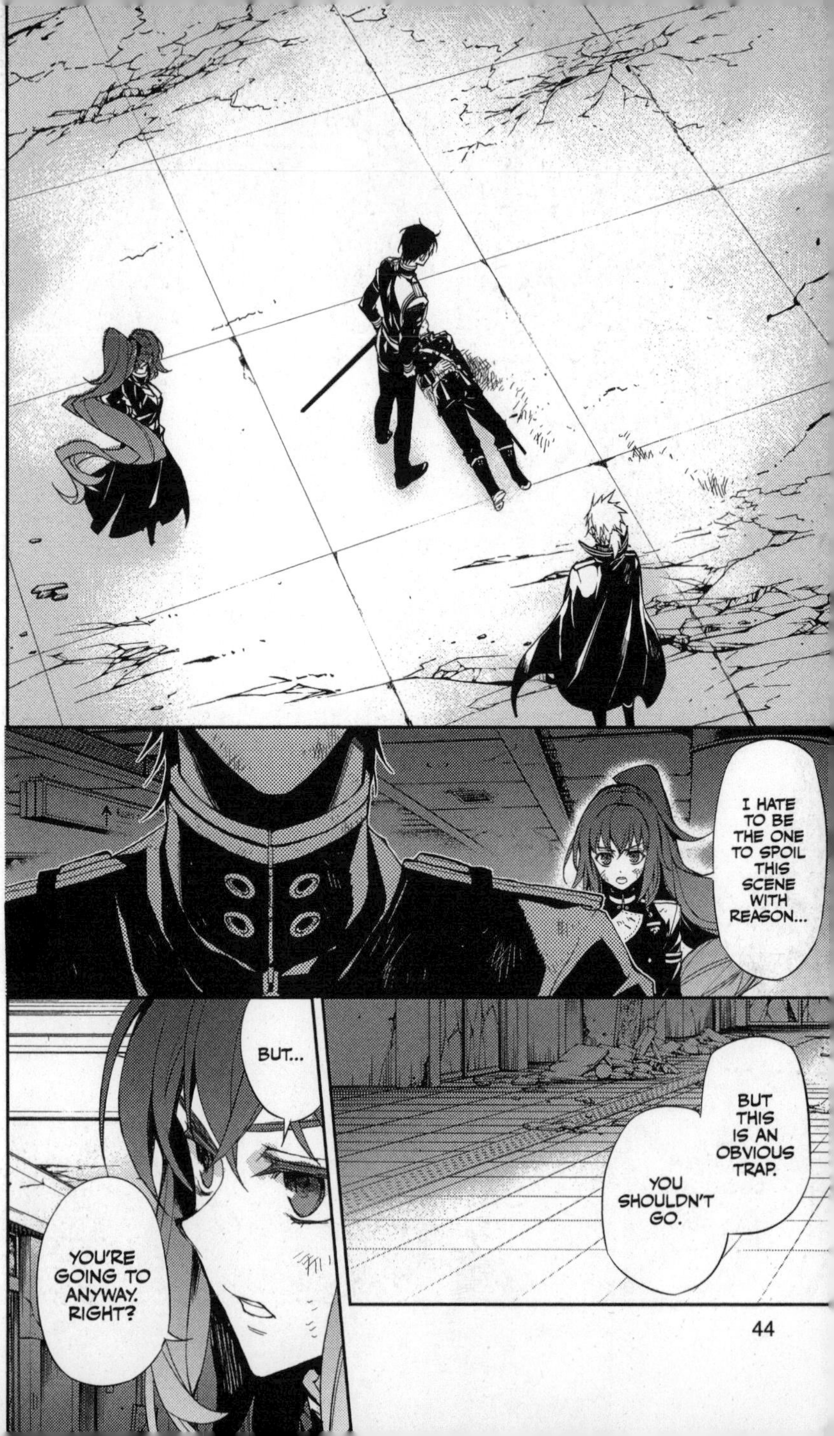
I HATE TO BE THE ONE TO SPOIL THIS SCENE WITH REASON...
BUT THIS IS AN OBVIOUS TRAP.
YOU SHOULDN'T GO.
BUT...
YOU'RE GOING TO ANYWAY. RIGHT?

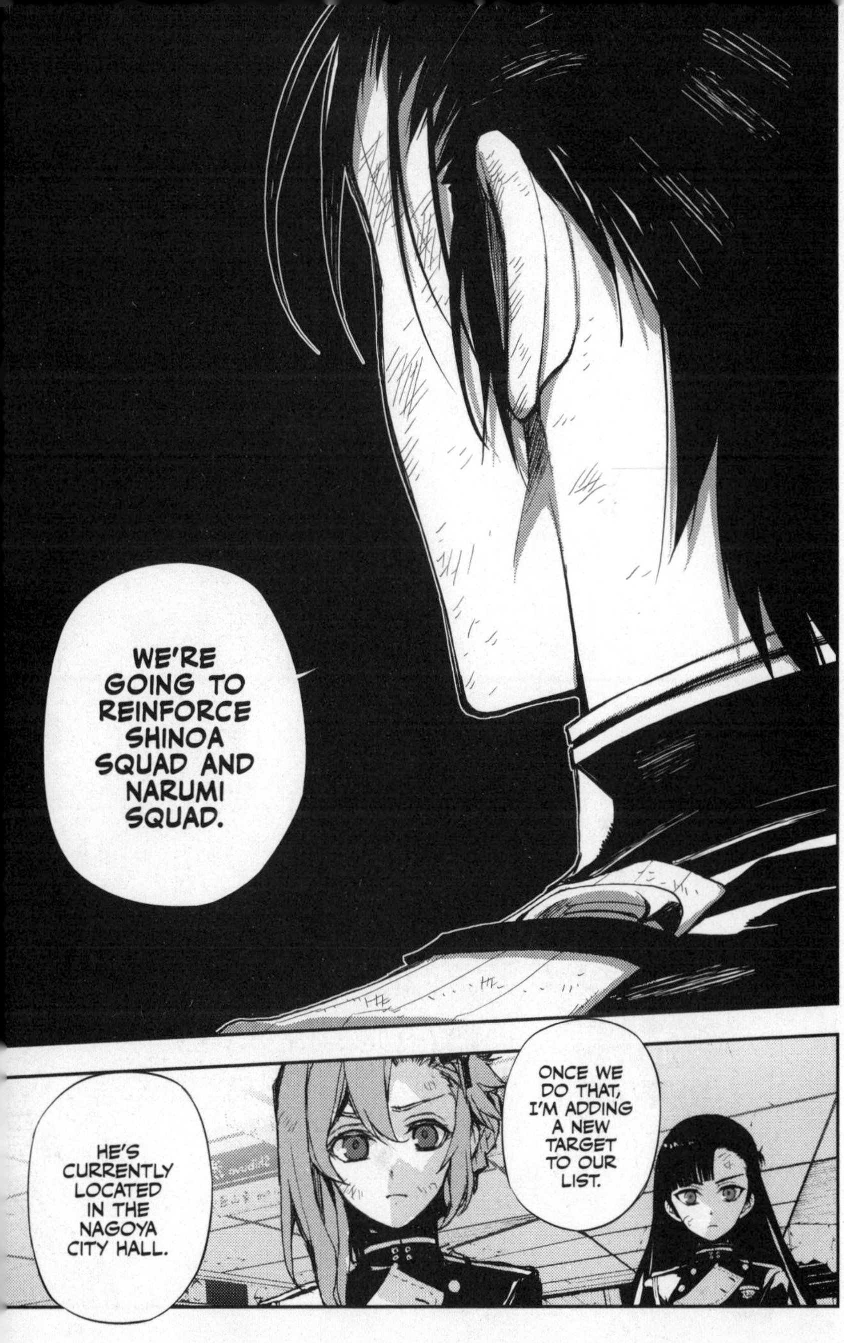
WE'RE GOING TO REINFORCE SHINOA SQUAD AND NARUMI SQUAD.
ONCE WE DO THAT, I'M ADDING A NEW TARGET TO OUR LIST.
HE'S CURRENTLY LOCATED IN THE NAGOYA CITY HALL.

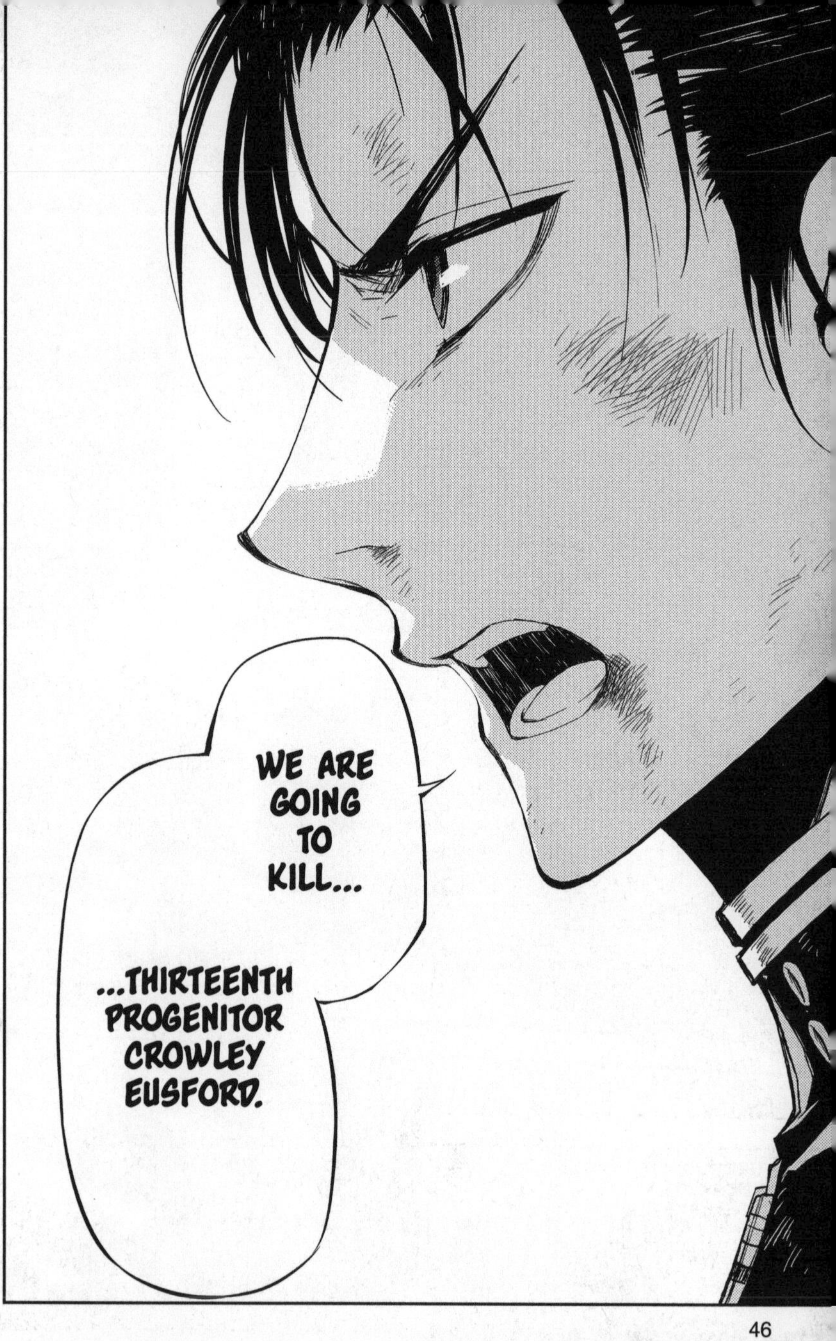
WE ARE GOING TO KILL...
...THIRTEENTH PROGENITOR CROWLEY EUSFORD.

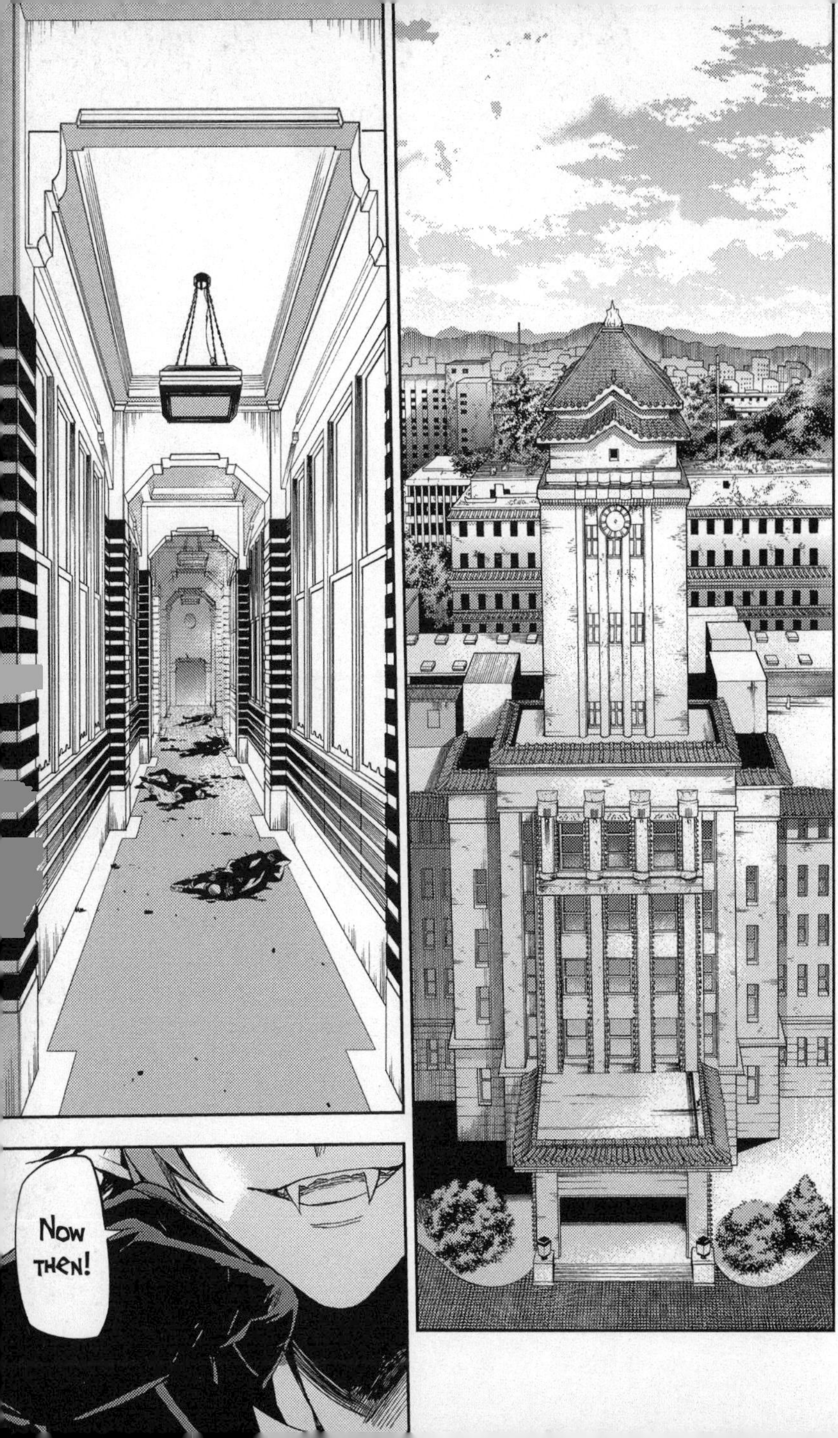
Now then!

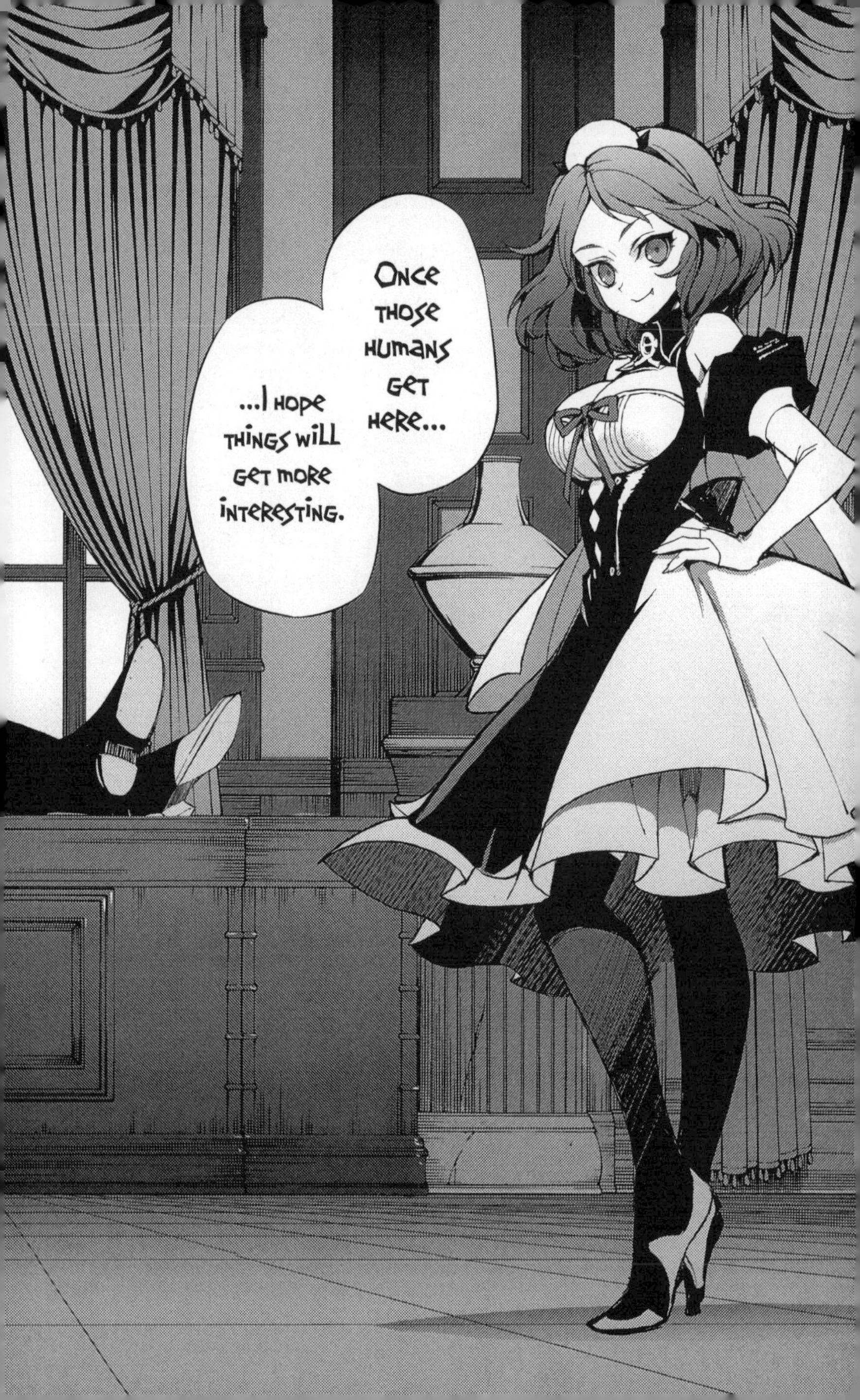
Once those humans get here...
...I hope things will get more interesting.

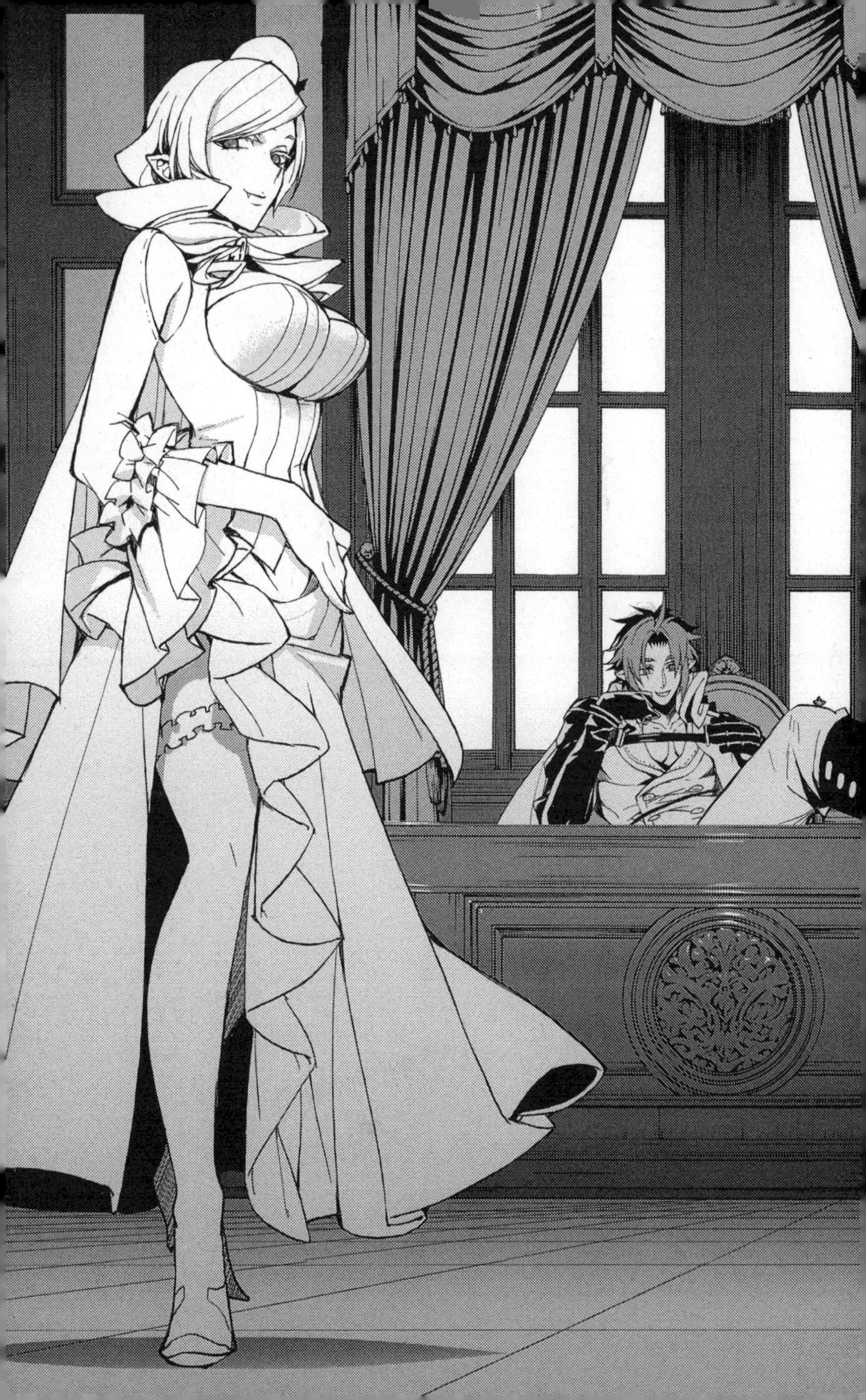

Seraph of the End
─VAMPIRE REIGN─

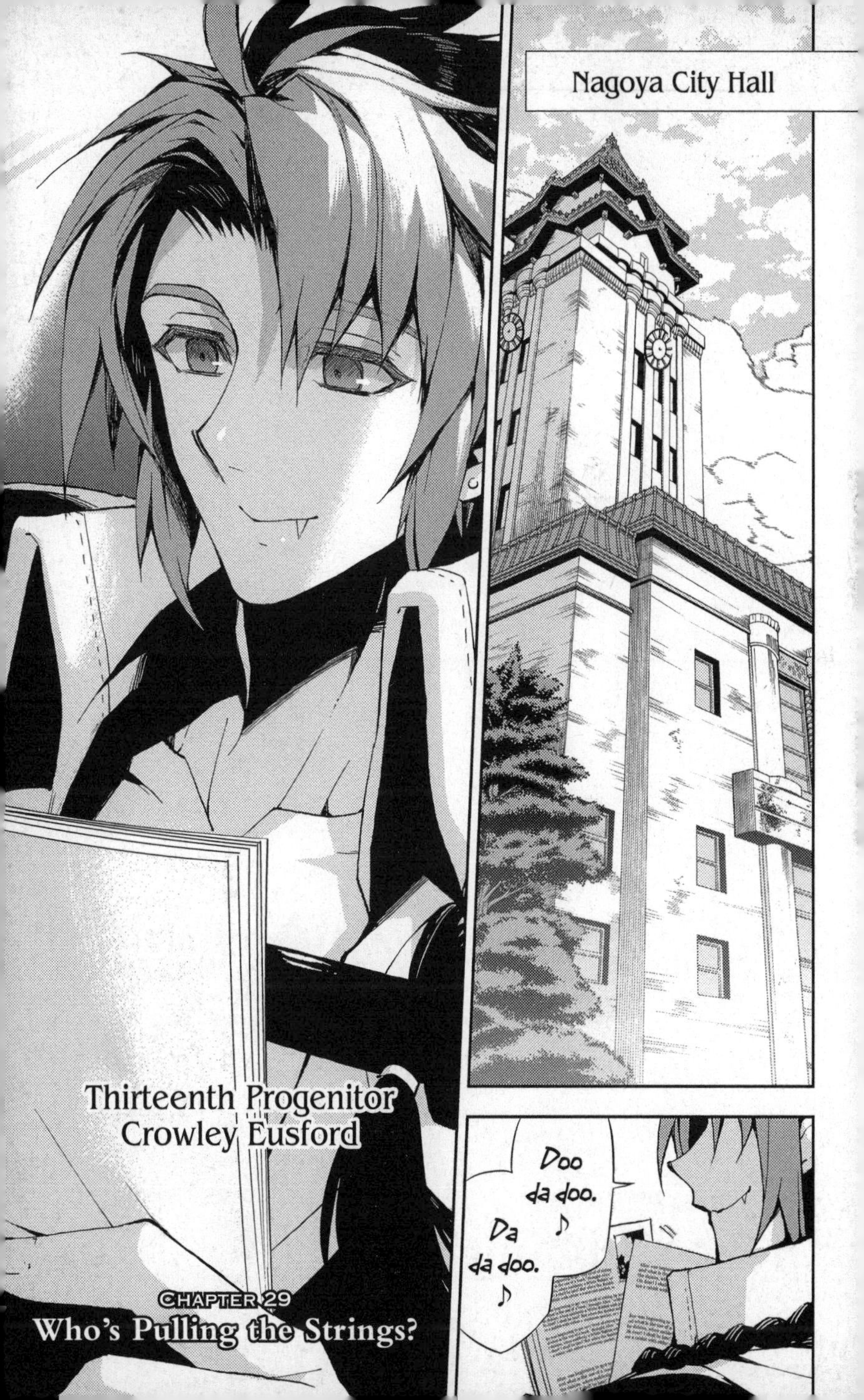
Nagoya City Hall
Doo da doo. ♪
Da da doo. ♪
Thirteenth Progenitor Crowley Eusford
CHAPTER 29
Who's Pulling the Strings?

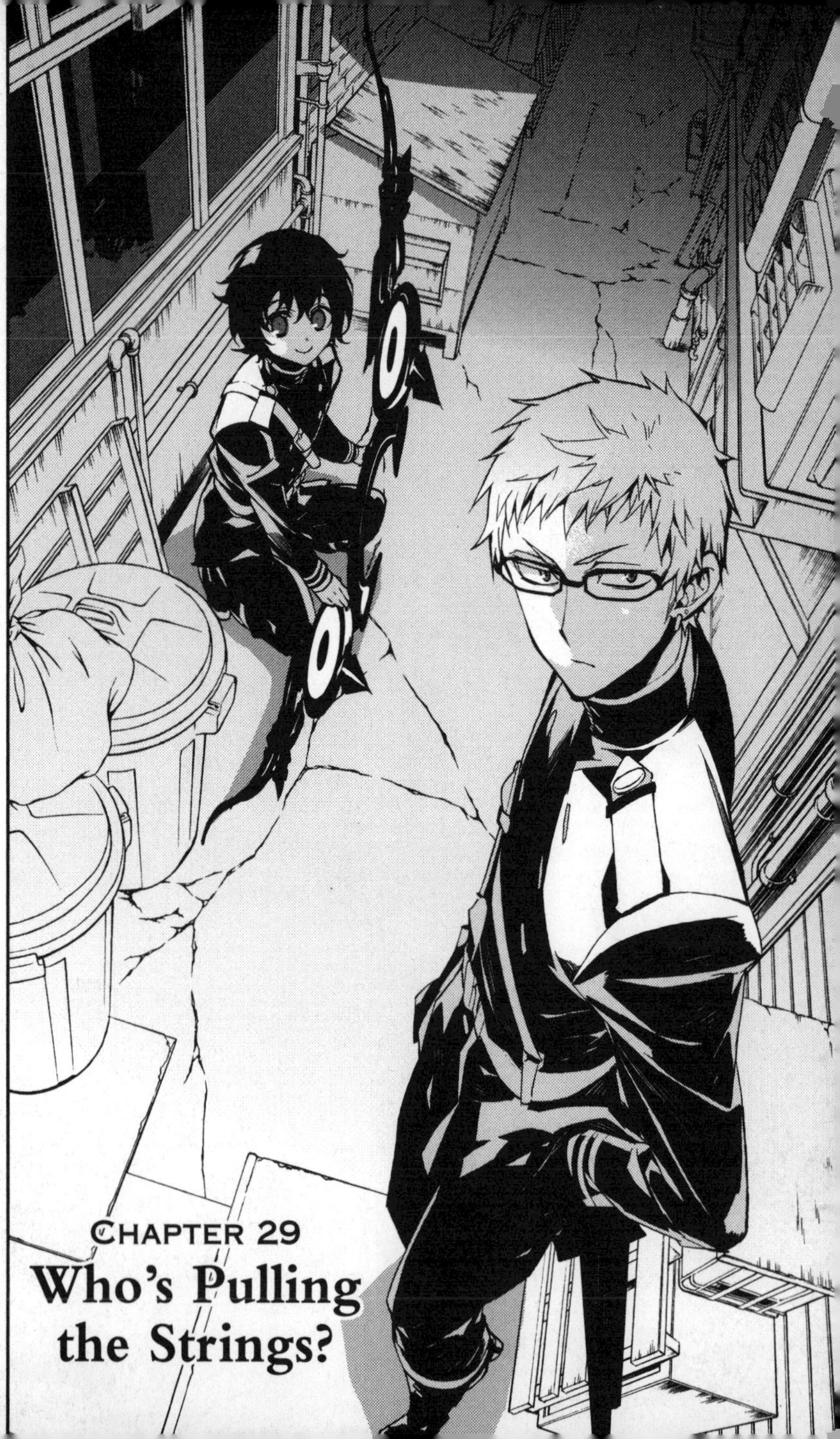
CHAPTER 29
Who's Pulling the Strings?

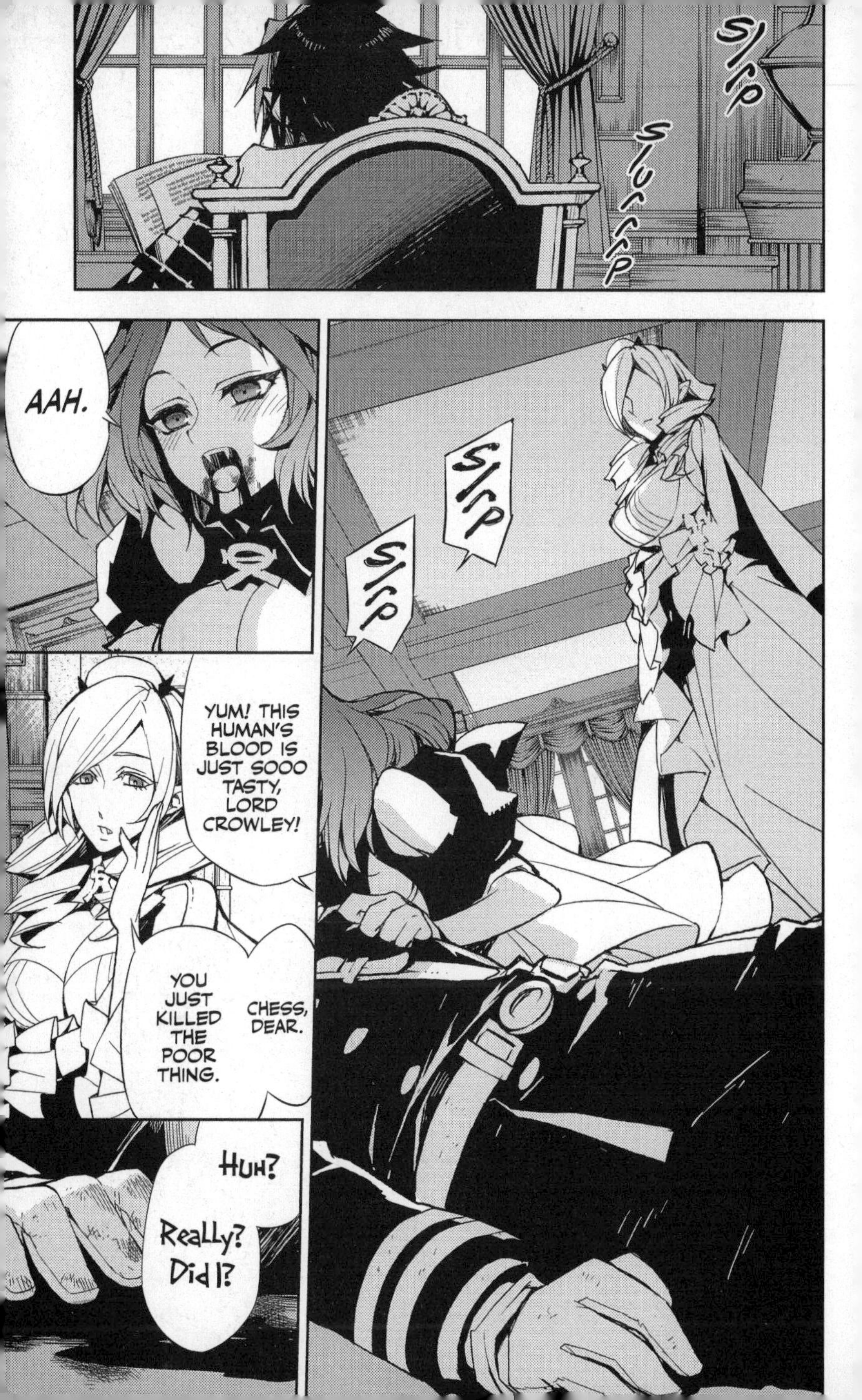
Slrp
Slurrrp
Slrp
Slrp
AAH.
YUM! THIS HUMAN'S BLOOD IS JUST SOOO TASTY, LORD CROWLEY!
CHESS, DEAR.
YOU JUST KILLED THE POOR THING.
Huh?
Really? Did I?

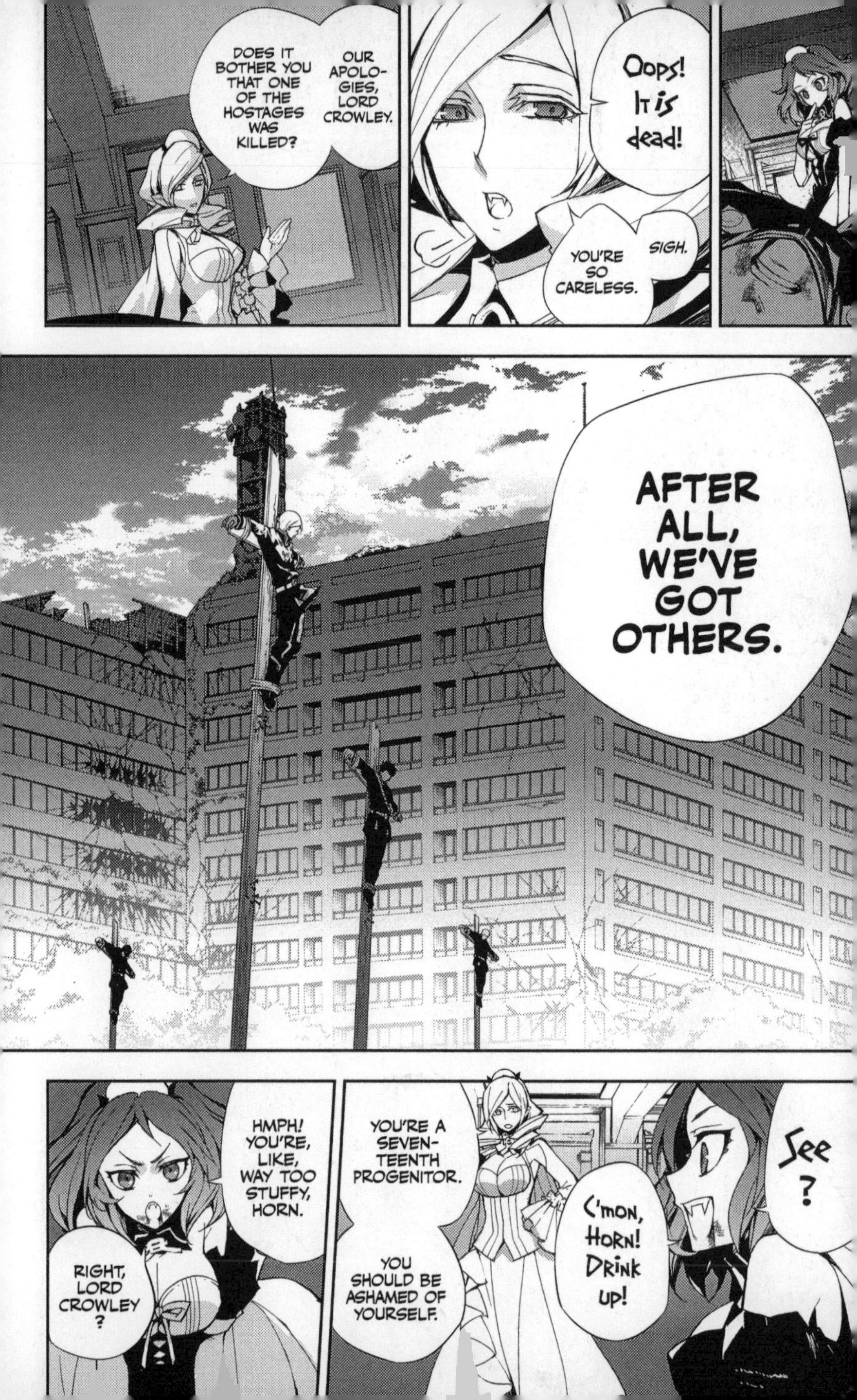
Oops! It is dead!
SIGH.
YOU'RE SO CARELESS.
OUR APOLOGIES, LORD CROWLEY.
DOES IT BOTHER YOU THAT ONE OF THE HOSTAGES WAS KILLED?
AFTER ALL, WE'VE GOT OTHERS.
See?
C'MON, HORN! DRINK UP!
YOU'RE A SEVENTEENTH PROGENITOR.
YOU SHOULD BE ASHAMED OF YOURSELF.
HMPH! YOU'RE, LIKE, WAY TOO STUFFY, HORN.
RIGHT, LORD CROWLEY?

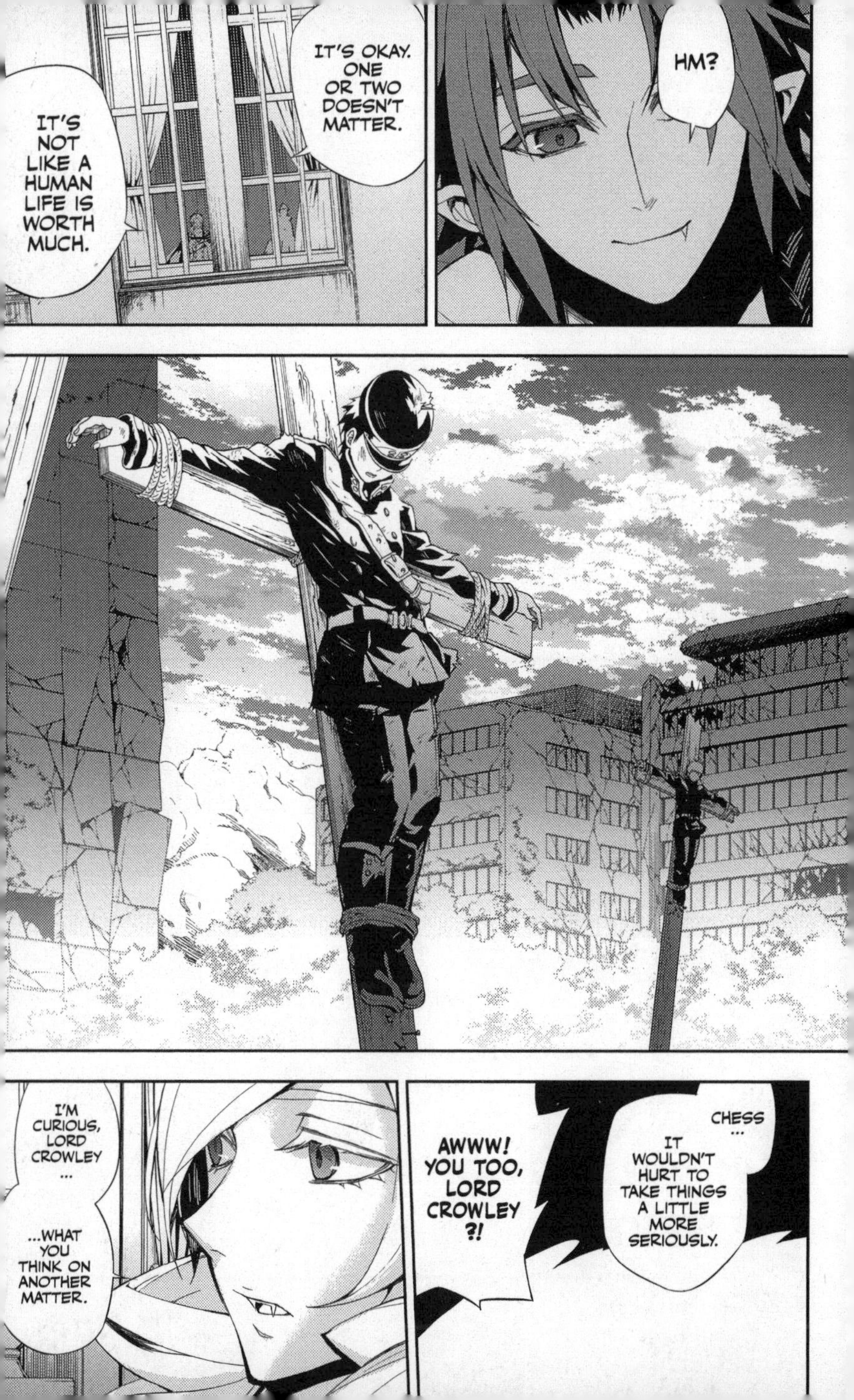
HM?
IT'S OKAY. ONE OR TWO DOESN'T MATTER.
IT'S NOT LIKE A HUMAN LIFE IS WORTH MUCH.
CHESS...
IT WOULDN'T HURT TO TAKE THINGS A LITTLE MORE SERIOUSLY.
AWWW! YOU TOO, LORD CROWLEY?!
I'M CURIOUS, LORD CROWLEY...
...WHAT YOU THINK ON ANOTHER MATTER.

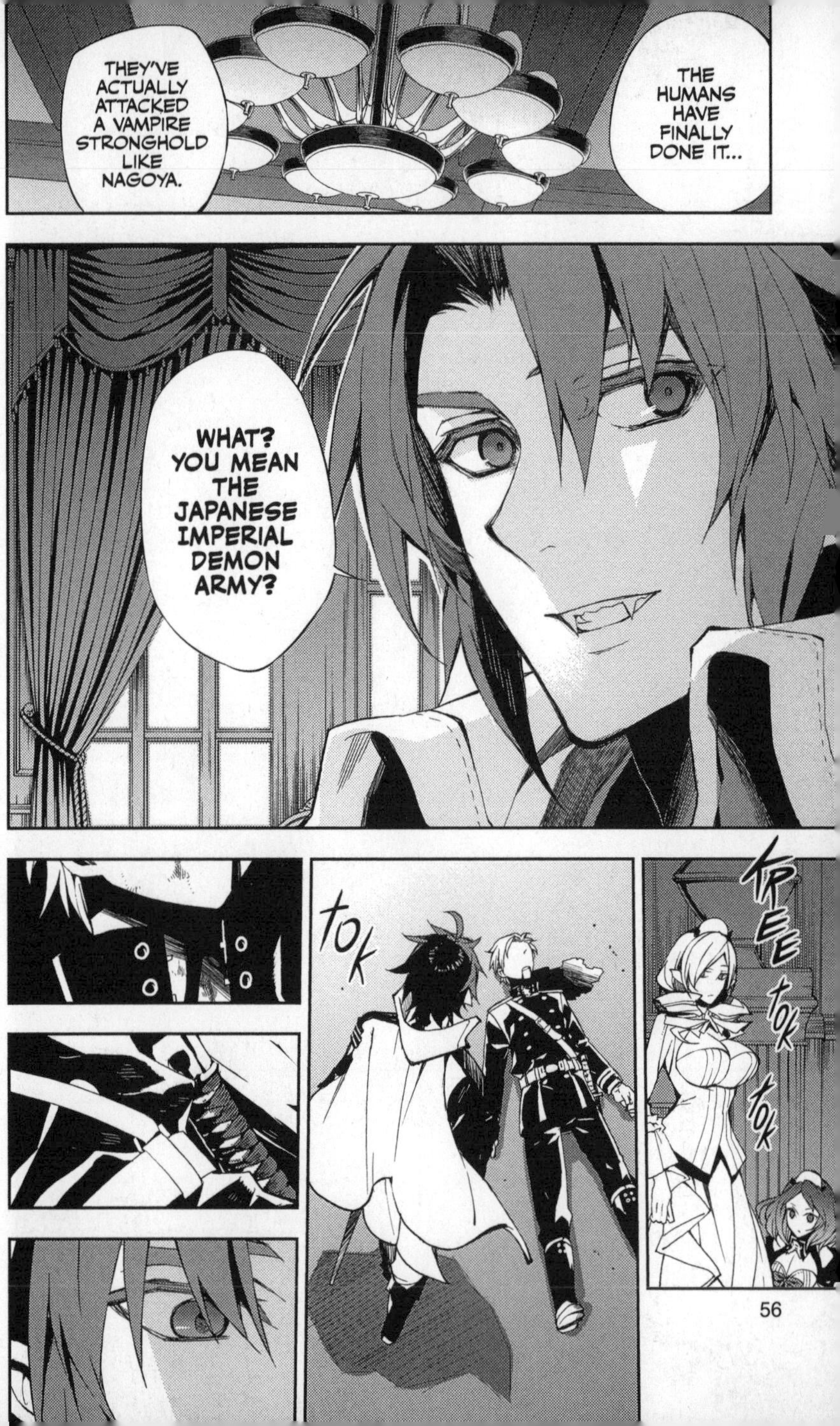
THE HUMANS HAVE FINALLY DONE IT...
THEY'VE ACTUALLY ATTACKED A VAMPIRE STRONGHOLD LIKE NAGOYA.
WHAT? YOU MEAN THE JAPANESE IMPERIAL DEMON ARMY?
KREE
TOK
TOK
TOK
TOK

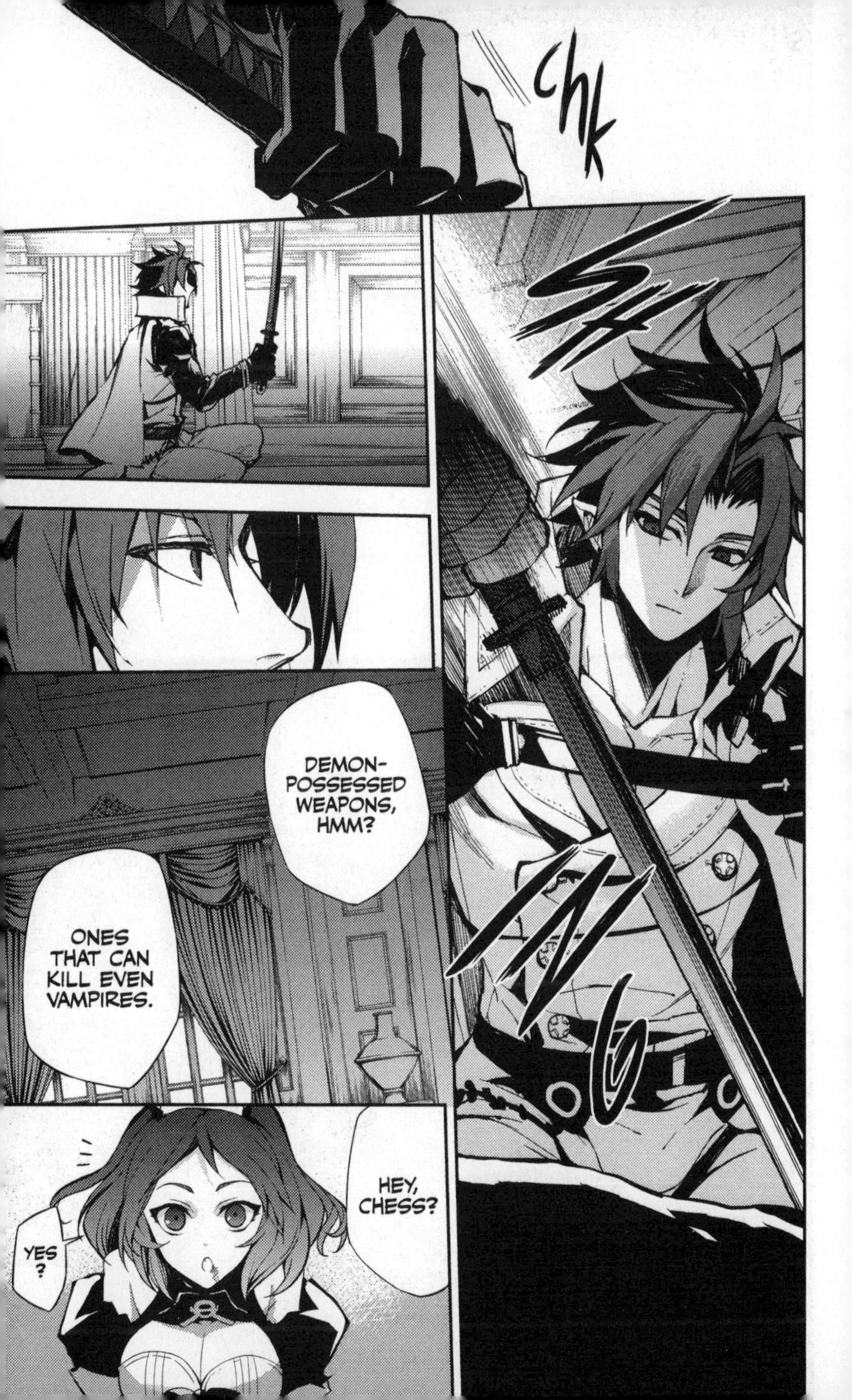
chk
DEMON-POSSESSED WEAPONS, HMM?
ONES THAT CAN KILL EVEN VAMPIRES.
HEY, CHESS?
YES?

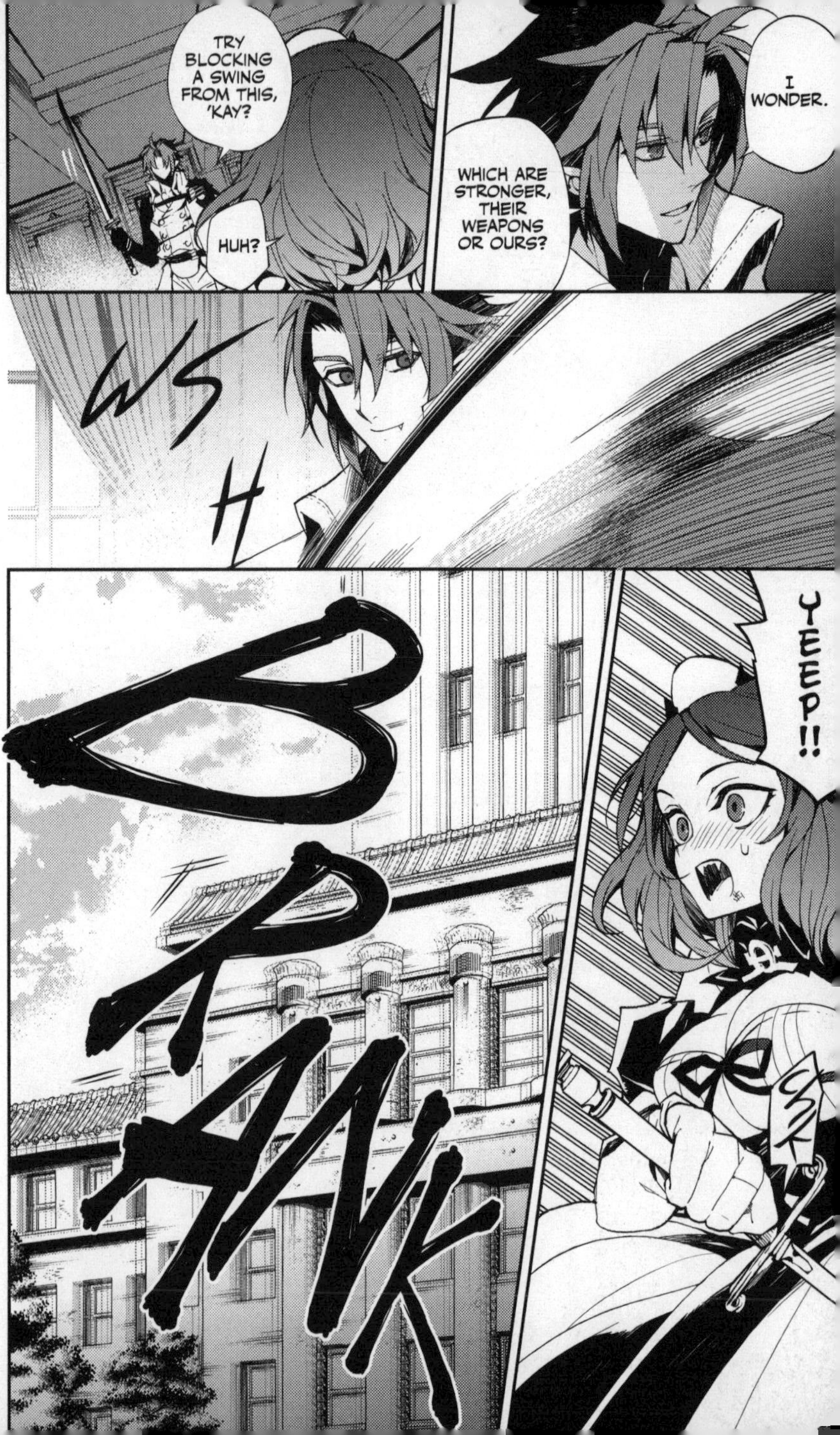
I WONDER.
WHICH ARE STRONGER, THEIR WEAPONS OR OURS?
TRY BLOCKING A SWING FROM THIS, 'KAY?
HUH?
WSH
YEEEP!!

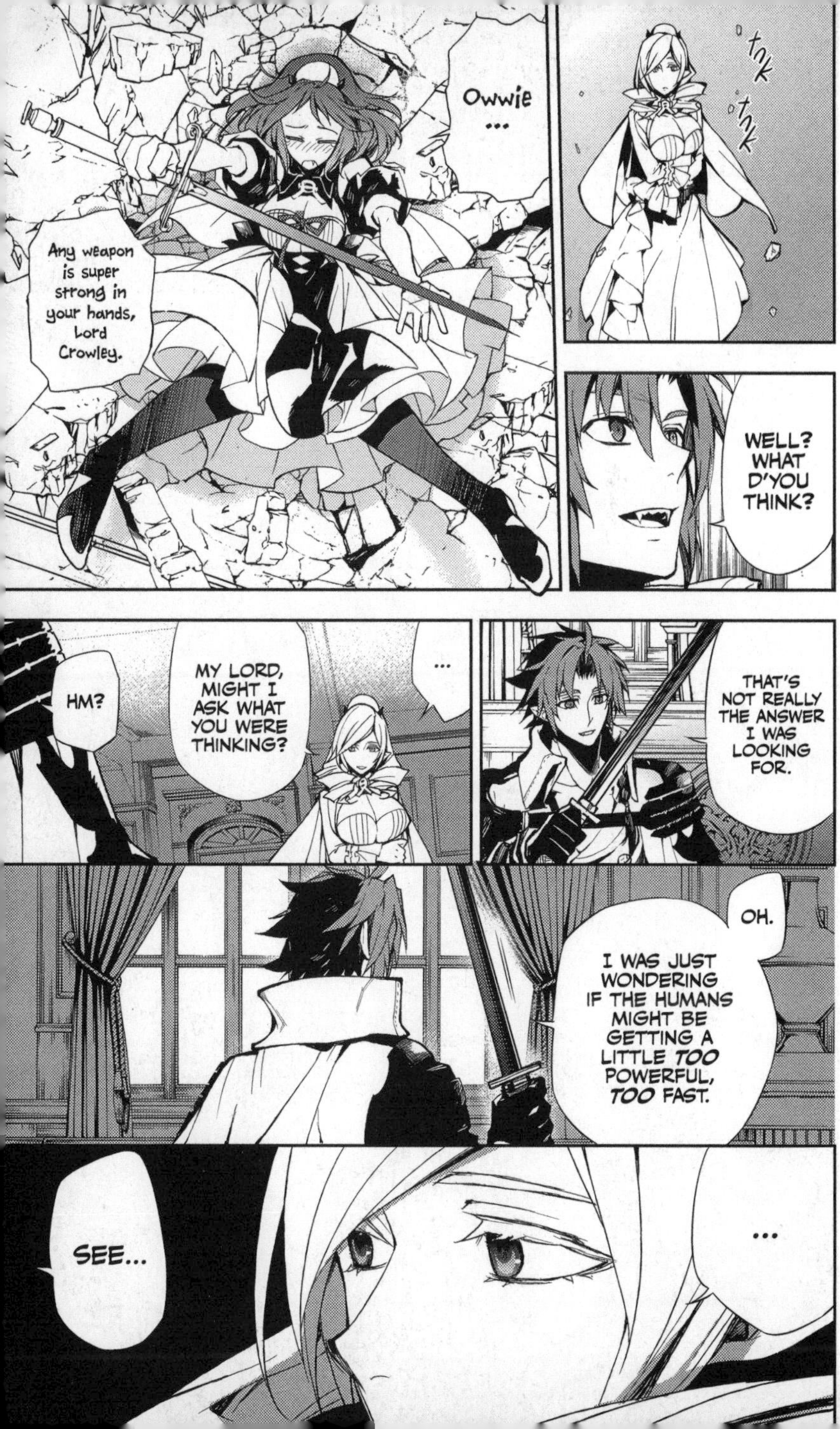

tnk tnk
WELL? WHAT D'YOU THINK?
Owwie...
Any weapon is super strong in your hands, Lord Crowley.
THAT'S NOT REALLY THE ANSWER I WAS LOOKING FOR.
...
MY LORD, MIGHT I ASK WHAT YOU WERE THINKING?
HM?
OH.
I WAS JUST WONDERING IF THE HUMANS MIGHT BE GETTING A LITTLE *TOO* POWERFUL, *TOO* FAST.
...
SEE...

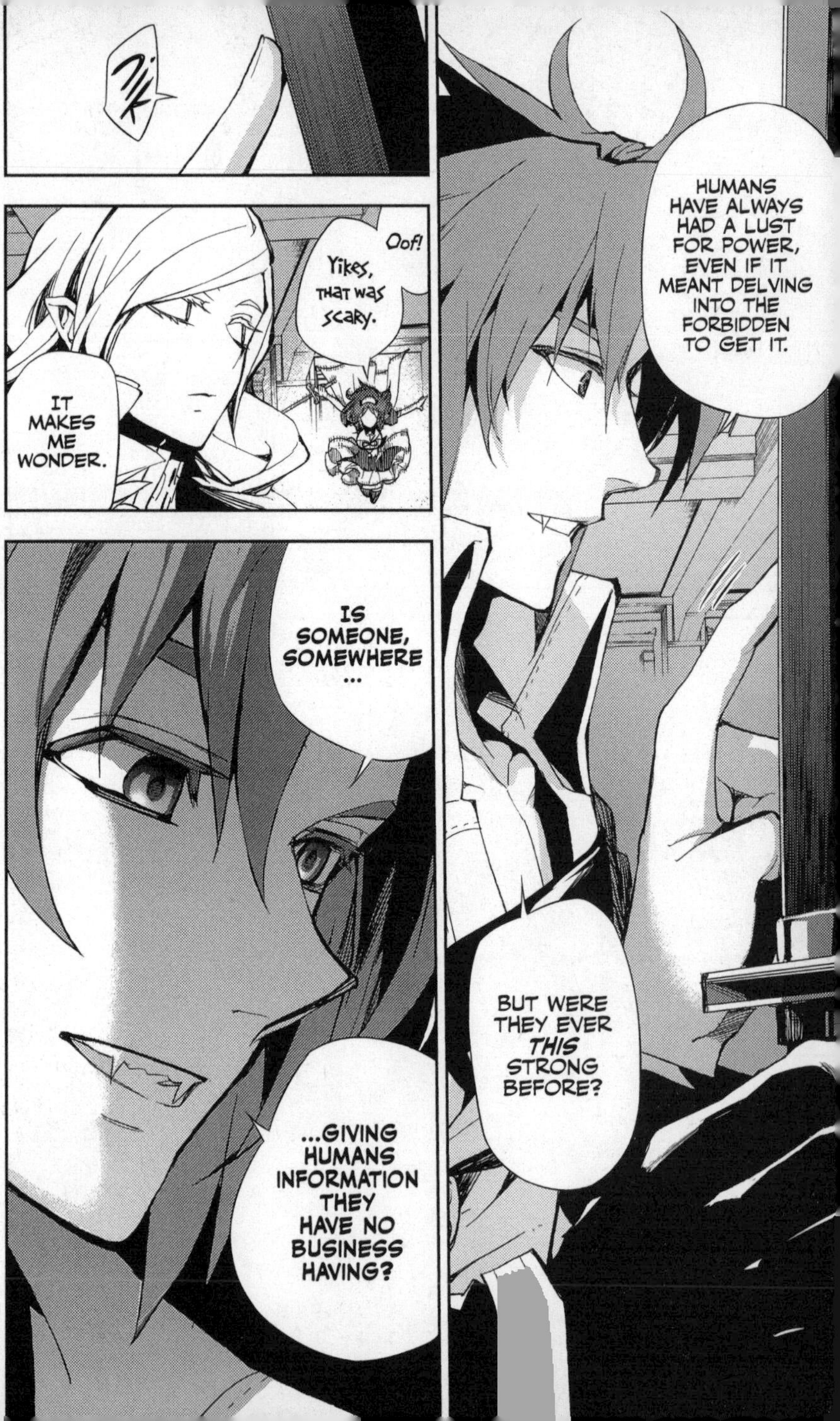
HUMANS HAVE ALWAYS HAD A LUST FOR POWER, EVEN IF IT MEANT DELVING INTO THE FORBIDDEN TO GET IT.
BUT WERE THEY EVER *THIS* STRONG BEFORE?
JIK
Oof!
Yikes, THAT WAS scary.
IT MAKES ME WONDER.
IS SOMEONE, SOMEWHERE...
...GIVING HUMANS INFORMATION THEY HAVE NO BUSINESS HAVING?

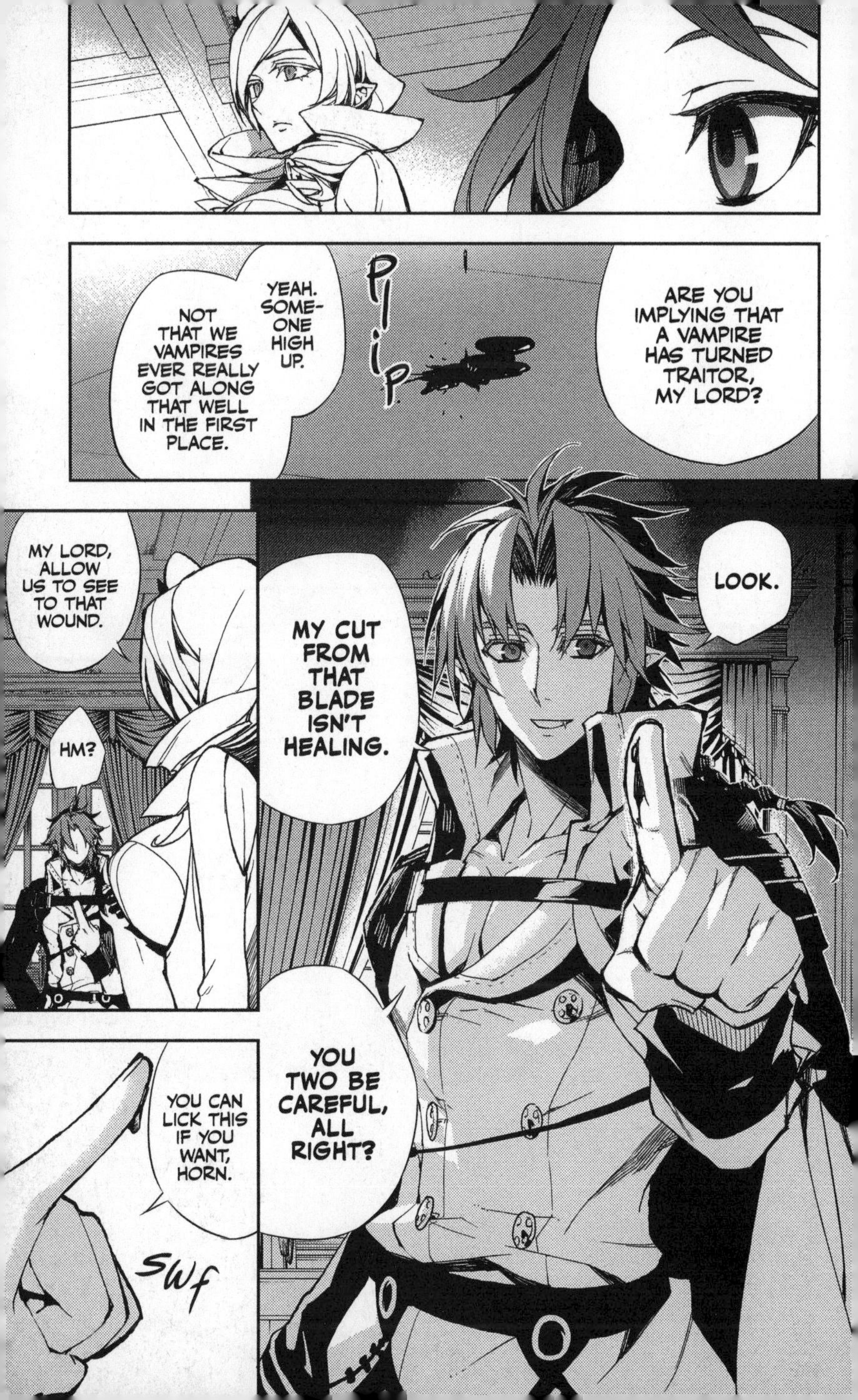

ARE YOU IMPLYING THAT A VAMPIRE HAS TURNED TRAITOR, MY LORD?
PIIP
YEAH. SOME-ONE HIGH UP.
NOT THAT WE VAMPIRES EVER REALLY GOT ALONG THAT WELL IN THE FIRST PLACE.
LOOK.
MY CUT FROM THAT BLADE ISN'T HEALING.
YOU TWO BE CAREFUL, ALL RIGHT?
MY LORD, ALLOW US TO SEE TO THAT WOUND.
HM?
YOU CAN LICK THIS IF YOU WANT, HORN.
SWF

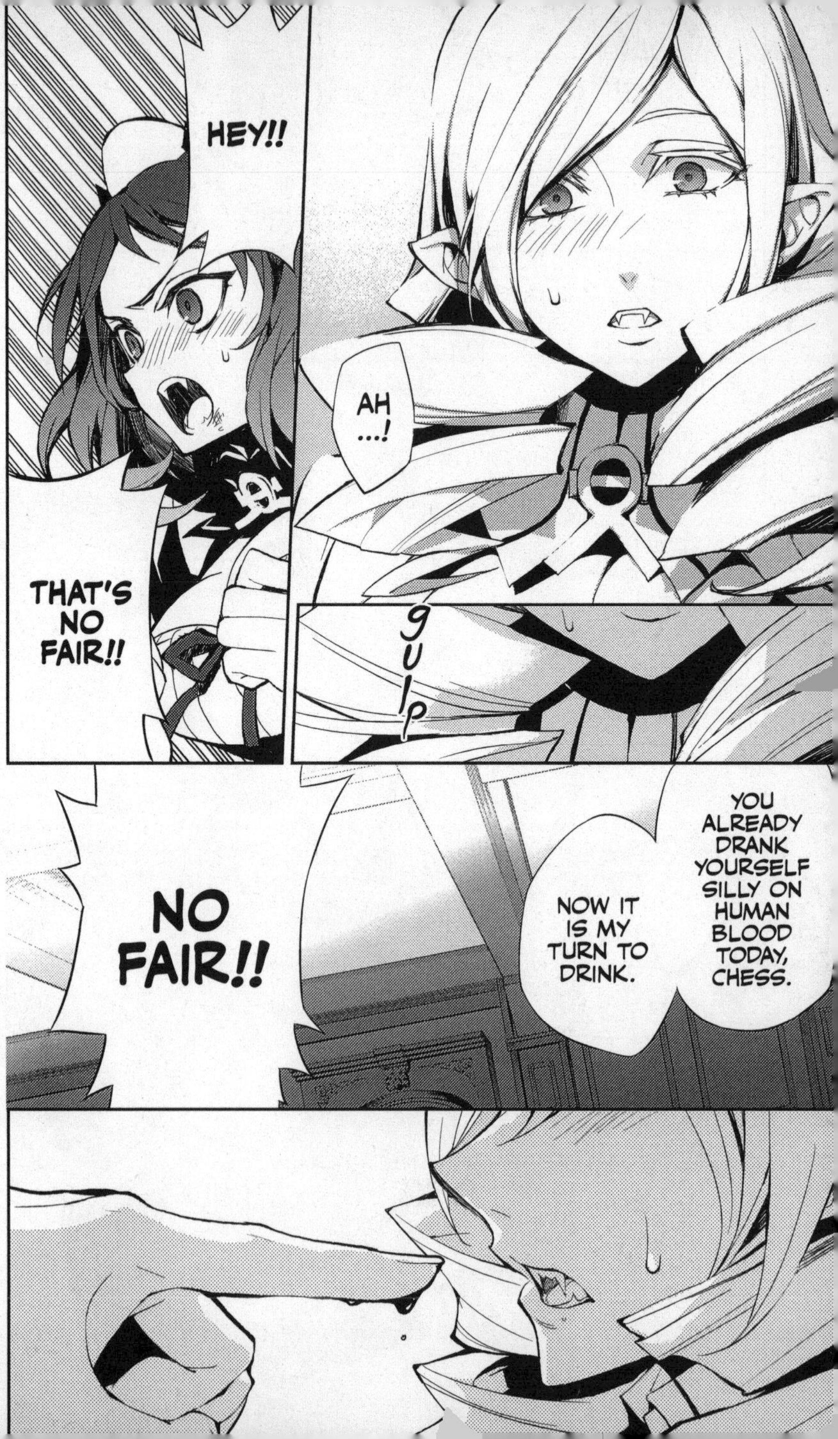
AH ...!
GULP
HEY!!
THAT'S NO FAIR!!
YOU ALREADY DRANK YOURSELF SILLY ON HUMAN BLOOD TODAY, CHESS.
NOW IT IS MY TURN TO DRINK.
NO FAIR!!

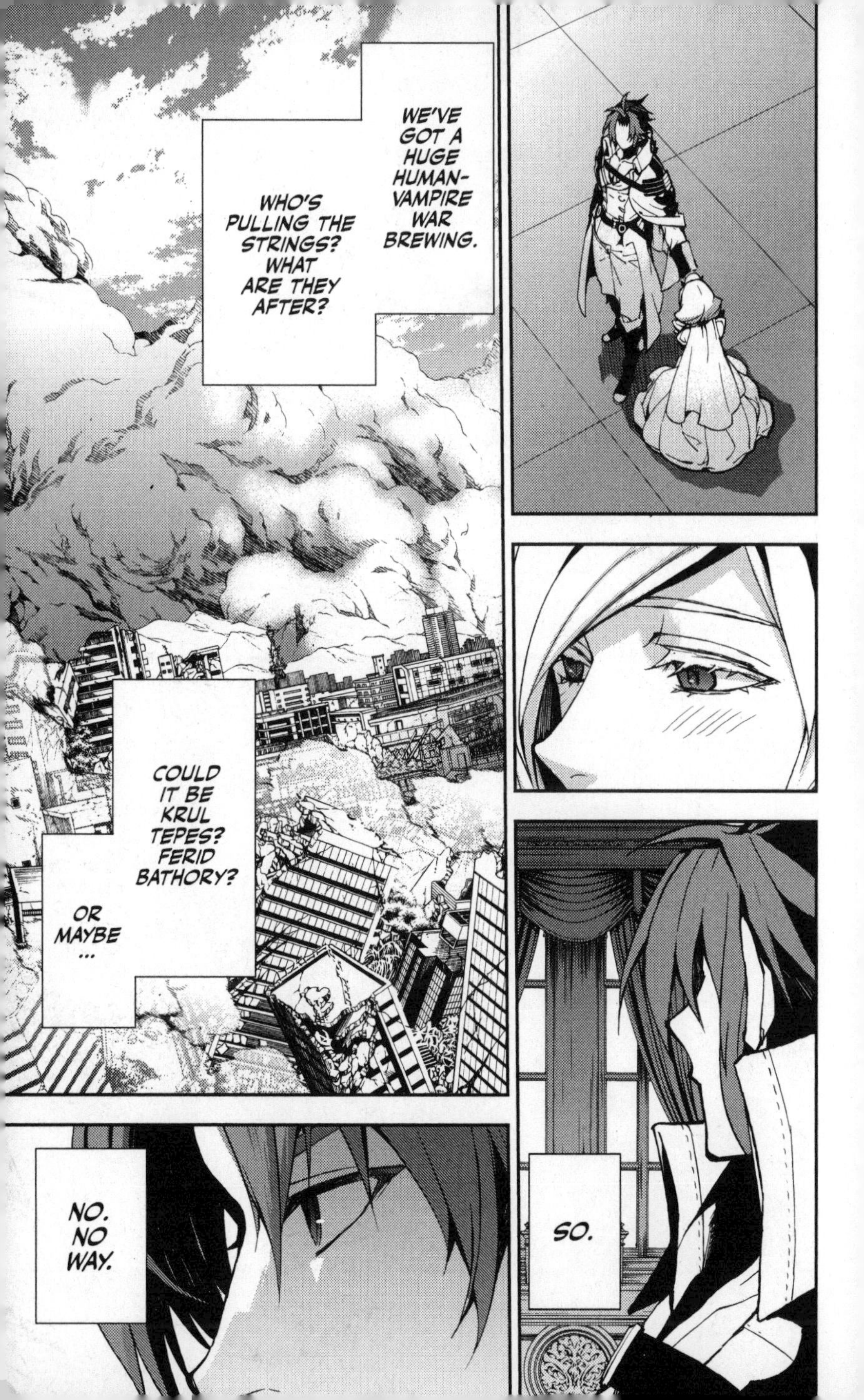
WE'VE GOT A HUGE HUMAN-VAMPIRE WAR BREWING.
WHO'S PULLING THE STRINGS? WHAT ARE THEY AFTER?
COULD IT BE KRUL TEPES? FERID BATHORY?
OR MAYBE ...
SO.
NO. NO WAY.

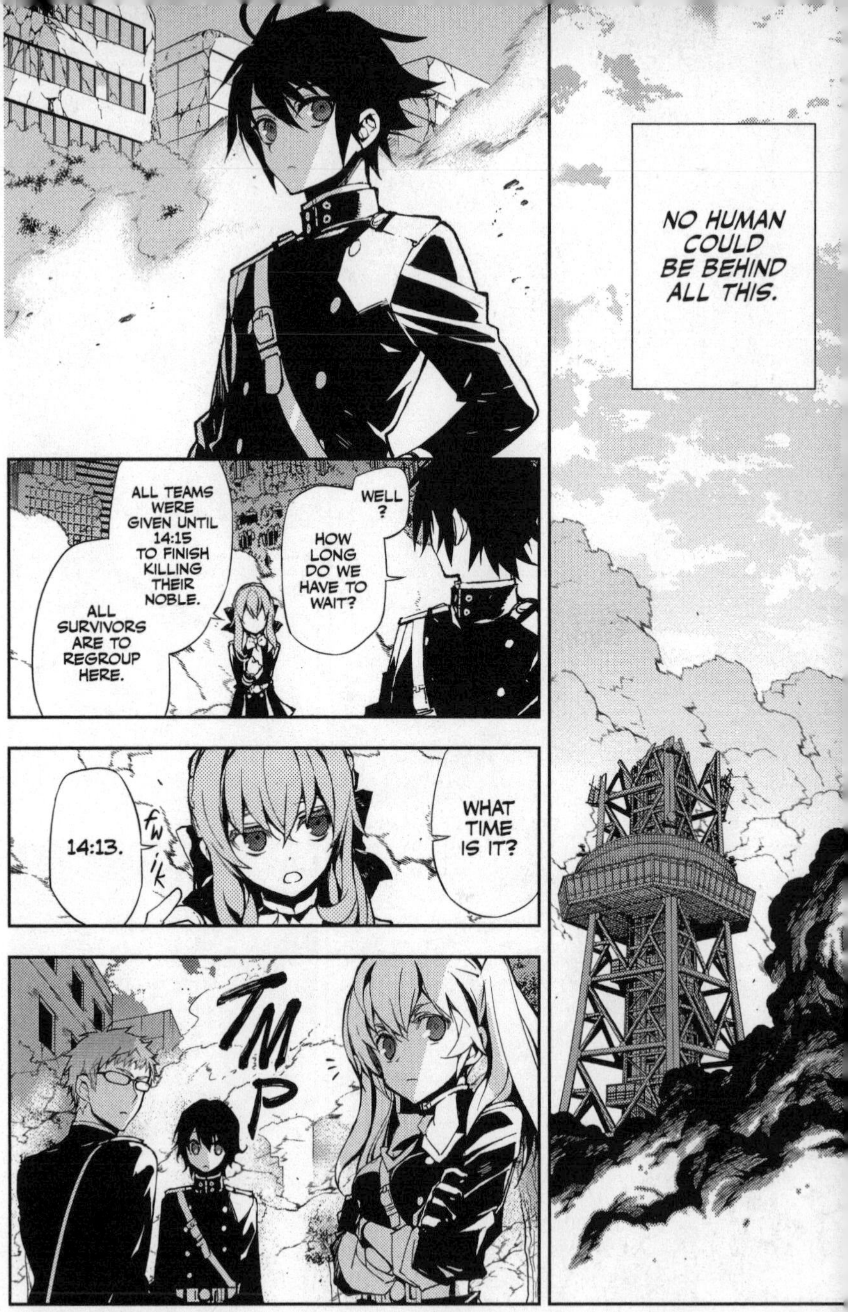
NO HUMAN COULD BE BEHIND ALL THIS.
WELL? HOW LONG DO WE HAVE TO WAIT?
ALL TEAMS WERE GIVEN UNTIL 14:15 TO FINISH KILLING THEIR NOBLE.
ALL SURVIVORS ARE TO REGROUP HERE.
WHAT TIME IS IT?
FWIK
14:13.
TMP

Team Leader Aiko Aihara

WHERE'S LT. COLONEL ICHINOSE?

SHINOA.

...

WE WAIT UNTIL 15 AFTER.

HE ISN'T HERE YET.

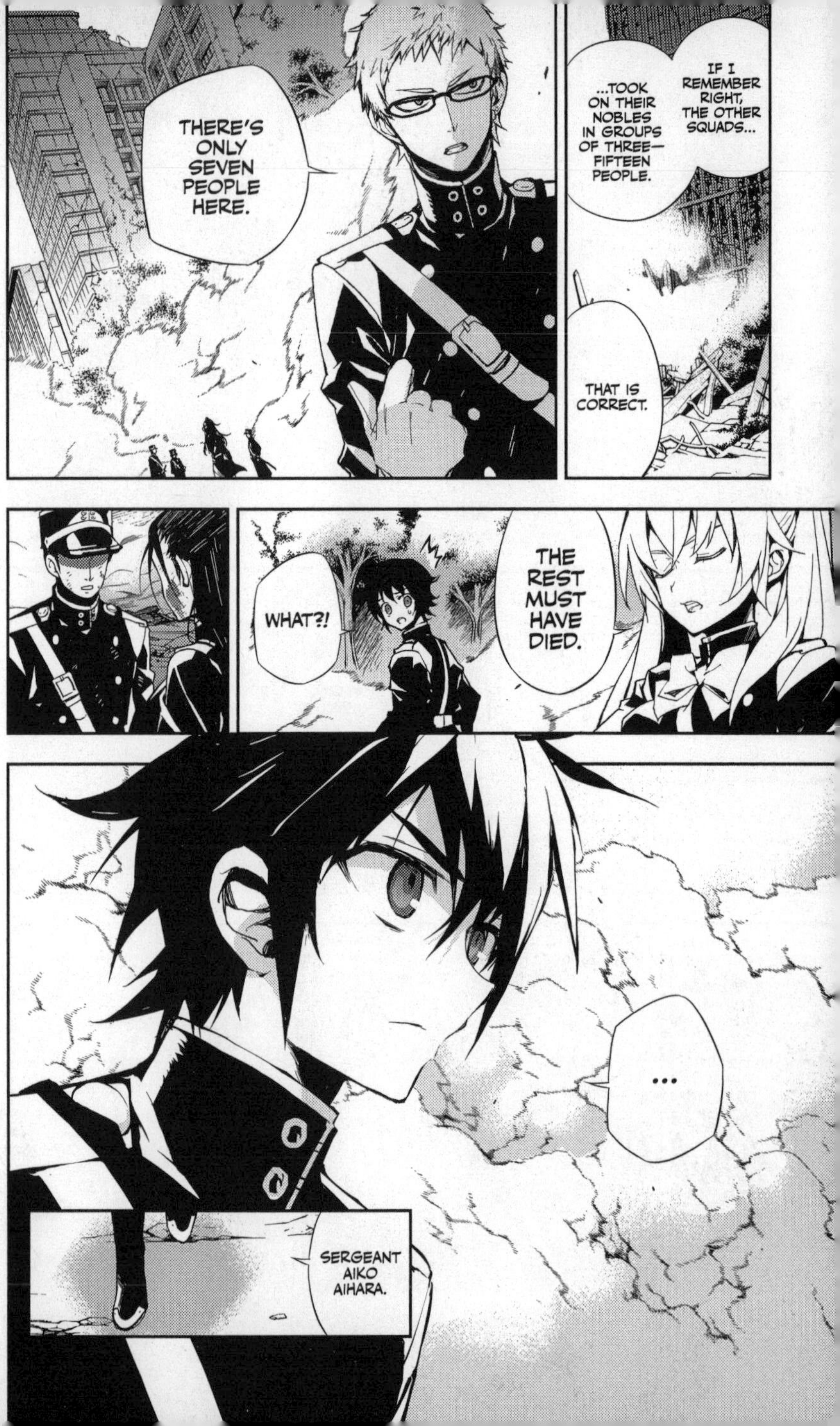
IF I REMEMBER RIGHT, THE OTHER SQUADS...
...TOOK ON THEIR NOBLES IN GROUPS OF THREE—FIFTEEN PEOPLE.
THAT IS CORRECT.
THERE'S ONLY SEVEN PEOPLE HERE.
THE REST MUST HAVE DIED.
WHAT?!
...
SERGEANT AIKO AIHARA.

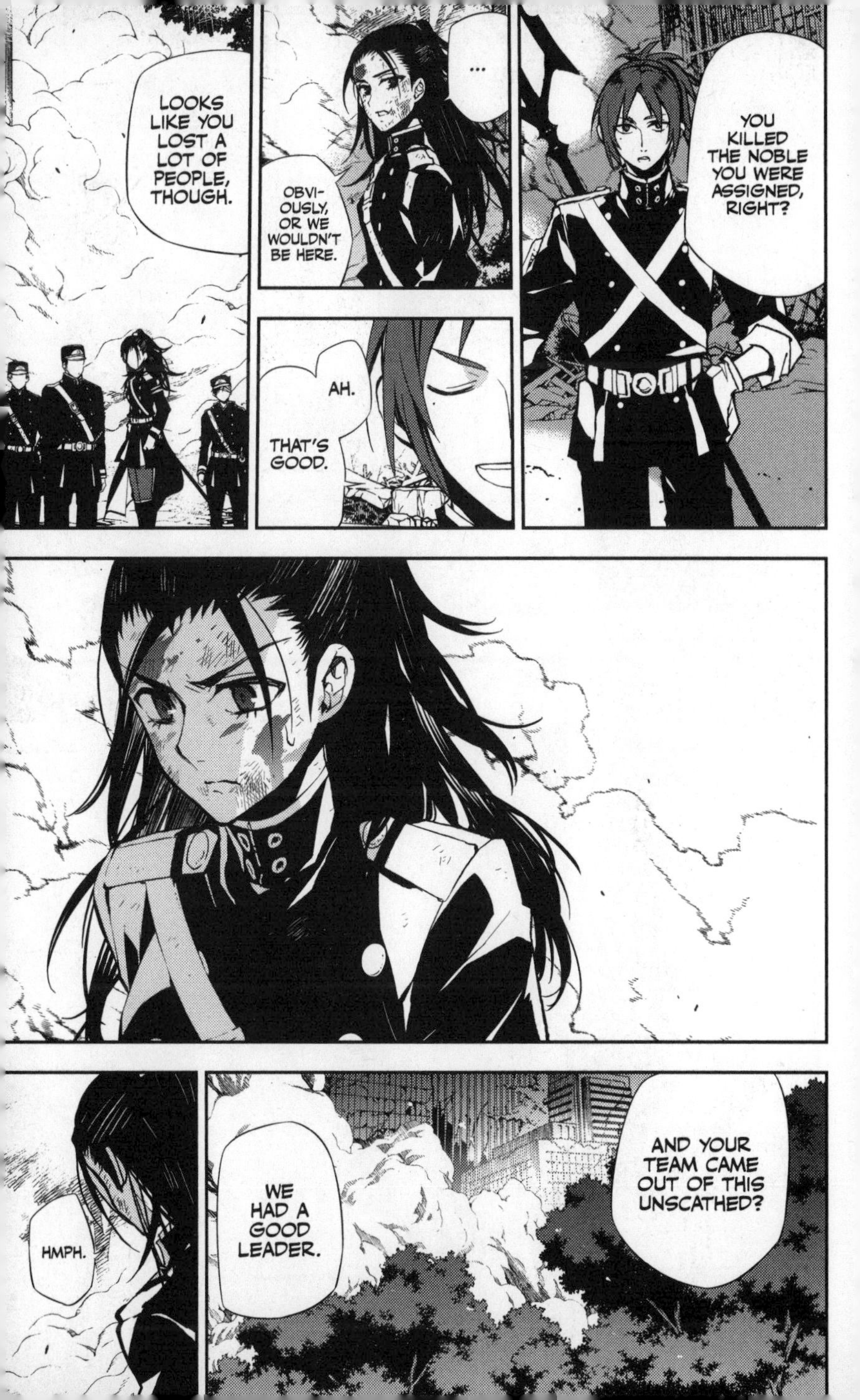
YOU KILLED THE NOBLE YOU WERE ASSIGNED, RIGHT?
...
OBVIOUSLY, OR WE WOULDN'T BE HERE.
AH.
THAT'S GOOD.
LOOKS LIKE YOU LOST A LOT OF PEOPLE, THOUGH.
AND YOUR TEAM CAME OUT OF THIS UNSCATHED?
WE HAD A GOOD LEADER.
HMPH.

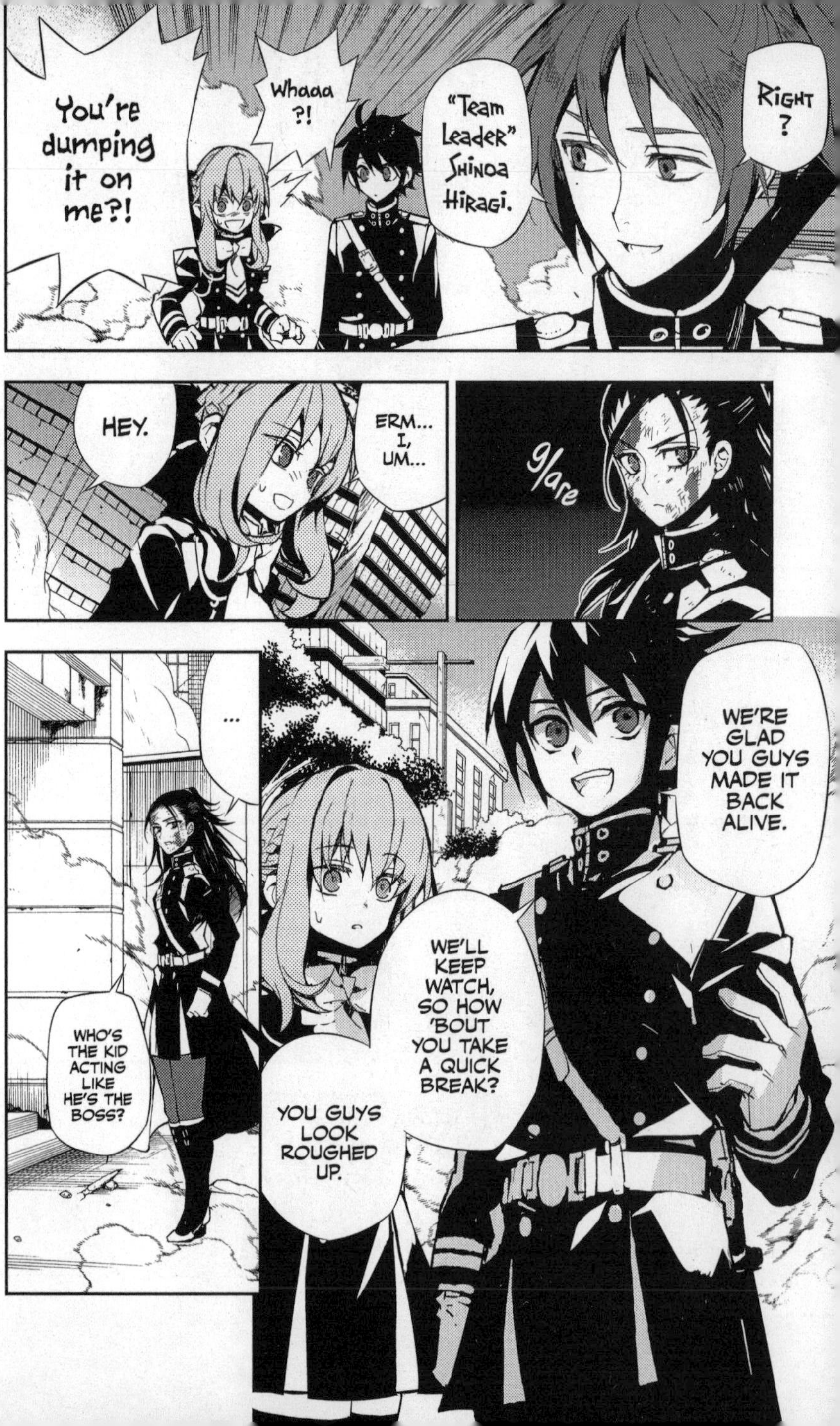
Right?
"Team Leader" Shinoa Hiragi.
Whaaa?!
You're dumping it on me?!
glare
ERM... I, UM...
HEY.
WE'RE GLAD YOU GUYS MADE IT BACK ALIVE.
WE'LL KEEP WATCH, SO HOW 'BOUT YOU TAKE A QUICK BREAK?
YOU GUYS LOOK ROUGHED UP.
...
WHO'S THE KID ACTING LIKE HE'S THE BOSS?

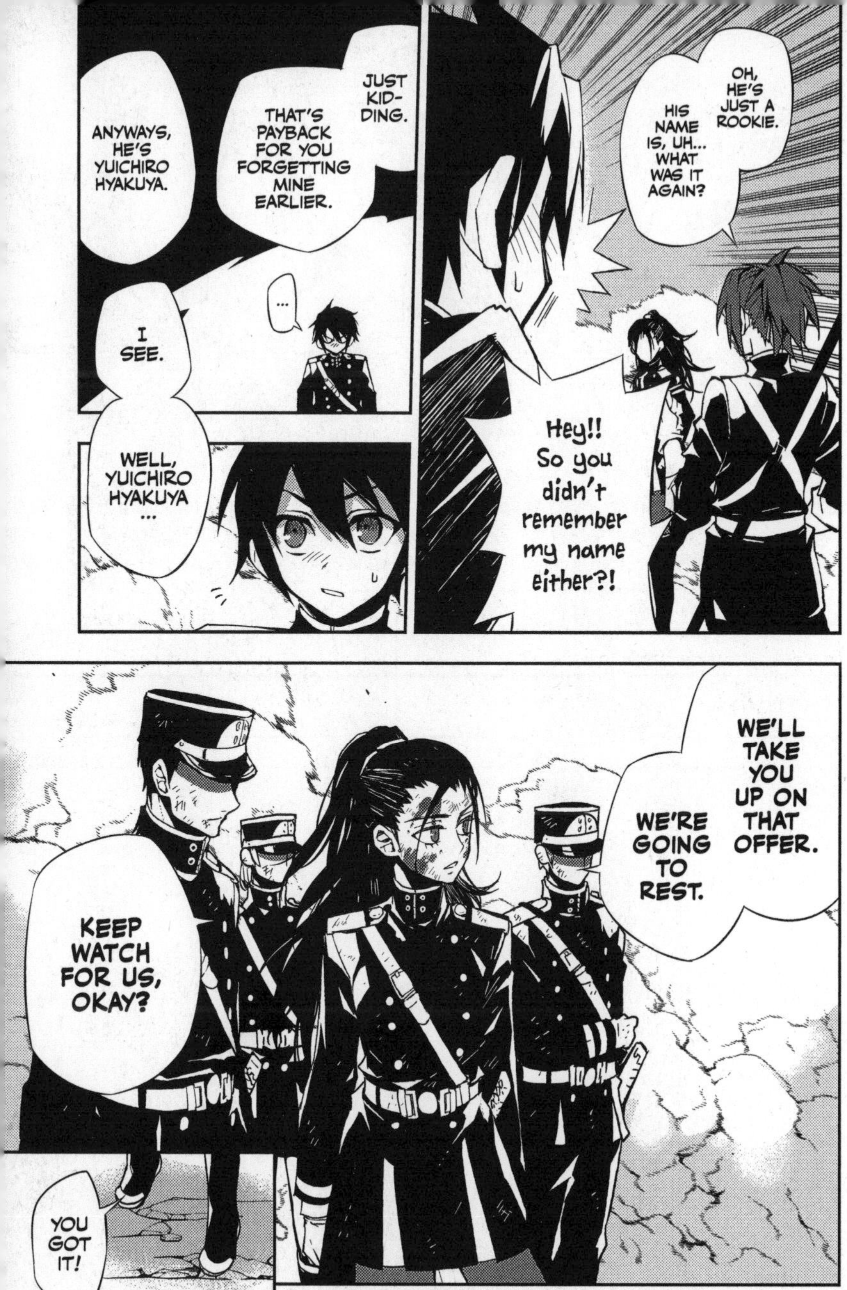
OH, HE'S JUST A ROOKIE.
HIS NAME IS, UH... WHAT WAS IT AGAIN?
Hey!! So you didn't remember my name either?!
JUST KID-DING.
THAT'S PAYBACK FOR YOU FORGETTING MINE EARLIER.
ANYWAYS, HE'S YUICHIRO HYAKUYA.
...
I SEE.
WELL, YUICHIRO HYAKUYA ...
WE'LL TAKE YOU UP ON THAT OFFER.
WE'RE GOING TO REST.
KEEP WATCH FOR US, OKAY?
YOU GOT IT!

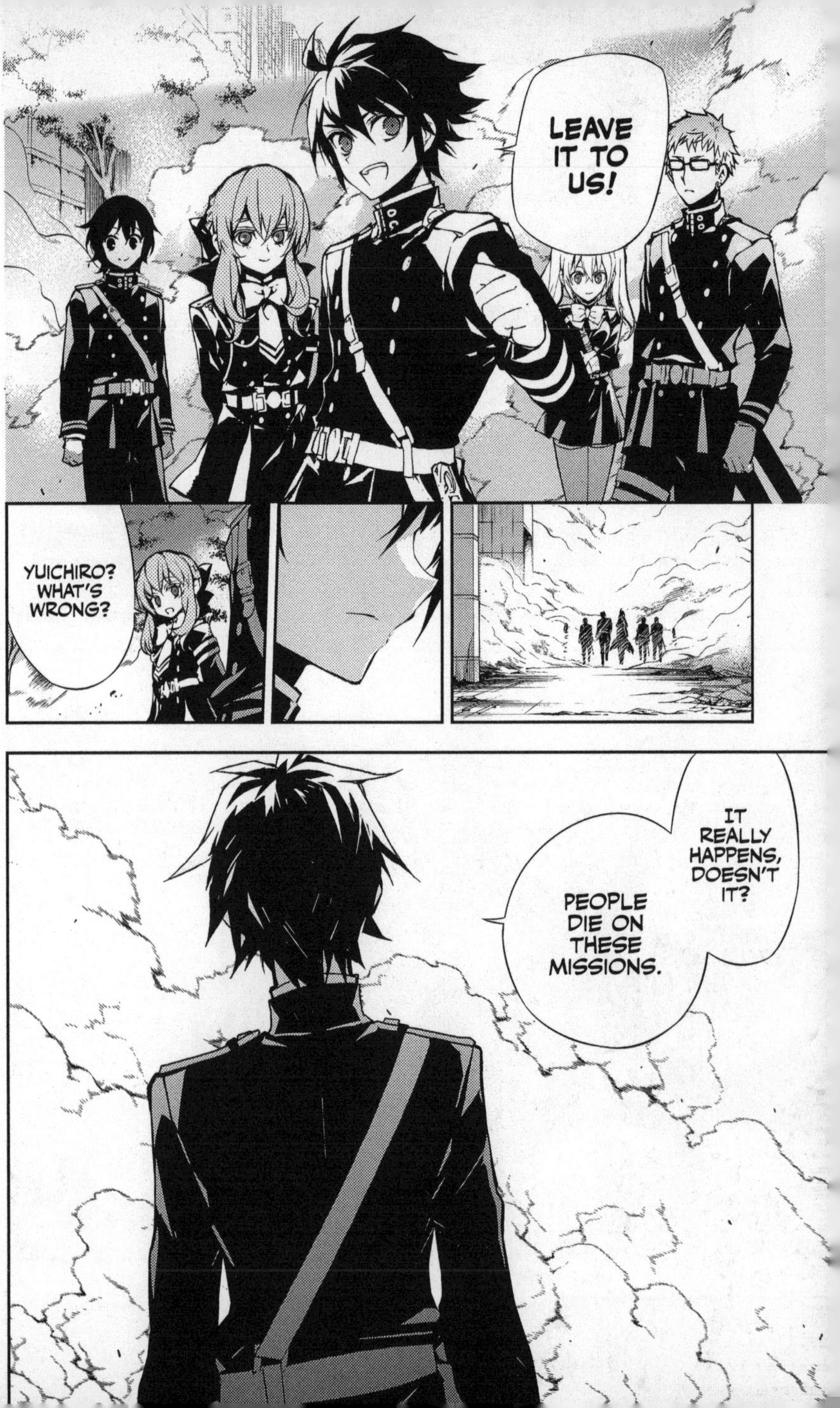
LEAVE IT TO US!
YUICHIRO? WHAT'S WRONG?
IT REALLY HAPPENS, DOESN'T IT?
PEOPLE DIE ON THESE MISSIONS.

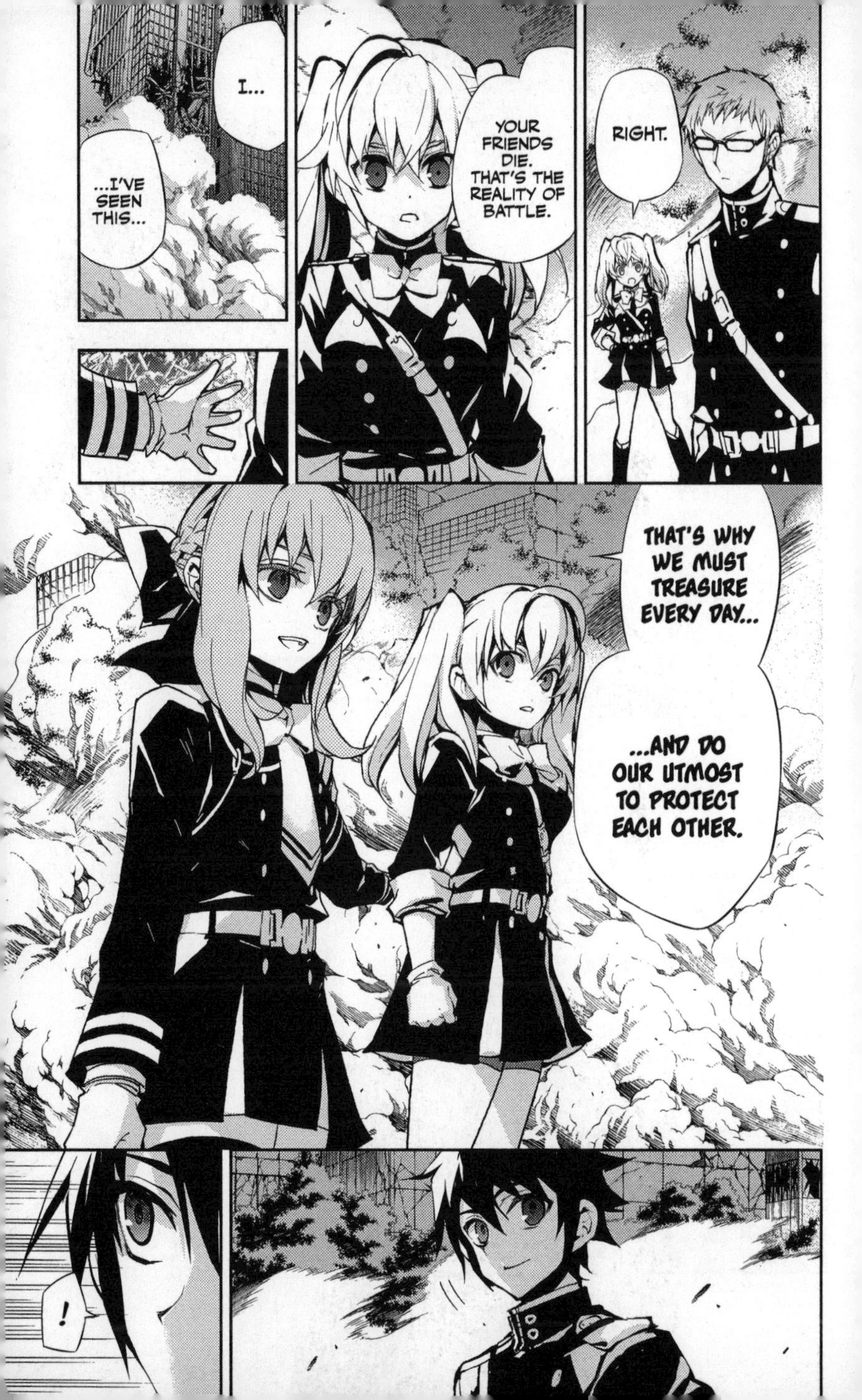
RIGHT.
YOUR FRIENDS DIE. THAT'S THE REALITY OF BATTLE.
I...
...I'VE SEEN THIS...
THAT'S WHY WE MUST TREASURE EVERY DAY...
...AND DO OUR UTMOST TO PROTECT EACH OTHER.
!

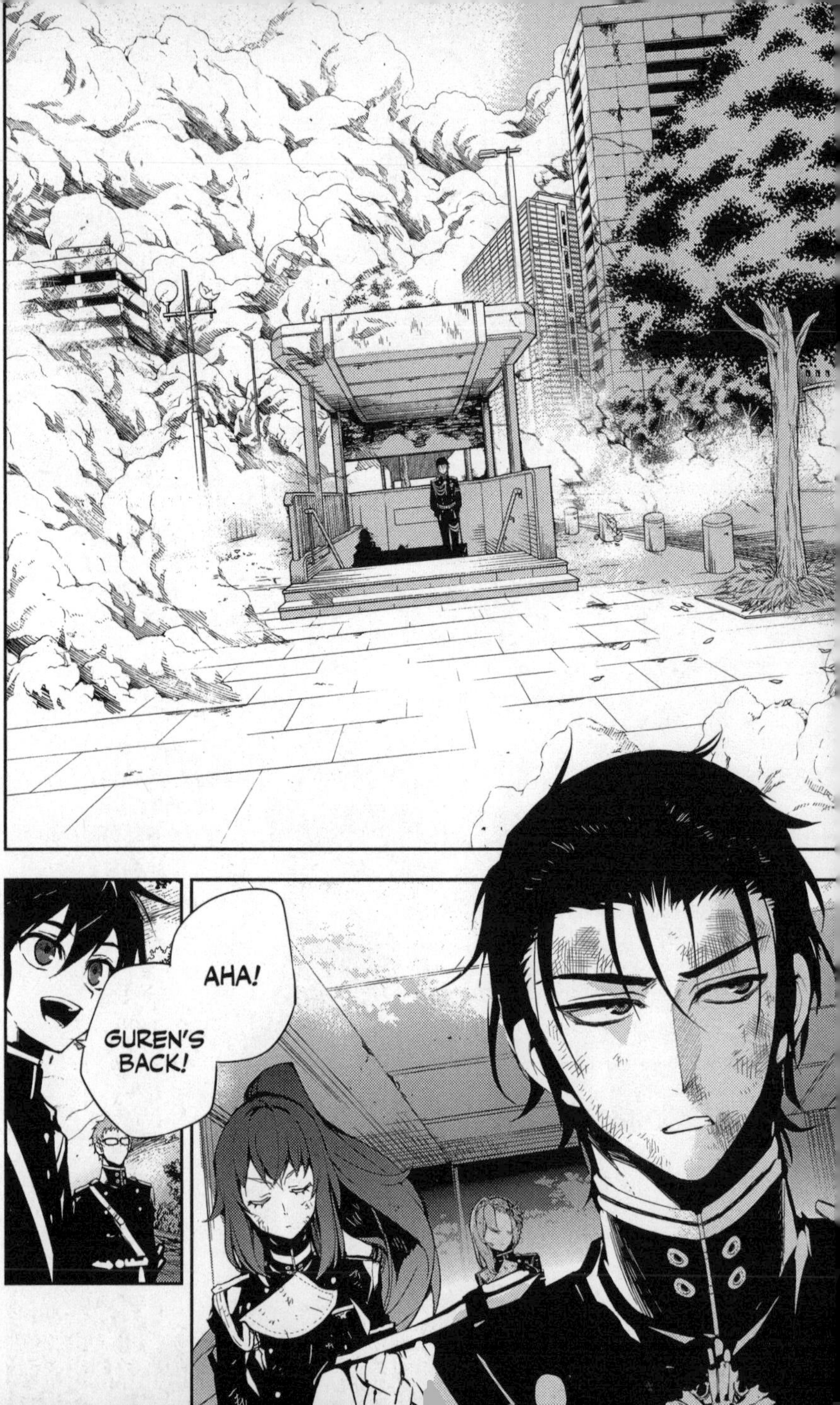
AHA!
GUREN'S BACK!

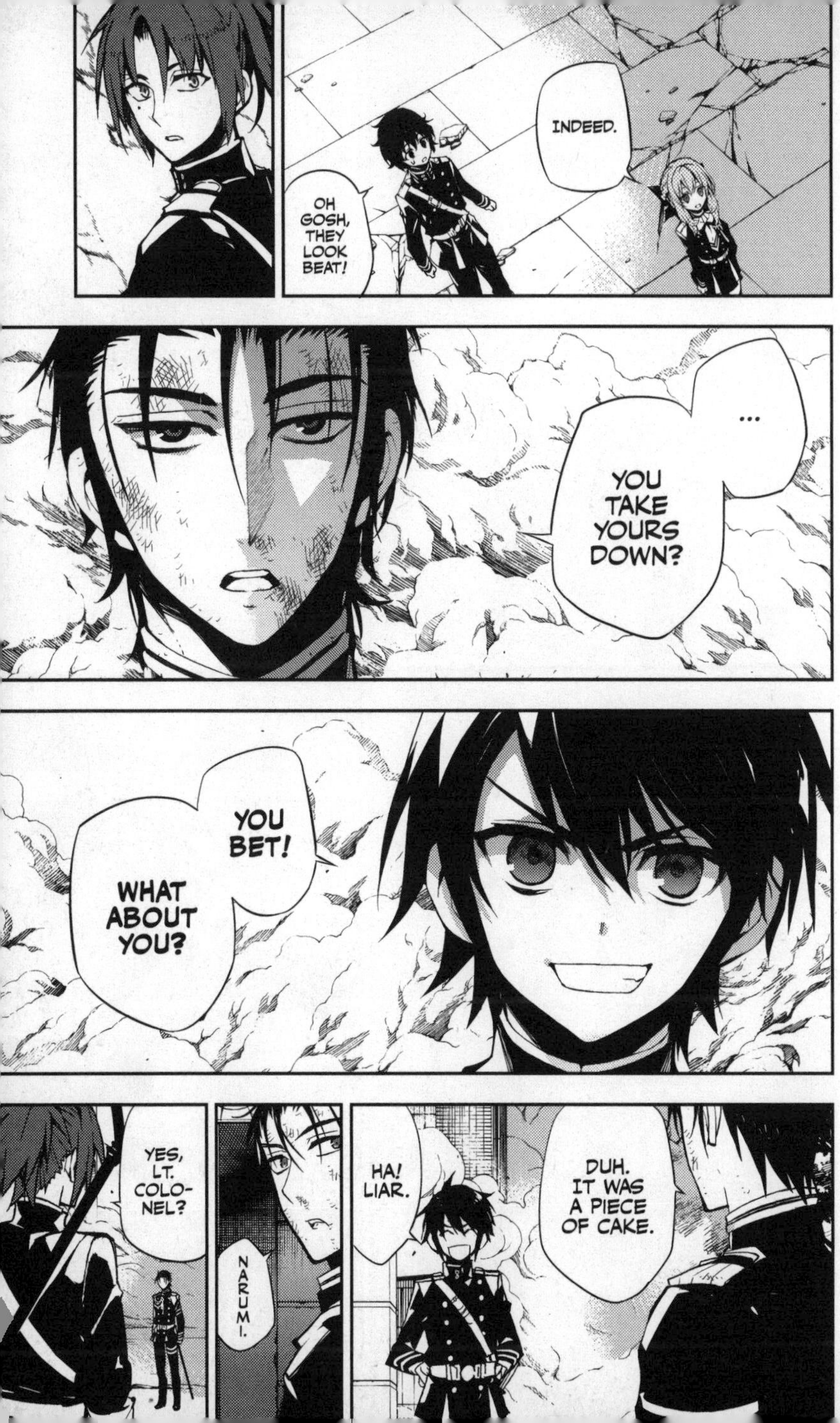
INDEED.
OH GOSH, THEY LOOK BEAT!
... YOU TAKE YOURS DOWN?
YOU BET! WHAT ABOUT YOU?
DUH. IT WAS A PIECE OF CAKE.
HA! LIAR.
NARUMI.
YES, LT. COLONEL?

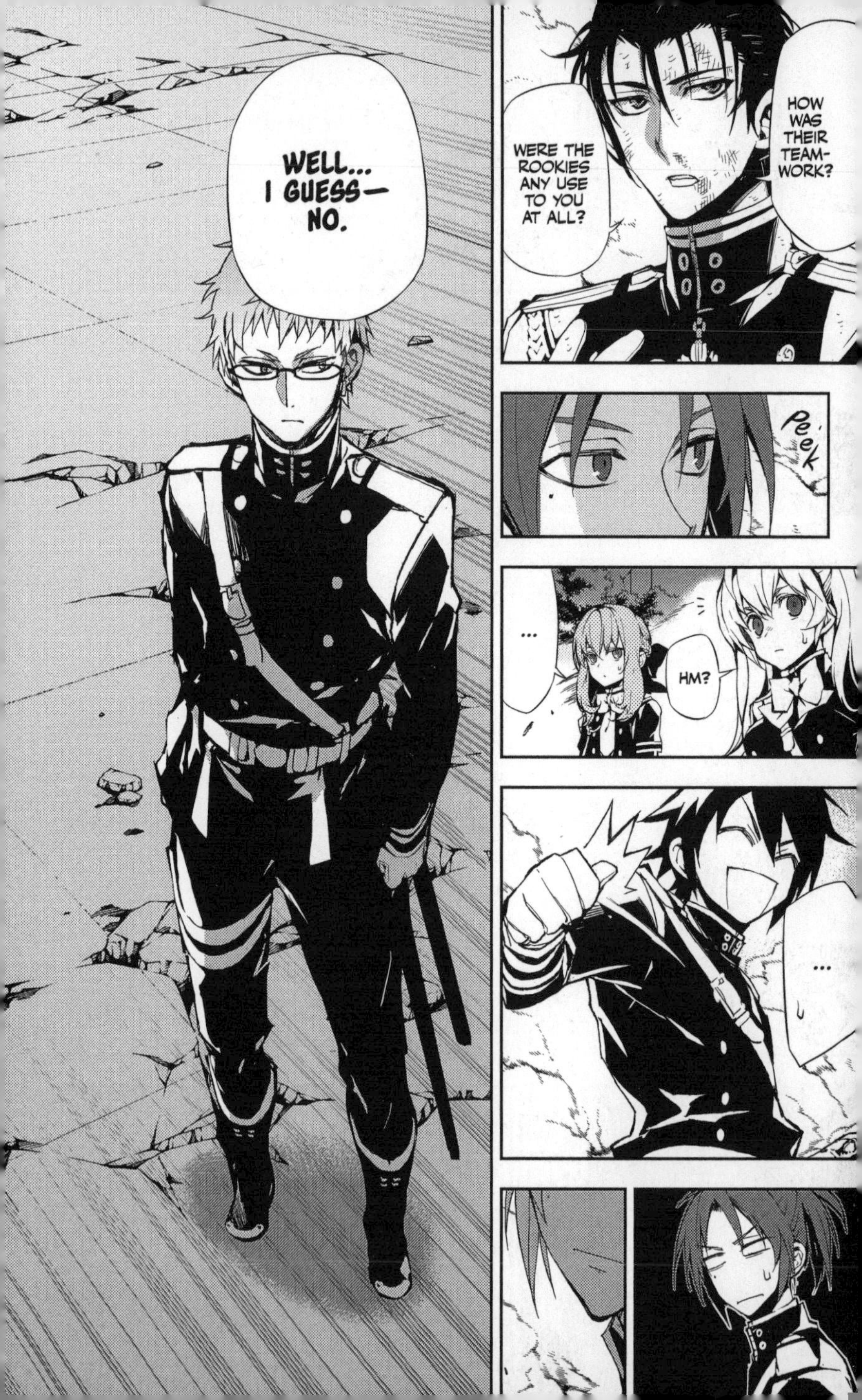
HOW WAS THEIR TEAM-WORK?
WERE THE ROOKIES ANY USE TO YOU AT ALL?
Peek
HM?
...
...
WELL... I GUESS— NO.

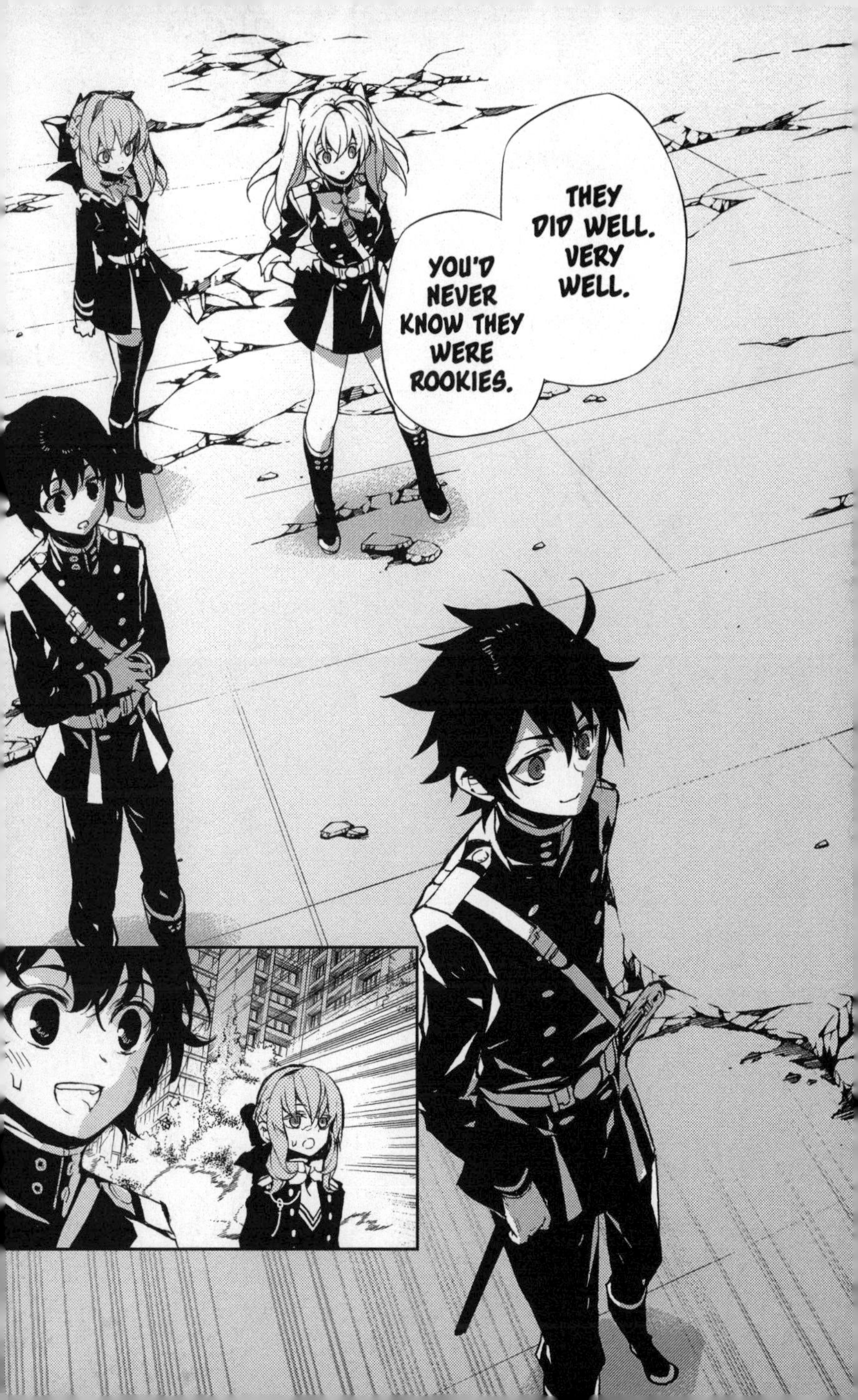
THEY DID WELL. VERY WELL.
YOU'D NEVER KNOW THEY WERE ROOKIES.

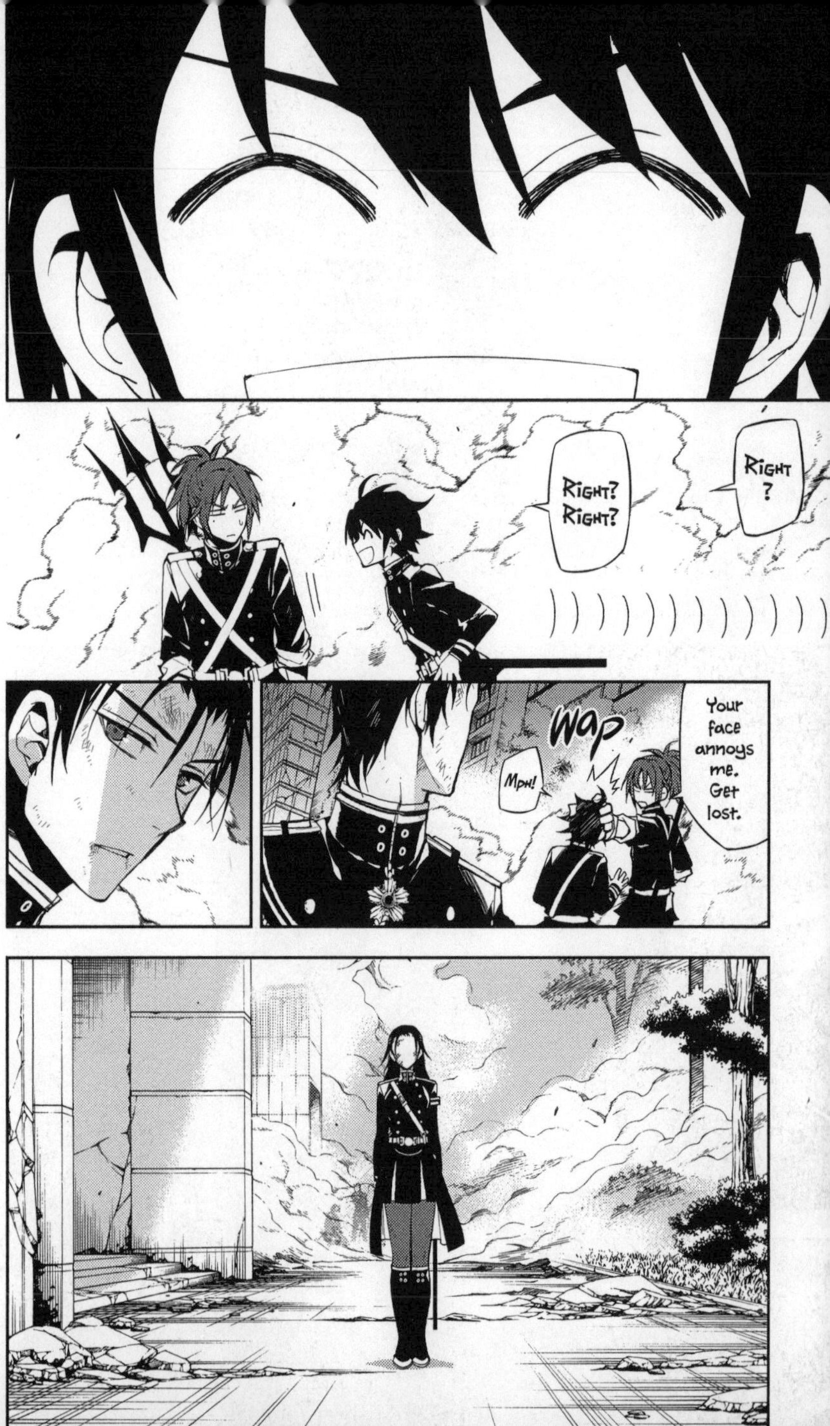
RIGHT ?
RIGHT? RIGHT?
Your face annoys me. Get lost.
WAP
MPH!

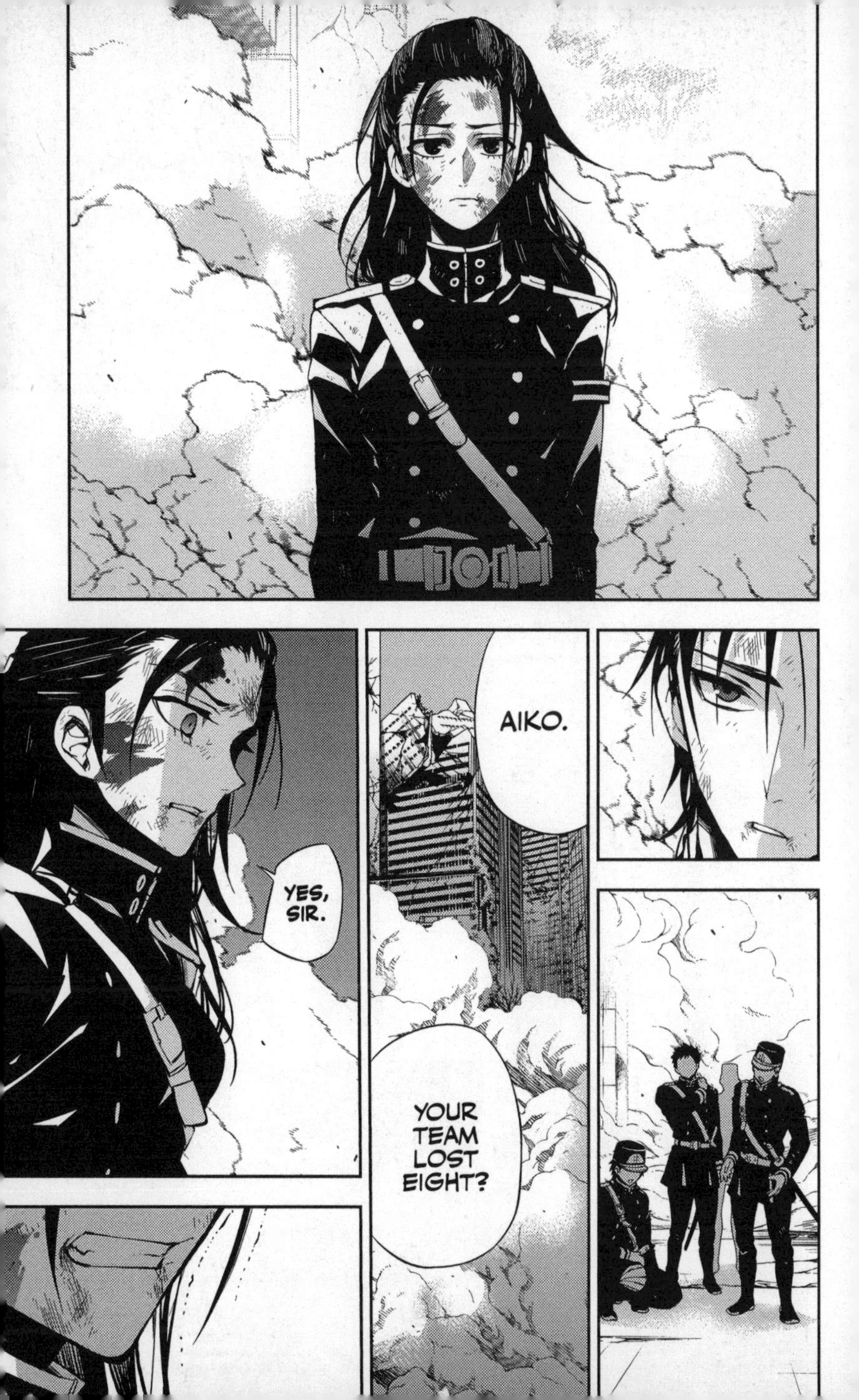
AIKO.
YOUR TEAM LOST EIGHT?
YES, SIR.

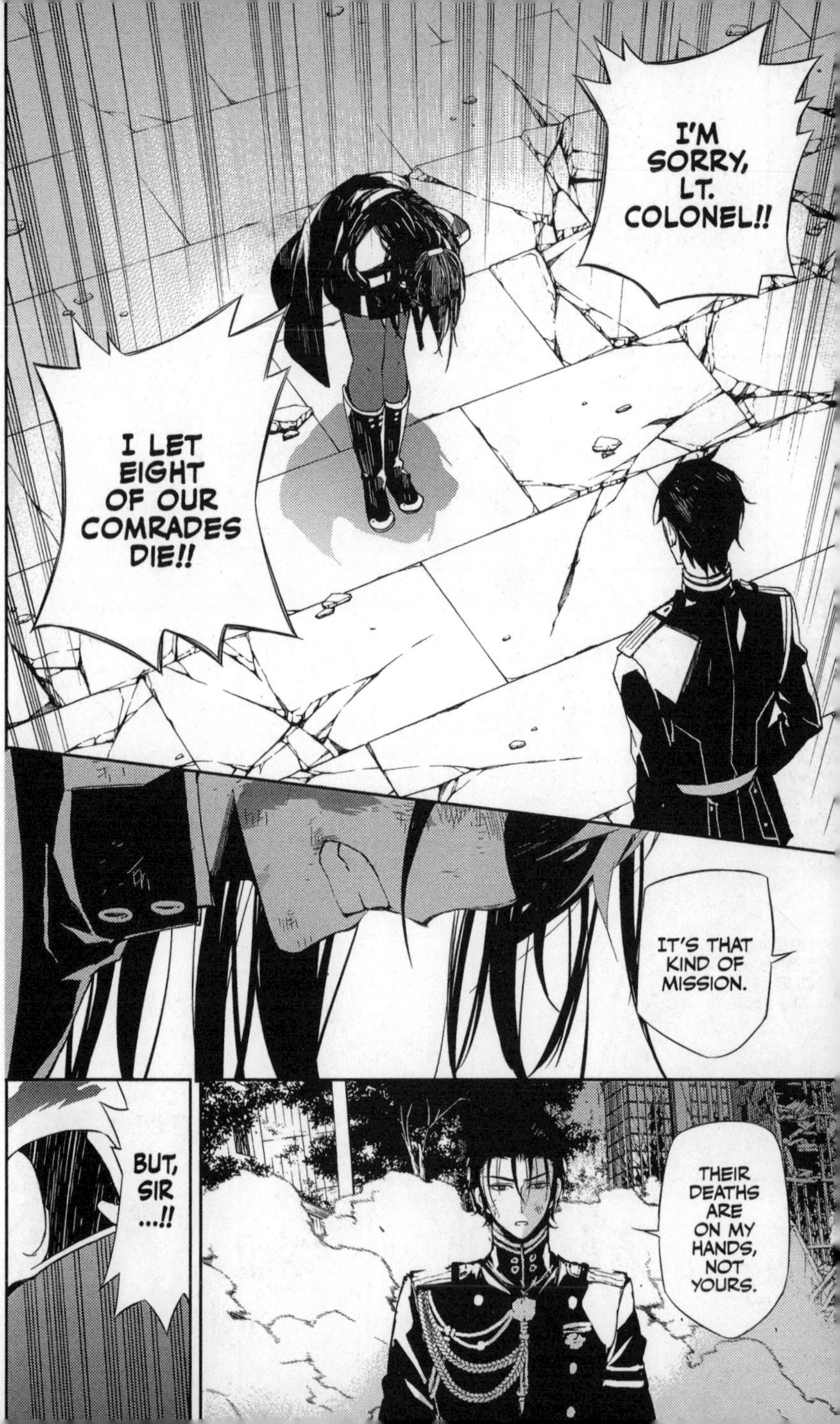
I'M SORRY, LT. COLONEL!!
I LET EIGHT OF OUR COMRADES DIE!!
IT'S THAT KIND OF MISSION.
THEIR DEATHS ARE ON MY HANDS, NOT YOURS.
BUT, SIR ...!!

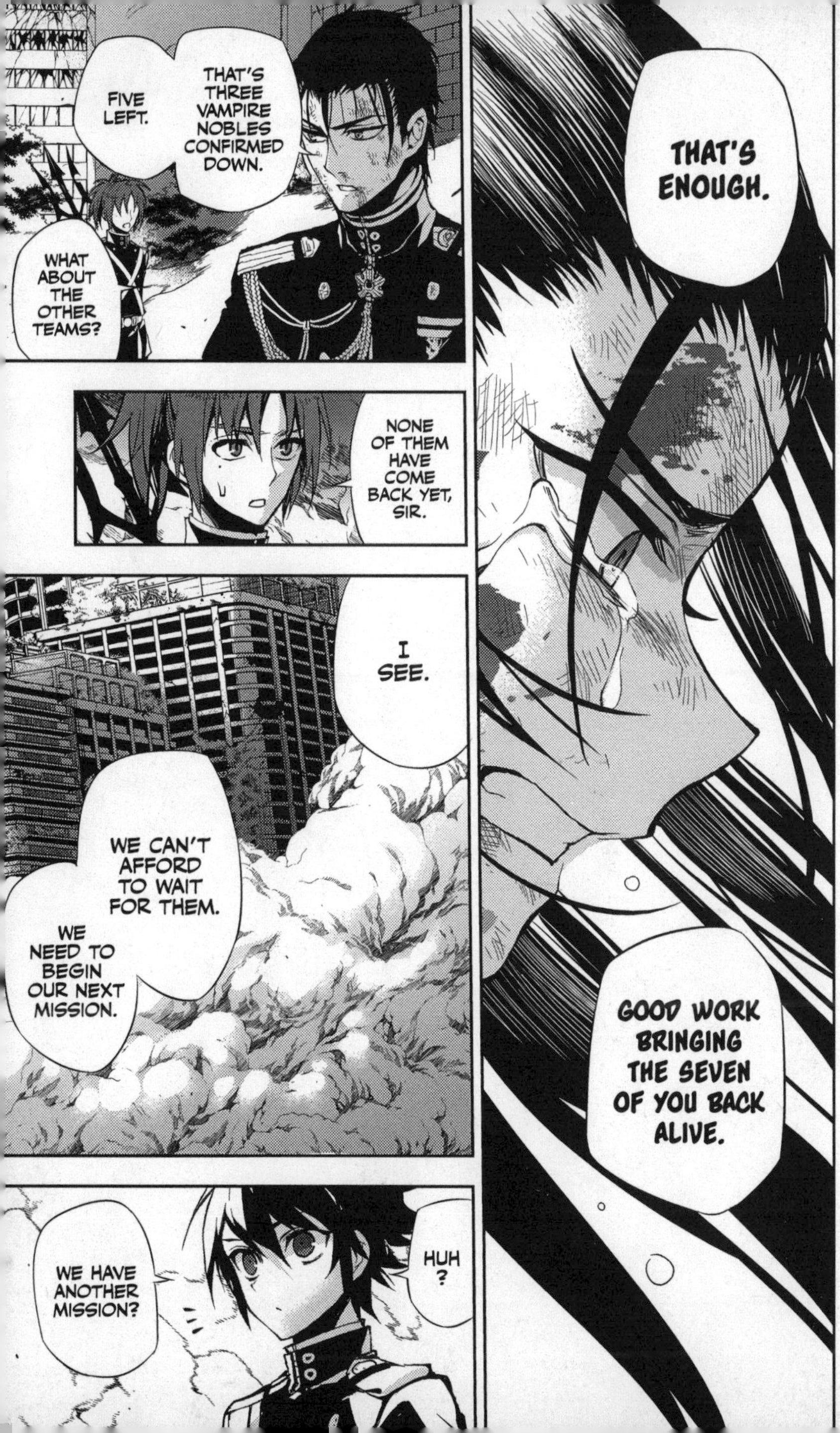
THAT'S ENOUGH.
GOOD WORK BRINGING THE SEVEN OF YOU BACK ALIVE.
THAT'S THREE VAMPIRE NOBLES CONFIRMED DOWN.
FIVE LEFT.
WHAT ABOUT THE OTHER TEAMS?
NONE OF THEM HAVE COME BACK YET, SIR.
I SEE.
WE CAN'T AFFORD TO WAIT FOR THEM.
WE NEED TO BEGIN OUR NEXT MISSION.
HUH?
WE HAVE ANOTHER MISSION?

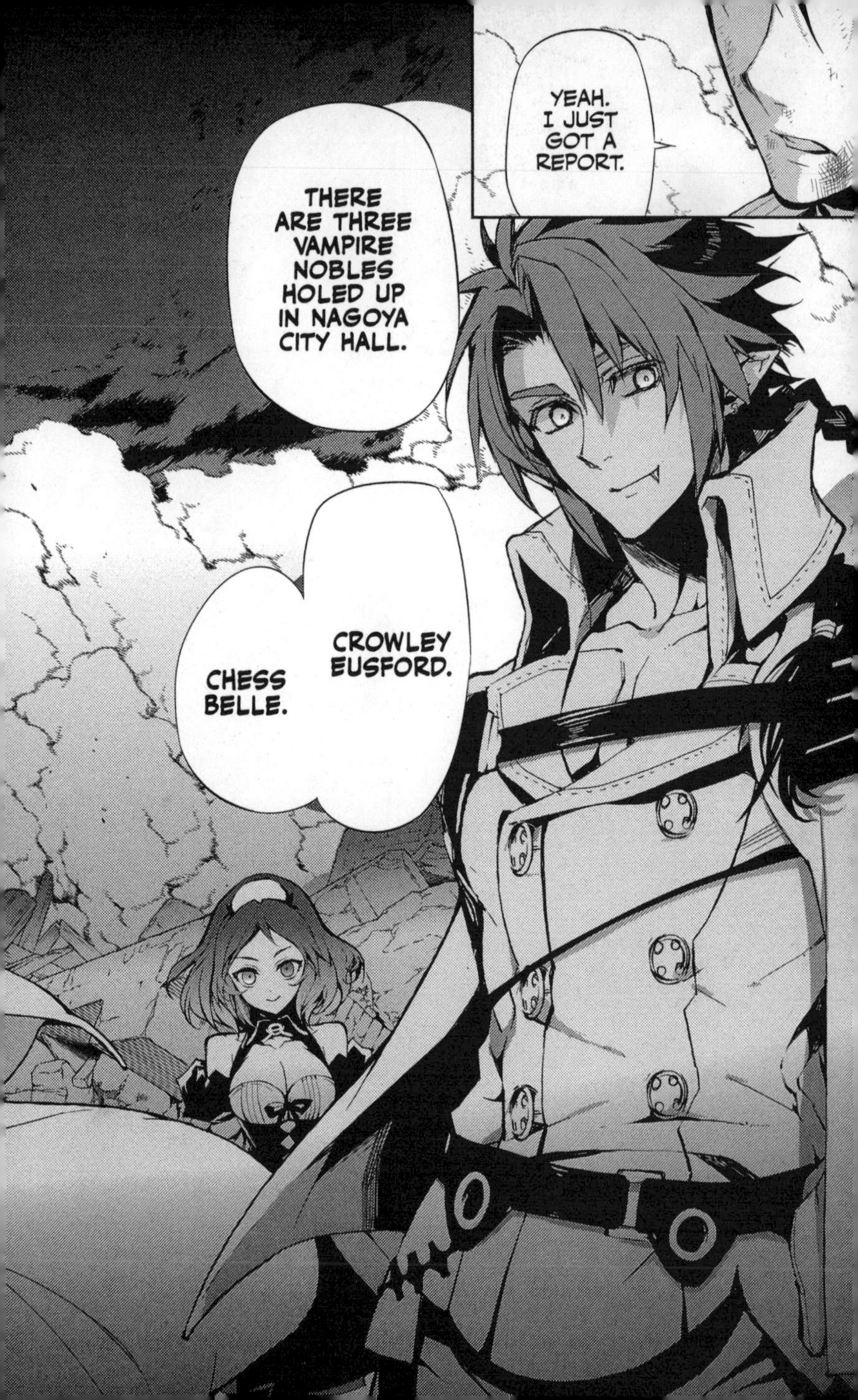
YEAH. I JUST GOT A REPORT.
THERE ARE THREE VAMPIRE NOBLES HOLED UP IN NAGOYA CITY HALL.
CROWLEY EUSFORD.
CHESS BELLE.

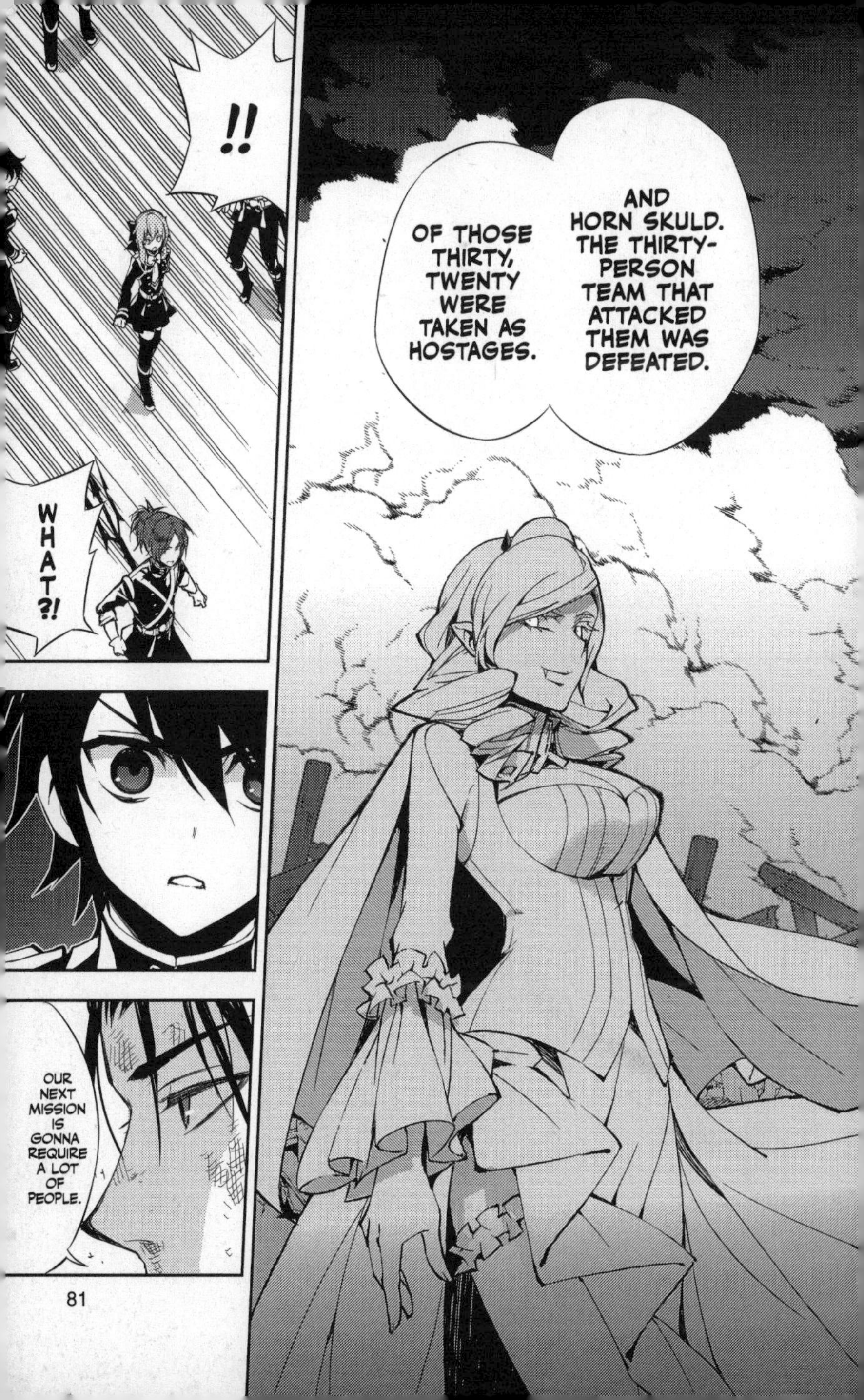
AND HORN SKULD. THE THIRTY-PERSON TEAM THAT ATTACKED THEM WAS DEFEATED.
OF THOSE THIRTY, TWENTY WERE TAKEN AS HOSTAGES.
!!
WHAT?!
OUR NEXT MISSION IS GONNA REQUIRE A LOT OF PEOPLE.

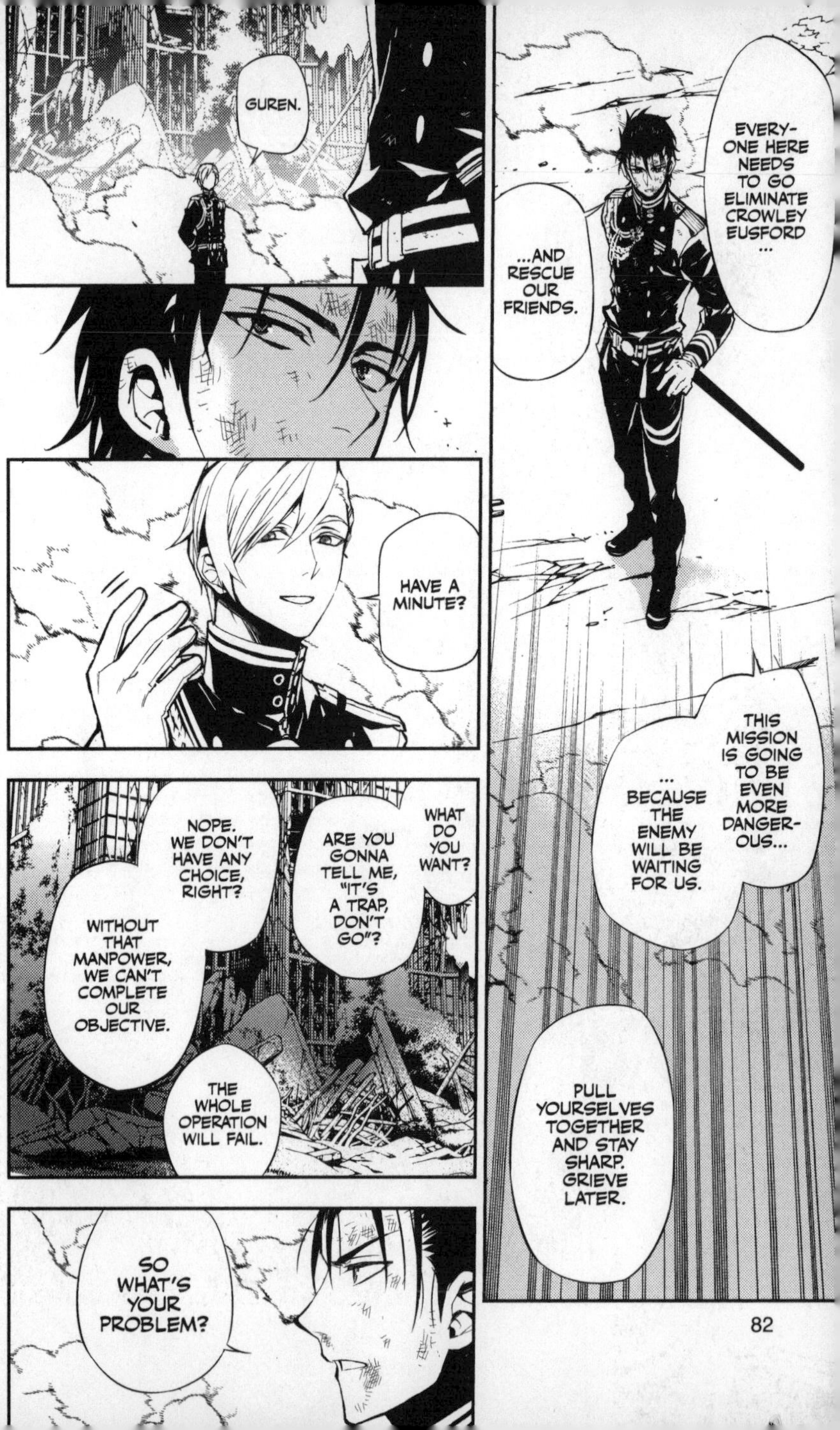
EVERY-ONE HERE NEEDS TO GO ELIMINATE CROWLEY EUSFORD ...
...AND RESCUE OUR FRIENDS.
THIS MISSION IS GOING TO BE EVEN MORE DANGER-OUS...
... BECAUSE THE ENEMY WILL BE WAITING FOR US.
PULL YOURSELVES TOGETHER AND STAY SHARP. GRIEVE LATER.
GUREN.
HAVE A MINUTE?
WHAT DO YOU WANT?
ARE YOU GONNA TELL ME, "IT'S A TRAP, DON'T GO"?
NOPE. WE DON'T HAVE ANY CHOICE, RIGHT?
WITHOUT THAT MANPOWER, WE CAN'T COMPLETE OUR OBJECTIVE.
THE WHOLE OPERATION WILL FAIL.
SO WHAT'S YOUR PROBLEM?

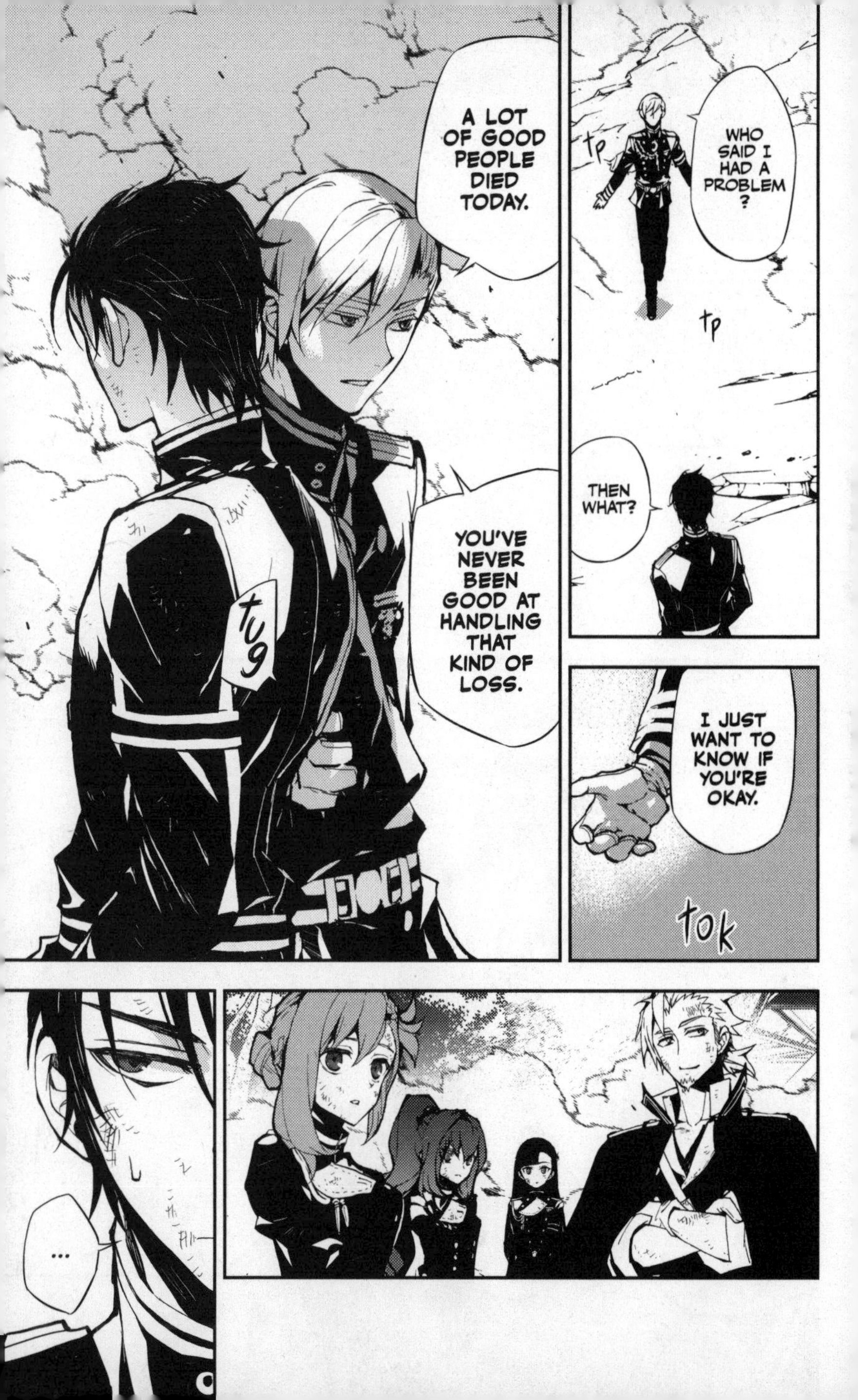
tp
WHO SAID I HAD A PROBLEM?
tp
THEN WHAT?
I JUST WANT TO KNOW IF YOU'RE OKAY.
tok
A LOT OF GOOD PEOPLE DIED TODAY.
tug
YOU'VE NEVER BEEN GOOD AT HANDLING THAT KIND OF LOSS.
...

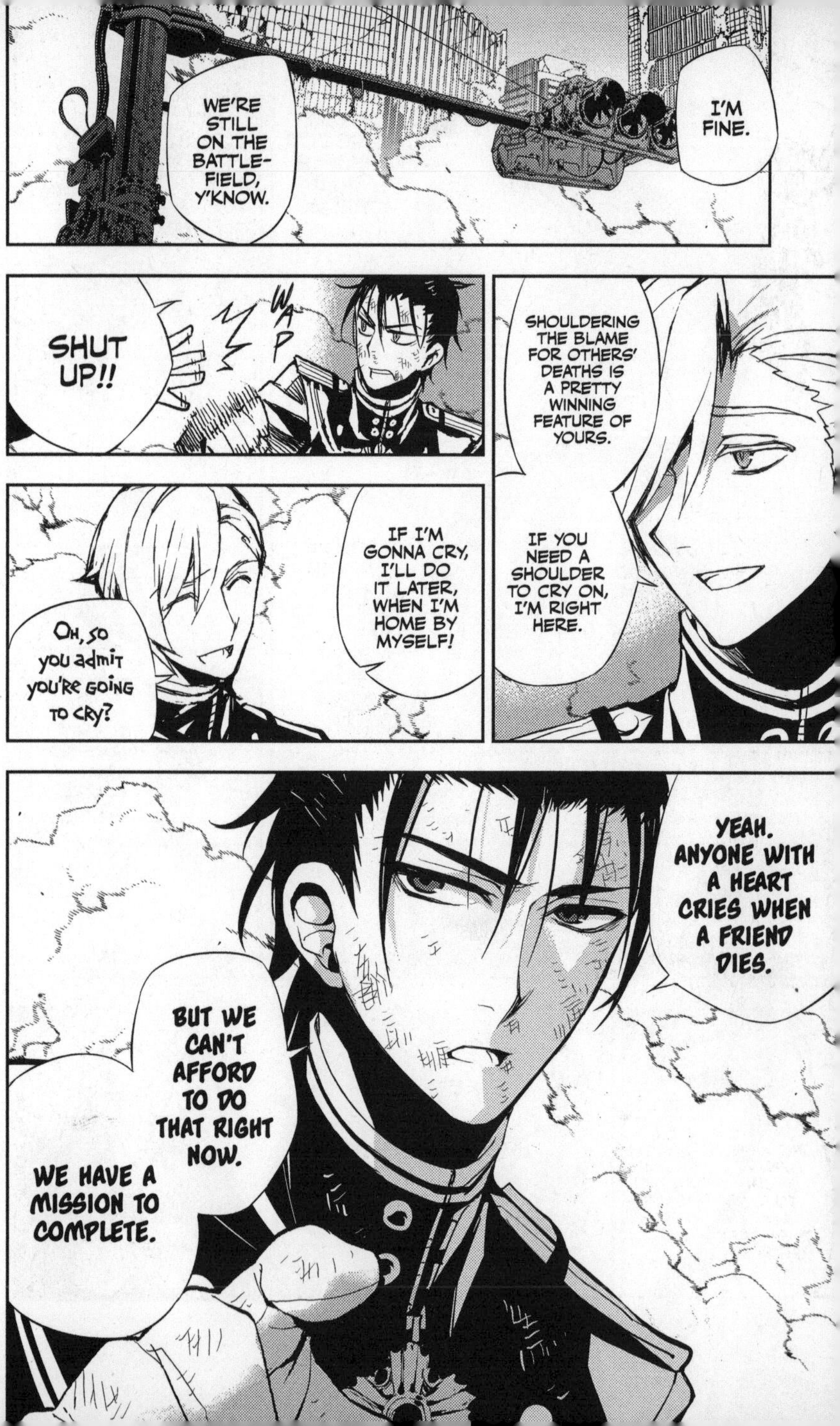
I'M FINE.
WE'RE STILL ON THE BATTLE-FIELD, Y'KNOW.
SHOULDERING THE BLAME FOR OTHERS' DEATHS IS A PRETTY WINNING FEATURE OF YOURS.
IF YOU NEED A SHOULDER TO CRY ON, I'M RIGHT HERE.
WAP
SHUT UP!!
IF I'M GONNA CRY, I'LL DO IT LATER, WHEN I'M HOME BY MYSELF!
Oh, so you admit you're going to cry?
YEAH. ANYONE WITH A HEART CRIES WHEN A FRIEND DIES.
BUT WE CAN'T AFFORD TO DO THAT RIGHT NOW.
WE HAVE A MISSION TO COMPLETE.

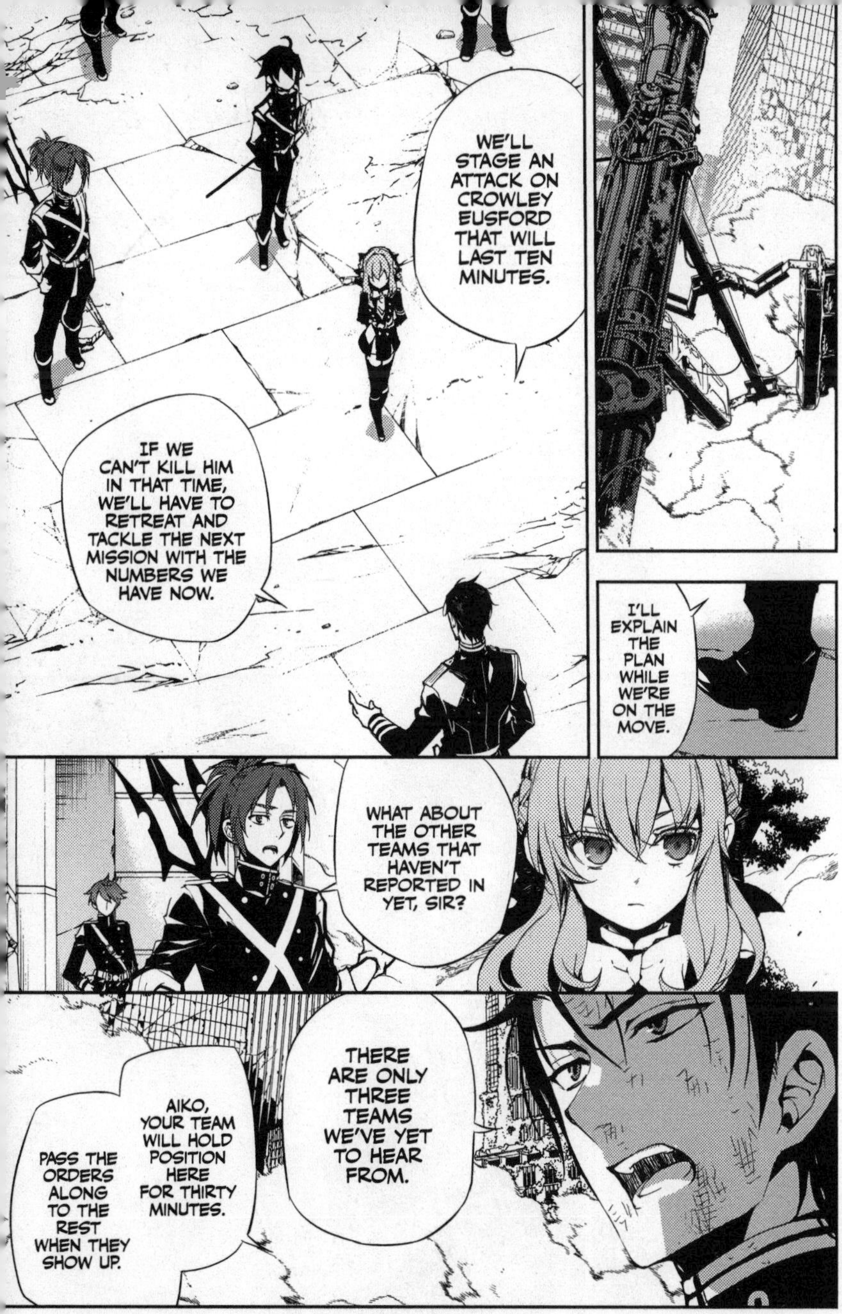
I'LL EXPLAIN THE PLAN WHILE WE'RE ON THE MOVE.
WE'LL STAGE AN ATTACK ON CROWLEY EUSFORD THAT WILL LAST TEN MINUTES.
IF WE CAN'T KILL HIM IN THAT TIME, WE'LL HAVE TO RETREAT AND TACKLE THE NEXT MISSION WITH THE NUMBERS WE HAVE NOW.
WHAT ABOUT THE OTHER TEAMS THAT HAVEN'T REPORTED IN YET, SIR?
THERE ARE ONLY THREE TEAMS WE'VE YET TO HEAR FROM.
AIKO, YOUR TEAM WILL HOLD POSITION HERE FOR THIRTY MINUTES.
PASS THE ORDERS ALONG TO THE REST WHEN THEY SHOW UP.

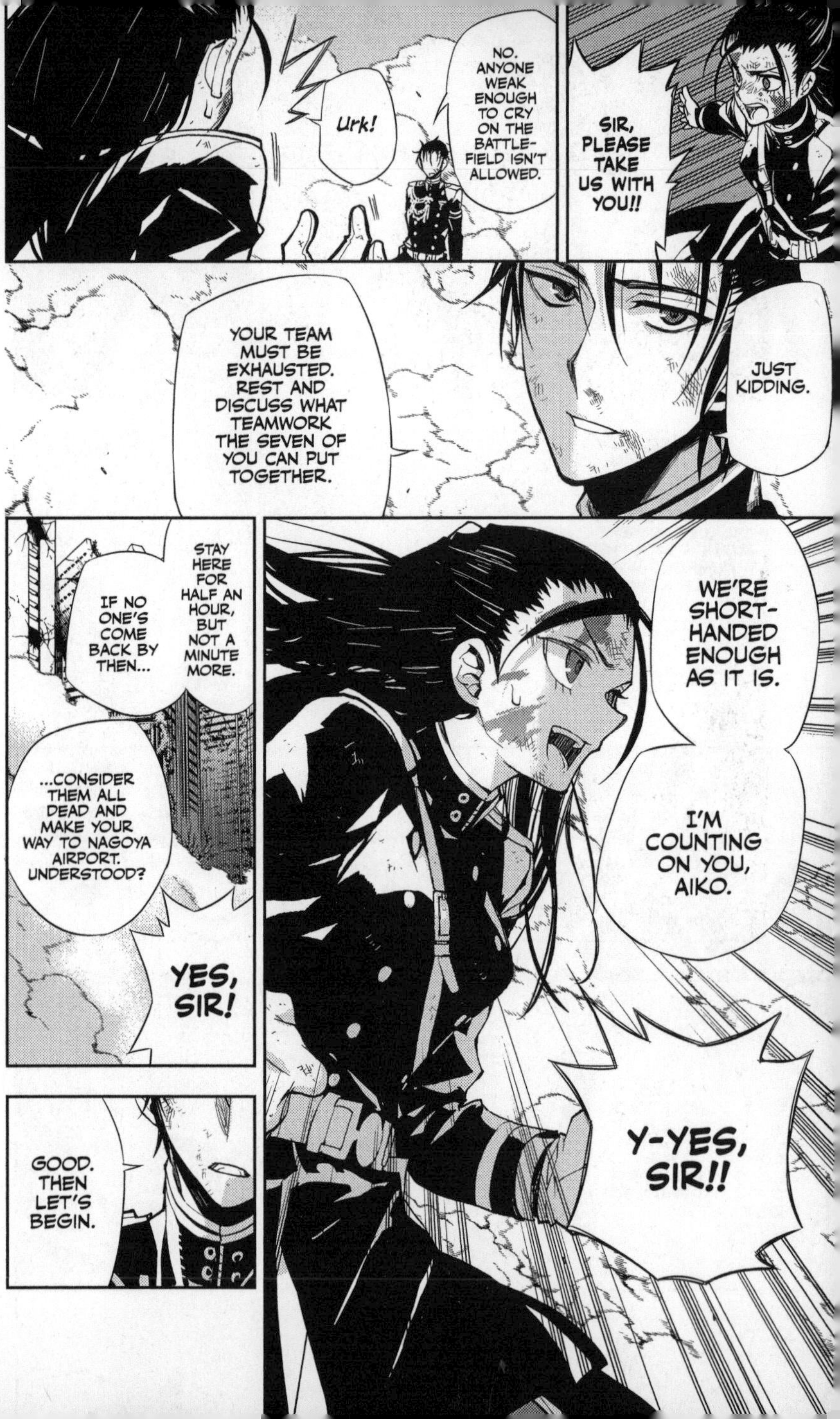
SIR, PLEASE TAKE US WITH YOU!!
NO. ANYONE WEAK ENOUGH TO CRY ON THE BATTLE-FIELD ISN'T ALLOWED.
Urk!
JUST KIDDING.
YOUR TEAM MUST BE EXHAUSTED. REST AND DISCUSS WHAT TEAMWORK THE SEVEN OF YOU CAN PUT TOGETHER.
WE'RE SHORT-HANDED ENOUGH AS IT IS.
I'M COUNTING ON YOU, AIKO.
Y-YES, SIR!!
STAY HERE FOR HALF AN HOUR, BUT NOT A MINUTE MORE.
IF NO ONE'S COME BACK BY THEN...
...CONSIDER THEM ALL DEAD AND MAKE YOUR WAY TO NAGOYA AIRPORT. UNDERSTOOD?
YES, SIR!
GOOD. THEN LET'S BEGIN.

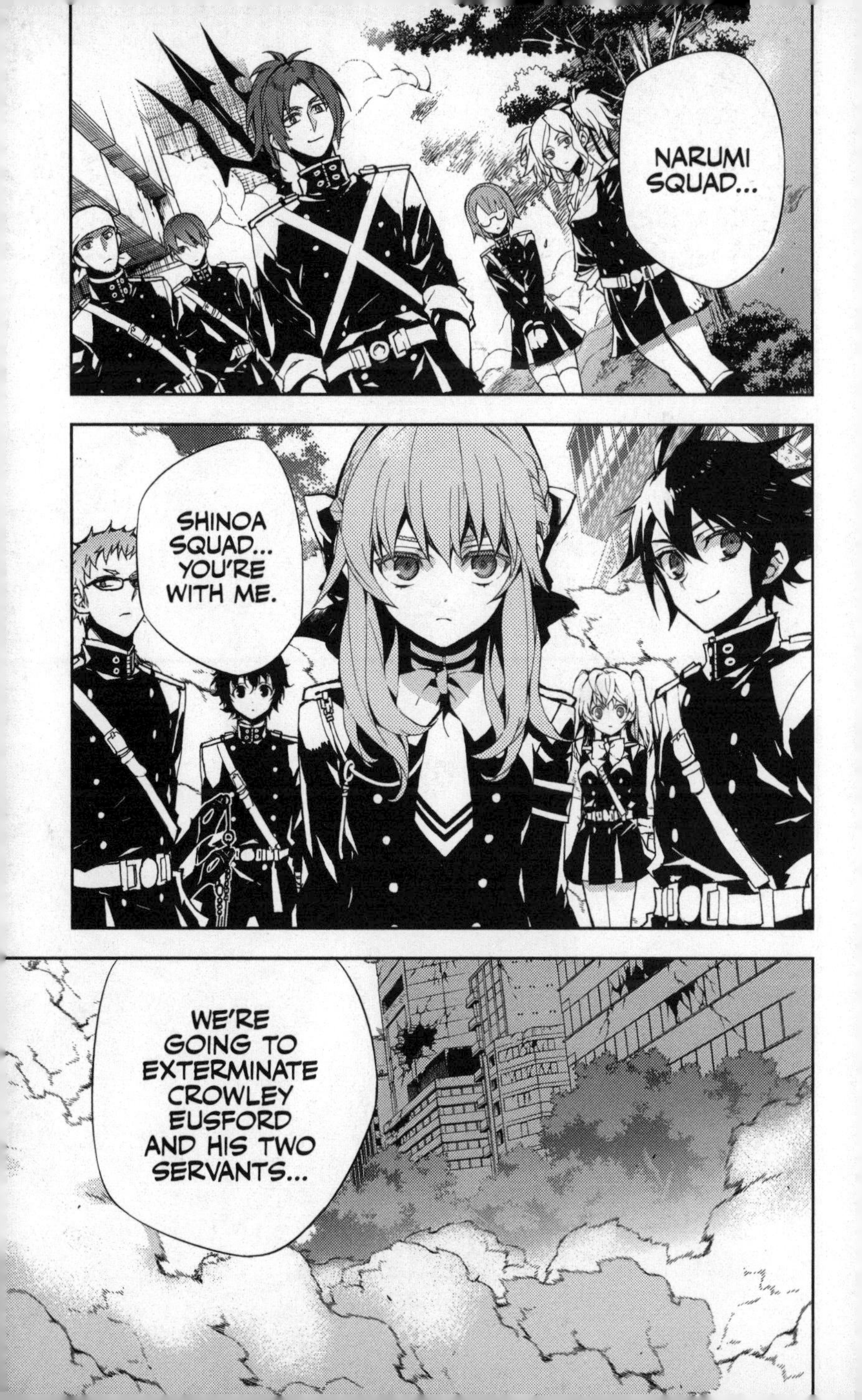
NARUMI SQUAD...
SHINOA SQUAD... YOU'RE WITH ME.
WE'RE GOING TO EXTERMINATE CROWLEY EUSFORD AND HIS TWO SERVANTS...

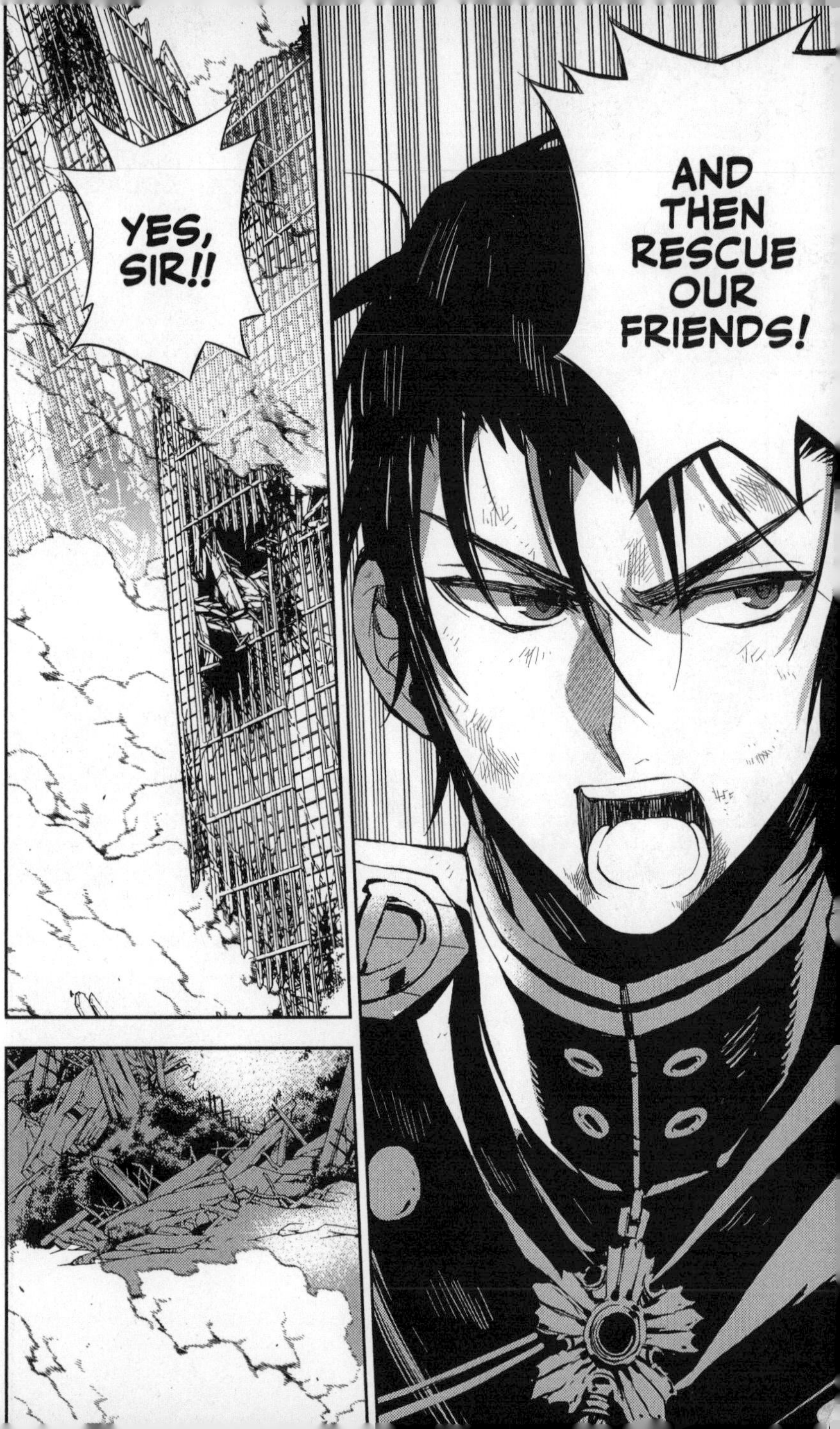
AND THEN RESCUE OUR FRIENDS!
YES, SIR!!

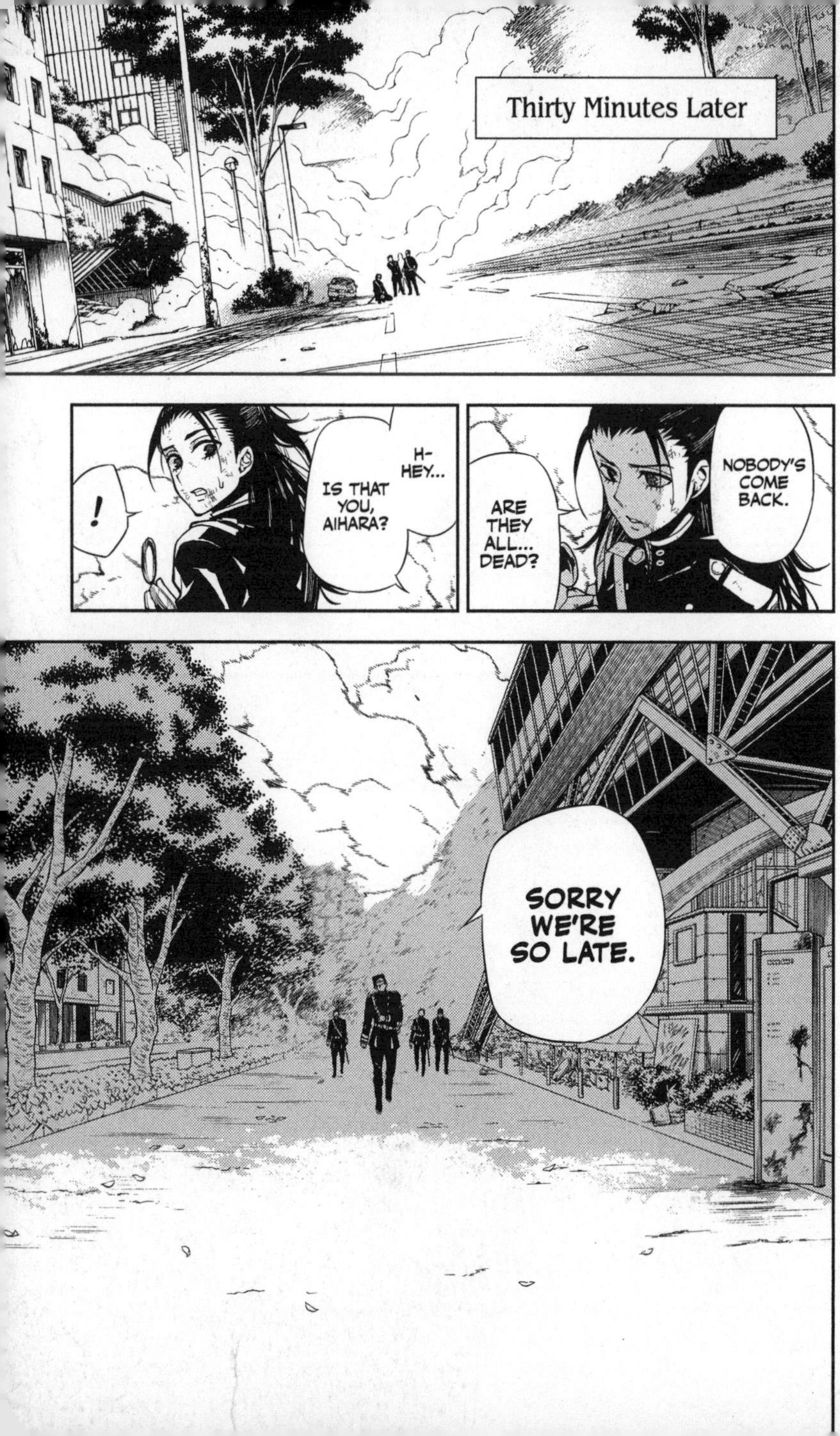
Thirty Minutes Later
NOBODY'S COME BACK.
ARE THEY ALL... DEAD?
H- HEY... IS THAT YOU, AIHARA?
!
SORRY WE'RE SO LATE.

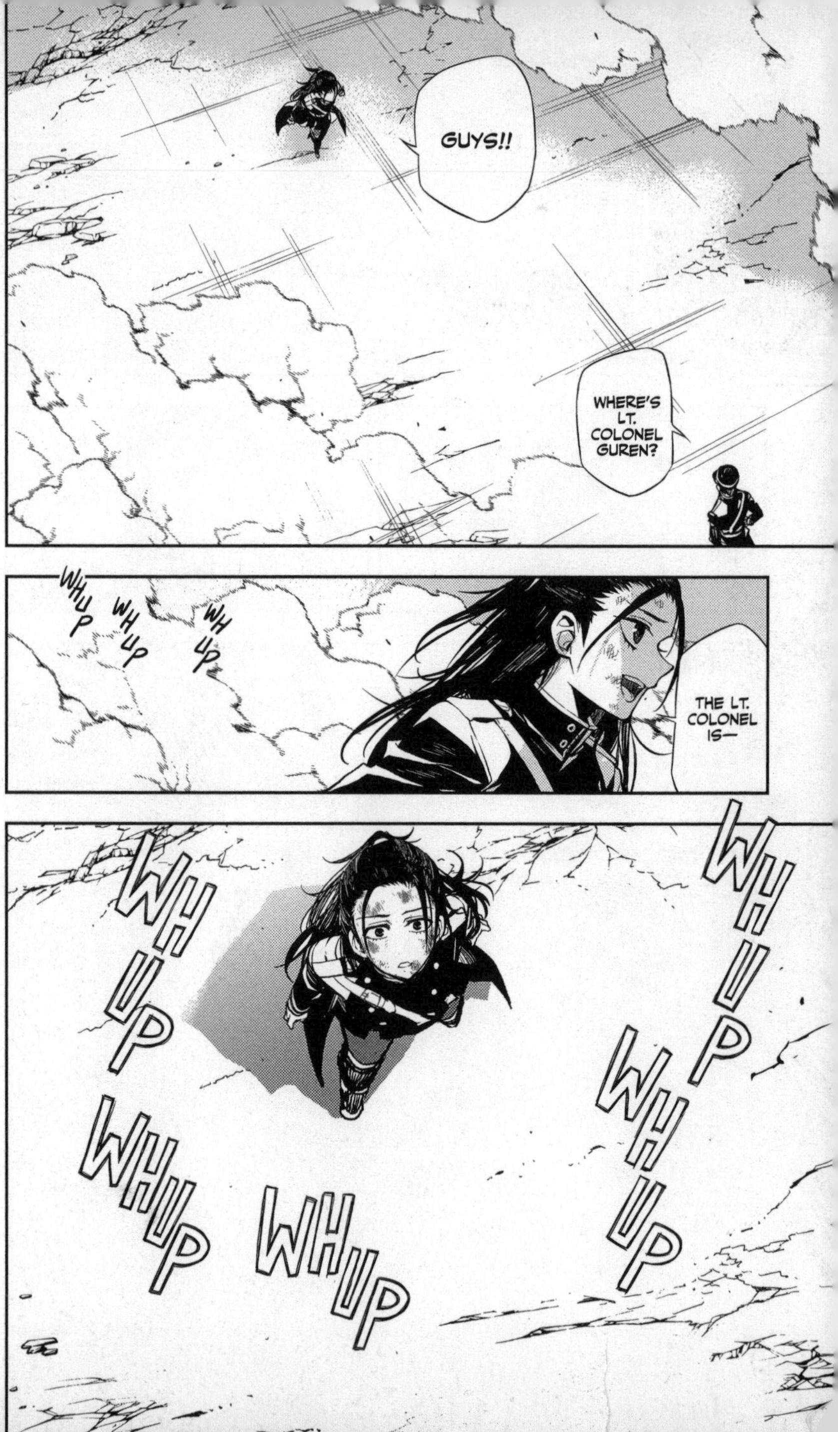
GUYS!!
WHERE'S LT. COLONEL GUREN?
THE LT. COLONEL IS—
WHUP WHUP WHUP
WHUP WHUP WHUP WHUP WHUP

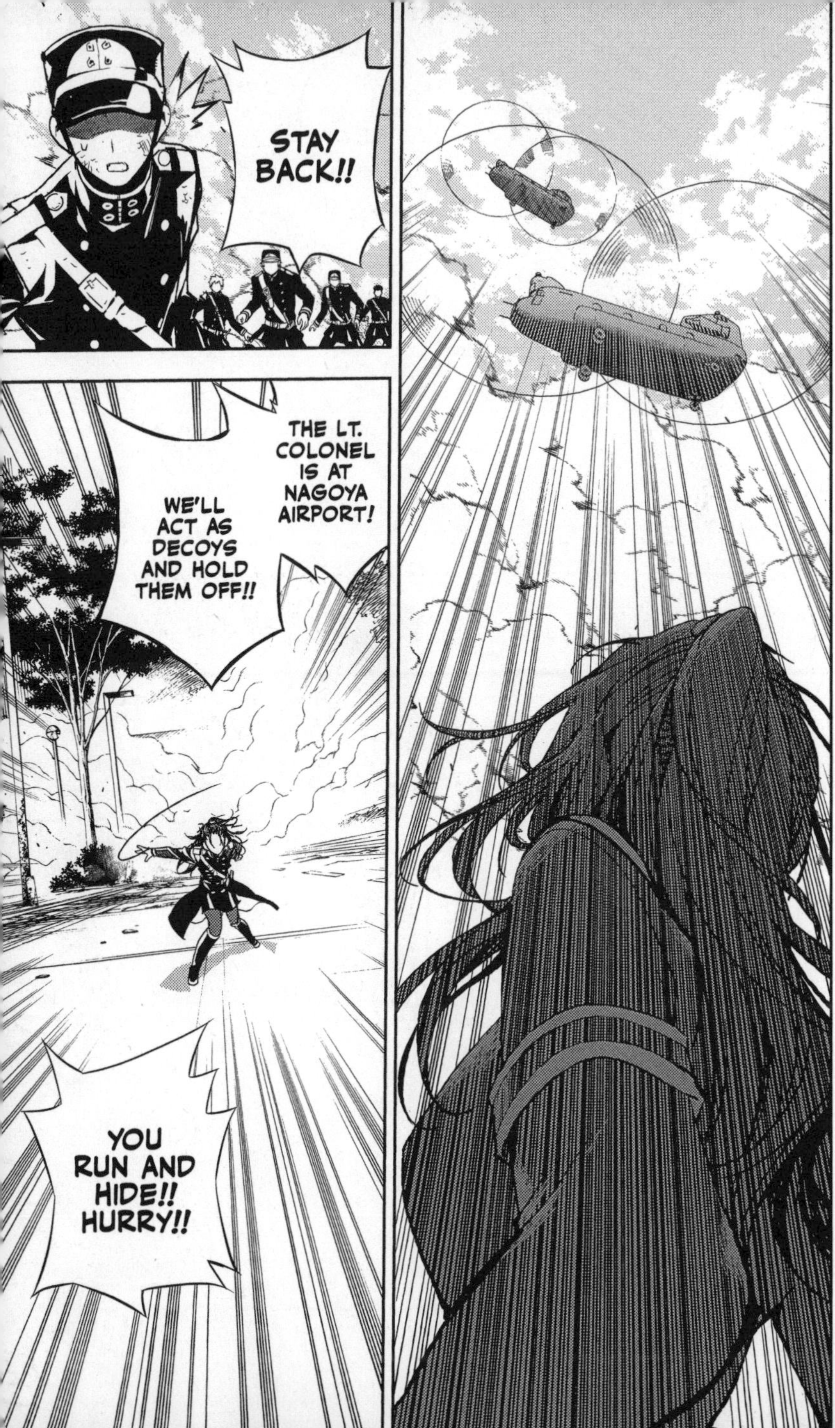
STAY BACK!!
THE LT. COLONEL IS AT NAGOYA AIRPORT!
WE'LL ACT AS DECOYS AND HOLD THEM OFF!!
YOU RUN AND HIDE!! HURRY!!

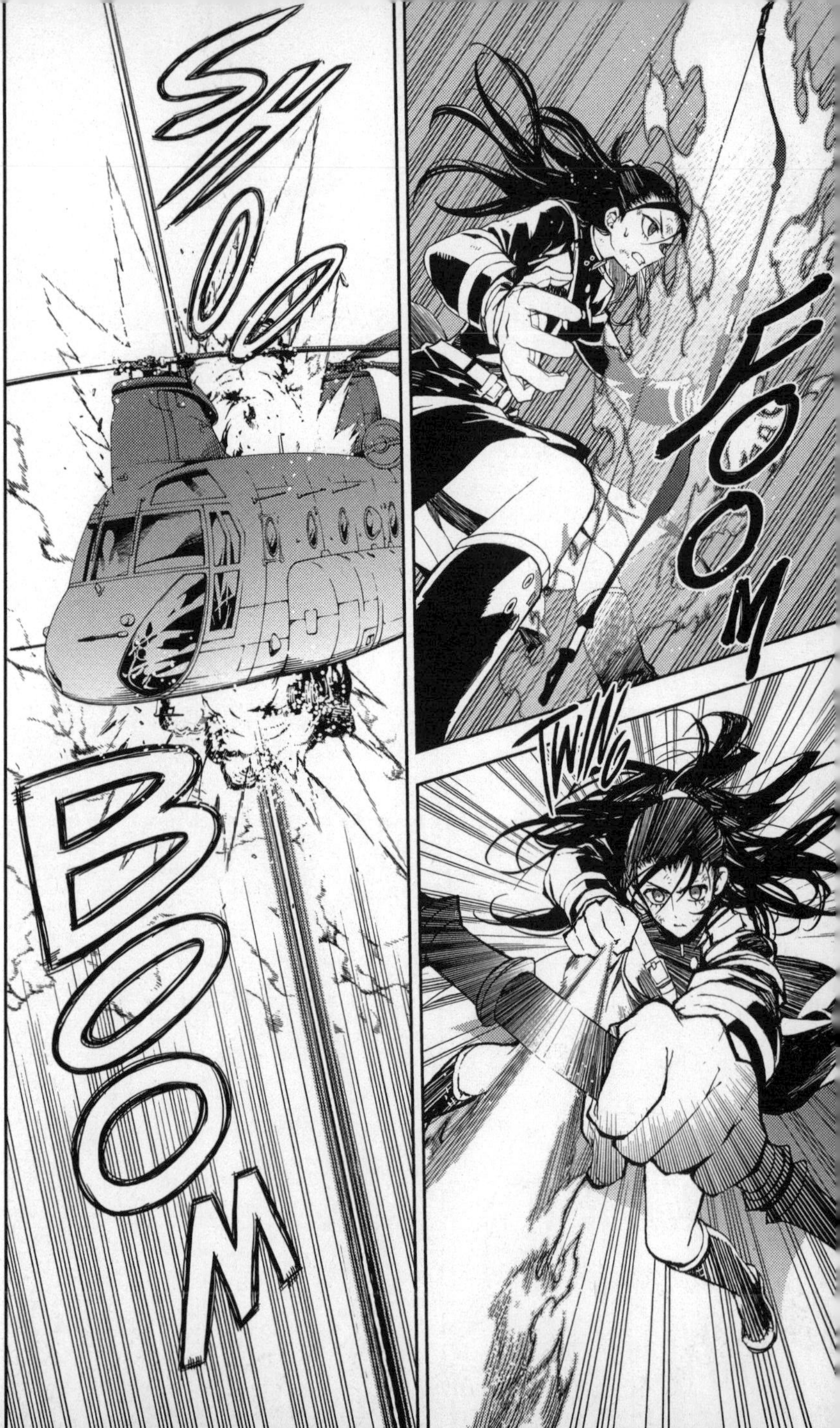
VOOM
TWING
SHOOO
BOOOM

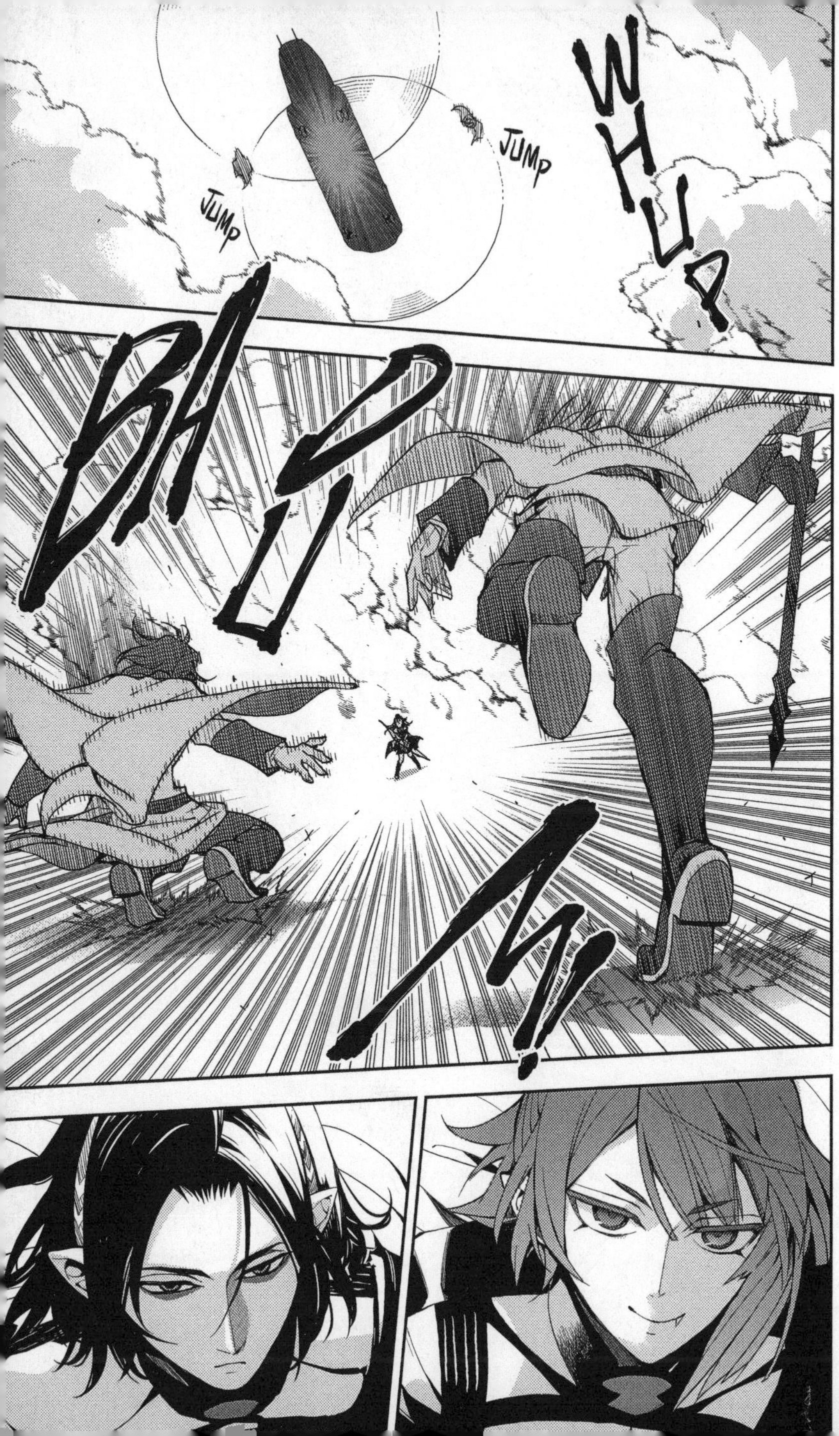
WHUA
JUMP
JUMP

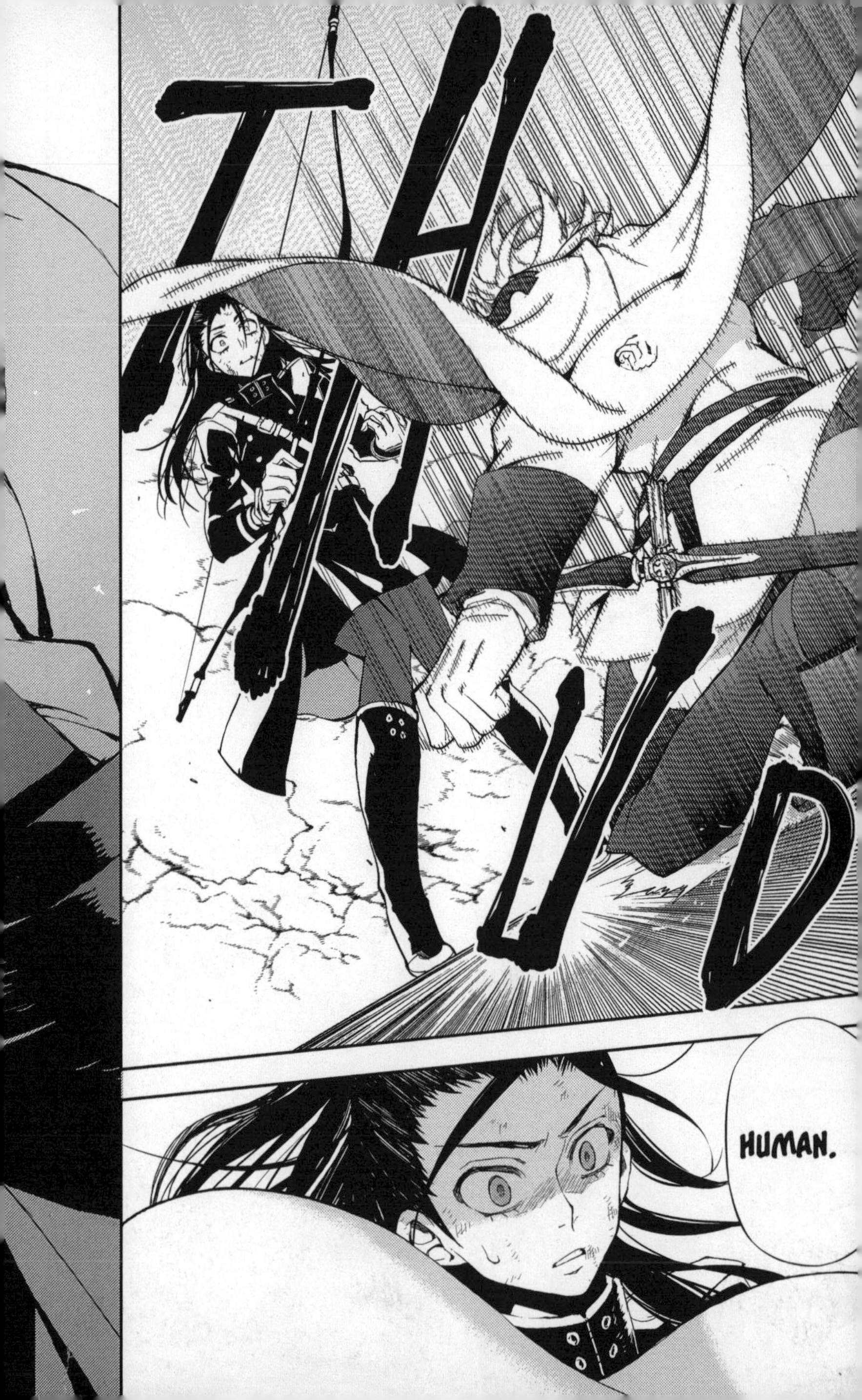
THUD
HUMAN.

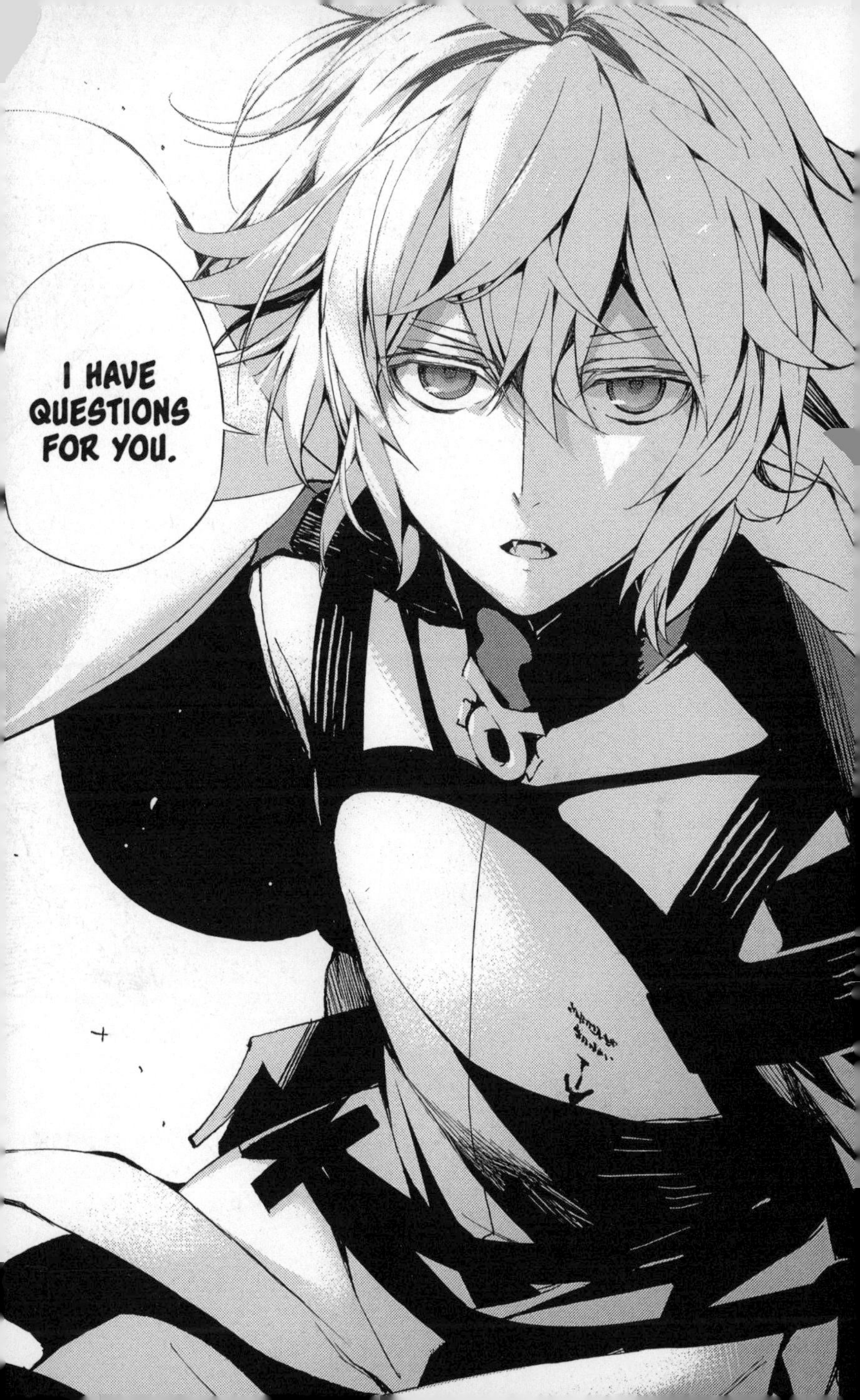
I HAVE QUESTIONS FOR YOU.

Seraph of the End
—VAMPIRE REIGN—

Chapter 30
Sword of Justice

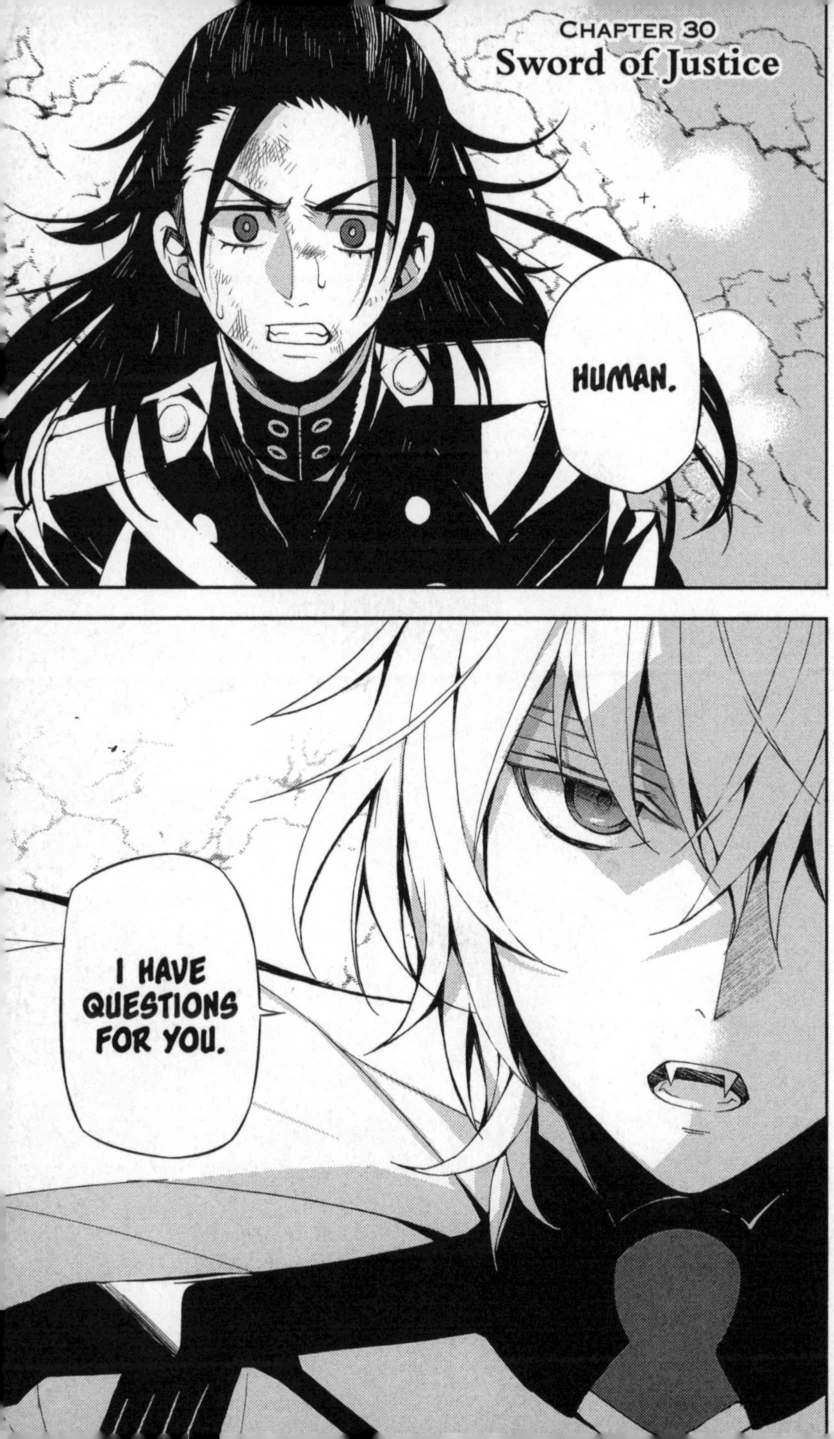
HUMAN.
I HAVE QUESTIONS FOR YOU.

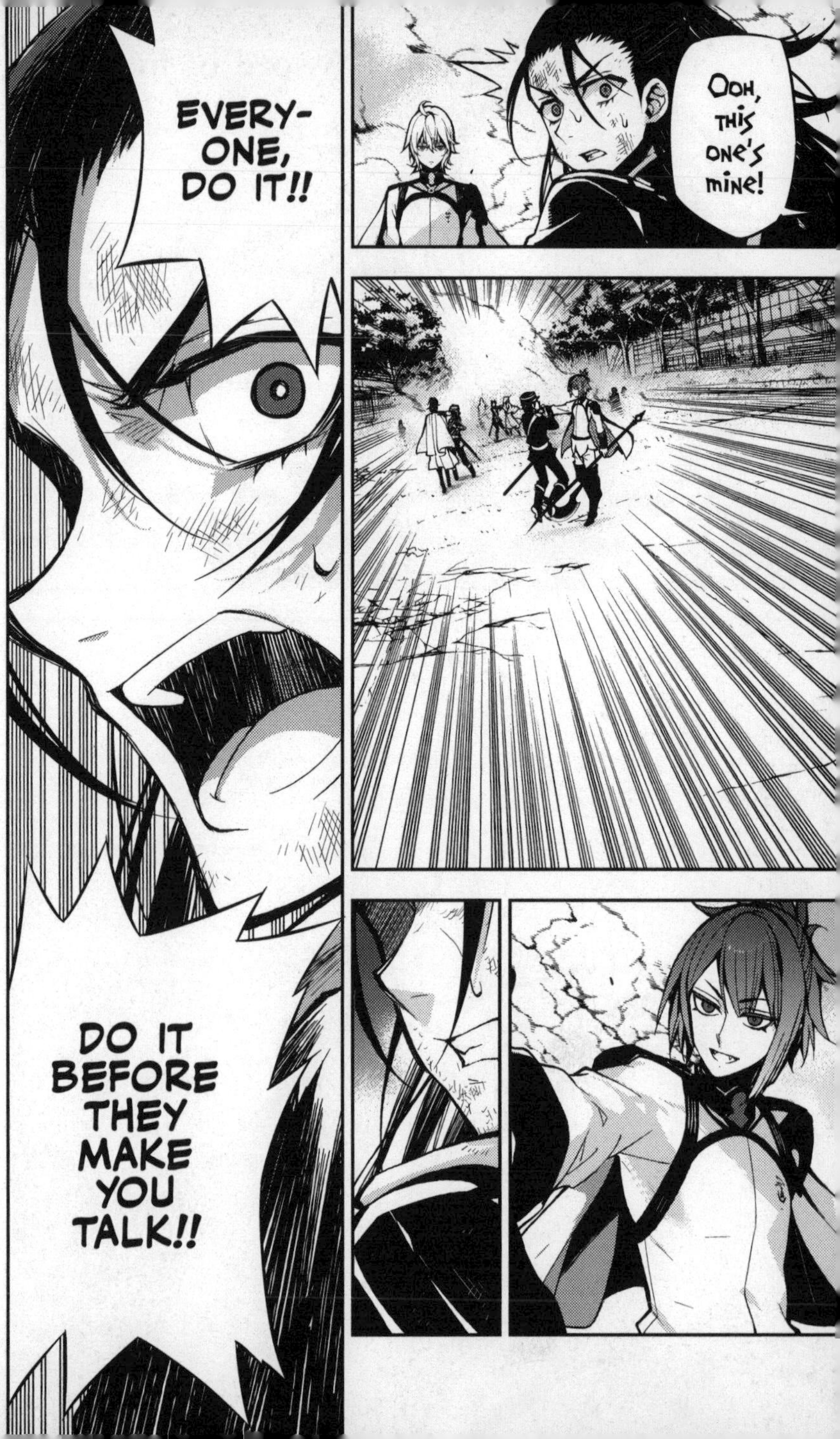
Ooh, this one's mine!
EVERY-ONE, DO IT!!
DO IT BEFORE THEY MAKE YOU TALK!!

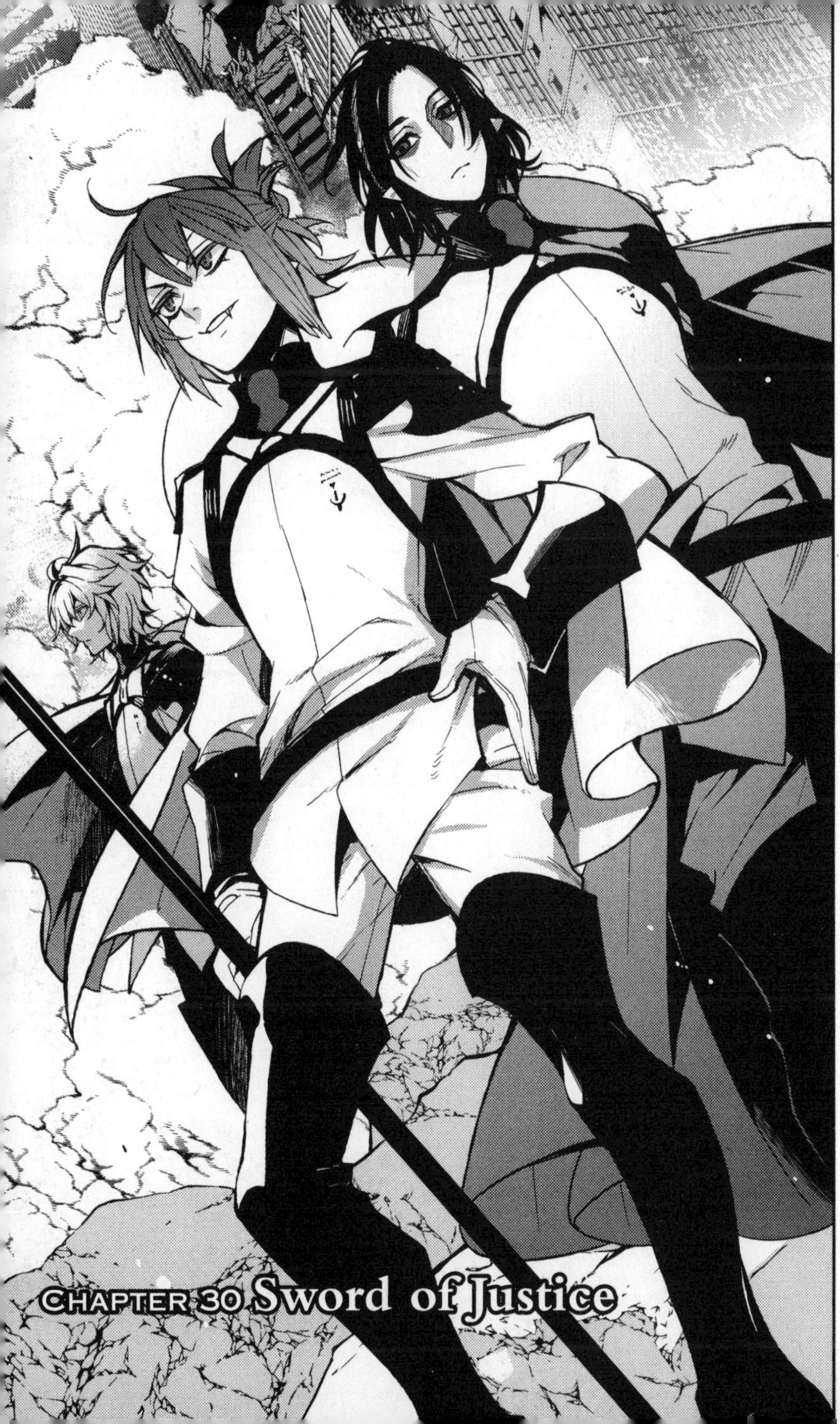

CHAPTER 30 Sword of Justice

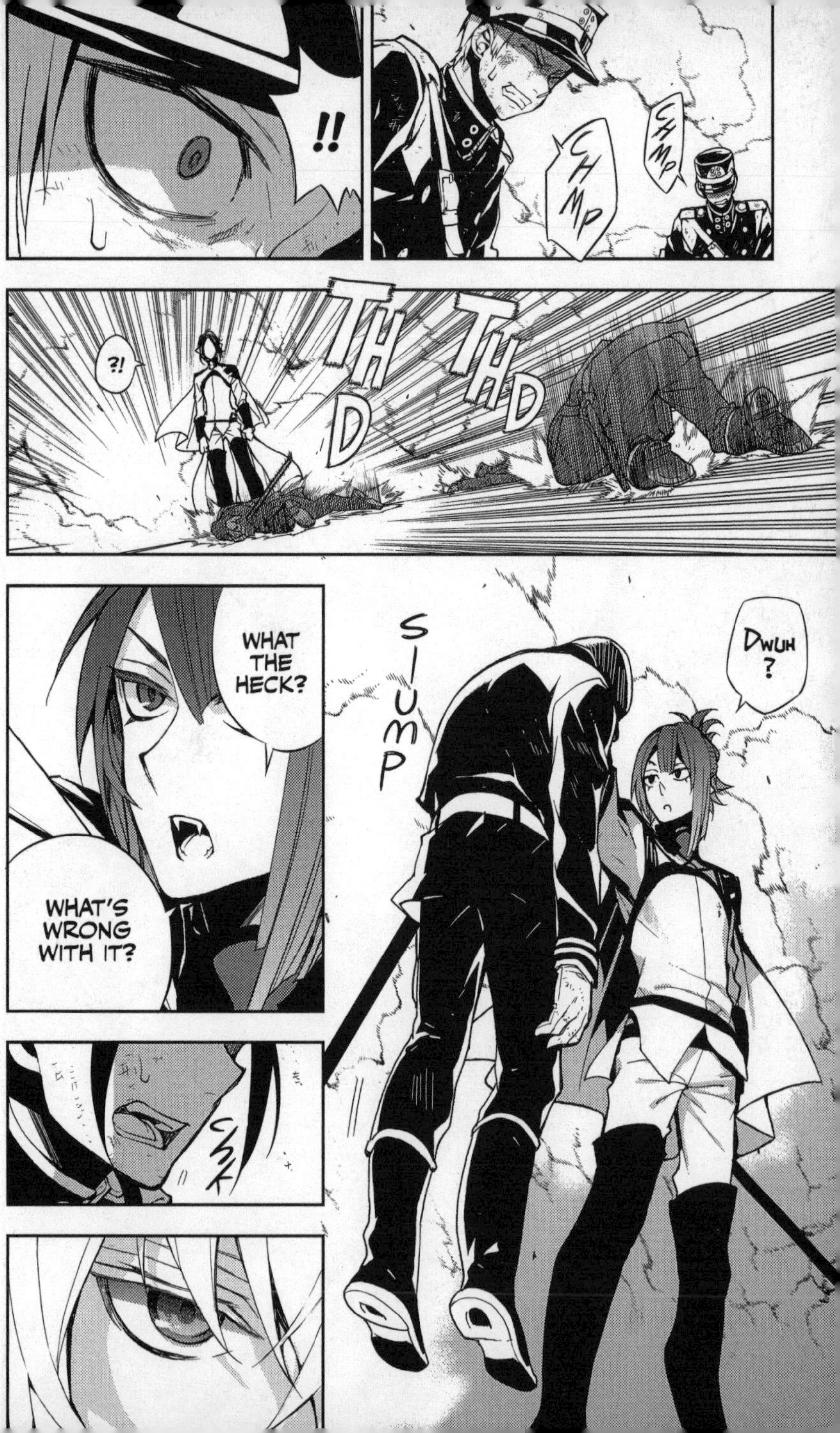
CHMP
CHMP
!!
THD
THD
?!
DWUH?
SLUMP
WHAT THE HECK?
WHAT'S WRONG WITH IT?
CHK

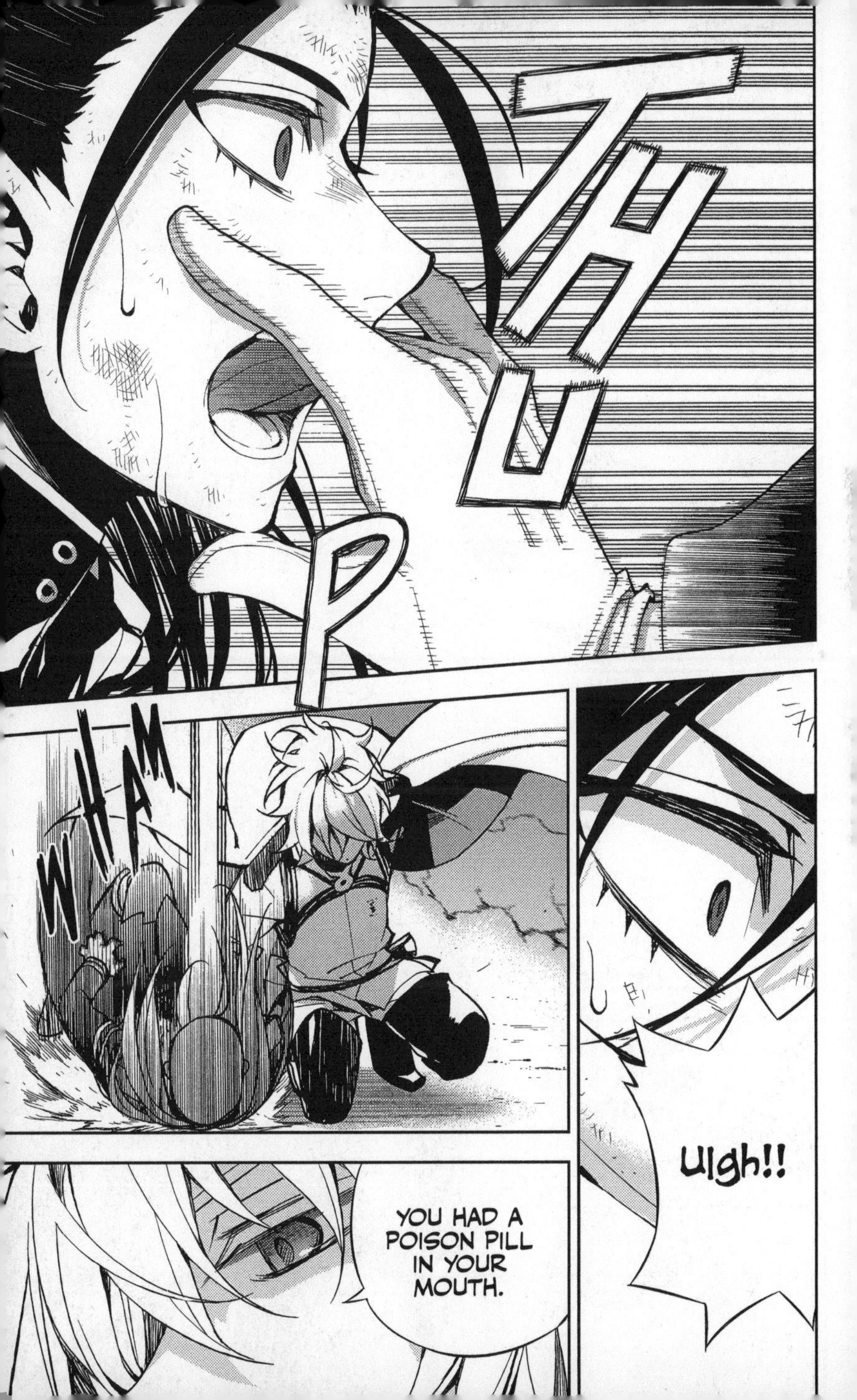
THUP
Ulgh!!
WHAM
YOU HAD A POISON PILL IN YOUR MOUTH.

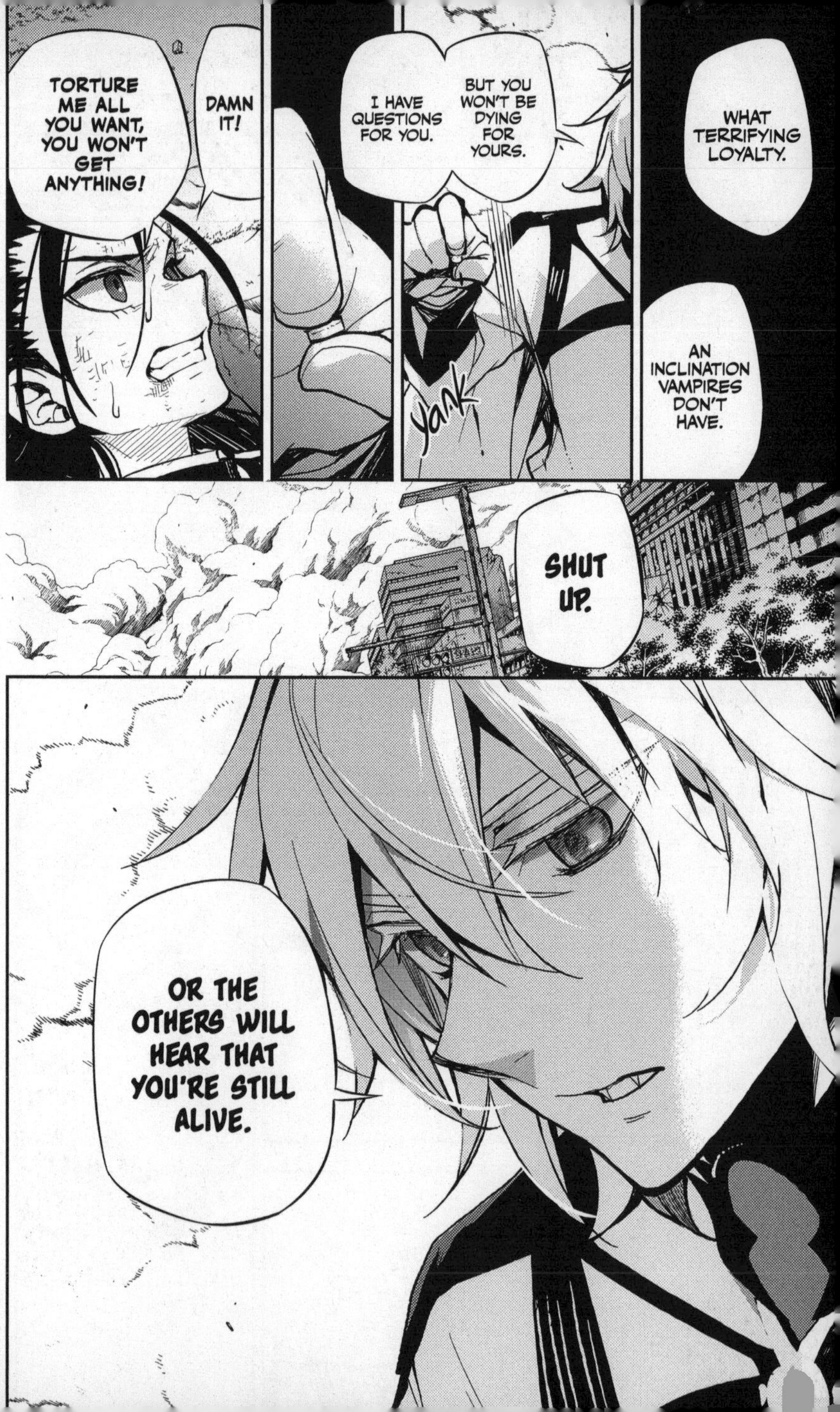
WHAT TERRIFYING LOYALTY.
AN INCLINATION VAMPIRES DON'T HAVE.
YANK
I HAVE QUESTIONS FOR YOU.
BUT YOU WON'T BE DYING FOR YOURS.
DAMN IT!
TORTURE ME ALL YOU WANT, YOU WON'T GET ANYTHING!
SHUT UP.
OR THE OTHERS WILL HEAR THAT YOU'RE STILL ALIVE.

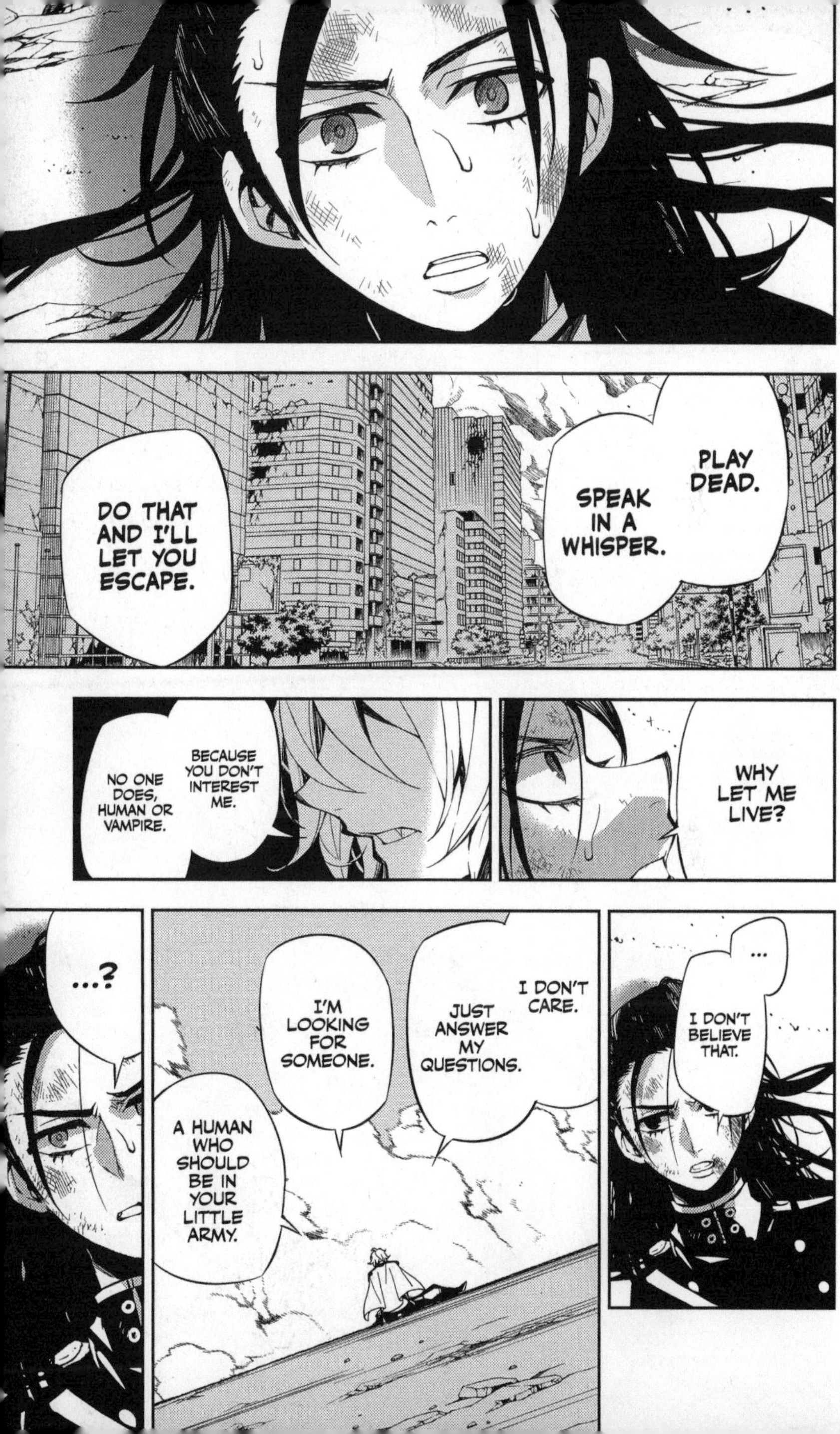
PLAY DEAD.
SPEAK IN A WHISPER.
DO THAT AND I'LL LET YOU ESCAPE.
WHY LET ME LIVE?
BECAUSE YOU DON'T INTEREST ME.
NO ONE DOES, HUMAN OR VAMPIRE.
...
I DON'T BELIEVE THAT.
I DON'T CARE.
JUST ANSWER MY QUESTIONS.
I'M LOOKING FOR SOMEONE.
A HUMAN WHO SHOULD BE IN YOUR LITTLE ARMY.
...?

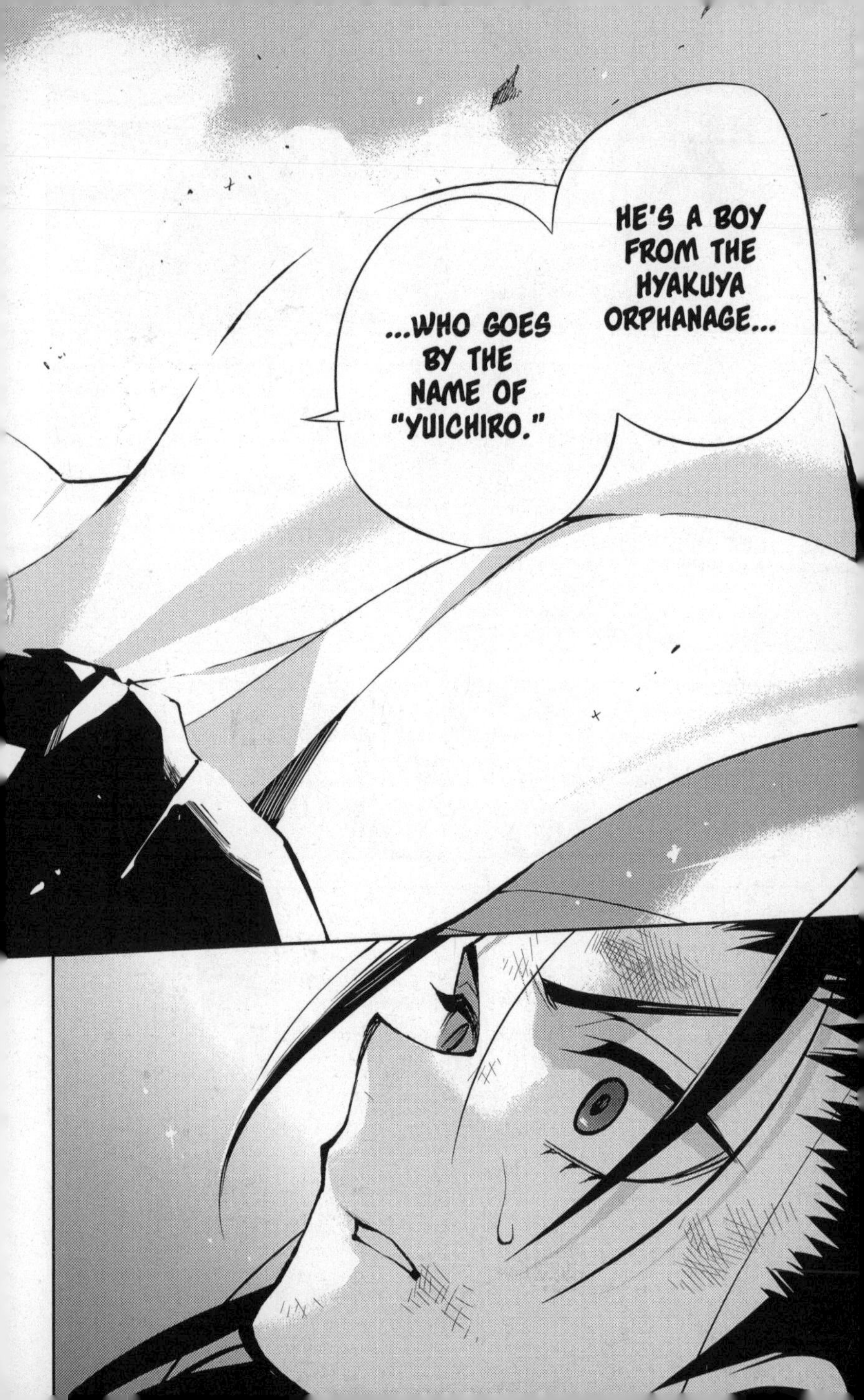
HE'S A BOY FROM THE HYAKUYA ORPHANAGE...
...WHO GOES BY THE NAME OF "YUICHIRO."

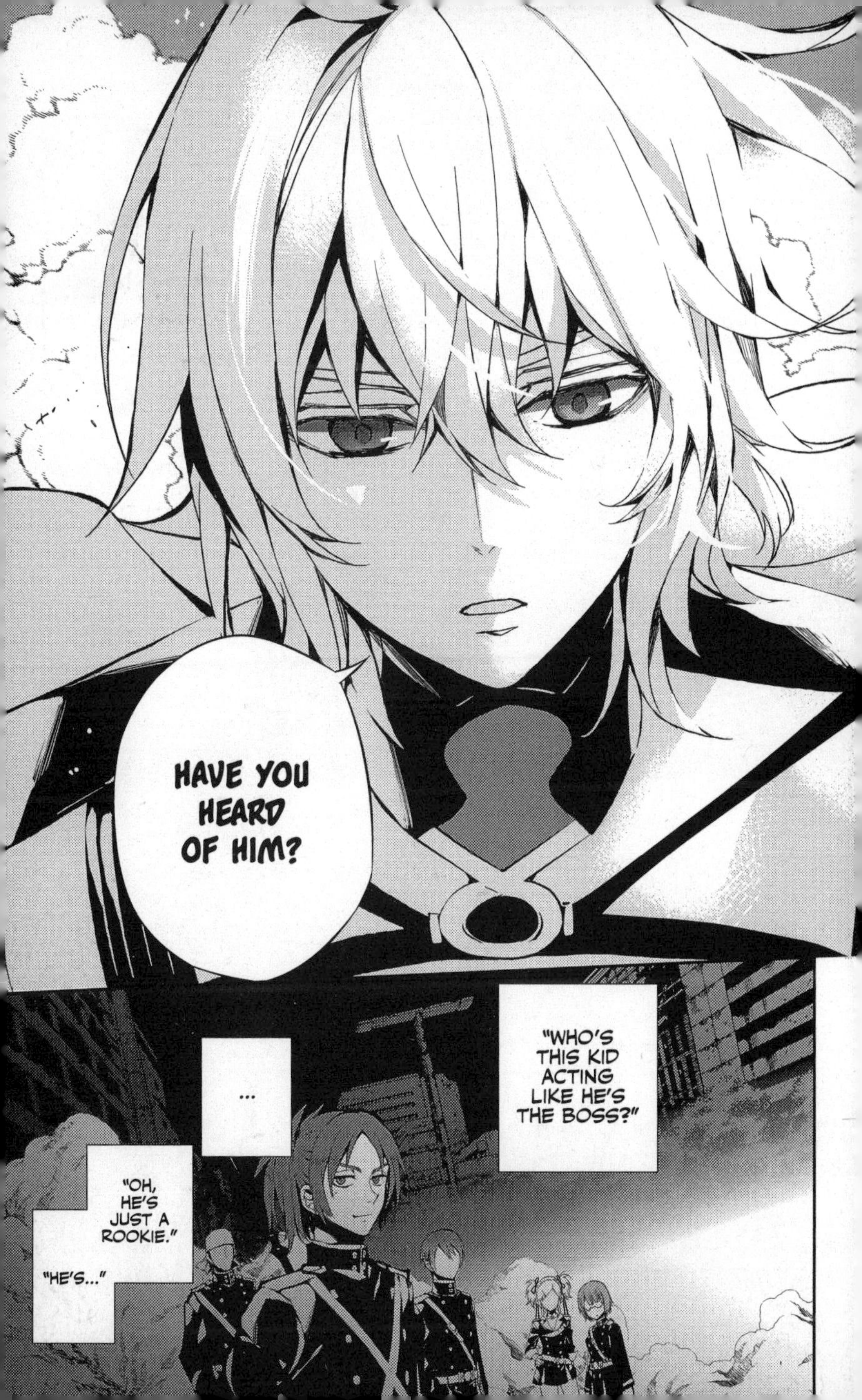
HAVE YOU HEARD OF HIM?
"WHO'S THIS KID ACTING LIKE HE'S THE BOSS?"
...
"OH, HE'S JUST A ROOKIE."
"HE'S..."

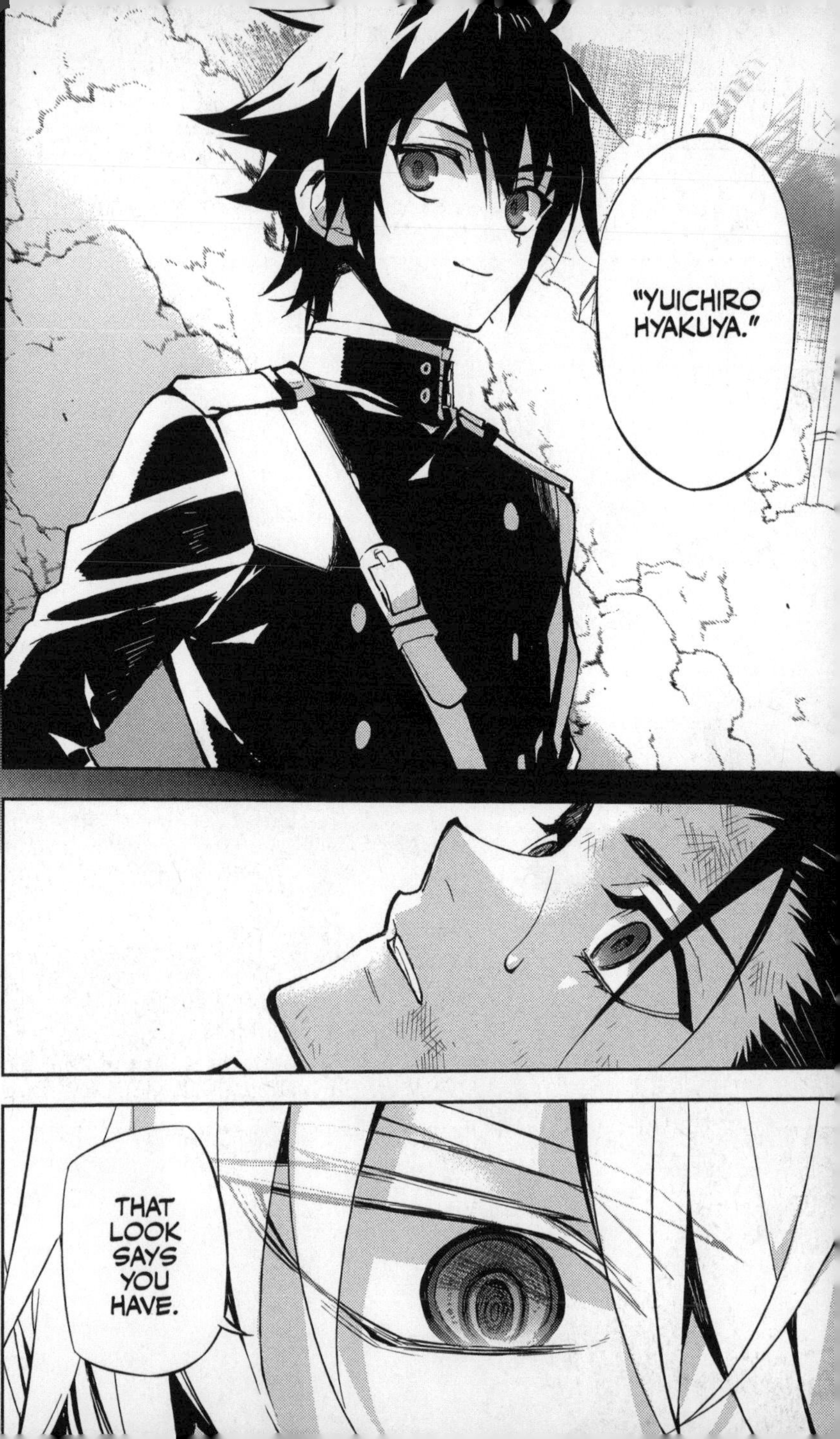
"YUICHIRO HYAKUYA."
THAT LOOK SAYS YOU HAVE.

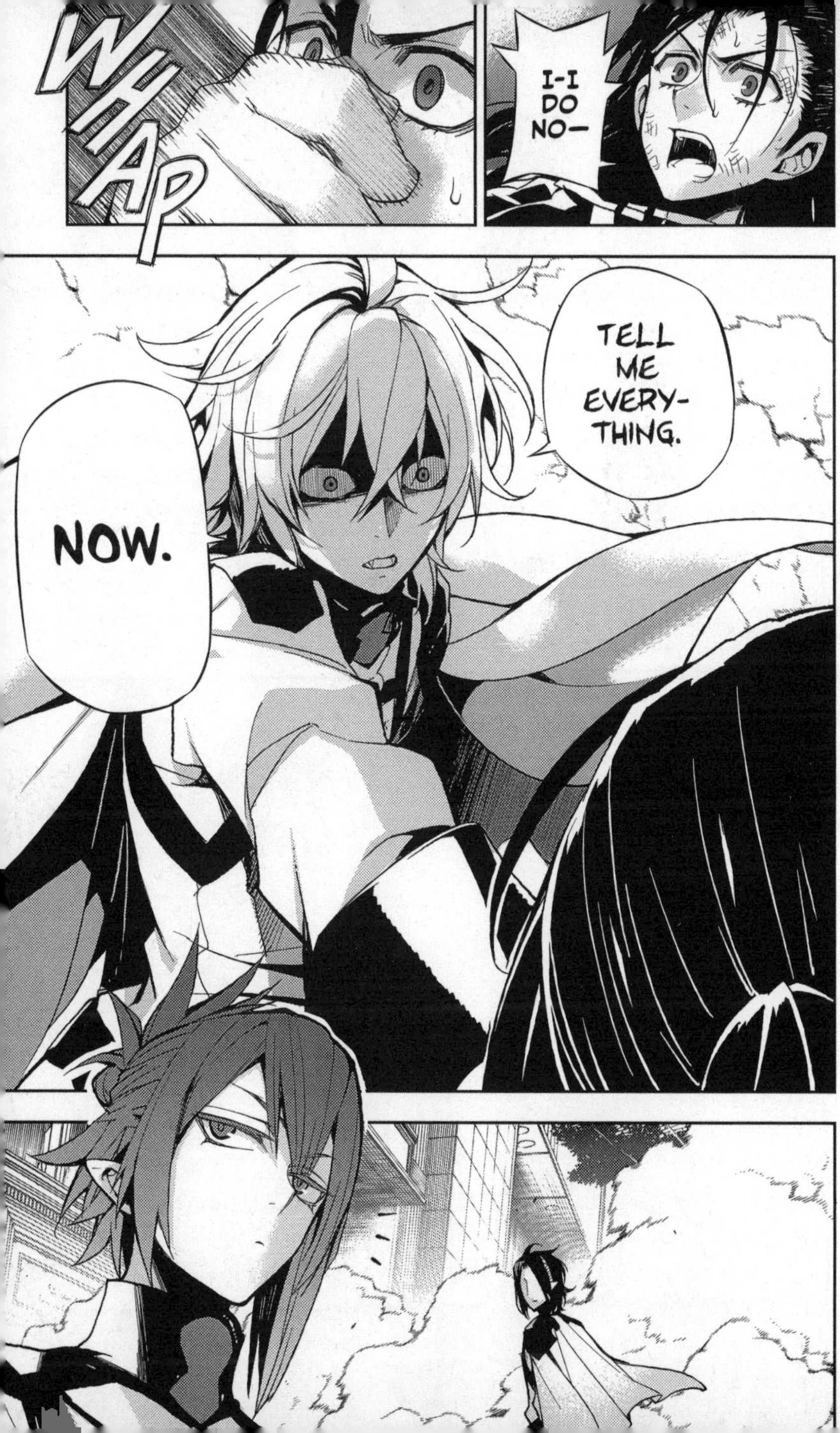
I-I DO NO—
WHAP
TELL ME EVERY-THING.
NOW.

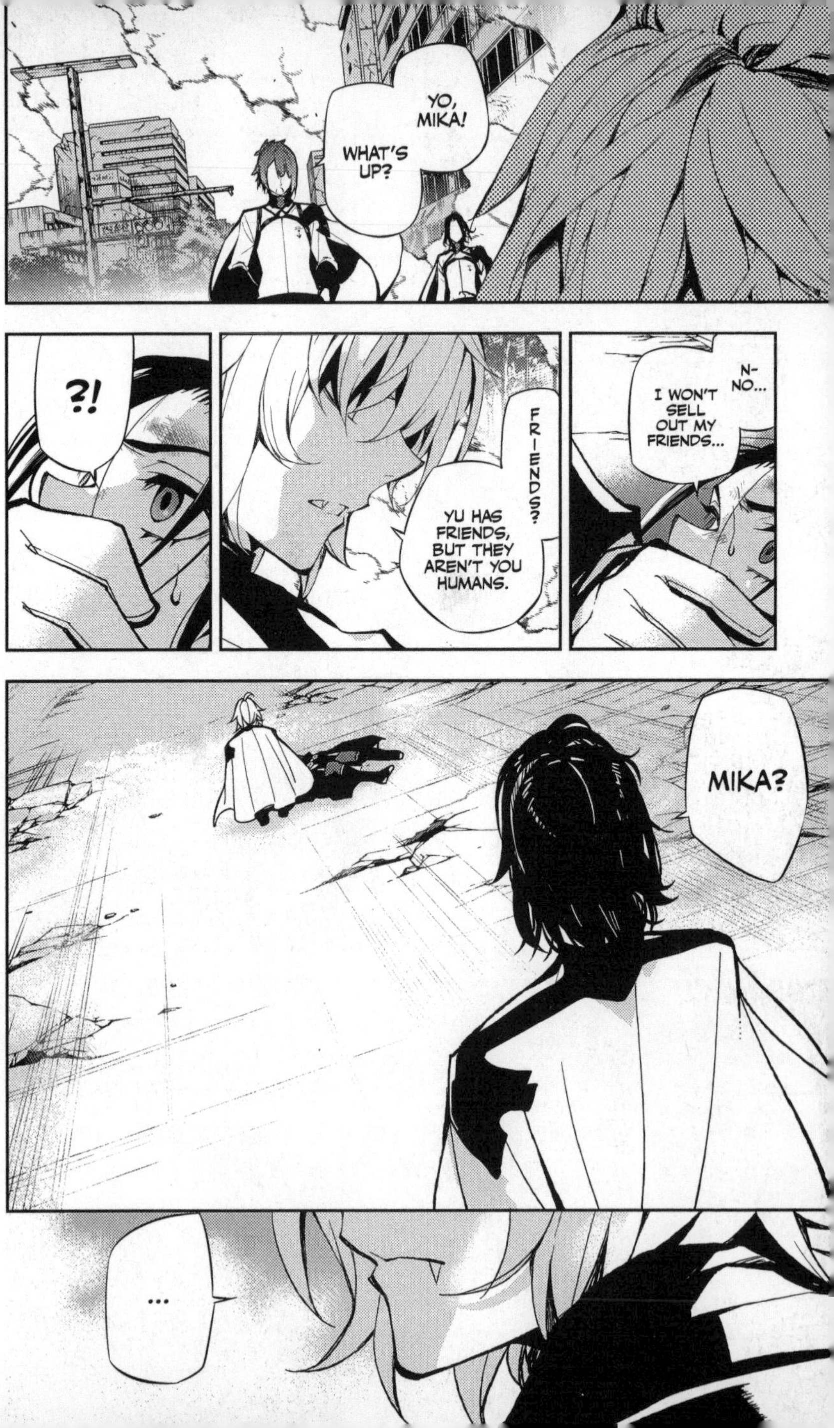
YO, MIKA!
WHAT'S UP?
N-NO... I WON'T SELL OUT MY FRIENDS...
FRIENDS?
YU HAS FRIENDS, BUT THEY AREN'T YOU HUMANS.
?!
MIKA?
...

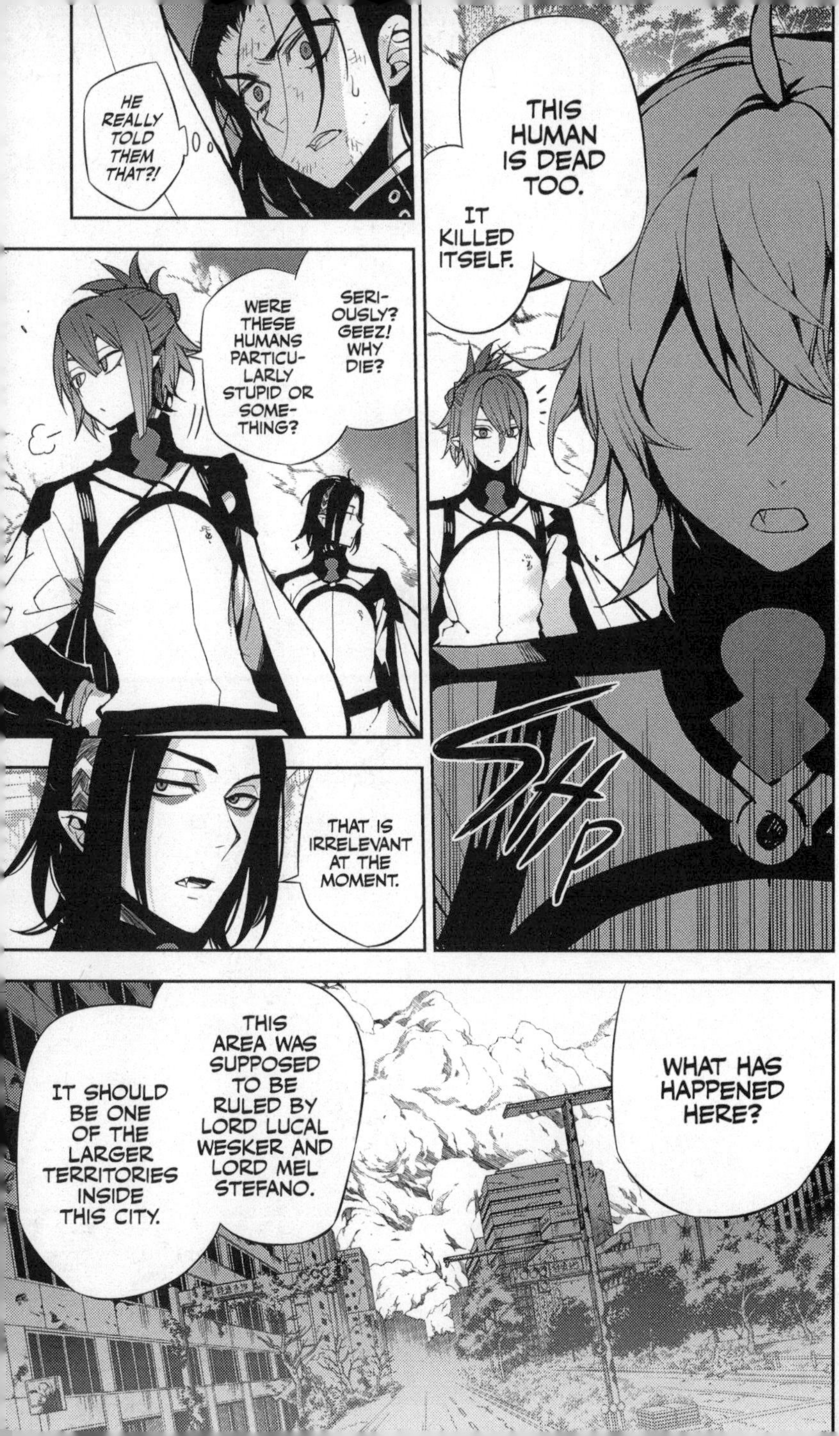
THIS HUMAN IS DEAD TOO.
IT KILLED ITSELF.
SHP
HE REALLY TOLD THEM THAT?!
SERI-OUSLY? GEEZ! WHY DIE?
WERE THESE HUMANS PARTICU-LARLY STUPID OR SOME-THING?
THAT IS IRRELEVANT AT THE MOMENT.
WHAT HAS HAPPENED HERE?
THIS AREA WAS SUPPOSED TO BE RULED BY LORD LUCAL WESKER AND LORD MEL STEFANO.
IT SHOULD BE ONE OF THE LARGER TERRITORIES INSIDE THIS CITY.

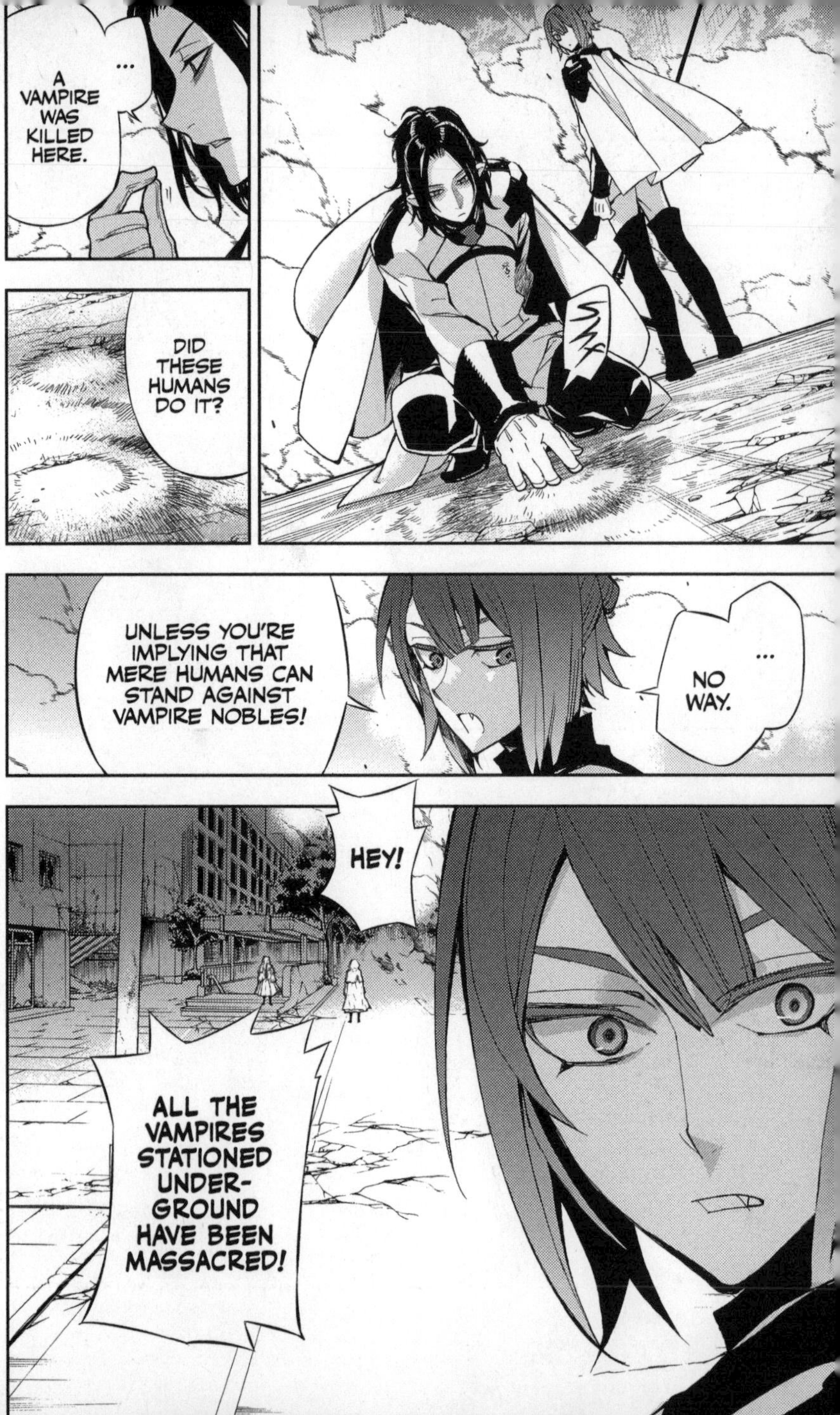
...
A VAMPIRE WAS KILLED HERE.
DID THESE HUMANS DO IT?
...
NO WAY.
UNLESS YOU'RE IMPLYING THAT MERE HUMANS CAN STAND AGAINST VAMPIRE NOBLES!
HEY!
ALL THE VAMPIRES STATIONED UNDER-GROUND HAVE BEEN MASSACRED!

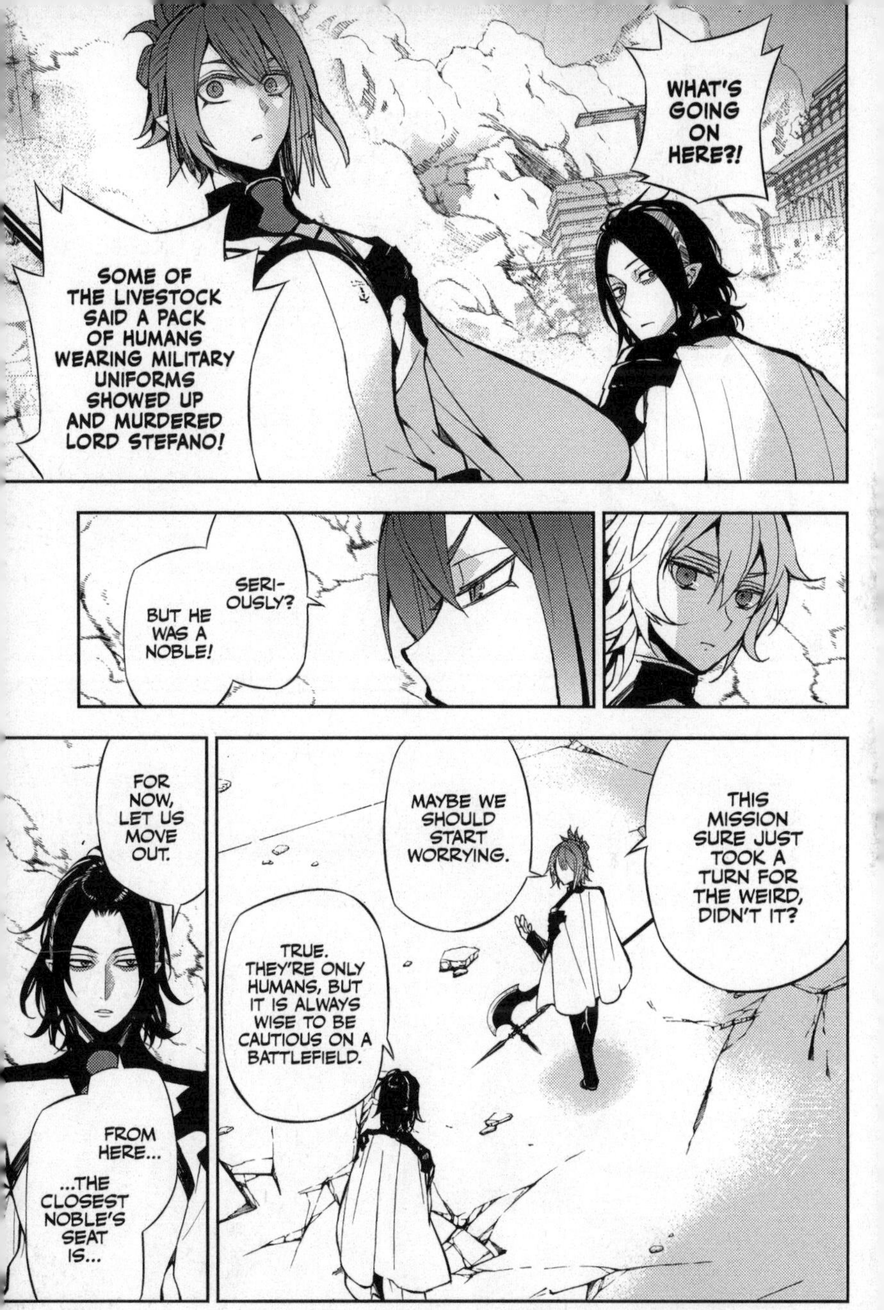
WHAT'S GOING ON HERE?!
SOME OF THE LIVESTOCK SAID A PACK OF HUMANS WEARING MILITARY UNIFORMS SHOWED UP AND MURDERED LORD STEFANO!
SERI-OUSLY?
BUT HE WAS A NOBLE!
THIS MISSION SURE JUST TOOK A TURN FOR THE WEIRD, DIDN'T IT?
MAYBE WE SHOULD START WORRYING.
TRUE. THEY'RE ONLY HUMANS, BUT IT IS ALWAYS WISE TO BE CAUTIOUS ON A BATTLEFIELD.
FOR NOW, LET US MOVE OUT.
FROM HERE...
...THE CLOSEST NOBLE'S SEAT IS...

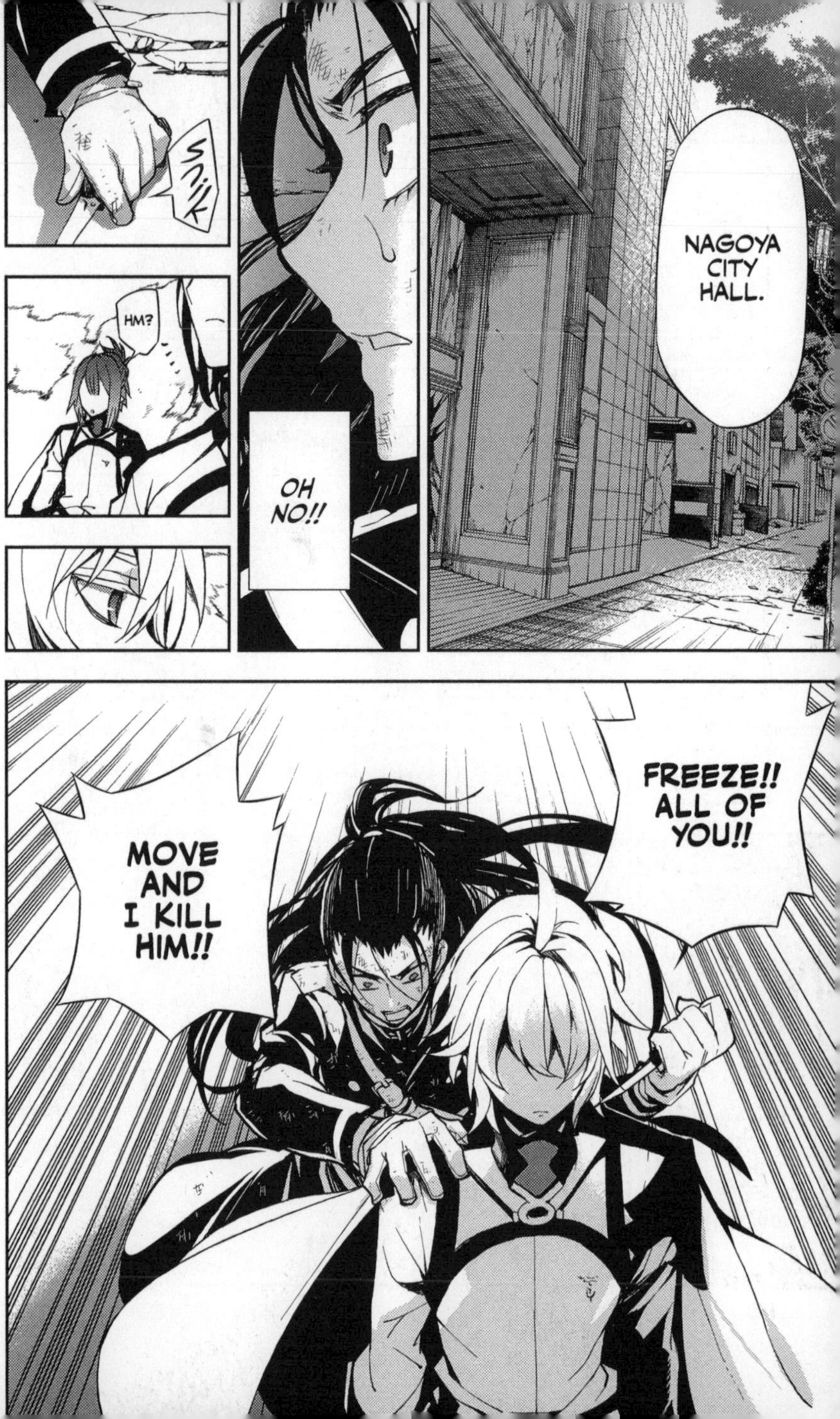
NAGOYA CITY HALL.
OH NO!!
SNIK
HM?
FREEZE!! ALL OF YOU!!
MOVE AND I KILL HIM!!

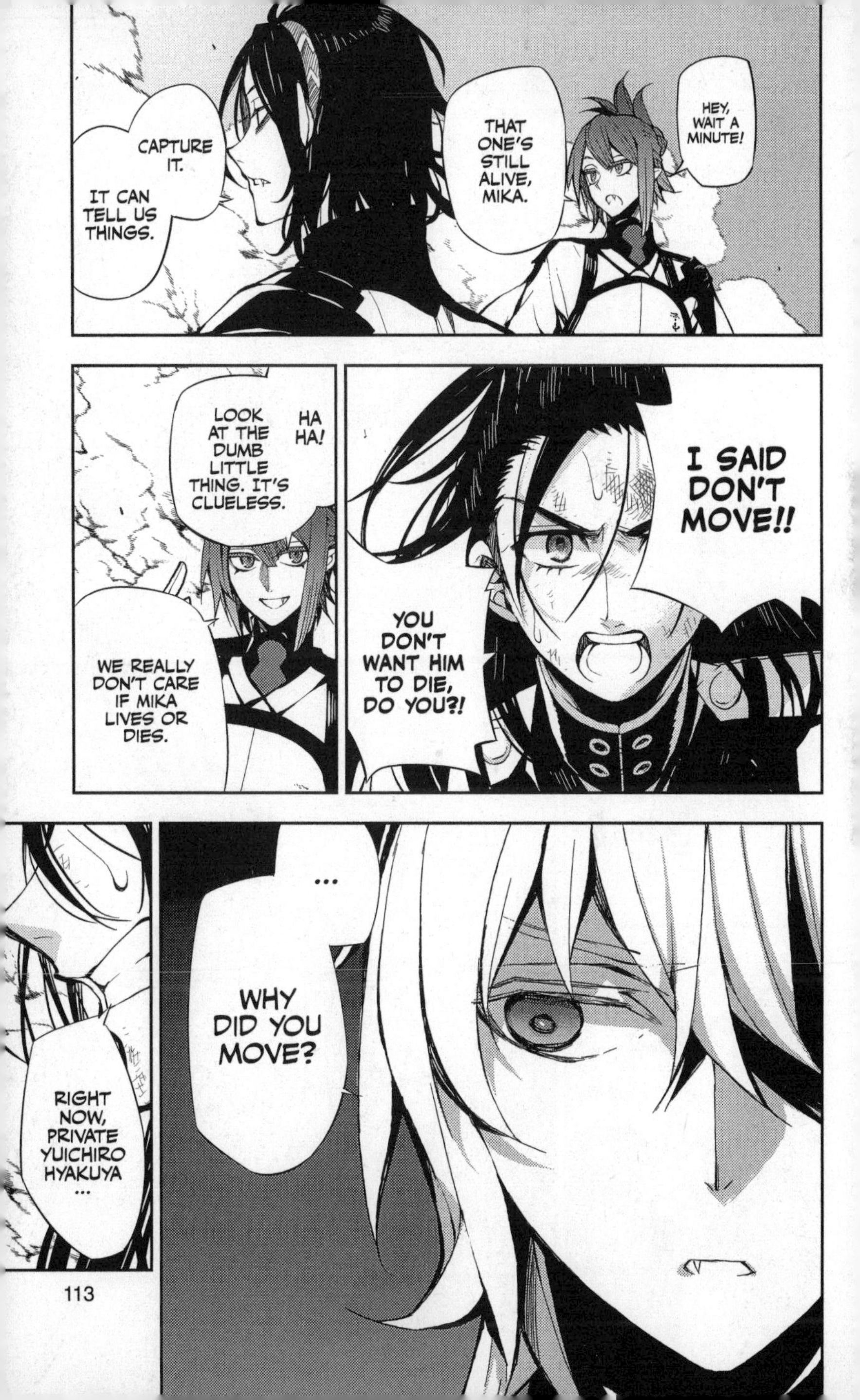
HEY, WAIT A MINUTE!
THAT ONE'S STILL ALIVE, MIKA.
CAPTURE IT.
IT CAN TELL US THINGS.
I SAID DON'T MOVE!!
YOU DON'T WANT HIM TO DIE, DO YOU?!
HA HA!
LOOK AT THE DUMB LITTLE THING. IT'S CLUELESS.
WE REALLY DON'T CARE IF MIKA LIVES OR DIES.
...
WHY DID YOU MOVE?
RIGHT NOW, PRIVATE YUICHIRO HYAKUYA ...

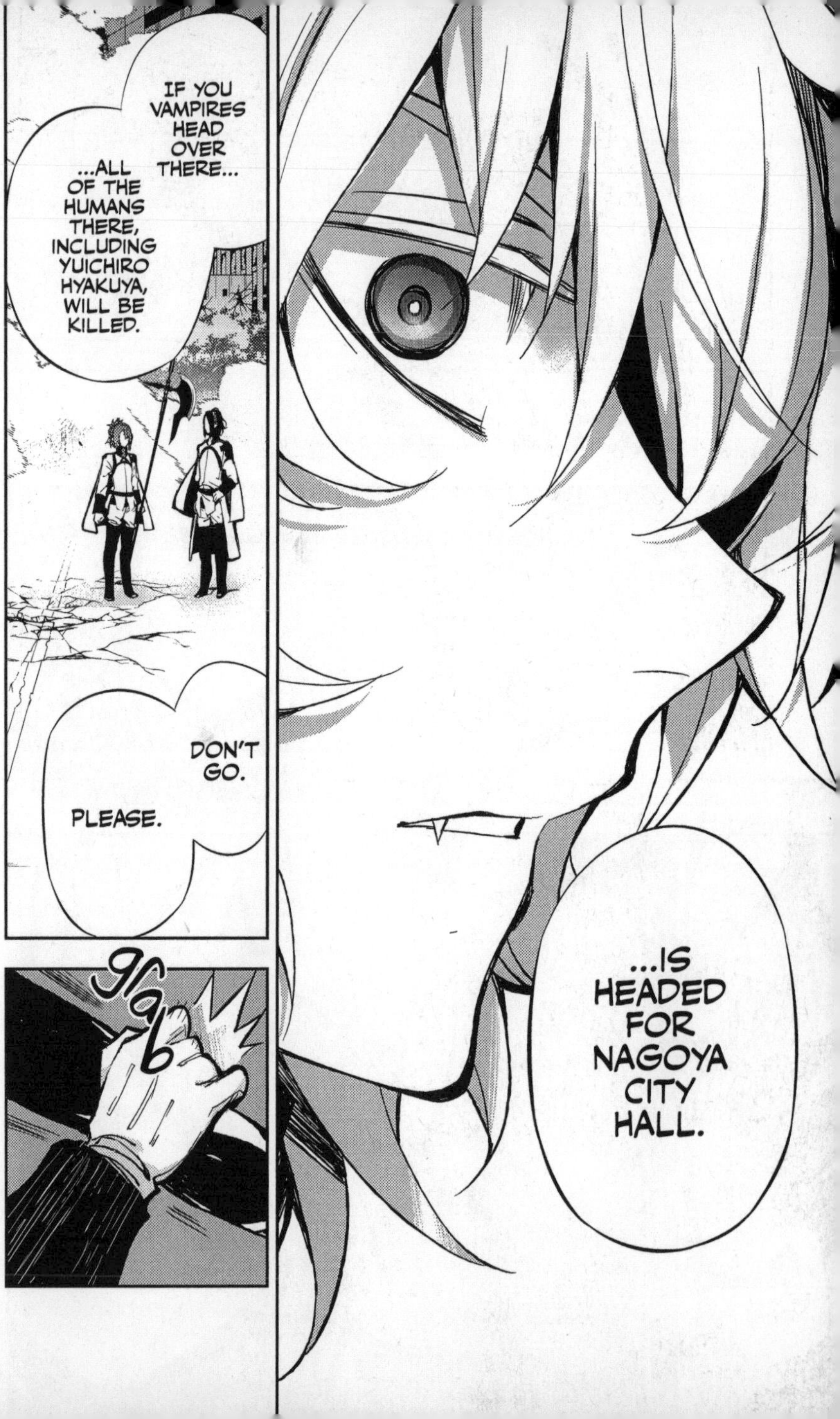
...IS HEADED FOR NAGOYA CITY HALL.
IF YOU VAMPIRES HEAD OVER THERE...
...ALL OF THE HUMANS THERE, INCLUDING YUICHIRO HYAKUYA, WILL BE KILLED.
DON'T GO.
PLEASE.
grab

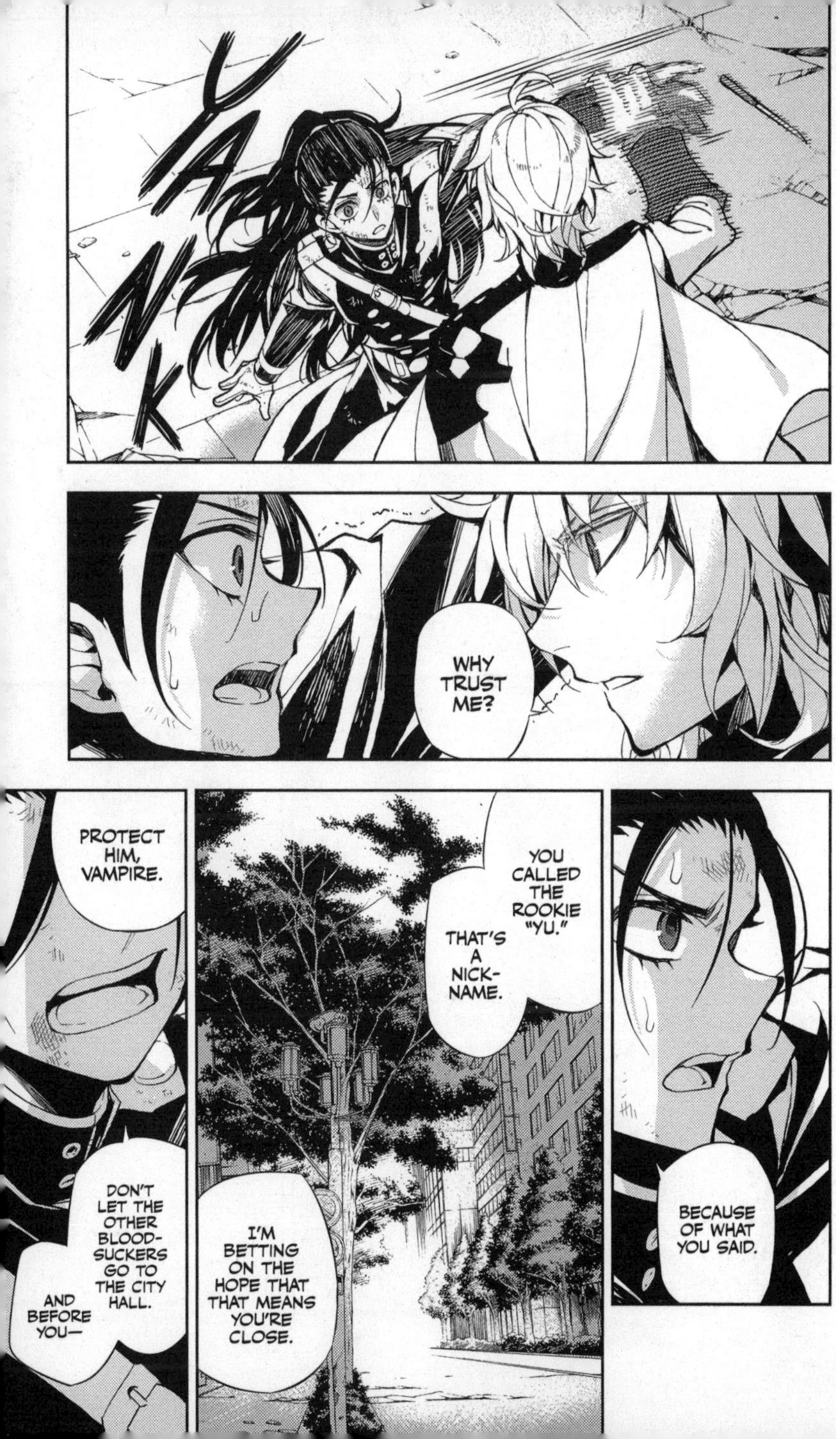
YANK
WHY TRUST ME?
BECAUSE OF WHAT YOU SAID.
YOU CALLED THE ROOKIE "YU."
THAT'S A NICK-NAME.
I'M BETTING ON THE HOPE THAT THAT MEANS YOU'RE CLOSE.
PROTECT HIM, VAMPIRE.
DON'T LET THE OTHER BLOOD-SUCKERS GO TO THE CITY HALL.
AND BEFORE YOU—

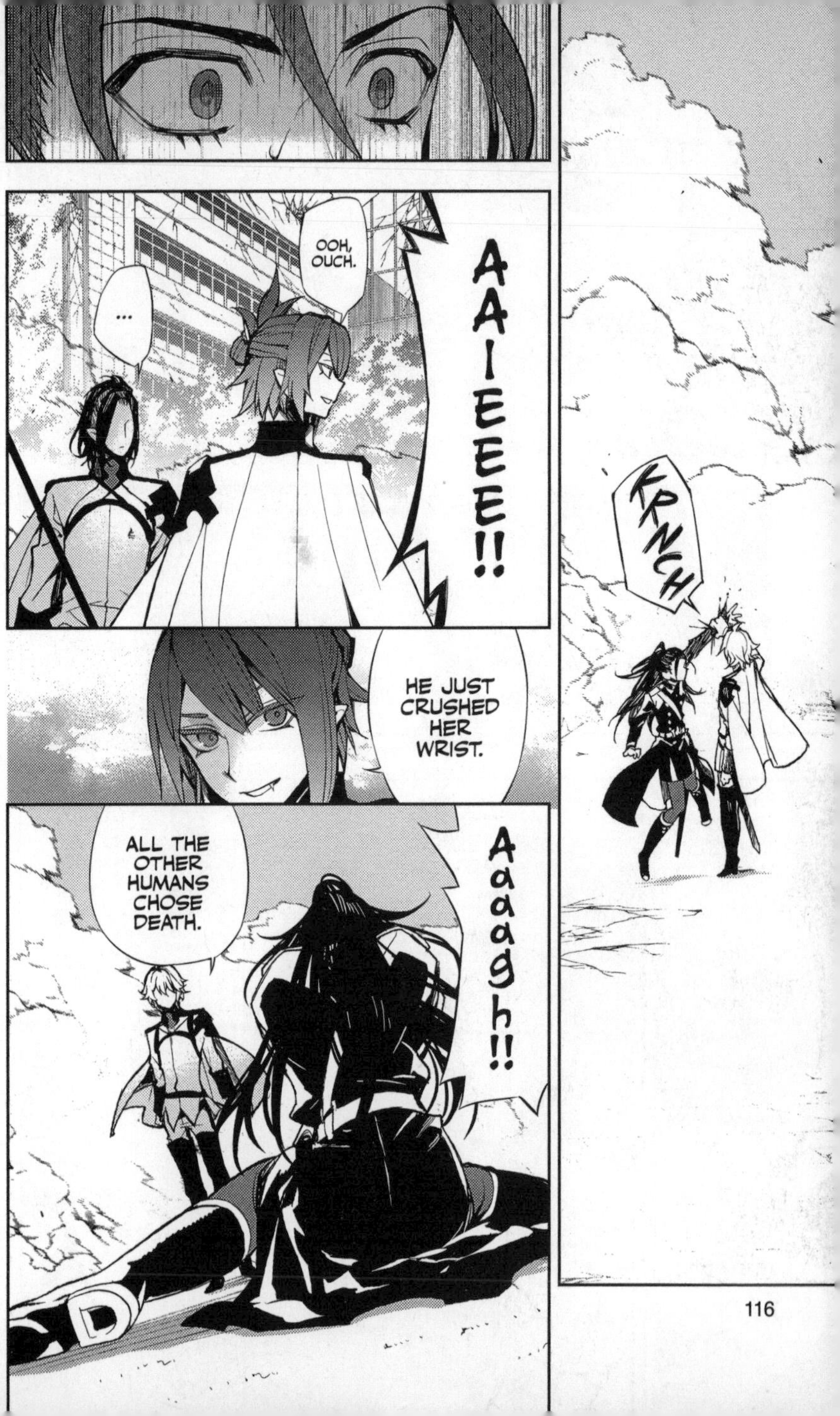
KRNCH
AAIEEEE!!
OOH, OUCH.
...
HE JUST CRUSHED HER WRIST.
Aaaagh!!
ALL THE OTHER HUMANS CHOSE DEATH.

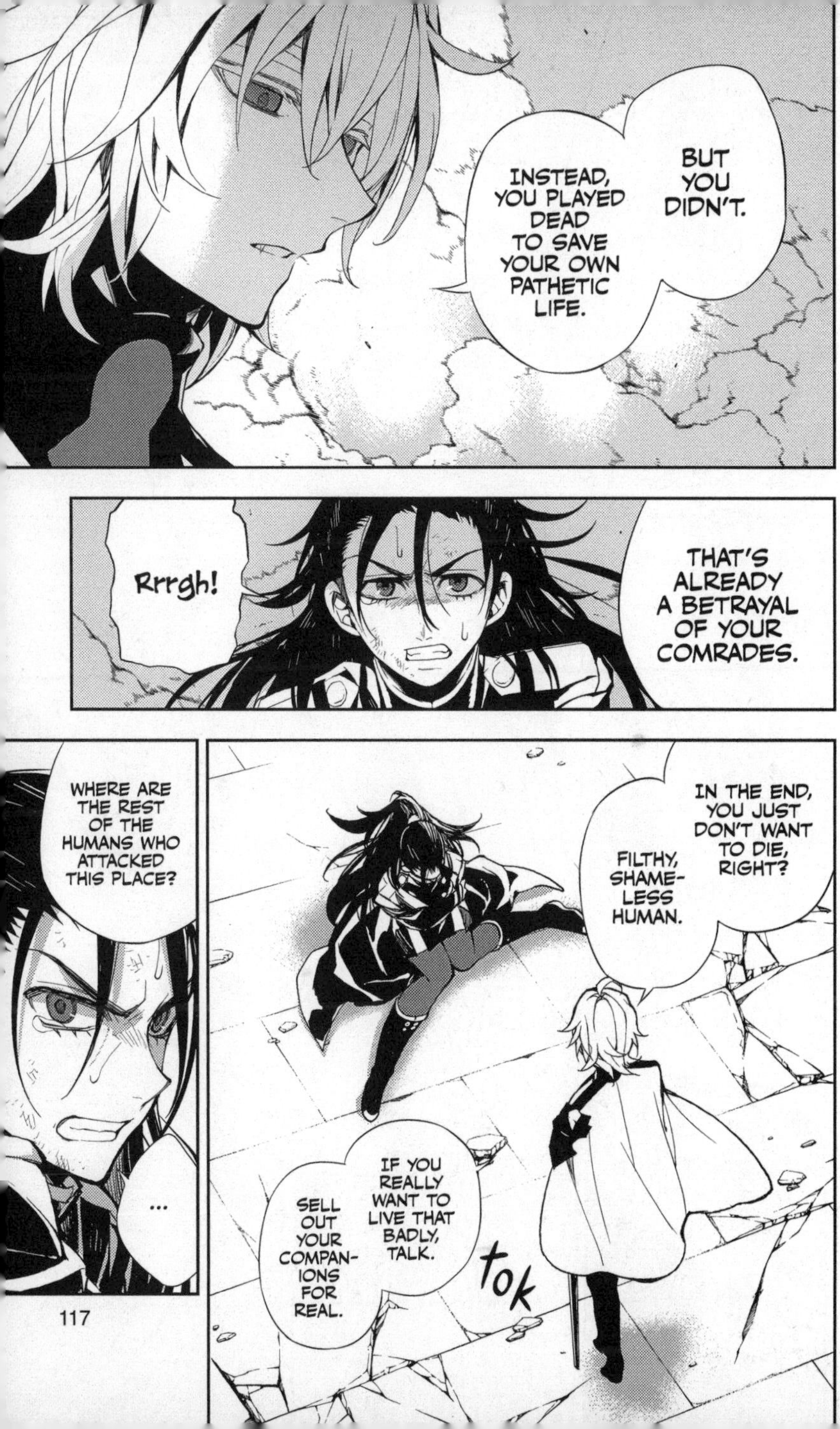
BUT YOU DIDN'T.
INSTEAD, YOU PLAYED DEAD TO SAVE YOUR OWN PATHETIC LIFE.
THAT'S ALREADY A BETRAYAL OF YOUR COMRADES.
Rrrgh!
IN THE END, YOU JUST DON'T WANT TO DIE, RIGHT?
FILTHY, SHAMELESS HUMAN.
IF YOU REALLY WANT TO LIVE THAT BADLY, TALK.
SELL OUT YOUR COMPANIONS FOR REAL.
tok
WHERE ARE THE REST OF THE HUMANS WHO ATTACKED THIS PLACE?
...

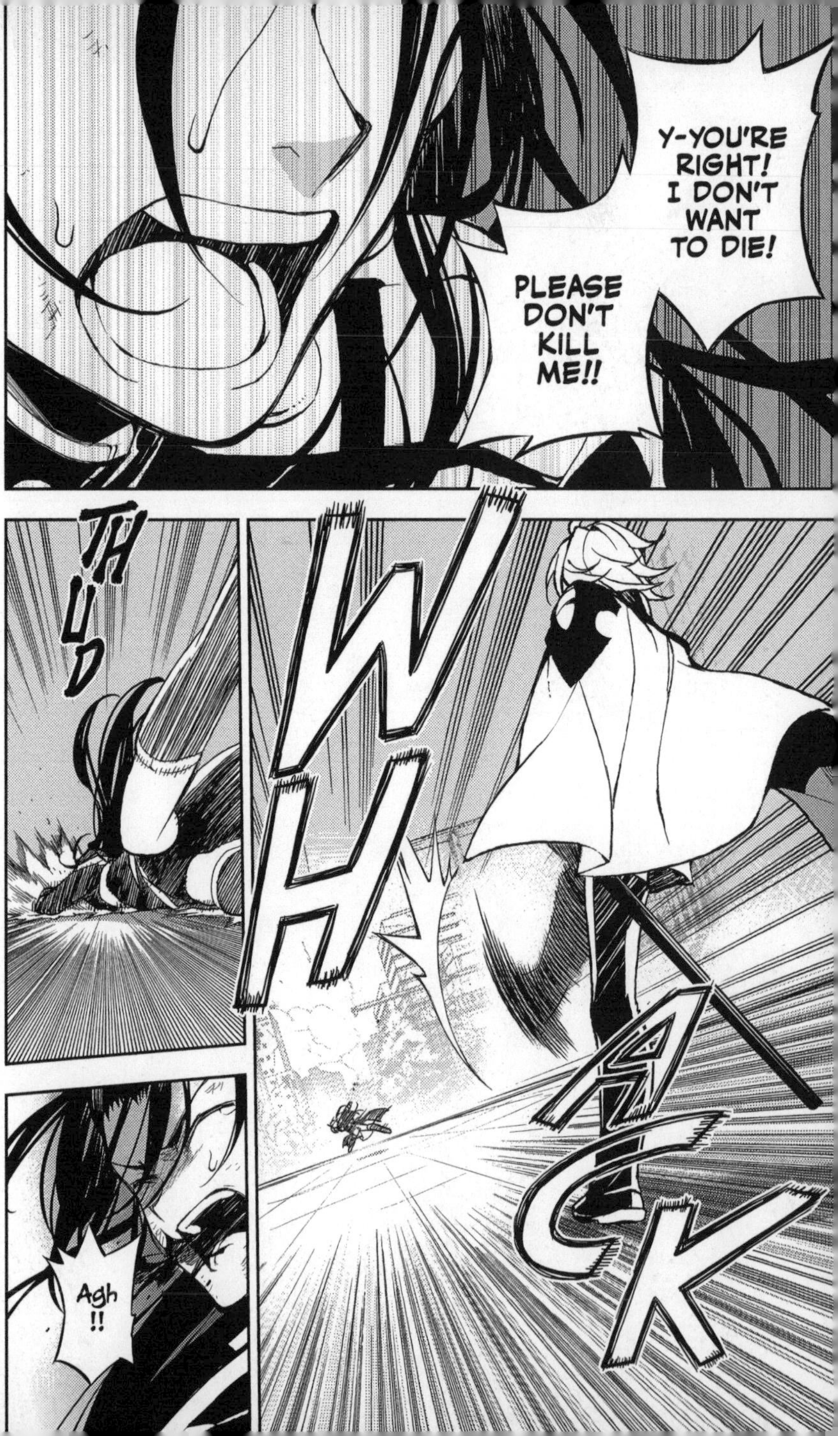
Y-YOU'RE RIGHT! I DON'T WANT TO DIE!
PLEASE DON'T KILL ME!!
WHACK
THUD
Agh !!

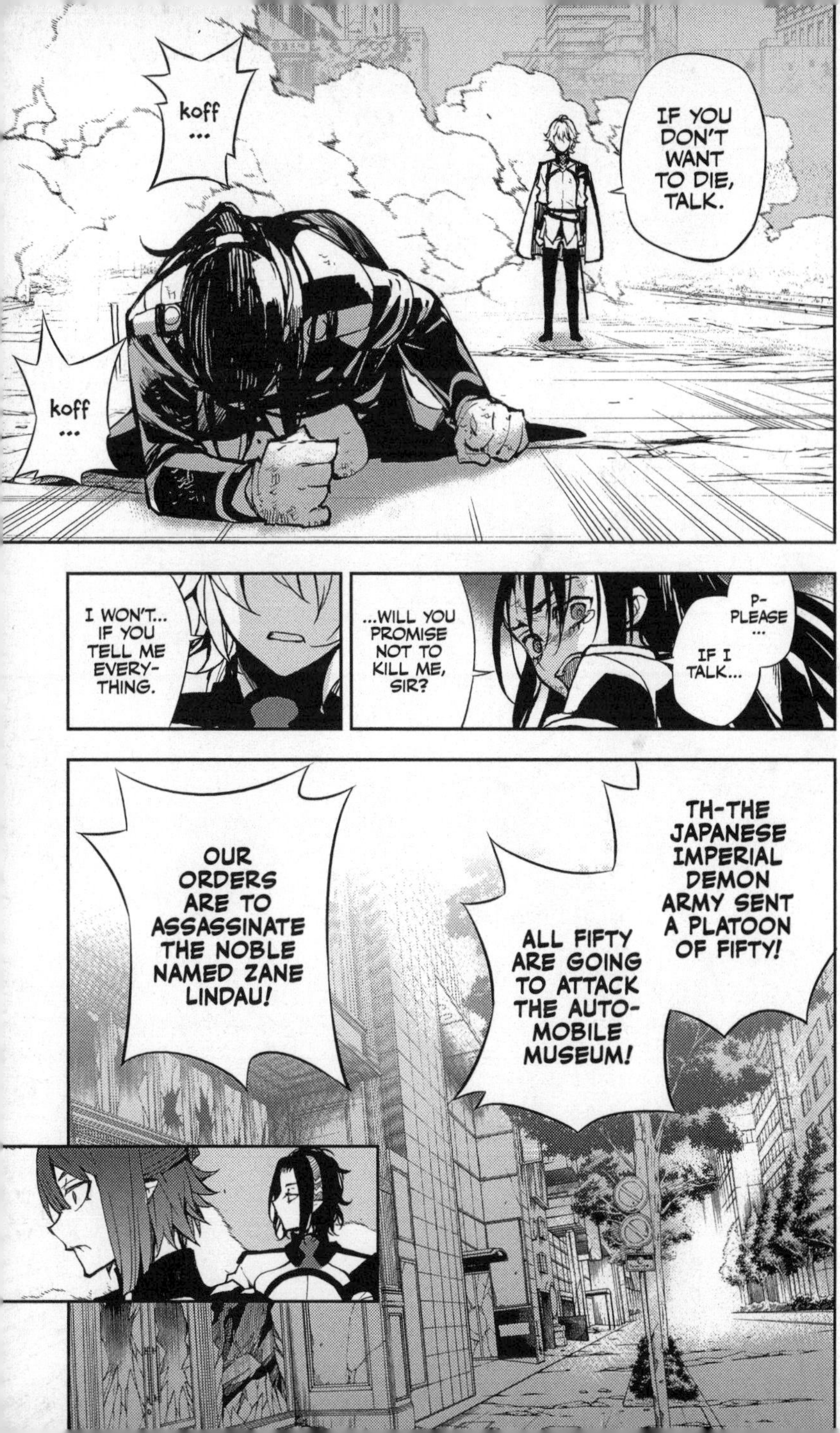
IF YOU DON'T WANT TO DIE, TALK.
koff...
koff...
P-PLEASE...
IF I TALK...
...WILL YOU PROMISE NOT TO KILL ME, SIR?
I WON'T... IF YOU TELL ME EVERY-THING.
TH-THE JAPANESE IMPERIAL DEMON ARMY SENT A PLATOON OF FIFTY!
ALL FIFTY ARE GOING TO ATTACK THE AUTO-MOBILE MUSEUM!
OUR ORDERS ARE TO ASSASSINATE THE NOBLE NAMED ZANE LINDAU!

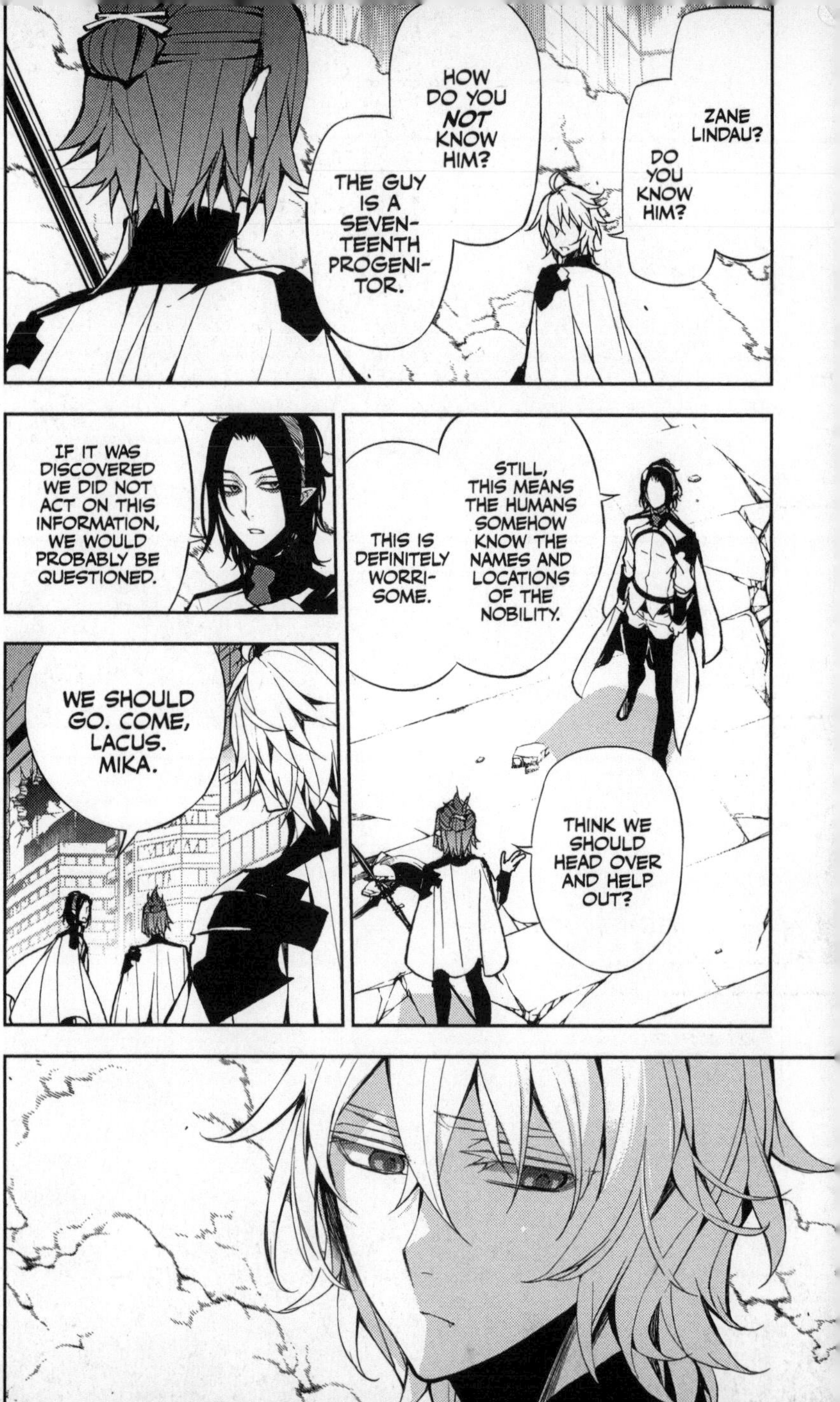
ZANE LINDAU?
DO YOU KNOW HIM?
HOW DO YOU *NOT* KNOW HIM?
THE GUY IS A SEVENTEENTH PROGENITOR.
STILL, THIS MEANS THE HUMANS SOMEHOW KNOW THE NAMES AND LOCATIONS OF THE NOBILITY.
THIS IS DEFINITELY WORRISOME.
THINK WE SHOULD HEAD OVER AND HELP OUT?
IF IT WAS DISCOVERED WE DID NOT ACT ON THIS INFORMATION, WE WOULD PROBABLY BE QUESTIONED.
WE SHOULD GO. COME, LACUS. MIKA.

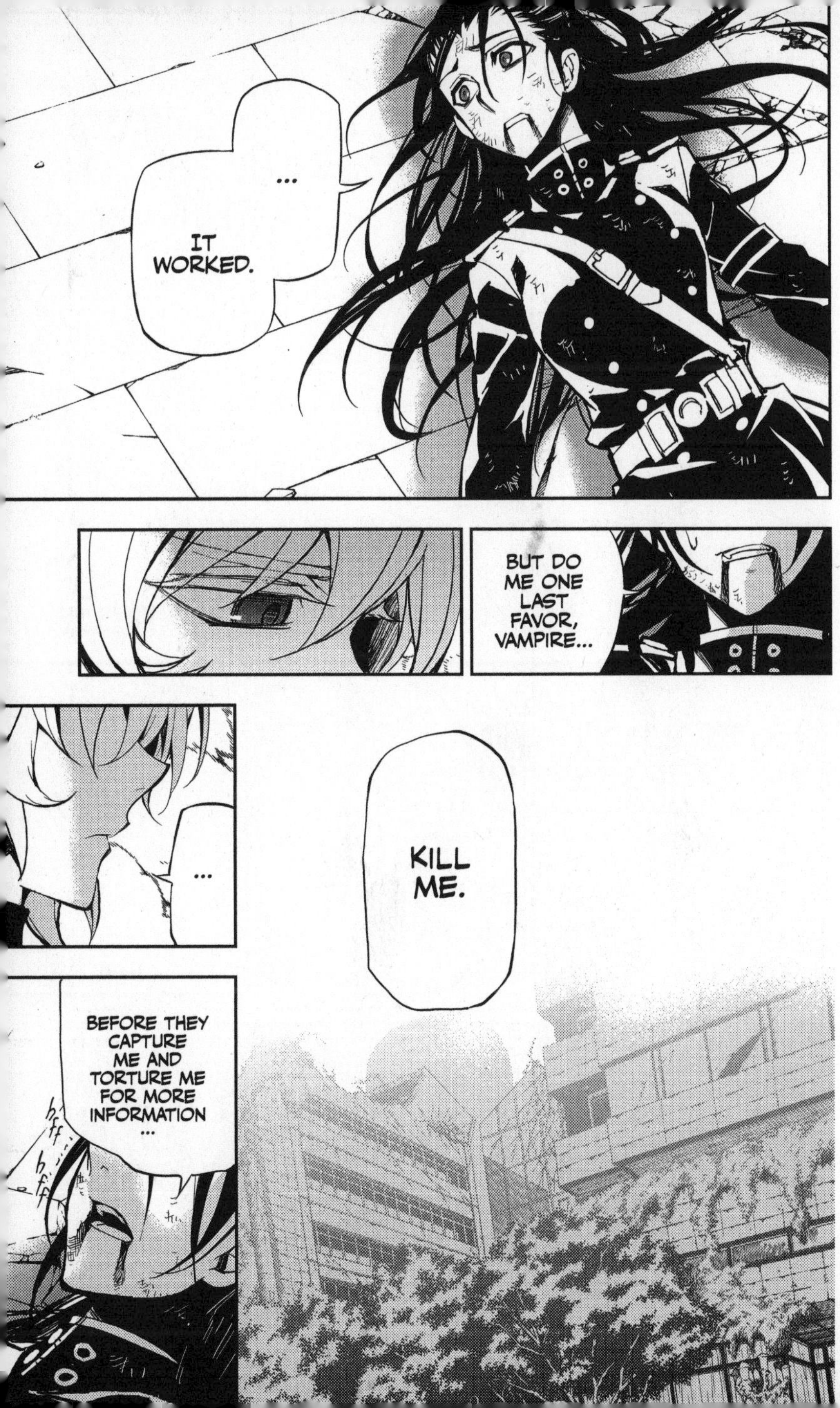
...
IT WORKED.
BUT DO ME ONE LAST FAVOR, VAMPIRE...
KILL ME.
...
BEFORE THEY CAPTURE ME AND TORTURE ME FOR MORE INFORMATION...
hff hff

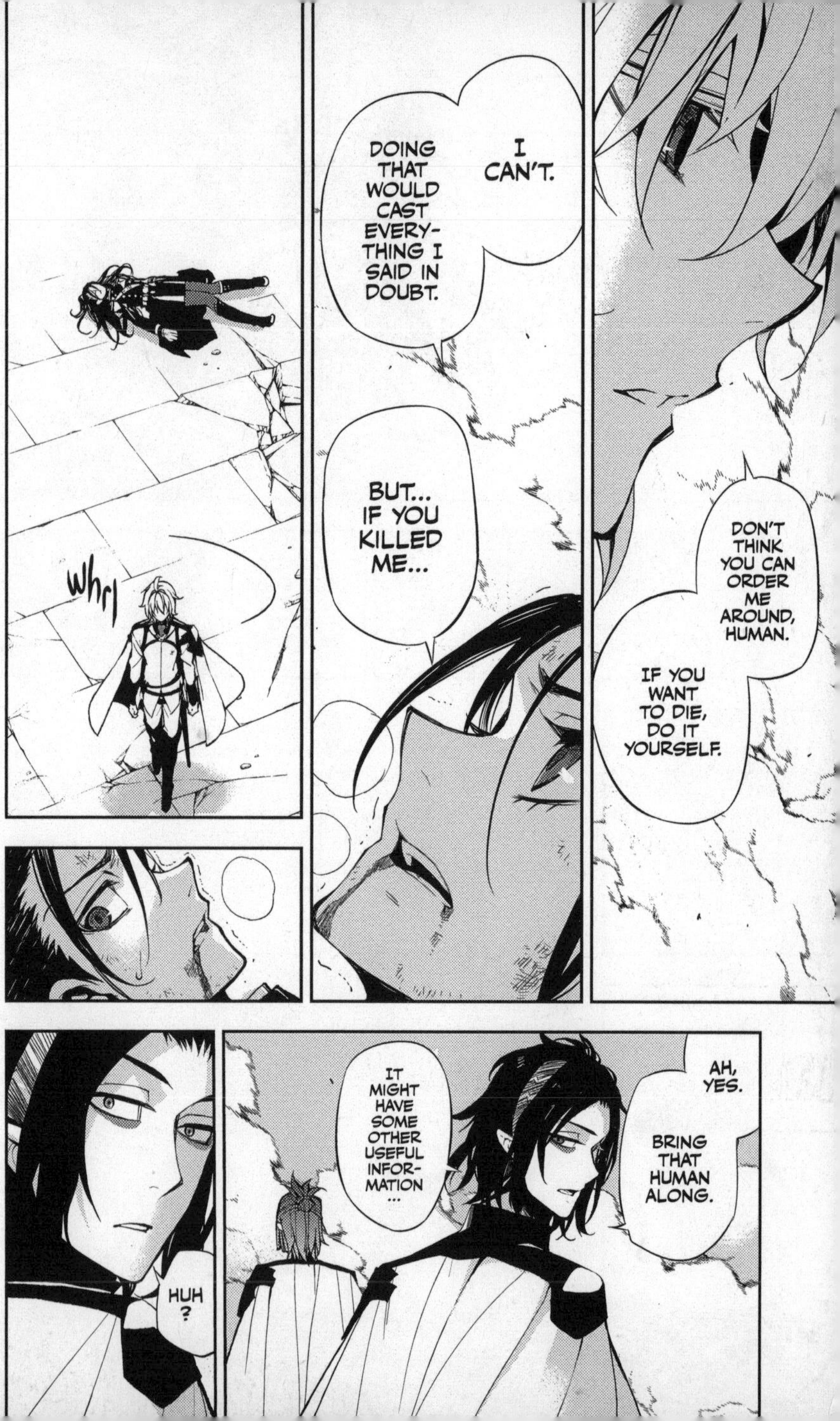
DON'T THINK YOU CAN ORDER ME AROUND, HUMAN.
IF YOU WANT TO DIE, DO IT YOURSELF.
I CAN'T.
DOING THAT WOULD CAST EVERYTHING I SAID IN DOUBT.
BUT... IF YOU KILLED ME...
whrl
AH, YES.
BRING THAT HUMAN ALONG.
IT MIGHT HAVE SOME OTHER USEFUL INFORMATION...
HUH?

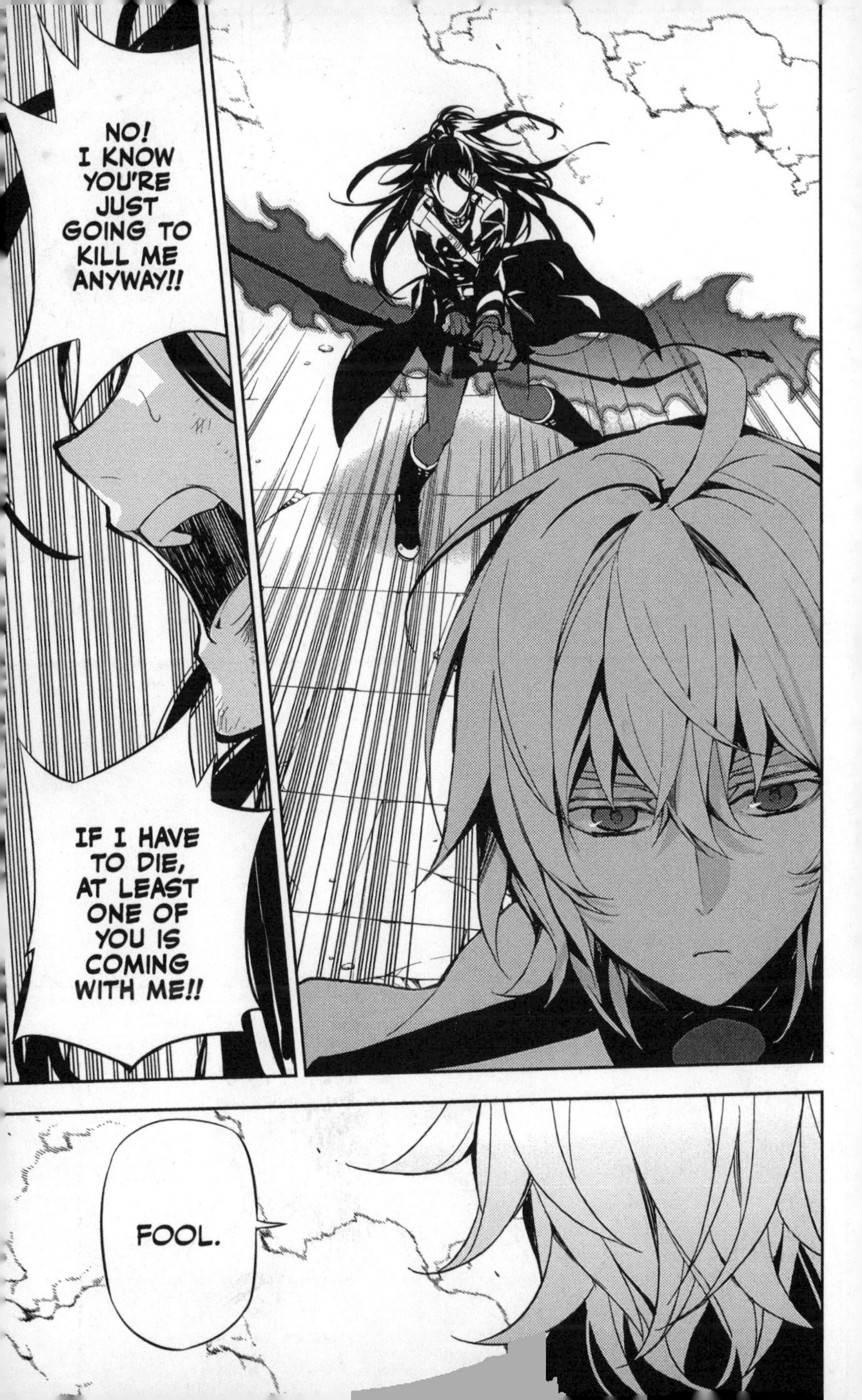
NO! I KNOW YOU'RE JUST GOING TO KILL ME ANYWAY!!
IF I HAVE TO DIE, AT LEAST ONE OF YOU IS COMING WITH ME!!
FOOL.

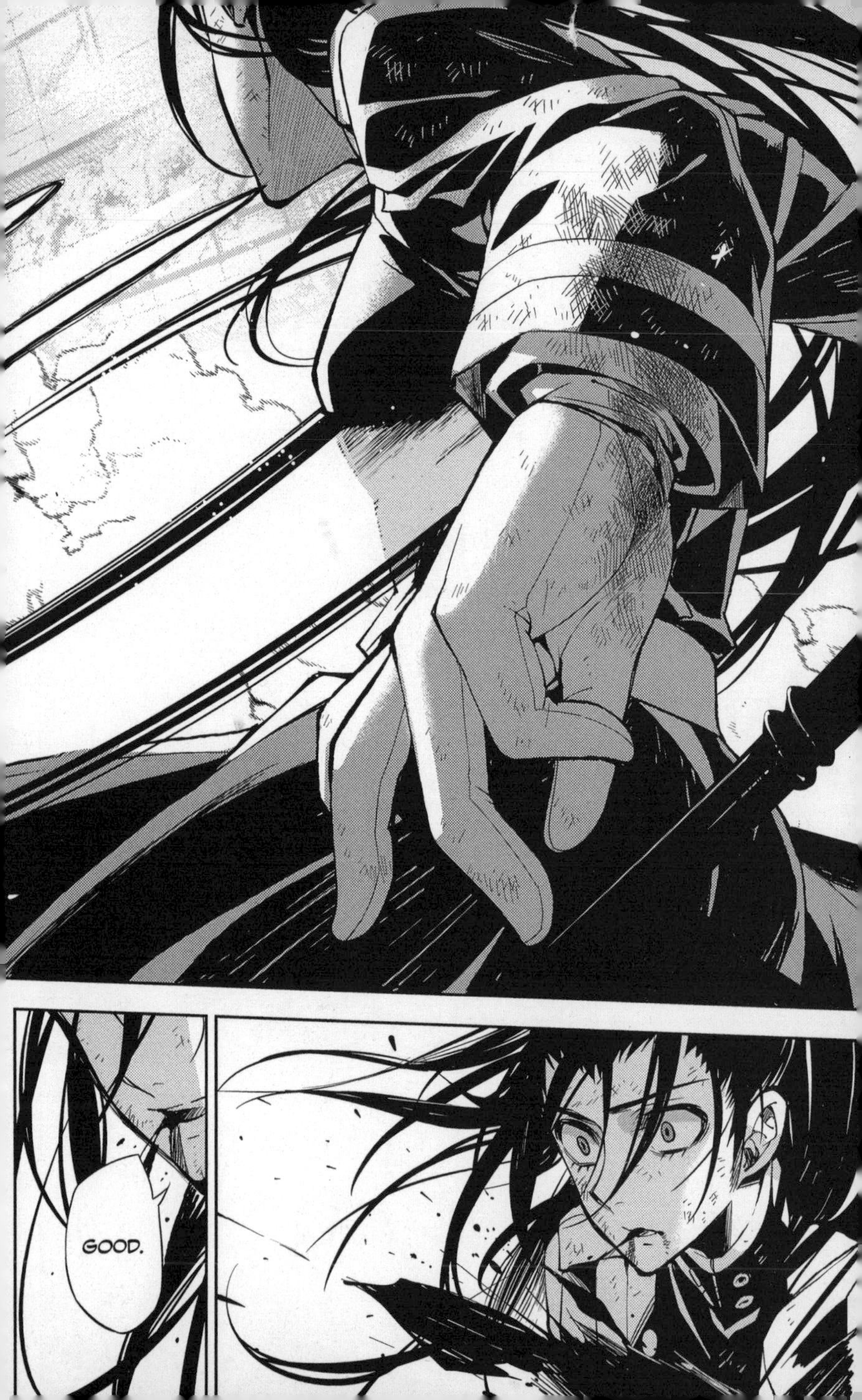
GOOD.

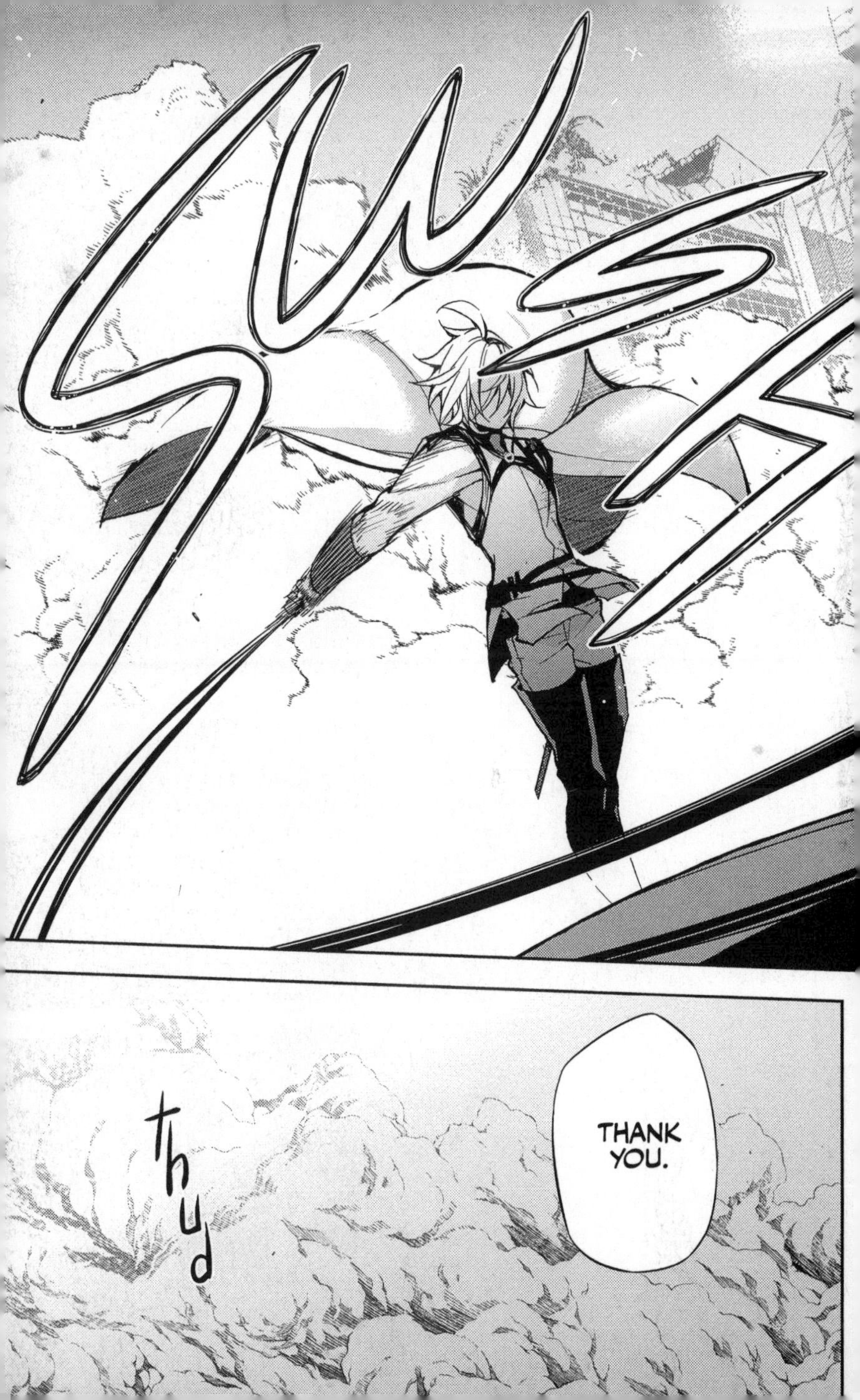
SWSH
THANK YOU.
thud

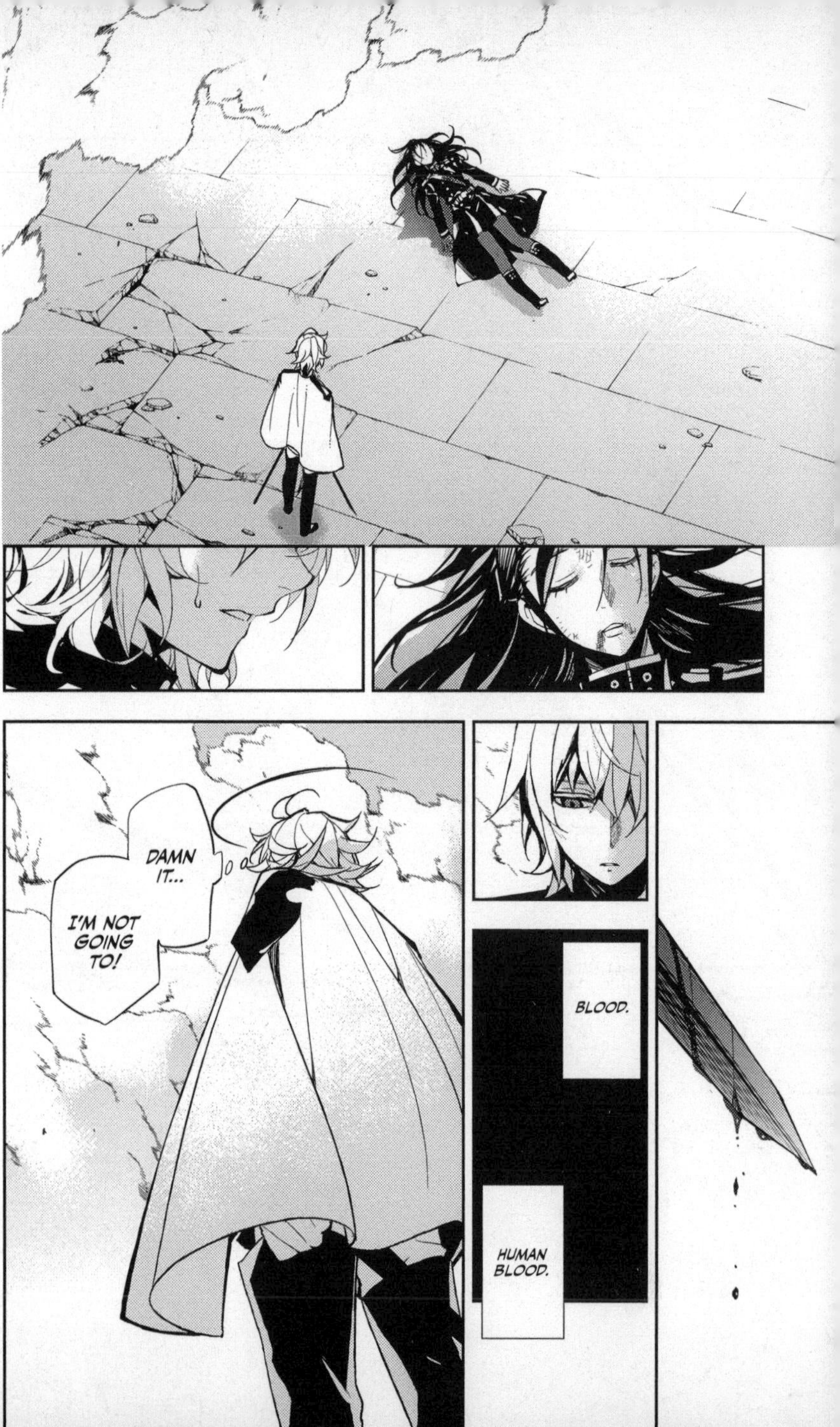
BLOOD.
HUMAN BLOOD.
DAMN IT...
I'M NOT GOING TO!

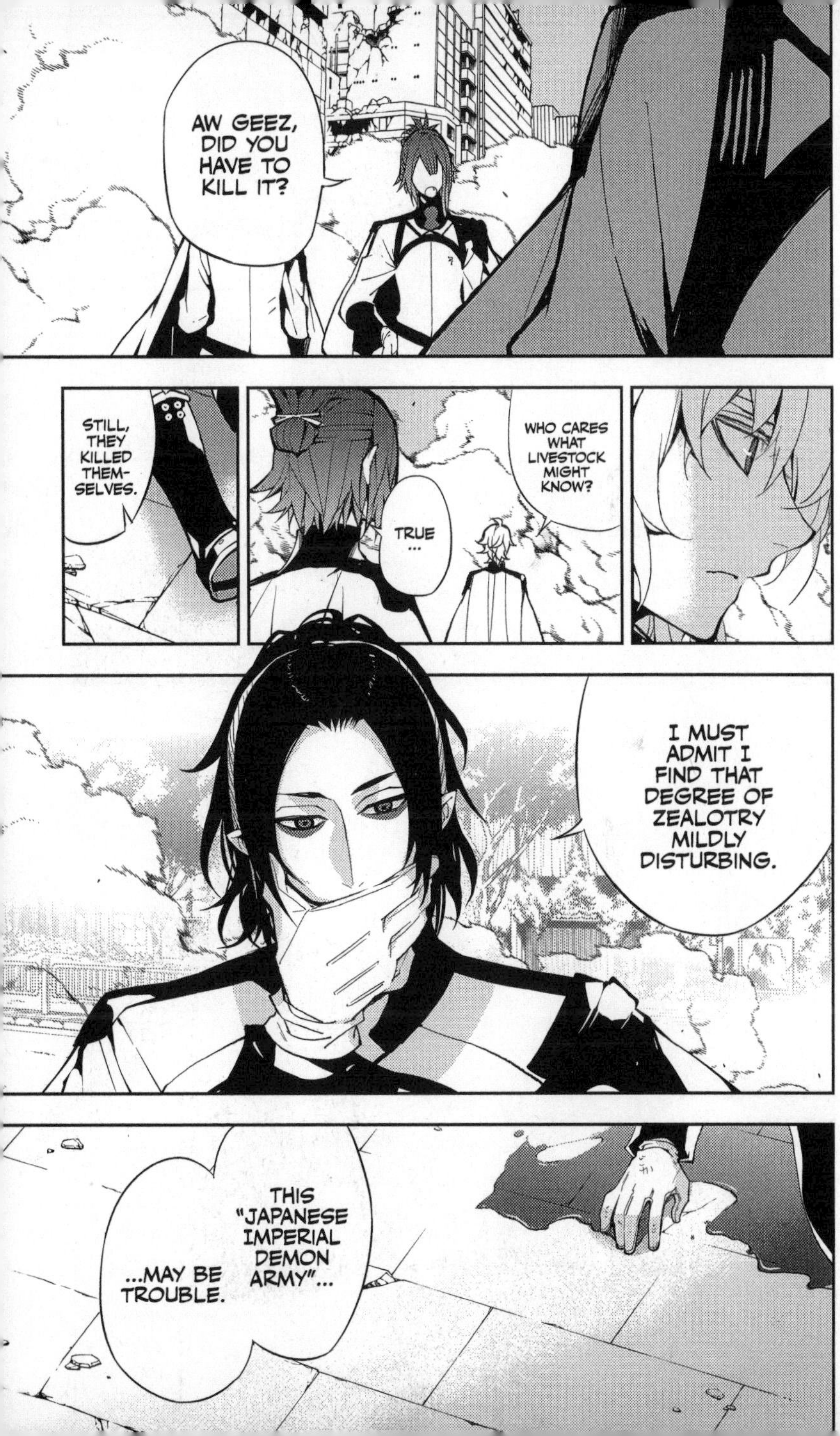
AW GEEZ, DID YOU HAVE TO KILL IT?
WHO CARES WHAT LIVESTOCK MIGHT KNOW?
TRUE...
STILL, THEY KILLED THEM-SELVES.
I MUST ADMIT I FIND THAT DEGREE OF ZEALOTRY MILDLY DISTURBING.
THIS "JAPANESE IMPERIAL DEMON ARMY"...
...MAY BE TROUBLE.

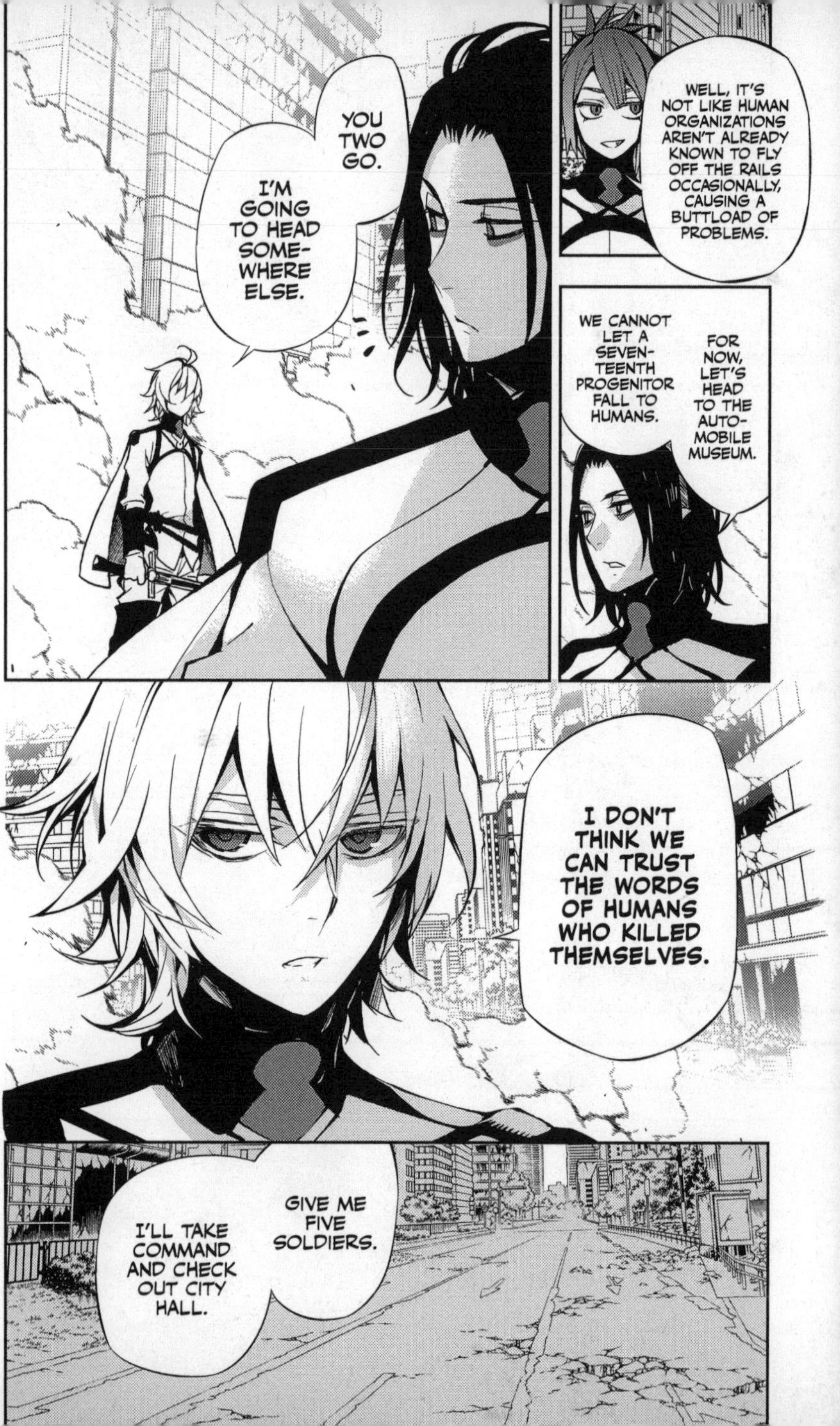
WELL, IT'S NOT LIKE HUMAN ORGANIZATIONS AREN'T ALREADY KNOWN TO FLY OFF THE RAILS OCCASIONALLY, CAUSING A BUTTLOAD OF PROBLEMS.
FOR NOW, LET'S HEAD TO THE AUTOMOBILE MUSEUM.
WE CANNOT LET A SEVENTEENTH PROGENITOR FALL TO HUMANS.
YOU TWO GO.
I'M GOING TO HEAD SOMEWHERE ELSE.
I DON'T THINK WE CAN TRUST THE WORDS OF HUMANS WHO KILLED THEMSELVES.
GIVE ME FIVE SOLDIERS.
I'LL TAKE COMMAND AND CHECK OUT CITY HALL.

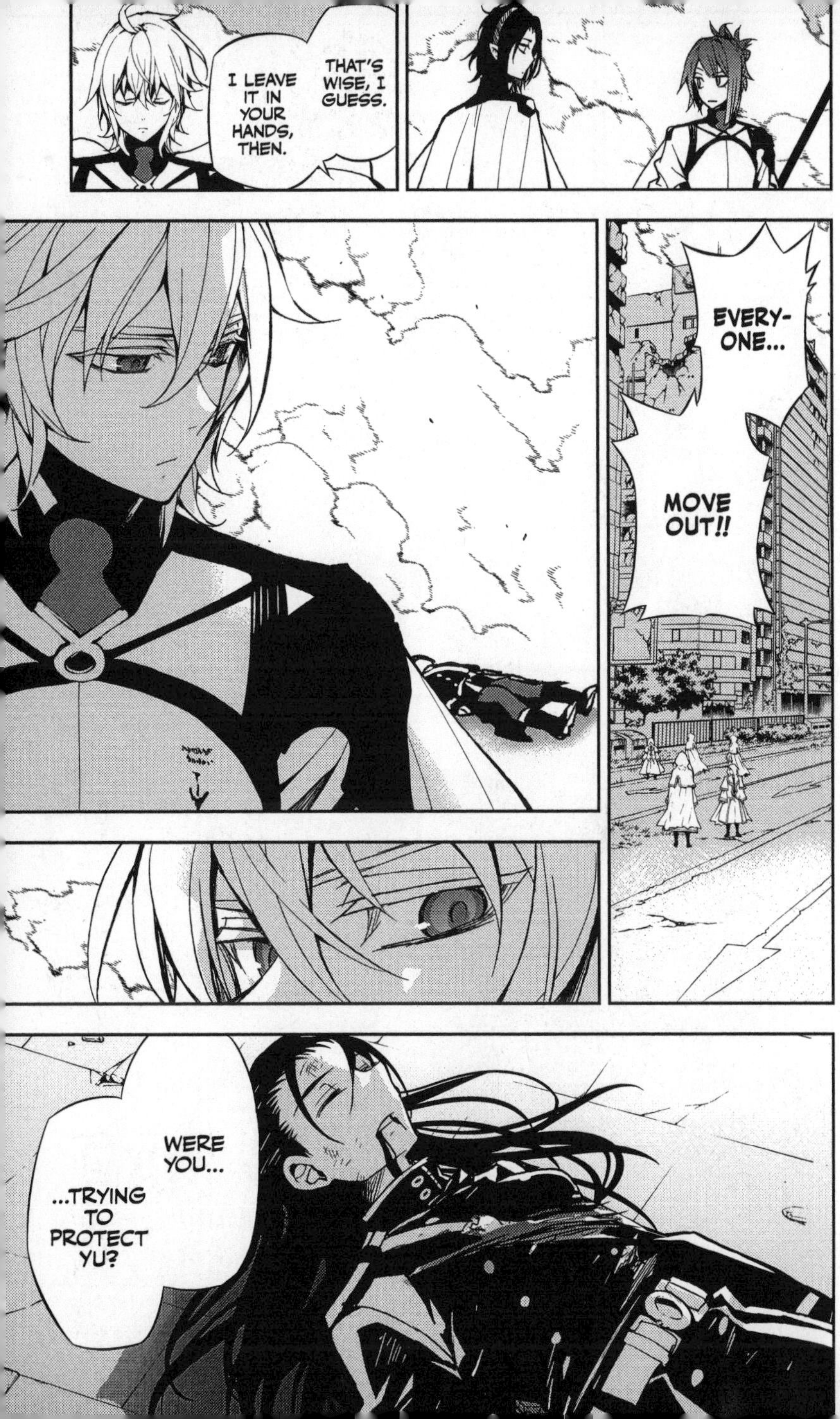
THAT'S WISE, I GUESS.
I LEAVE IT IN YOUR HANDS, THEN.
EVERY-ONE...
MOVE OUT!!
WERE YOU...
...TRYING TO PROTECT YU?

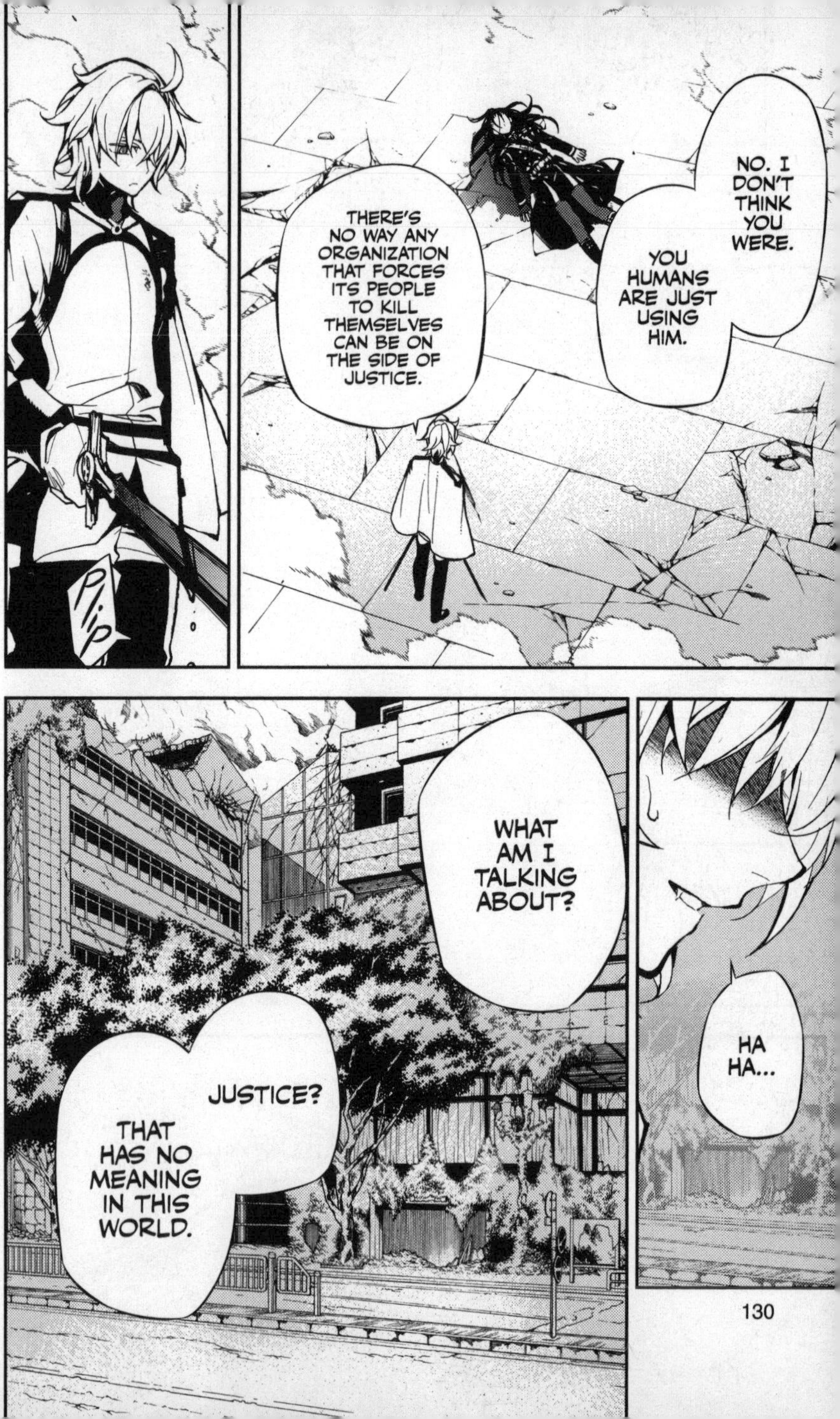
NO. I DON'T THINK YOU WERE.
YOU HUMANS ARE JUST USING HIM.
THERE'S NO WAY ANY ORGANIZATION THAT FORCES ITS PEOPLE TO KILL THEMSELVES CAN BE ON THE SIDE OF JUSTICE.
PLIP
HA HA...
WHAT AM I TALKING ABOUT?
JUSTICE?
THAT HAS NO MEANING IN THIS WORLD.

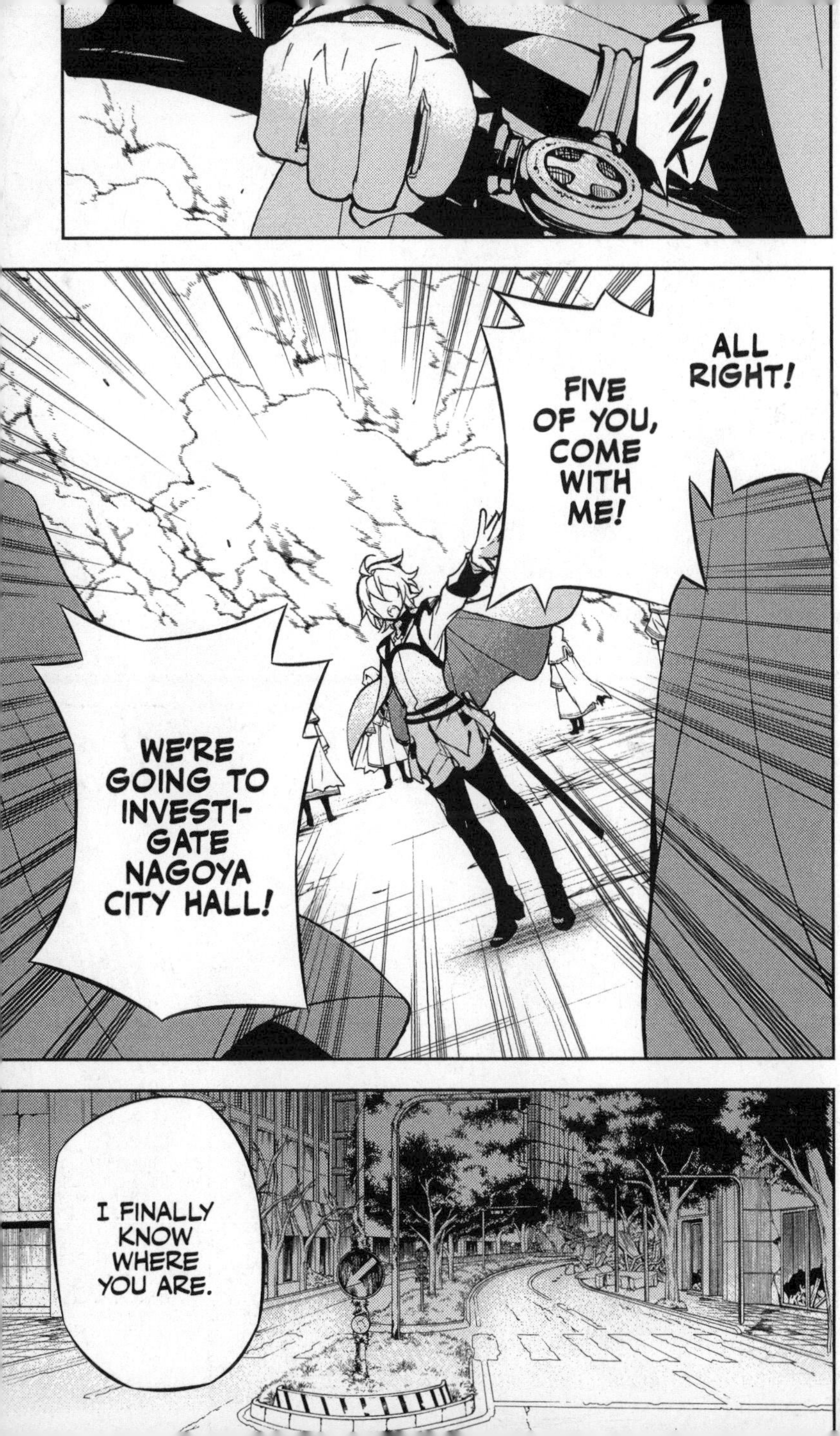
SNIK
ALL RIGHT!
FIVE OF YOU, COME WITH ME!
WE'RE GOING TO INVESTI-GATE NAGOYA CITY HALL!
I FINALLY KNOW WHERE YOU ARE.

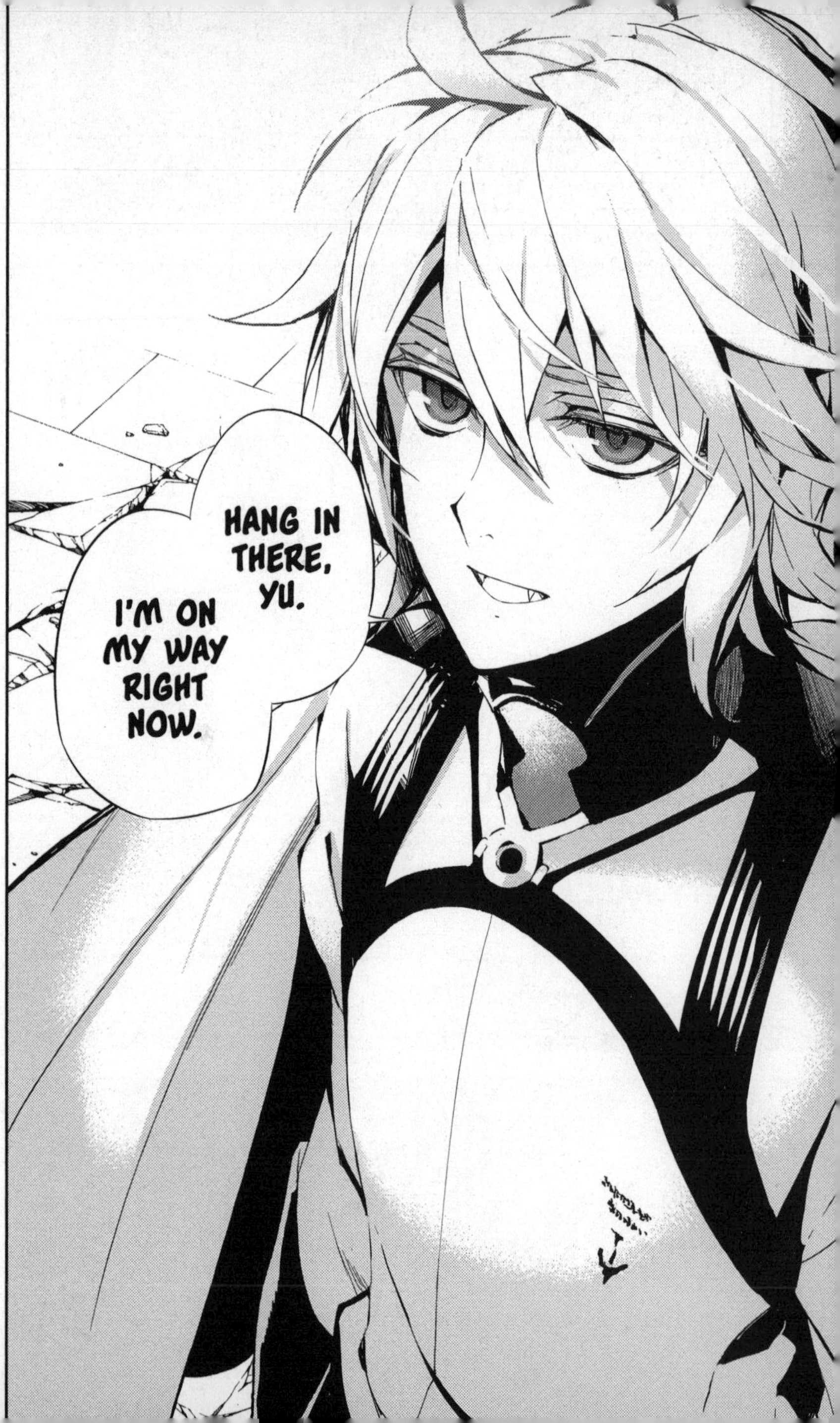
HANG IN THERE, YU.
I'M ON MY WAY RIGHT NOW.

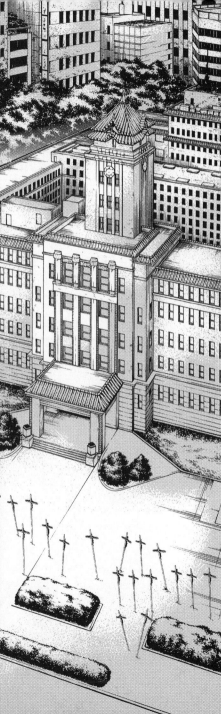

WELL, WELL.

THIS SCREAMS "AMBUSH" AT THE TOP OF ITS LUNGS.

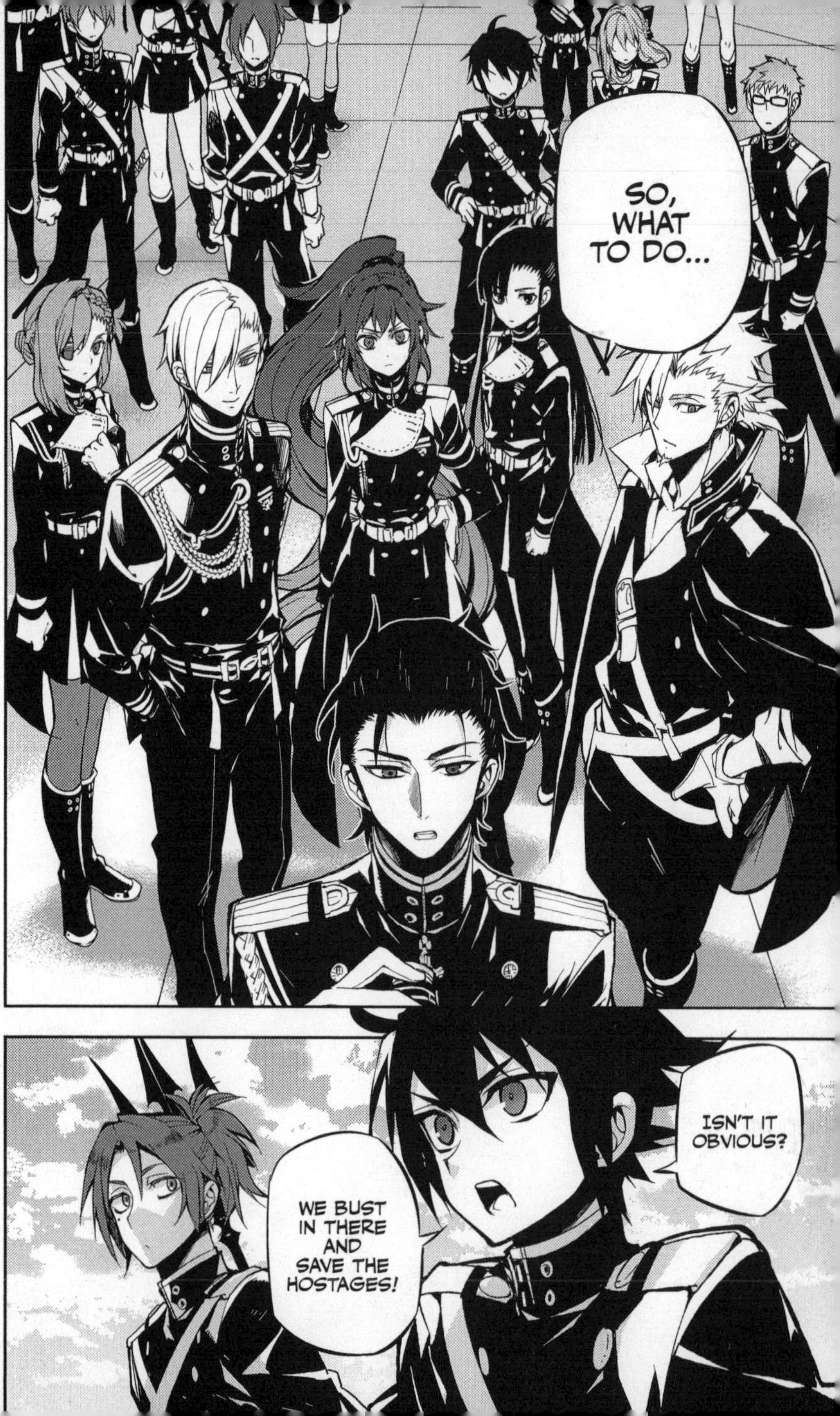
SO, WHAT TO DO...
ISN'T IT OBVIOUS?
WE BUST IN THERE AND SAVE THE HOSTAGES!

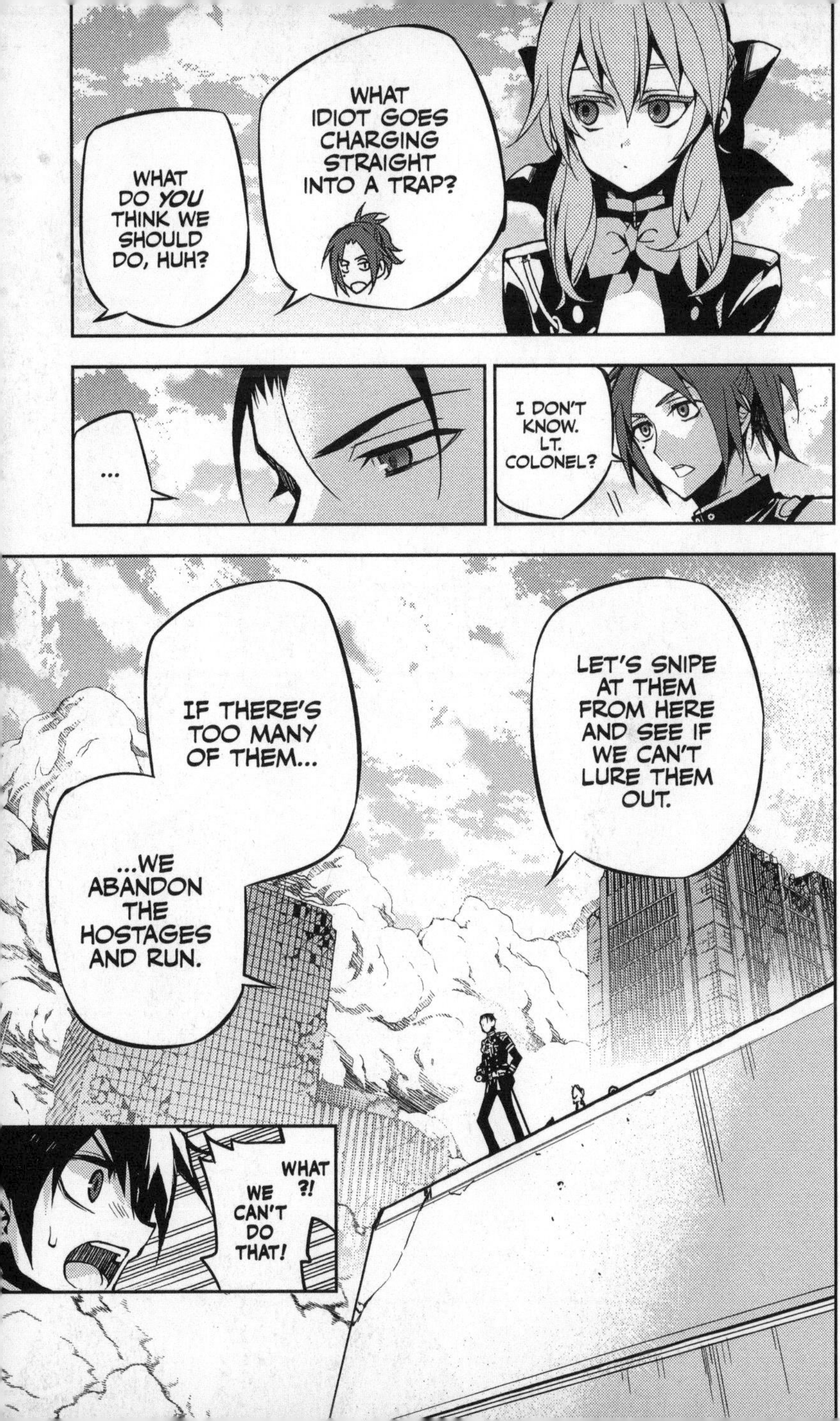
WHAT IDIOT GOES CHARGING STRAIGHT INTO A TRAP?
WHAT DO *YOU* THINK WE SHOULD DO, HUH?
I DON'T KNOW. LT. COLONEL?
...
LET'S SNIPE AT THEM FROM HERE AND SEE IF WE CAN'T LURE THEM OUT.
IF THERE'S TOO MANY OF THEM...
...WE ABANDON THE HOSTAGES AND RUN.
WHAT ?!
WE CAN'T DO THAT!

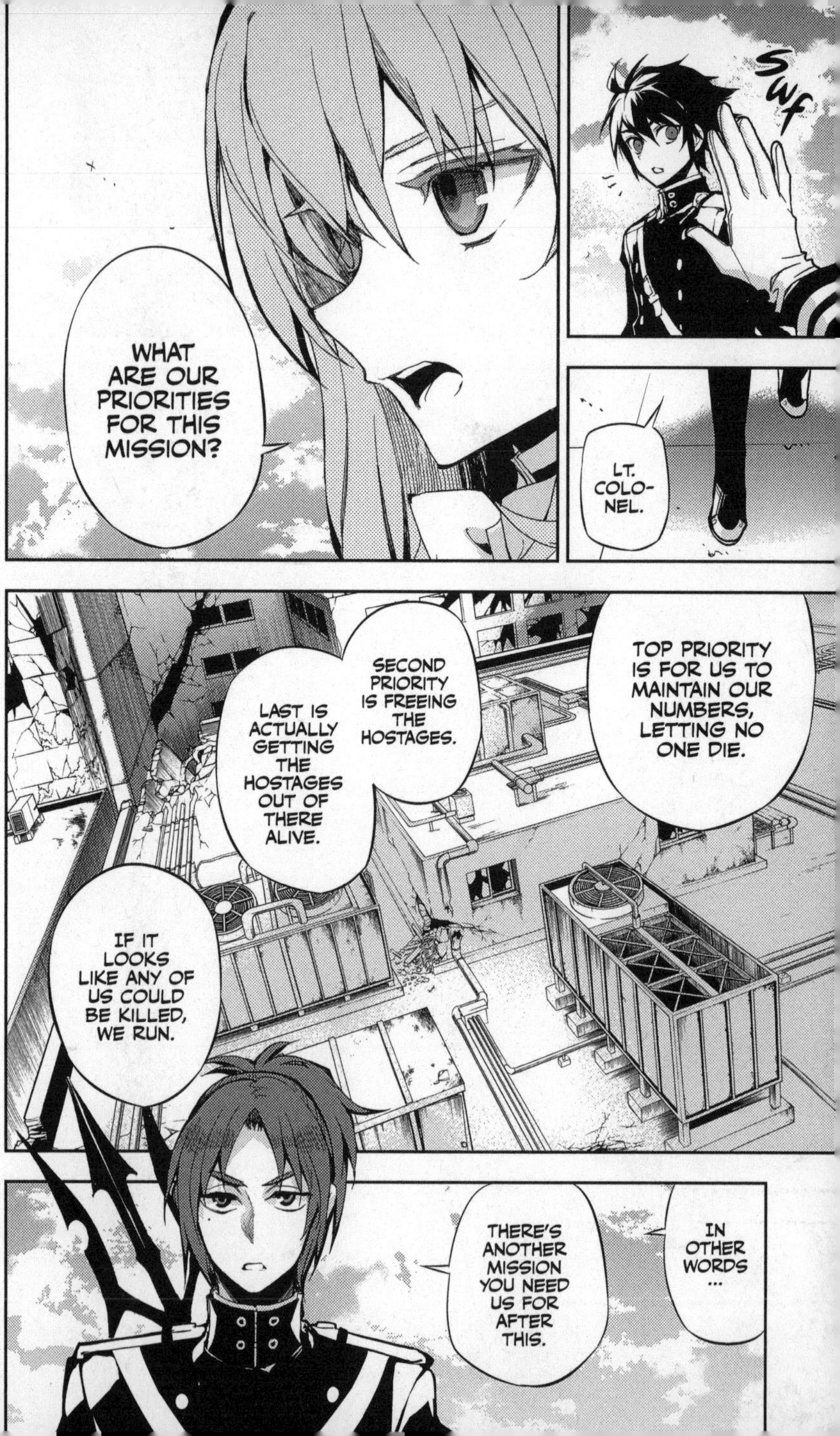
SWF
LT. COLO-NEL.
WHAT ARE OUR PRIORITIES FOR THIS MISSION?
TOP PRIORITY IS FOR US TO MAINTAIN OUR NUMBERS, LETTING NO ONE DIE.
SECOND PRIORITY IS FREEING THE HOSTAGES.
LAST IS ACTUALLY GETTING THE HOSTAGES OUT OF THERE ALIVE.
IF IT LOOKS LIKE ANY OF US COULD BE KILLED, WE RUN.
IN OTHER WORDS...
THERE'S ANOTHER MISSION YOU NEED US FOR AFTER THIS.

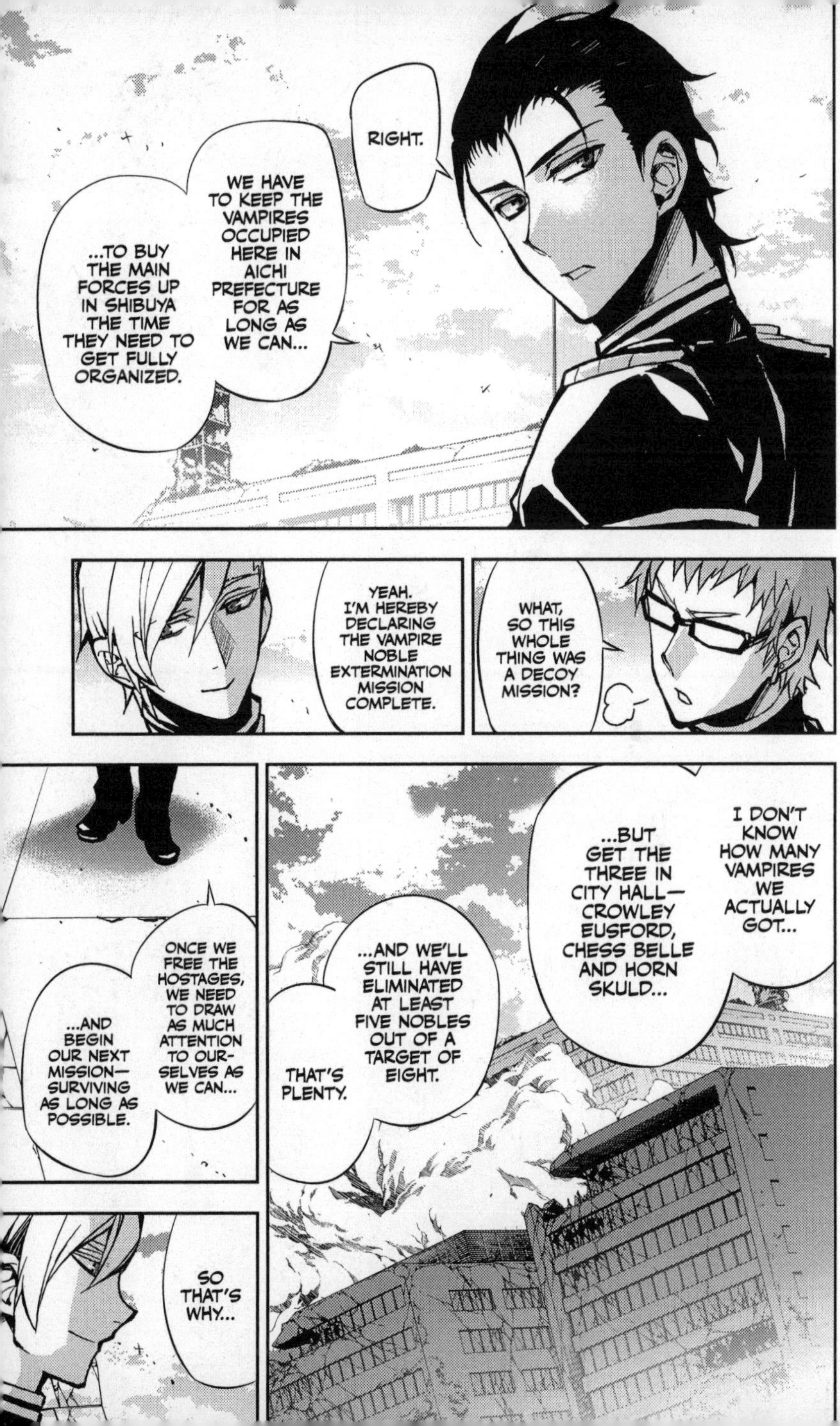
RIGHT.
WE HAVE TO KEEP THE VAMPIRES OCCUPIED HERE IN AICHI PREFECTURE FOR AS LONG AS WE CAN...
...TO BUY THE MAIN FORCES UP IN SHIBUYA THE TIME THEY NEED TO GET FULLY ORGANIZED.
WHAT, SO THIS WHOLE THING WAS A DECOY MISSION?
YEAH. I'M HEREBY DECLARING THE VAMPIRE NOBLE EXTERMINATION MISSION COMPLETE.
I DON'T KNOW HOW MANY VAMPIRES WE ACTUALLY GOT...
...BUT GET THE THREE IN CITY HALL—CROWLEY EUSFORD, CHESS BELLE AND HORN SKULD...
...AND WE'LL STILL HAVE ELIMINATED AT LEAST FIVE NOBLES OUT OF A TARGET OF EIGHT.
THAT'S PLENTY.
ONCE WE FREE THE HOSTAGES, WE NEED TO DRAW AS MUCH ATTENTION TO OURSELVES AS WE CAN...
...AND BEGIN OUR NEXT MISSION—SURVIVING AS LONG AS POSSIBLE.
SO THAT'S WHY...

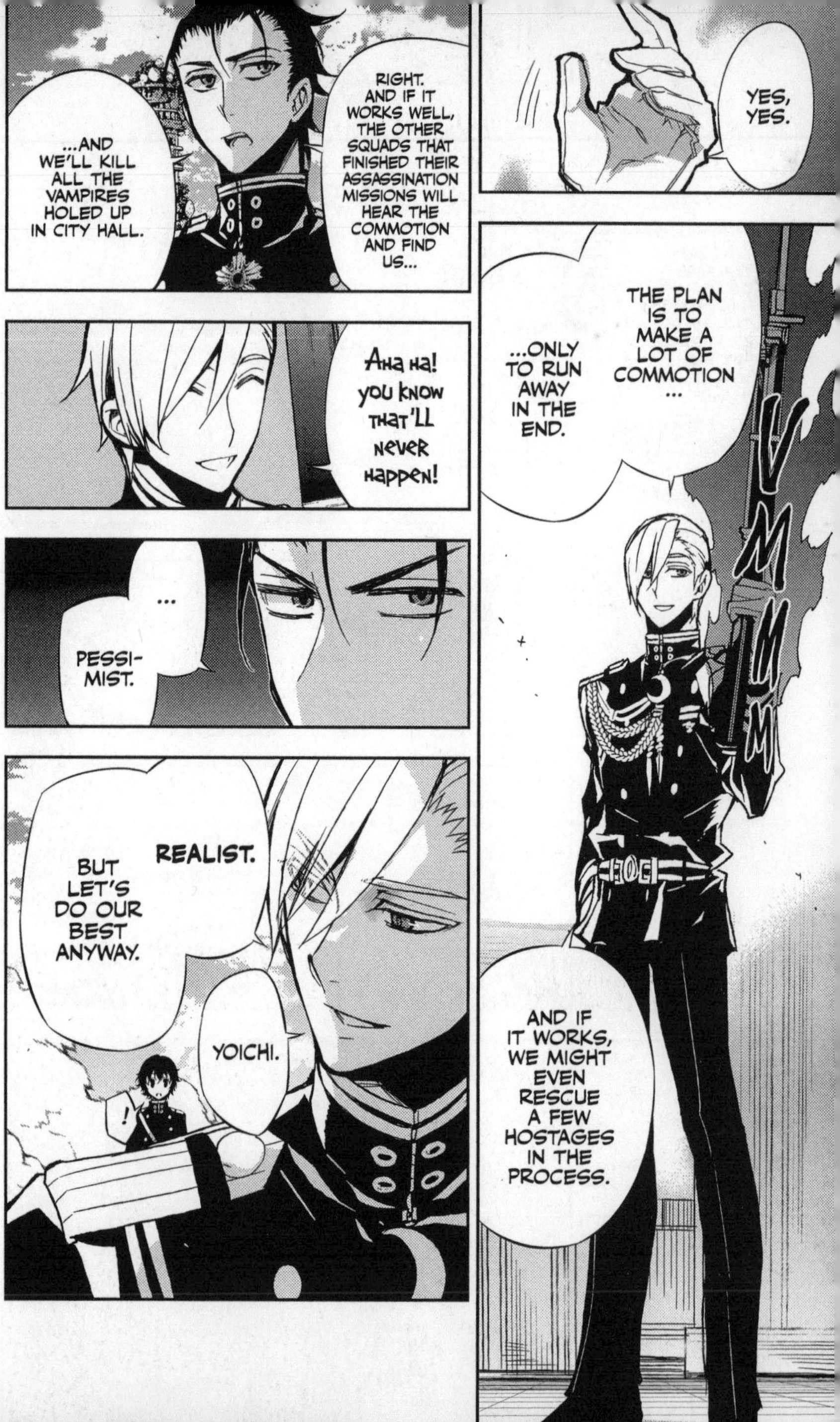
YES, YES.
THE PLAN IS TO MAKE A LOT OF COMMOTION...
...ONLY TO RUN AWAY IN THE END.
VMMMMM
AND IF IT WORKS, WE MIGHT EVEN RESCUE A FEW HOSTAGES IN THE PROCESS.
...AND WE'LL KILL ALL THE VAMPIRES HOLED UP IN CITY HALL.
RIGHT. AND IF IT WORKS WELL, THE OTHER SQUADS THAT FINISHED THEIR ASSASSINATION MISSIONS WILL HEAR THE COMMOTION AND FIND US...
AHA HA! YOU KNOW THAT'LL NEVER HAPPEN!
...
PESSI-MIST.
REALIST.
BUT LET'S DO OUR BEST ANYWAY.
YOICHI.
!

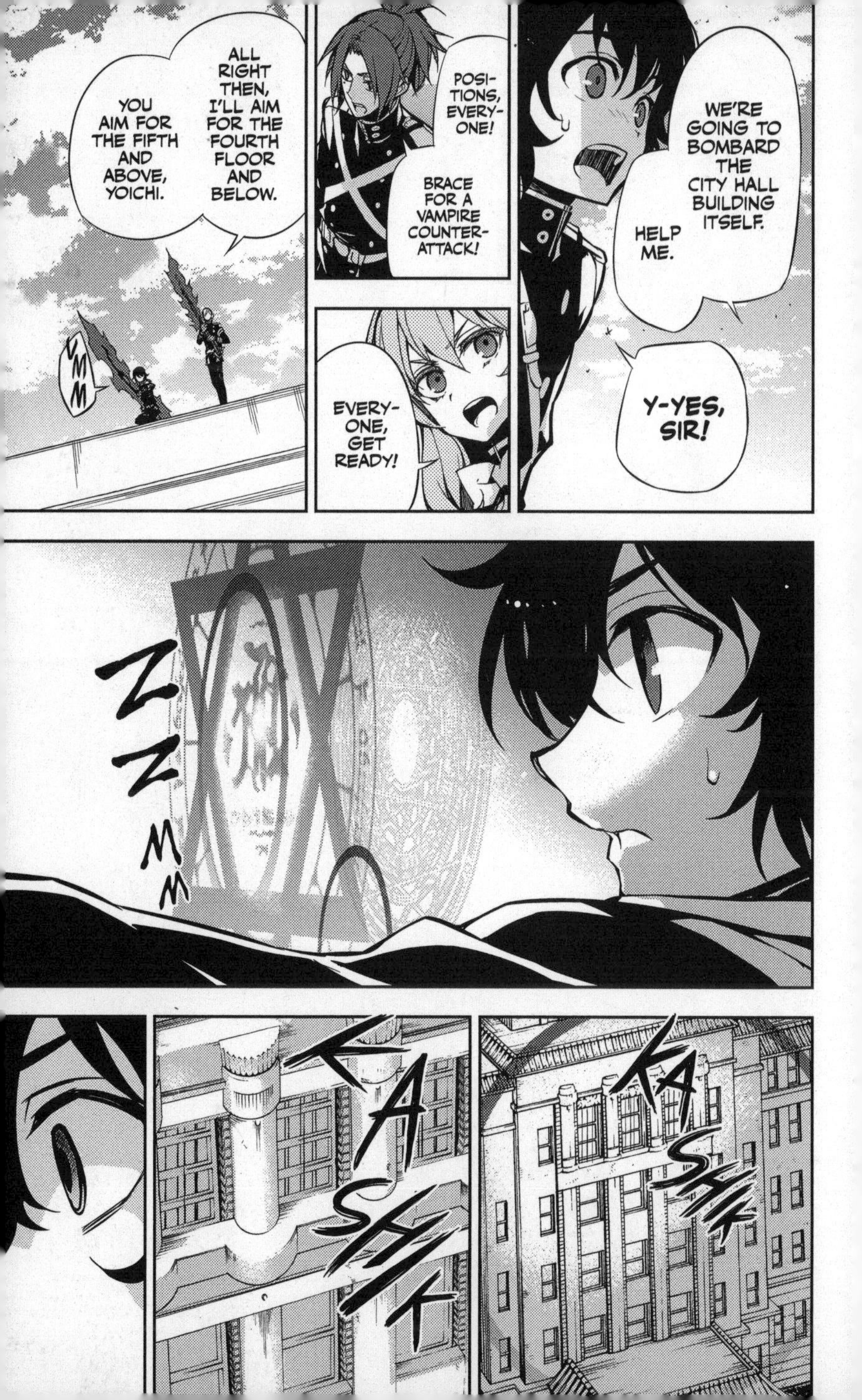
WE'RE GOING TO BOMBARD THE CITY HALL BUILDING ITSELF.
HELP ME.
Y-YES, SIR!
POSI-TIONS, EVERY-ONE!
BRACE FOR A VAMPIRE COUNTER-ATTACK!
EVERY-ONE, GET READY!
ALL RIGHT THEN, I'LL AIM FOR THE FOURTH FLOOR AND BELOW.
YOU AIM FOR THE FIFTH AND ABOVE, YOICHI.
VMM
NNNMM
KASHK
KASHK

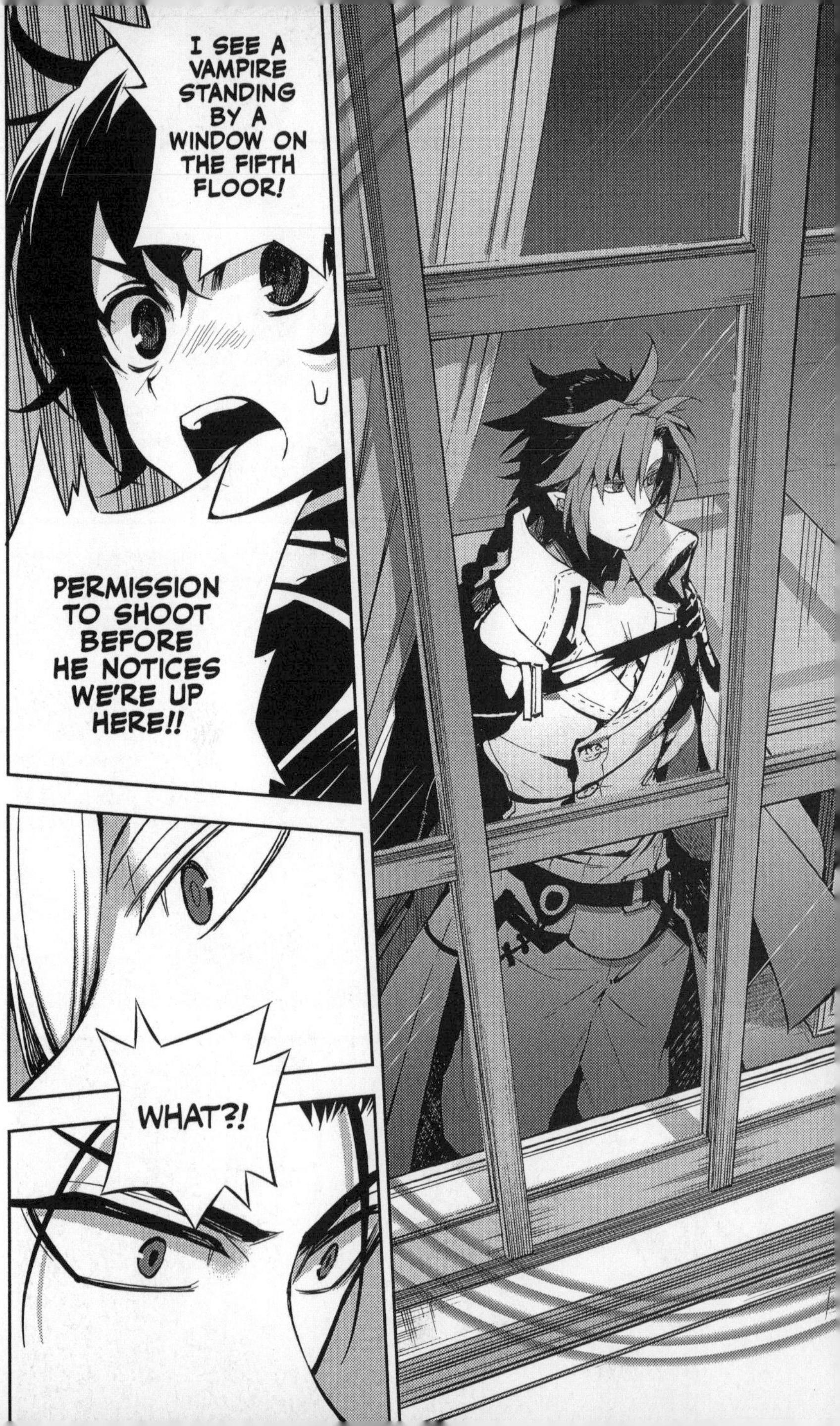
I SEE A VAMPIRE STANDING BY A WINDOW ON THE FIFTH FLOOR!
PERMISSION TO SHOOT BEFORE HE NOTICES WE'RE UP HERE!!
WHAT?!

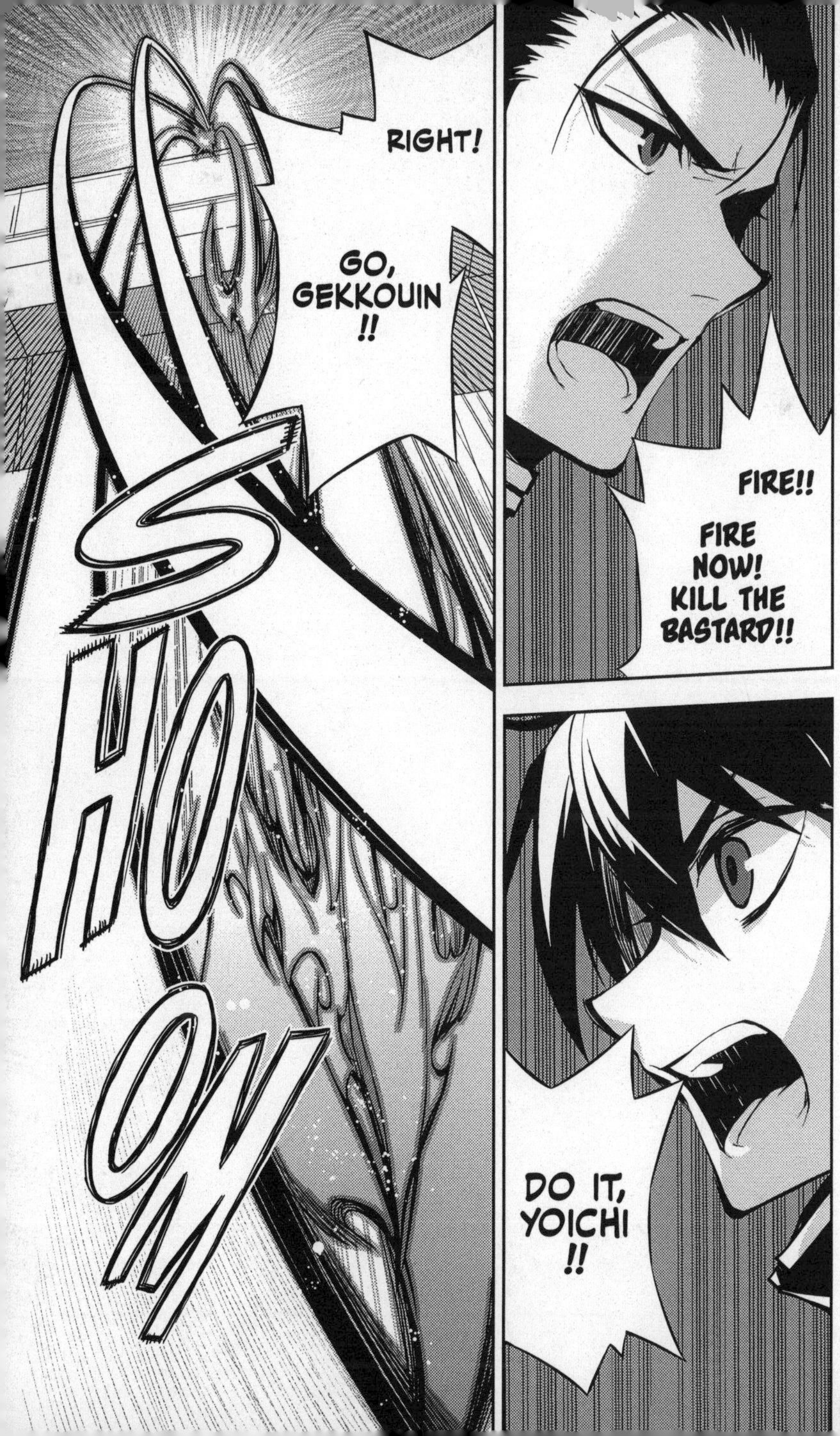
FIRE!!
FIRE NOW! KILL THE BASTARD!!
DO IT, YOICHI!!
RIGHT!
GO, GEKKOUIN!!
SHOOM

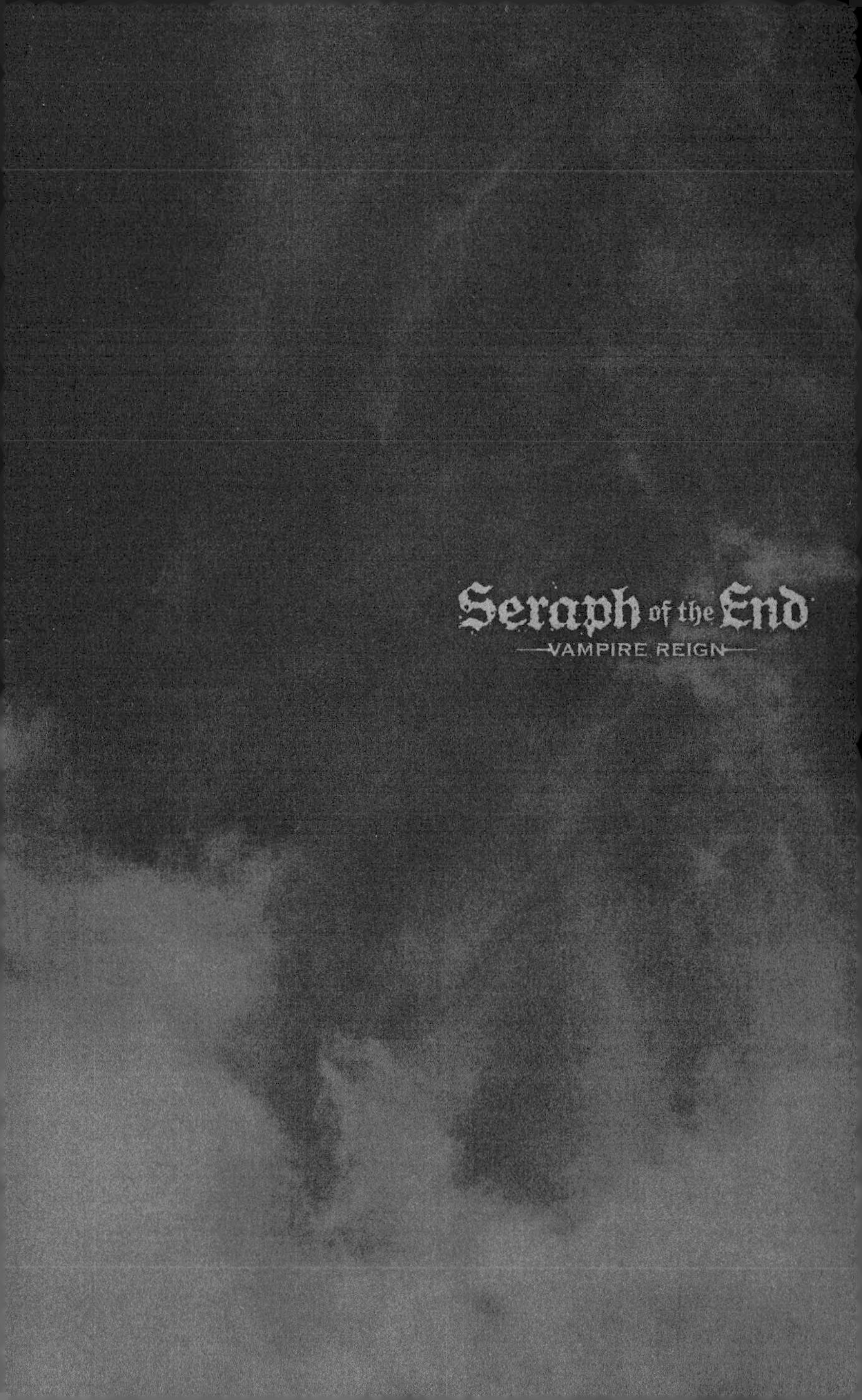
Seraph of the End
VAMPIRE REIGN

FIRE!!

FIRE NOW! KILL THE BASTARD!!

GO, GEKKOUIN!!

RIGHT!

DO IT, YOICHI!!

CHAPTER 31
Shinya and Guren

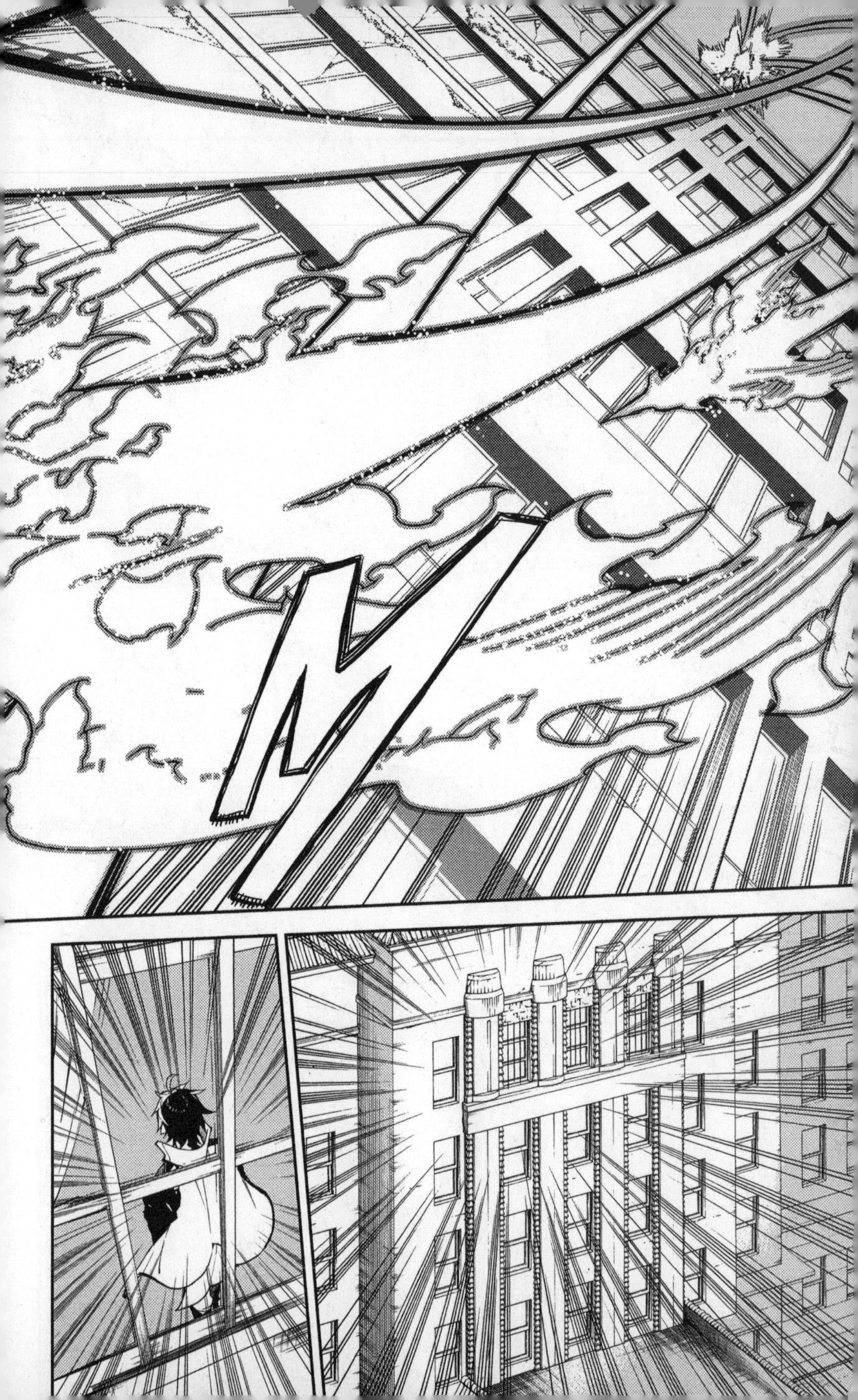
N

CHAPTER 31 Shinya and Guren

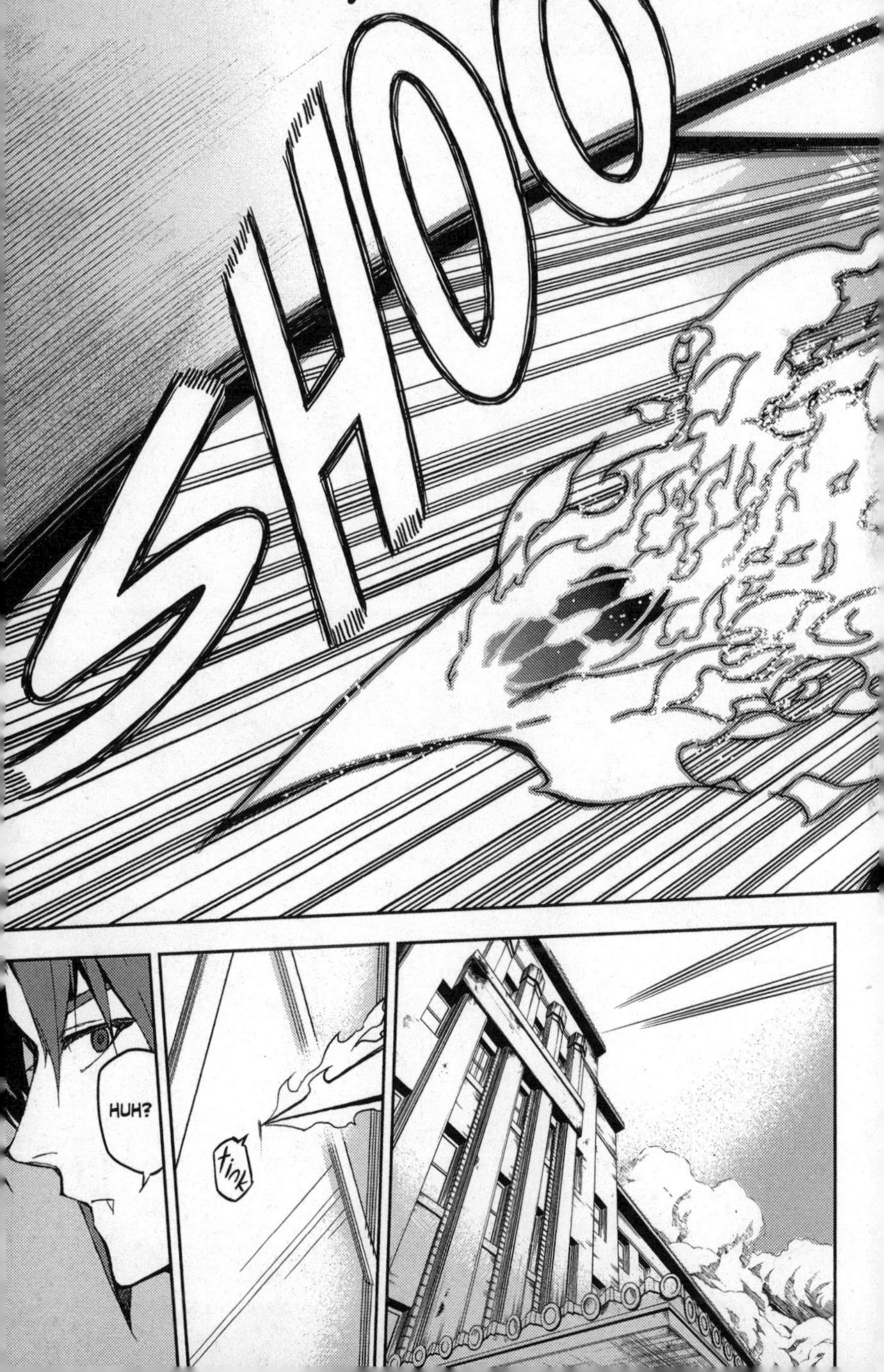
SHOO
tink
HUH?

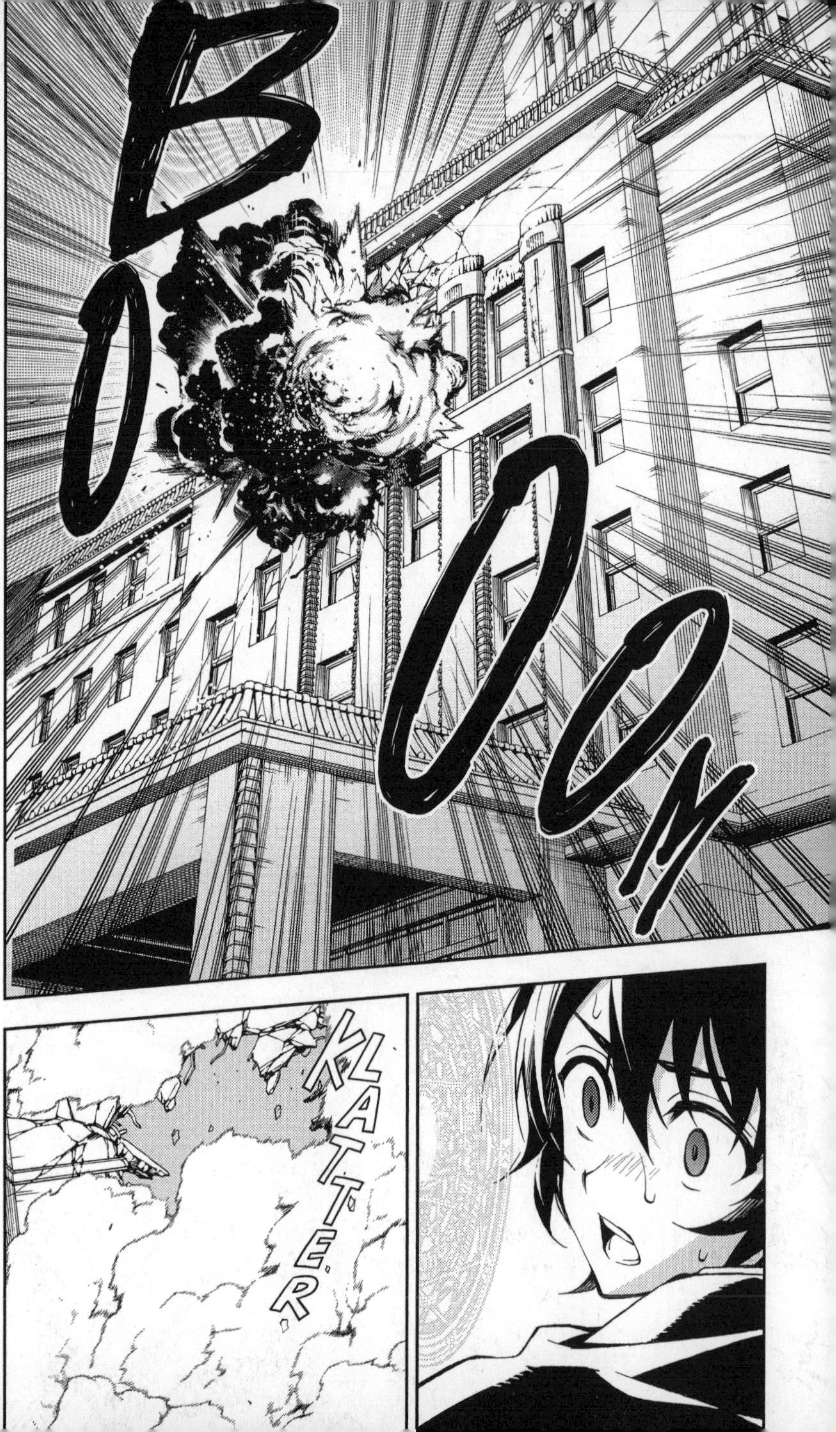
BOOOM
KLATTER

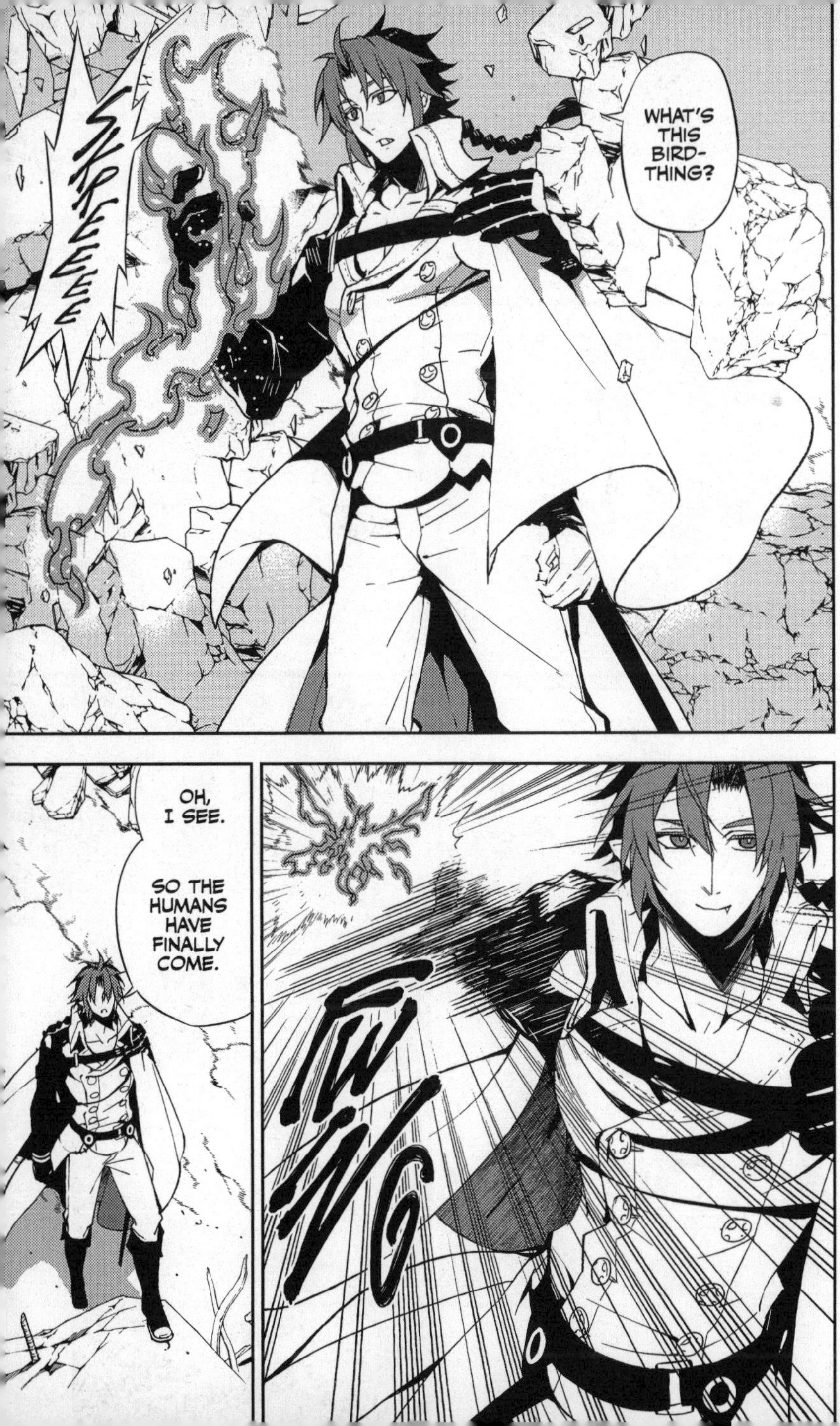
SKREEEEE
WHAT'S THIS BIRD-THING?
FWING
OH, I SEE.
SO THE HUMANS HAVE FINALLY COME.

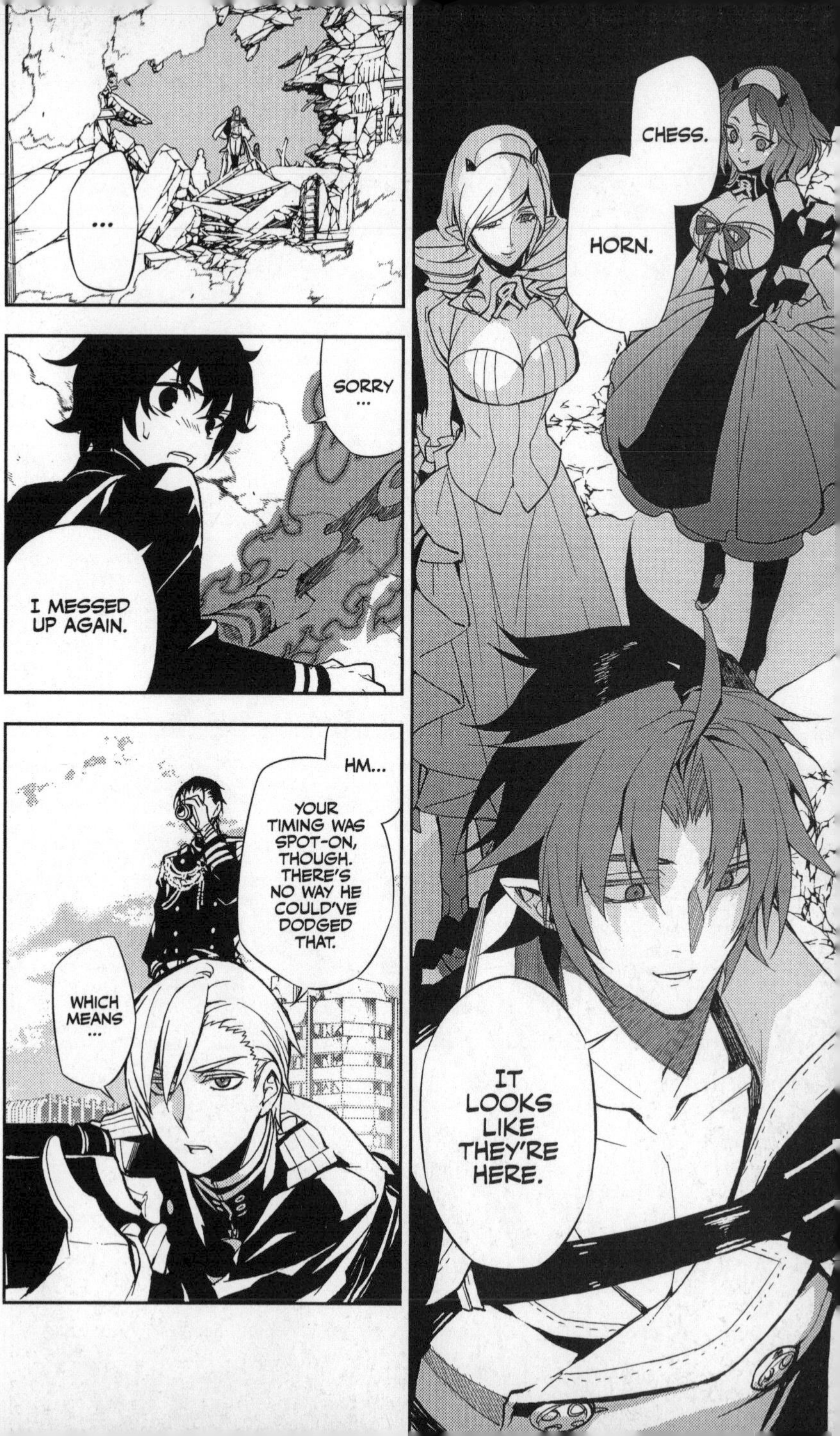
CHESS.
HORN.
IT LOOKS LIKE THEY'RE HERE.
...
SORRY ...
I MESSED UP AGAIN.
HM...
YOUR TIMING WAS SPOT-ON, THOUGH. THERE'S NO WAY HE COULD'VE DODGED THAT.
WHICH MEANS ...

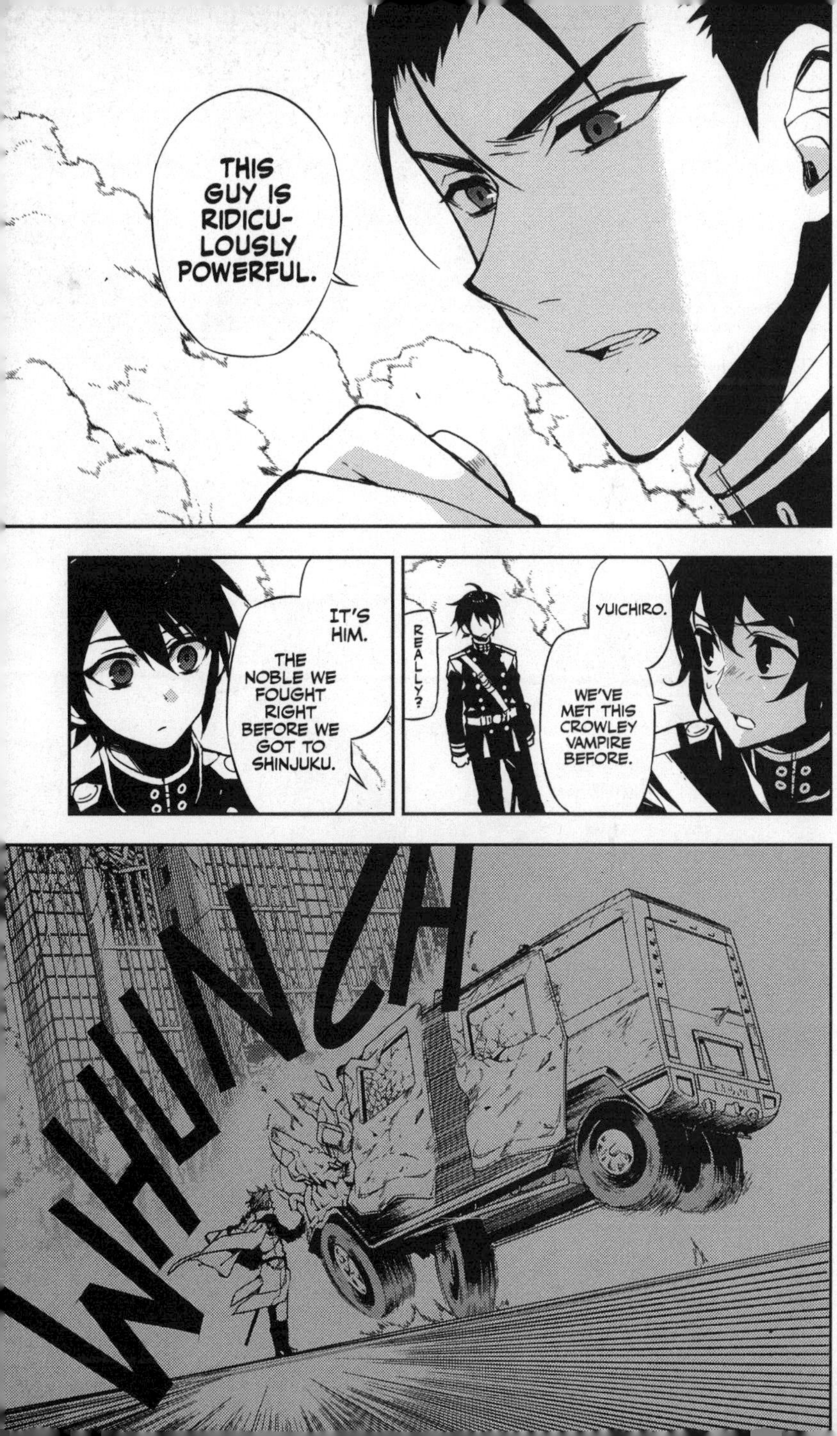
THIS GUY IS RIDICU-LOUSLY POWERFUL.
YUICHIRO.
WE'VE MET THIS CROWLEY VAMPIRE BEFORE.
REALLY?
IT'S HIM.
THE NOBLE WE FOUGHT RIGHT BEFORE WE GOT TO SHINJUKU.
WHUNCH

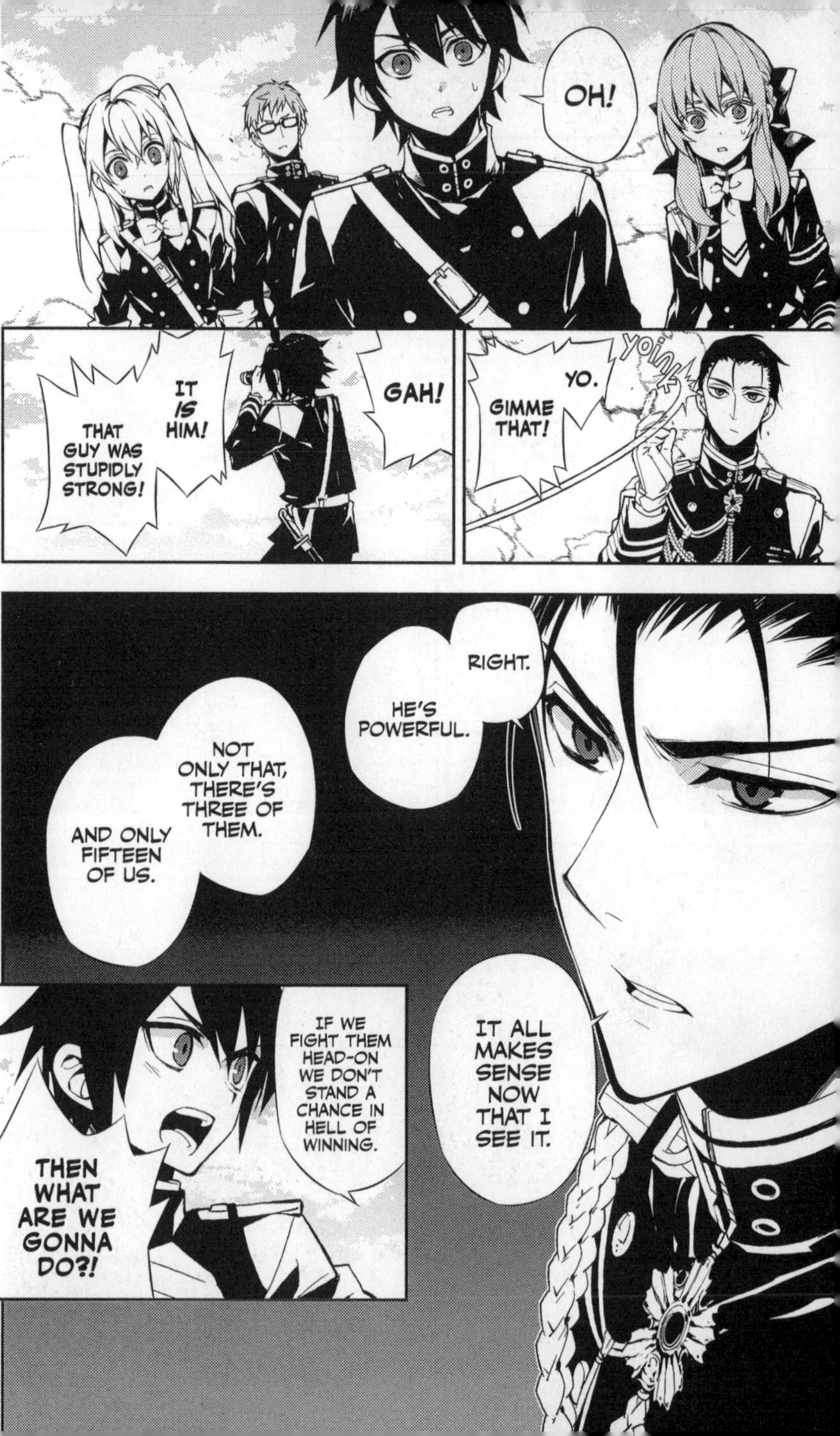
OH!
yoink
YO.
GIMME THAT!
GAH!
IT IS HIM!
THAT GUY WAS STUPIDLY STRONG!
RIGHT.
HE'S POWERFUL.
NOT ONLY THAT, THERE'S THREE OF THEM.
AND ONLY FIFTEEN OF US.
IT ALL MAKES SENSE NOW THAT I SEE IT.
IF WE FIGHT THEM HEAD-ON WE DON'T STAND A CHANCE IN HELL OF WINNING.
THEN WHAT ARE WE GONNA DO?!

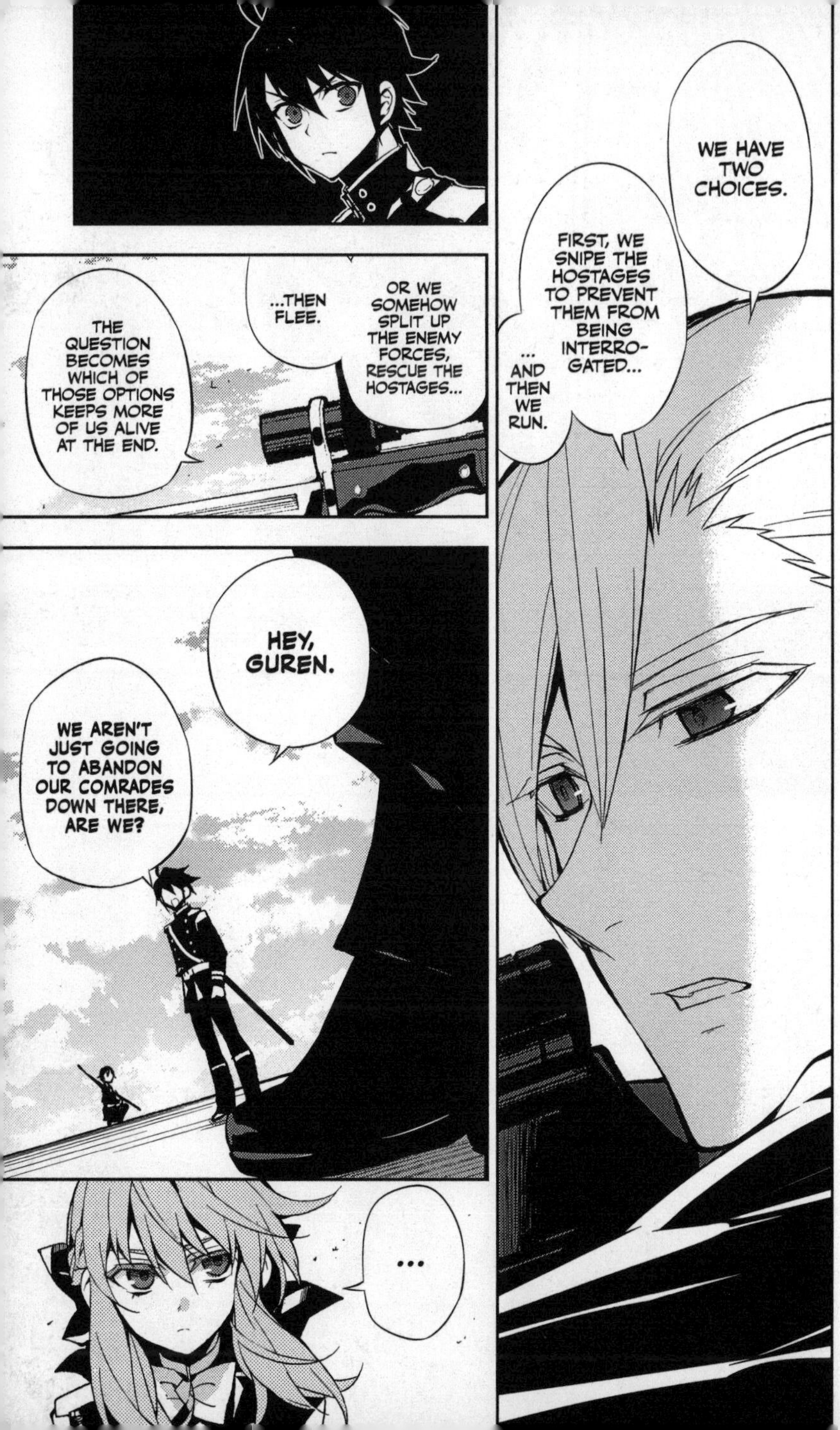
WE HAVE TWO CHOICES.
FIRST, WE SNIPE THE HOSTAGES TO PREVENT THEM FROM BEING INTERRO-GATED...
... AND THEN WE RUN.
OR WE SOMEHOW SPLIT UP THE ENEMY FORCES, RESCUE THE HOSTAGES...
...THEN FLEE.
THE QUESTION BECOMES WHICH OF THOSE OPTIONS KEEPS MORE OF US ALIVE AT THE END.
HEY, GUREN.
WE AREN'T JUST GOING TO ABANDON OUR COMRADES DOWN THERE, ARE WE?
...

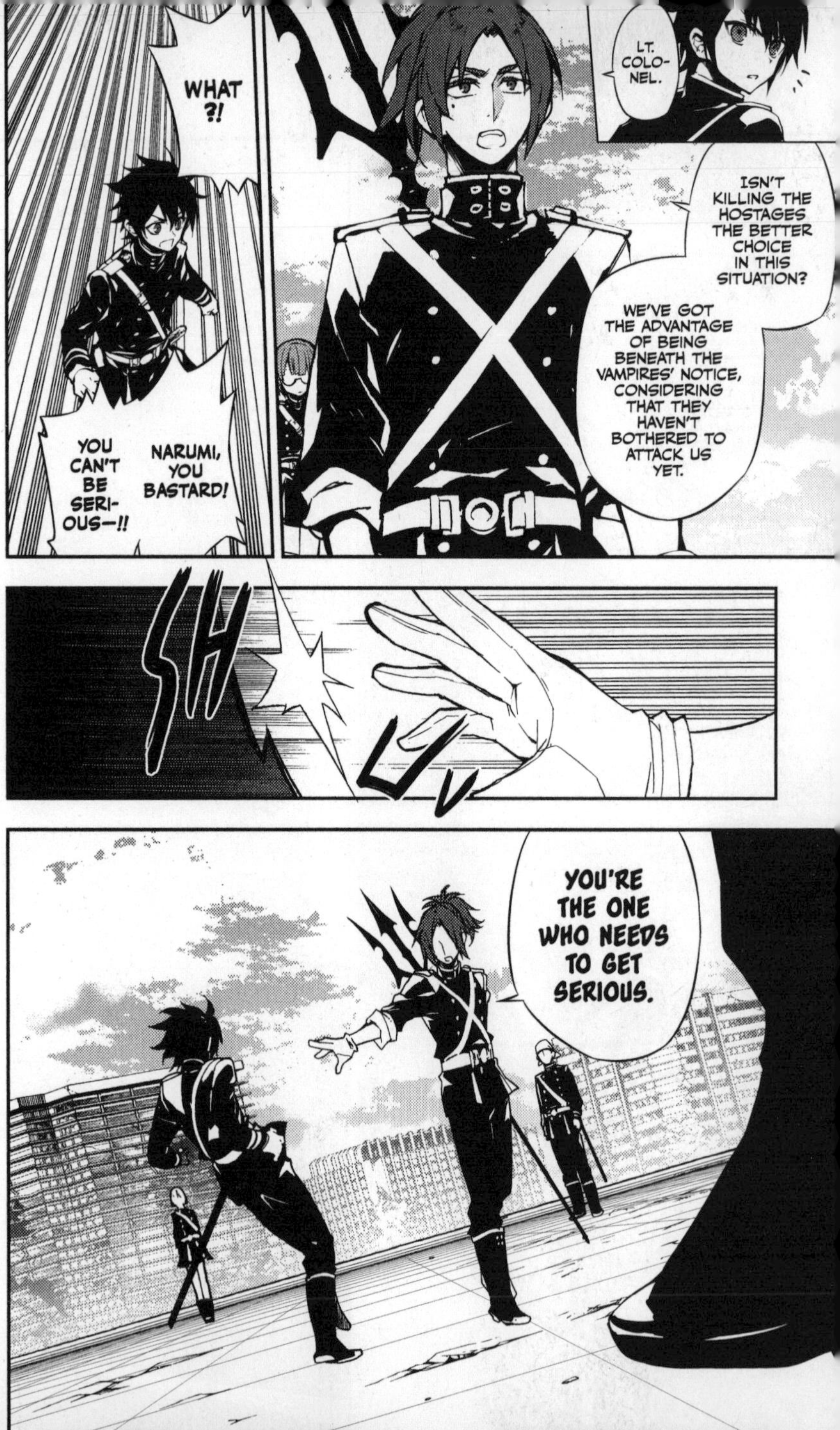
LT. COLONEL.
ISN'T KILLING THE HOSTAGES THE BETTER CHOICE IN THIS SITUATION?
WE'VE GOT THE ADVANTAGE OF BEING BENEATH THE VAMPIRES' NOTICE, CONSIDERING THAT THEY HAVEN'T BOTHERED TO ATTACK US YET.
WHAT?!
NARUMI, YOU BASTARD!
YOU CAN'T BE SERIOUS—!!
SHUV
YOU'RE THE ONE WHO NEEDS TO GET SERIOUS.

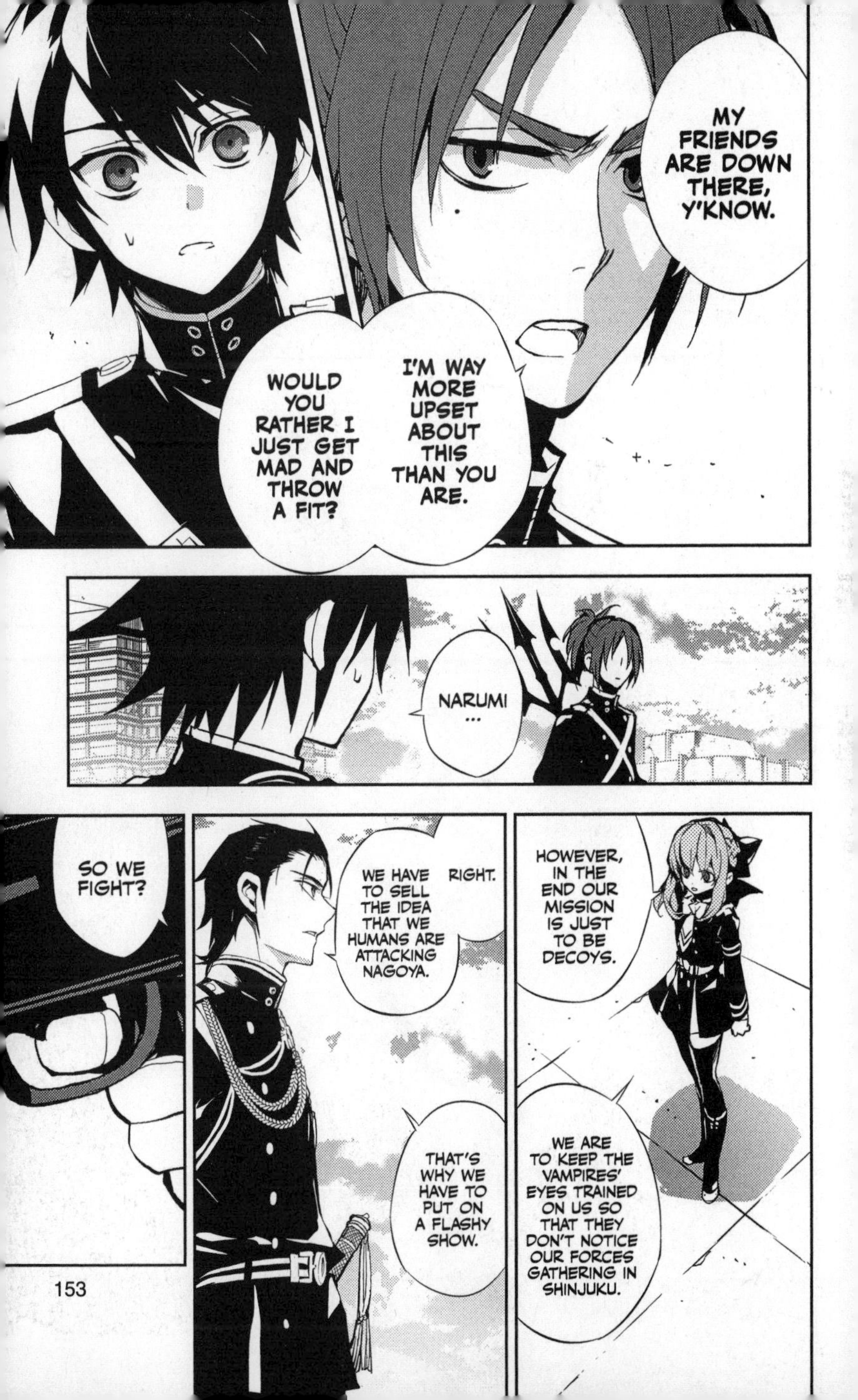
MY FRIENDS ARE DOWN THERE, Y'KNOW.
I'M WAY MORE UPSET ABOUT THIS THAN YOU ARE.
WOULD YOU RATHER I JUST GET MAD AND THROW A FIT?
NARUMI...
HOWEVER, IN THE END OUR MISSION IS JUST TO BE DECOYS.
WE ARE TO KEEP THE VAMPIRES' EYES TRAINED ON US SO THAT THEY DON'T NOTICE OUR FORCES GATHERING IN SHINJUKU.
RIGHT.
WE HAVE TO SELL THE IDEA THAT WE HUMANS ARE ATTACKING NAGOYA.
THAT'S WHY WE HAVE TO PUT ON A FLASHY SHOW.
SO WE FIGHT?

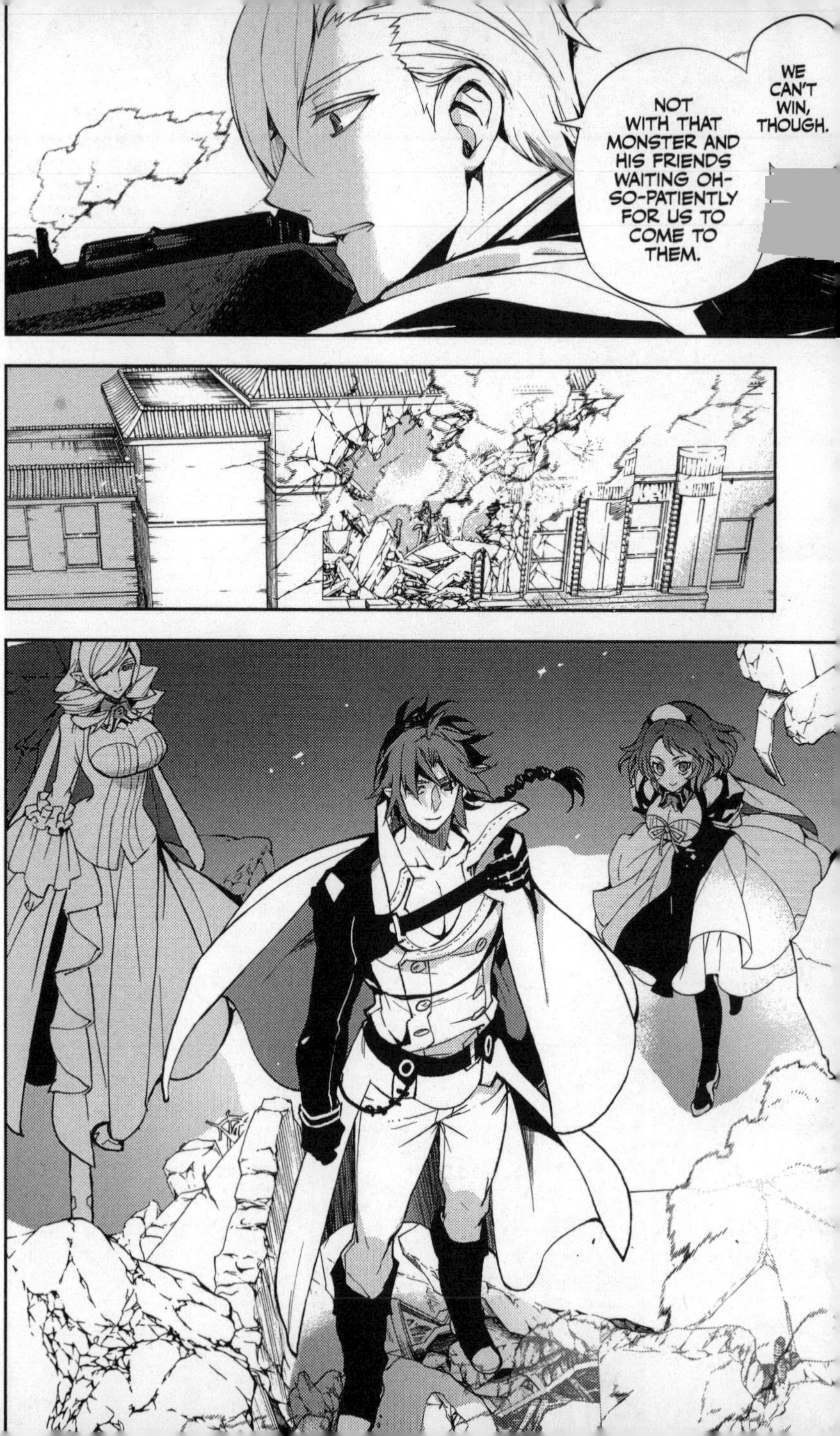
WE CAN'T WIN, THOUGH.
NOT WITH THAT MONSTER AND HIS FRIENDS WAITING OH-SO-PATIENTLY FOR US TO COME TO THEM.

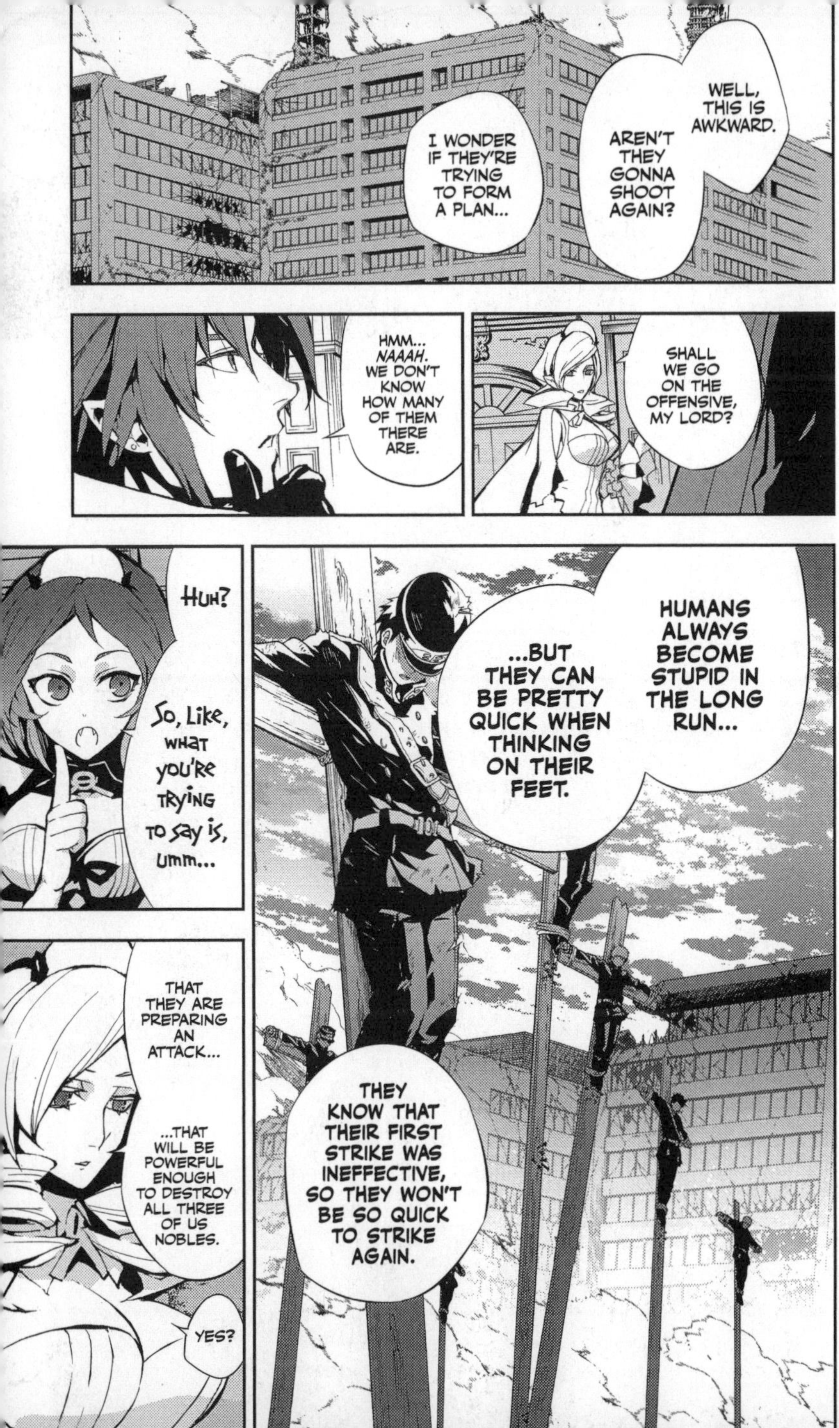
WELL, THIS IS AWKWARD.
AREN'T THEY GONNA SHOOT AGAIN?
I WONDER IF THEY'RE TRYING TO FORM A PLAN...
SHALL WE GO ON THE OFFENSIVE, MY LORD?
HMM... *NAAAH.* WE DON'T KNOW HOW MANY OF THEM THERE ARE.
HUMANS ALWAYS BECOME STUPID IN THE LONG RUN...
...BUT THEY CAN BE PRETTY QUICK WHEN THINKING ON THEIR FEET.
THEY KNOW THAT THEIR FIRST STRIKE WAS INEFFECTIVE, SO THEY WON'T BE SO QUICK TO STRIKE AGAIN.
HUH?
SO, LIKE, WHAT YOU'RE TRYING TO SAY IS, UMM...
THAT THEY ARE PREPARING AN ATTACK...
...THAT WILL BE POWERFUL ENOUGH TO DESTROY ALL THREE OF US NOBLES.
YES?

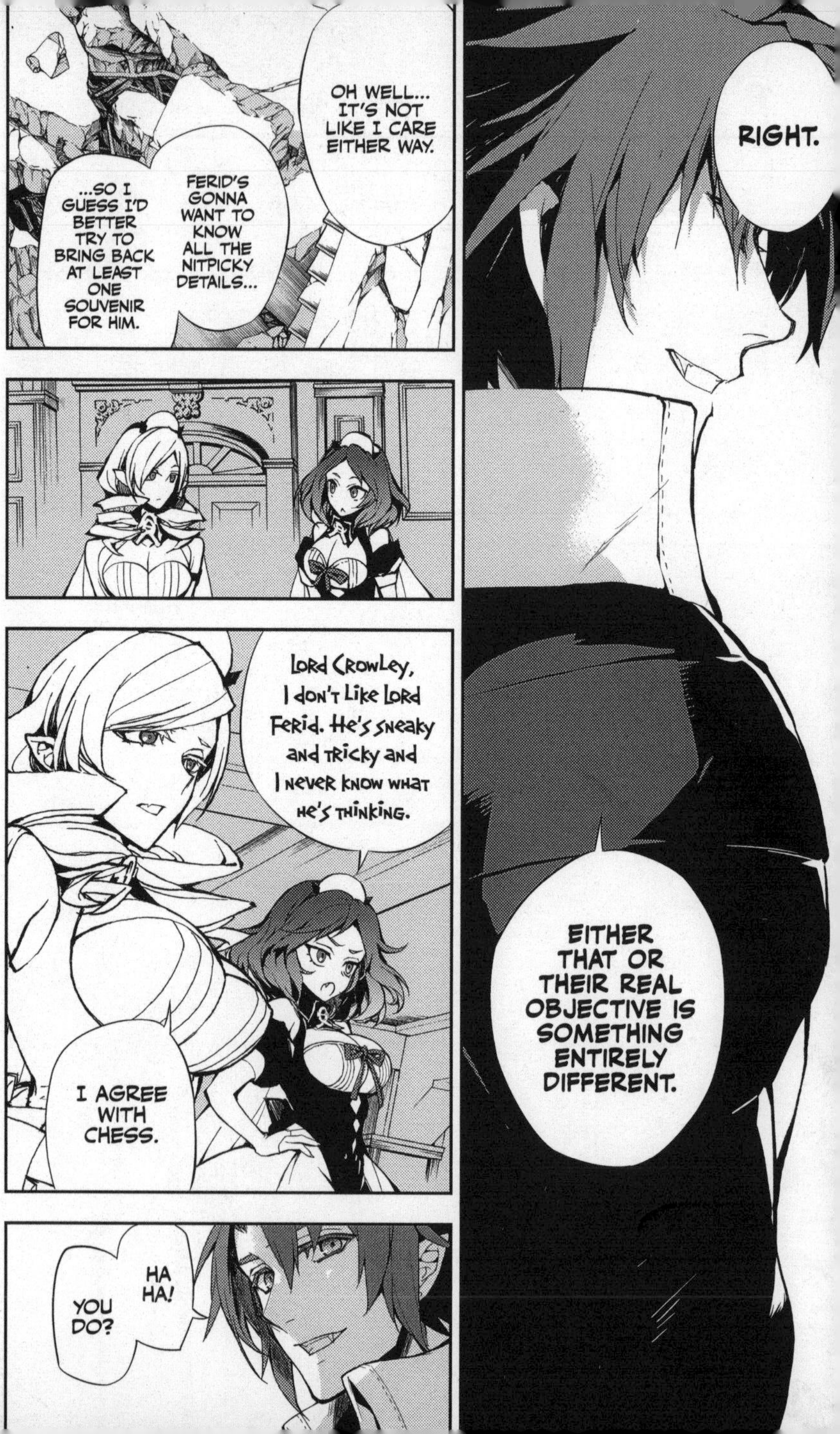
RIGHT.
EITHER THAT OR THEIR REAL OBJECTIVE IS SOMETHING ENTIRELY DIFFERENT.
OH WELL... IT'S NOT LIKE I CARE EITHER WAY.
FERID'S GONNA WANT TO KNOW ALL THE NITPICKY DETAILS...
...SO I GUESS I'D BETTER TRY TO BRING BACK AT LEAST ONE SOUVENIR FOR HIM.
Lord Crowley, I don't like Lord Ferid. He's sneaky and tricky and I never know what he's thinking.
I AGREE WITH CHESS.
HA HA!
YOU DO?

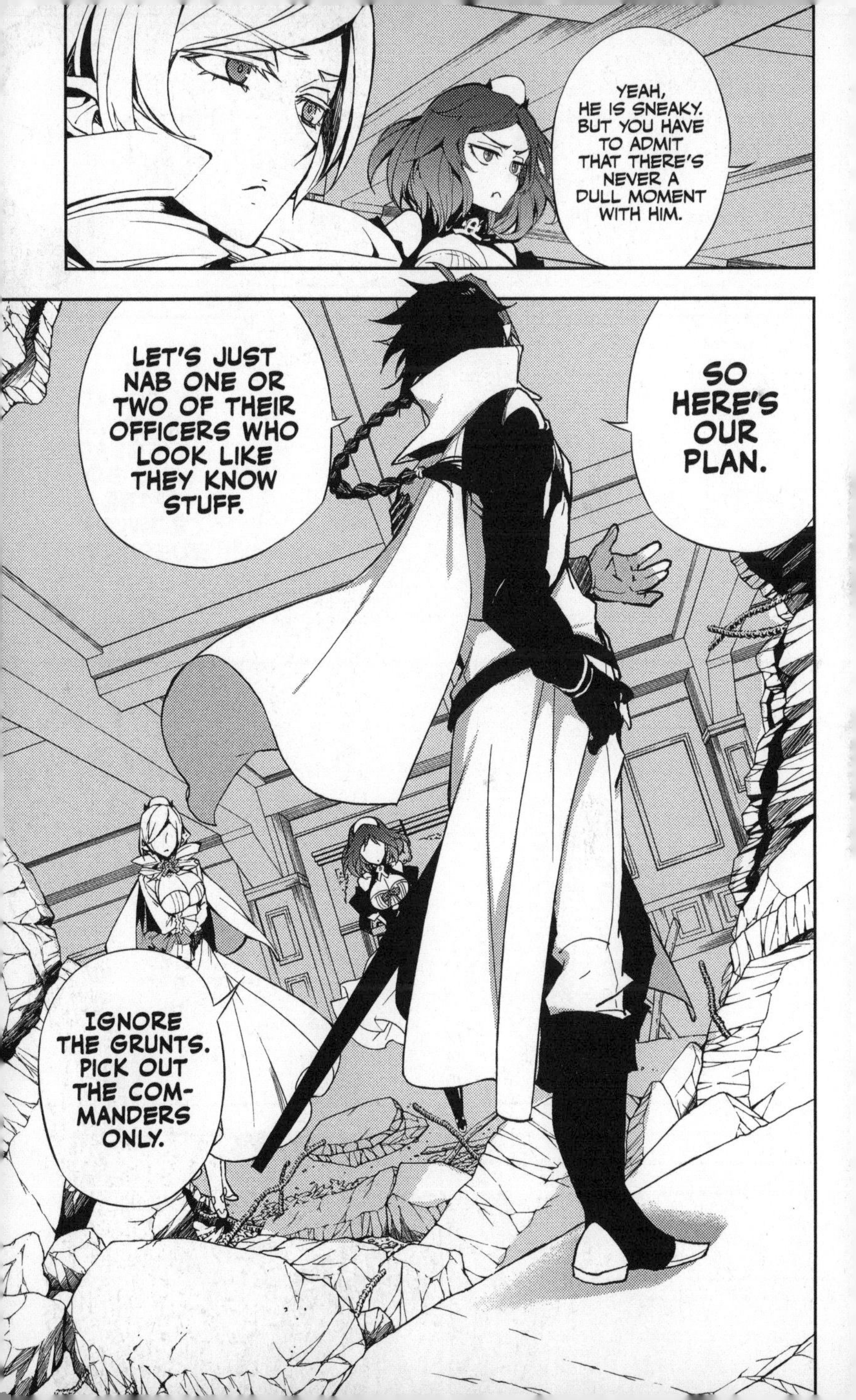
YEAH, HE IS SNEAKY. BUT YOU HAVE TO ADMIT THAT THERE'S NEVER A DULL MOMENT WITH HIM.
SO HERE'S OUR PLAN.
LET'S JUST NAB ONE OR TWO OF THEIR OFFICERS WHO LOOK LIKE THEY KNOW STUFF.
IGNORE THE GRUNTS. PICK OUT THE COM- MANDERS ONLY.

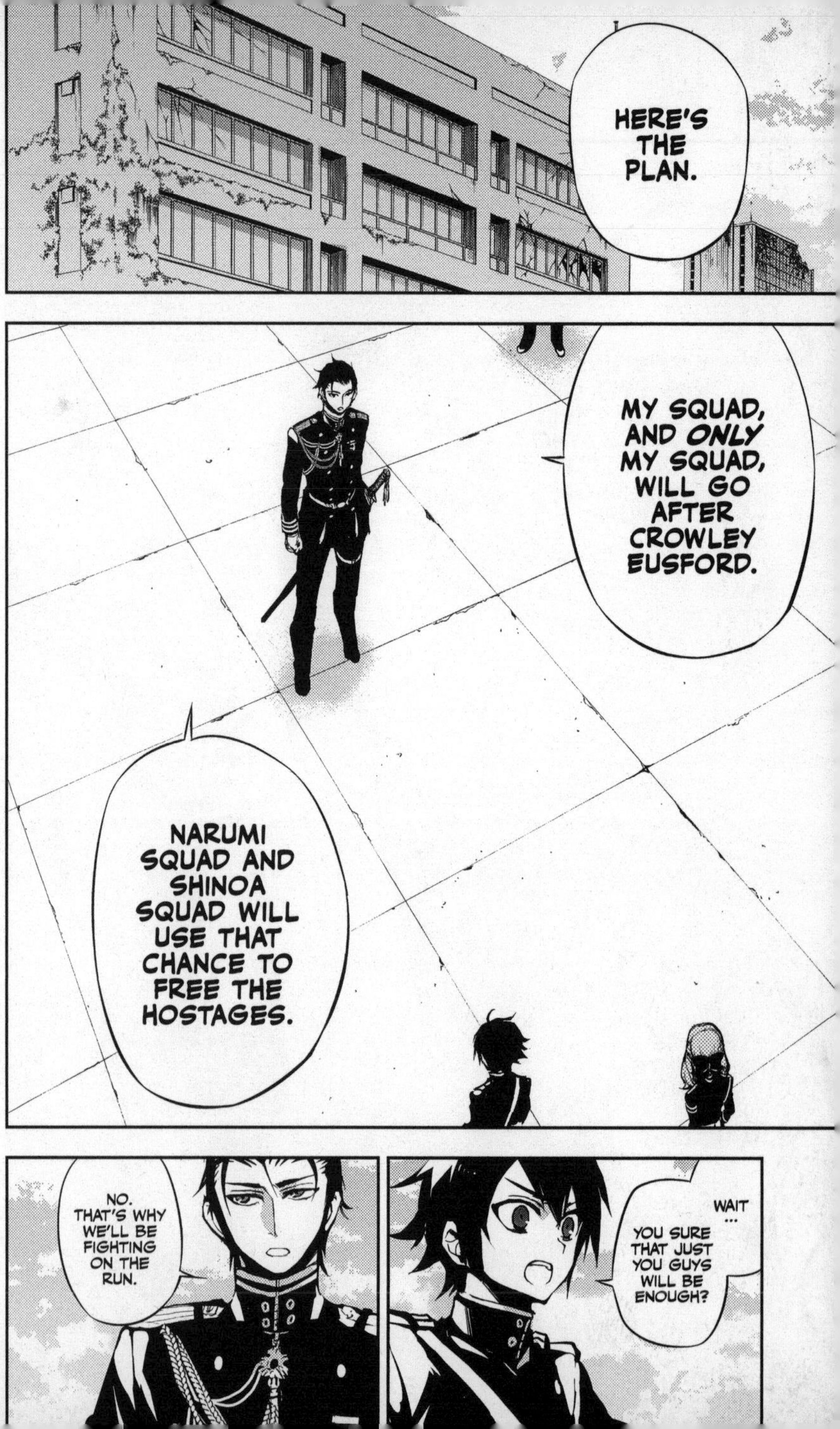
HERE'S THE PLAN.
MY SQUAD, AND ONLY MY SQUAD, WILL GO AFTER CROWLEY EUSFORD.
NARUMI SQUAD AND SHINOA SQUAD WILL USE THAT CHANCE TO FREE THE HOSTAGES.
WAIT... YOU SURE THAT JUST YOU GUYS WILL BE ENOUGH?
NO. THAT'S WHY WE'LL BE FIGHTING ON THE RUN.

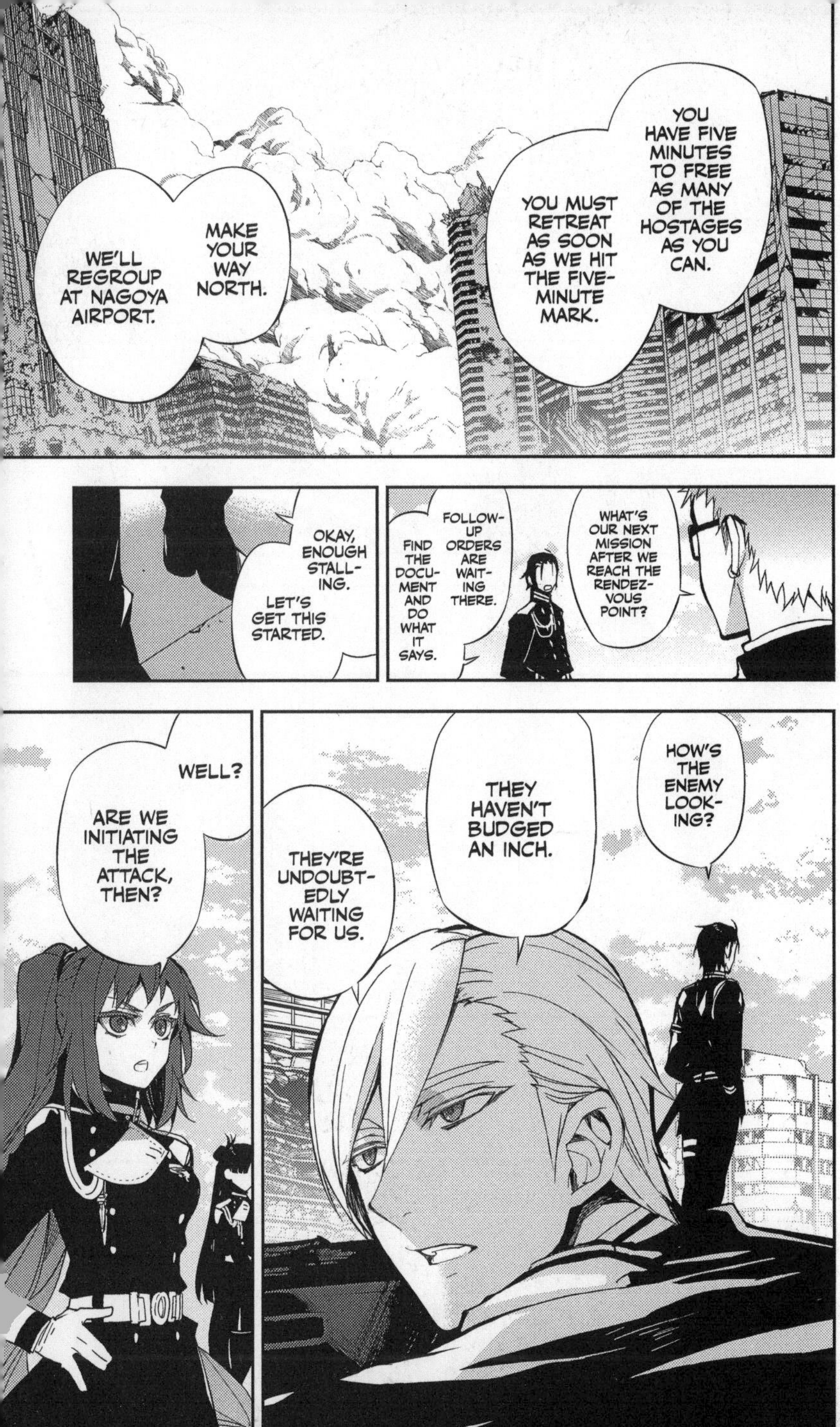

YOU HAVE FIVE MINUTES TO FREE AS MANY OF THE HOSTAGES AS YOU CAN.
YOU MUST RETREAT AS SOON AS WE HIT THE FIVE-MINUTE MARK.
MAKE YOUR WAY NORTH.
WE'LL REGROUP AT NAGOYA AIRPORT.
WHAT'S OUR NEXT MISSION AFTER WE REACH THE RENDEZVOUS POINT?
FOLLOW-UP ORDERS ARE WAITING THERE.
FIND THE DOCUMENT AND DO WHAT IT SAYS.
OKAY, ENOUGH STALLING.
LET'S GET THIS STARTED.
HOW'S THE ENEMY LOOKING?
THEY HAVEN'T BUDGED AN INCH.
THEY'RE UNDOUBTEDLY WAITING FOR US.
WELL?
ARE WE INITIATING THE ATTACK, THEN?

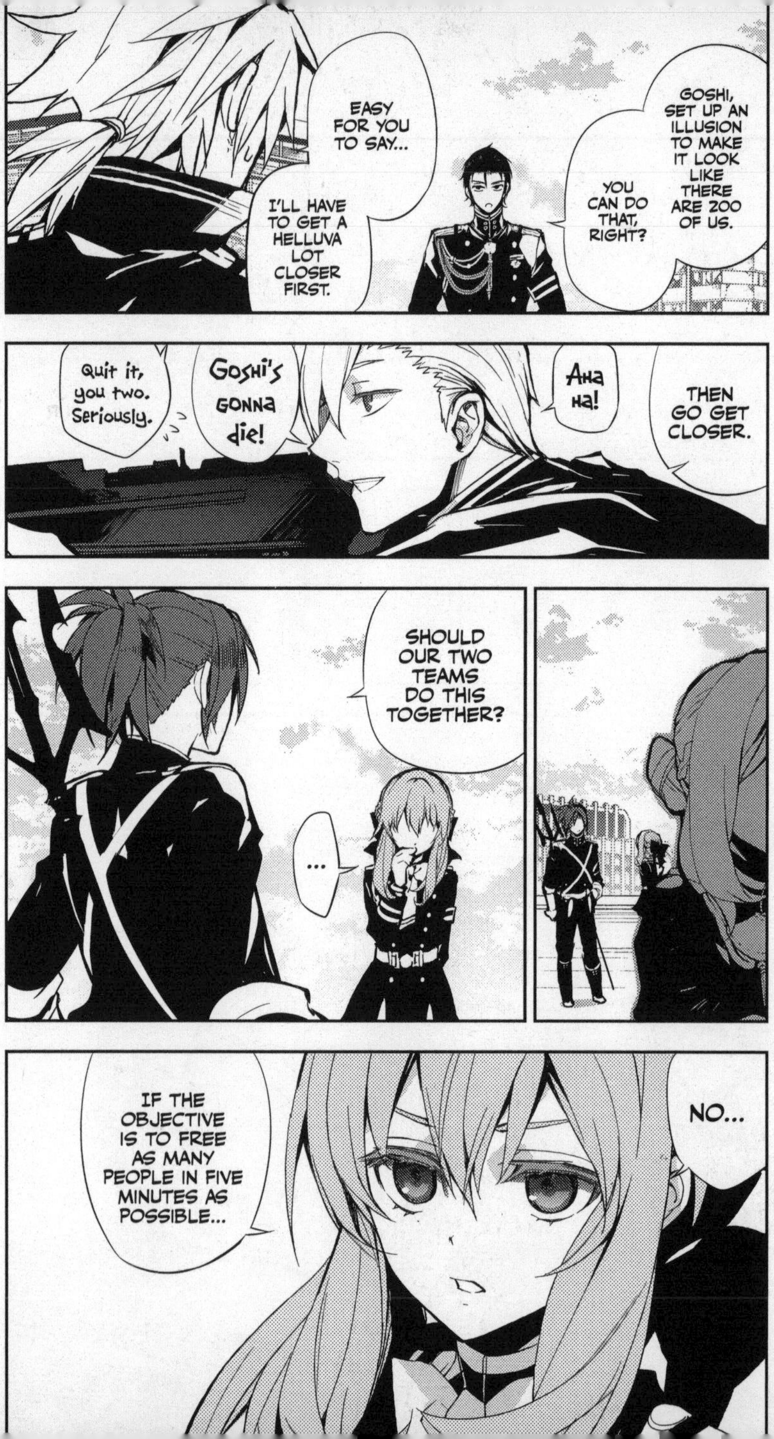
GOSHI, SET UP AN ILLUSION TO MAKE IT LOOK LIKE THERE ARE 200 OF US.
YOU CAN DO THAT, RIGHT?
EASY FOR YOU TO SAY...
I'LL HAVE TO GET A HELLUVA LOT CLOSER FIRST.
THEN GO GET CLOSER.
Aha ha!
Goshi's gonna die!
Quit it, you two. Seriously.
SHOULD OUR TWO TEAMS DO THIS TOGETHER?
...
NO...
IF THE OBJECTIVE IS TO FREE AS MANY PEOPLE IN FIVE MINUTES AS POSSIBLE...

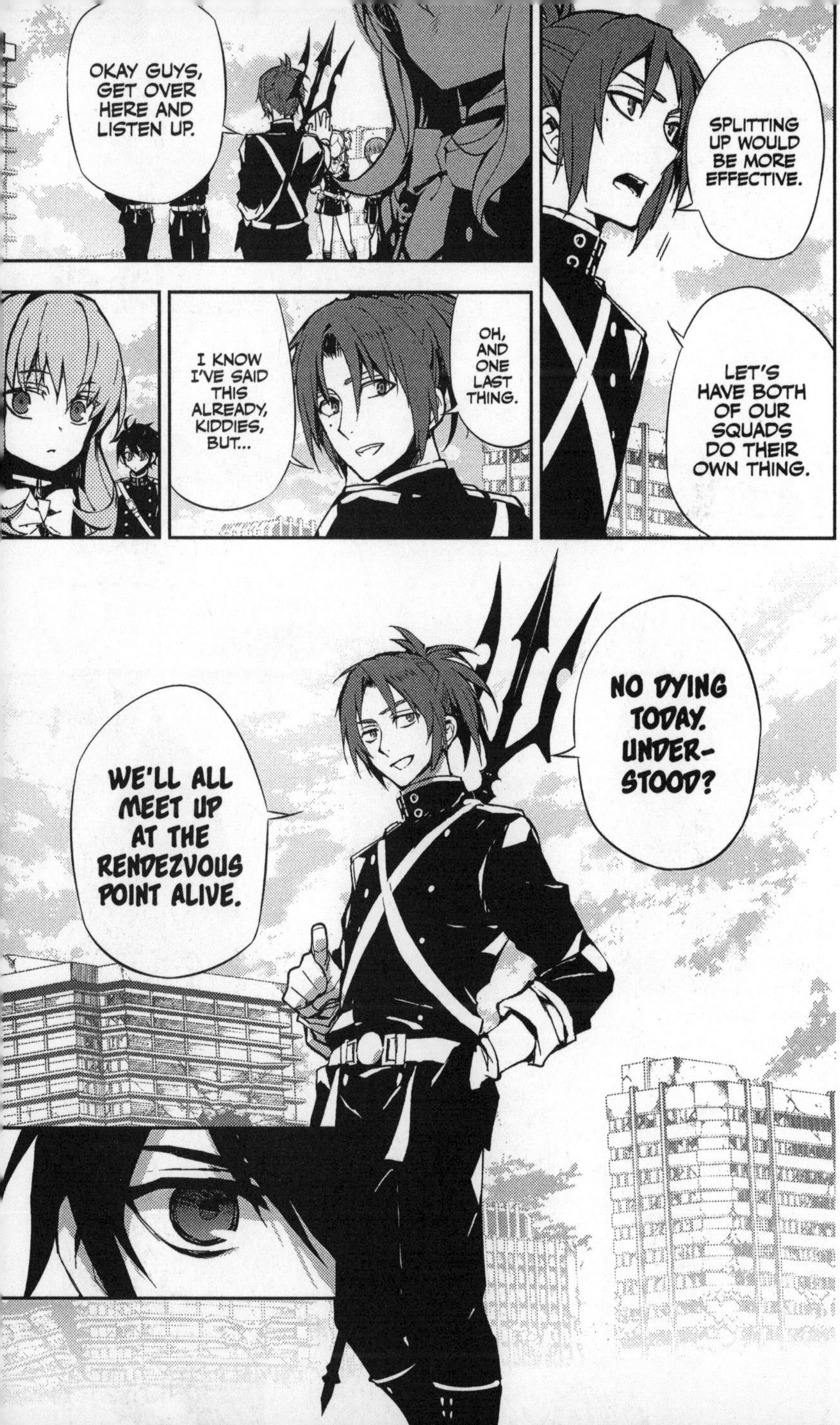
SPLITTING UP WOULD BE MORE EFFECTIVE.
LET'S HAVE BOTH OF OUR SQUADS DO THEIR OWN THING.
OKAY GUYS, GET OVER HERE AND LISTEN UP.
OH, AND ONE LAST THING.
I KNOW I'VE SAID THIS ALREADY, KIDDIES, BUT...
NO DYING TODAY. UNDER-STOOD?
WE'LL ALL MEET UP AT THE RENDEZVOUS POINT ALIVE.

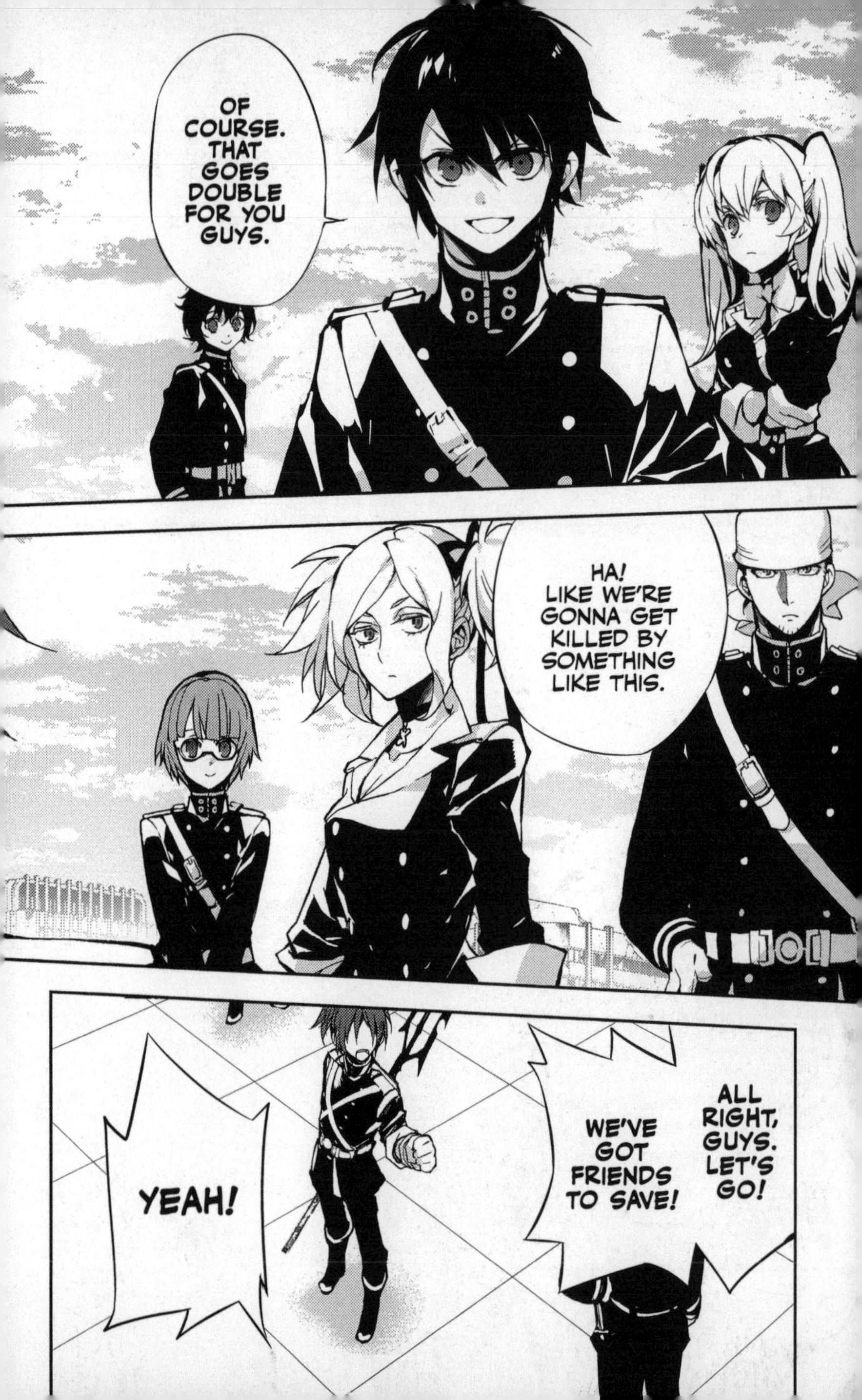
OF COURSE. THAT GOES DOUBLE FOR YOU GUYS.
HA! LIKE WE'RE GONNA GET KILLED BY SOMETHING LIKE THIS.
ALL RIGHT, GUYS. LET'S GO!
WE'VE GOT FRIENDS TO SAVE!
YEAH!

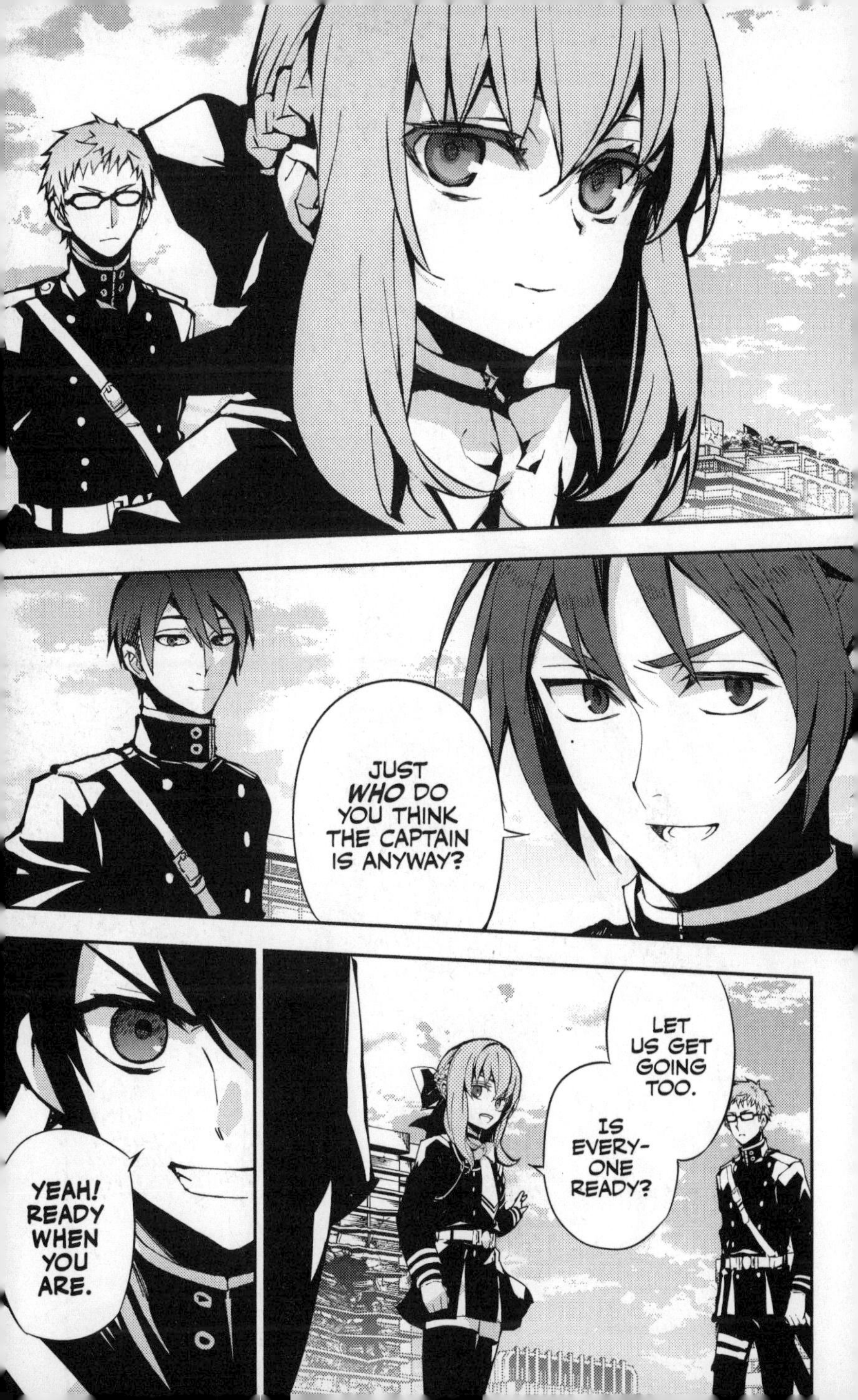
JUST *WHO* DO YOU THINK THE CAPTAIN IS ANYWAY?
LET US GET GOING TOO.
IS EVERY-ONE READY?
YEAH! READY WHEN YOU ARE.

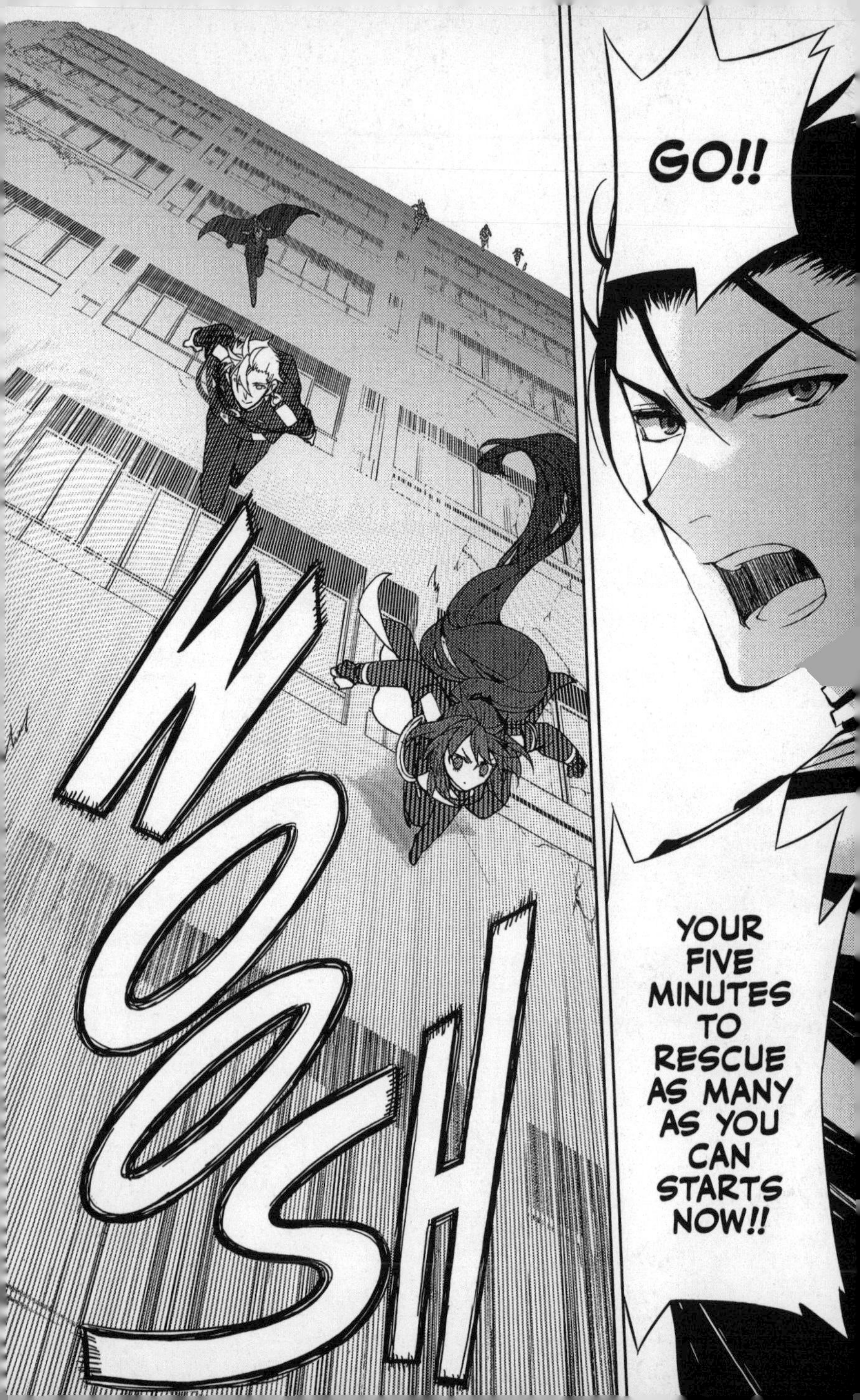
GO!!
YOUR FIVE MINUTES TO RESCUE AS MANY AS YOU CAN STARTS NOW!!
WHOOSH

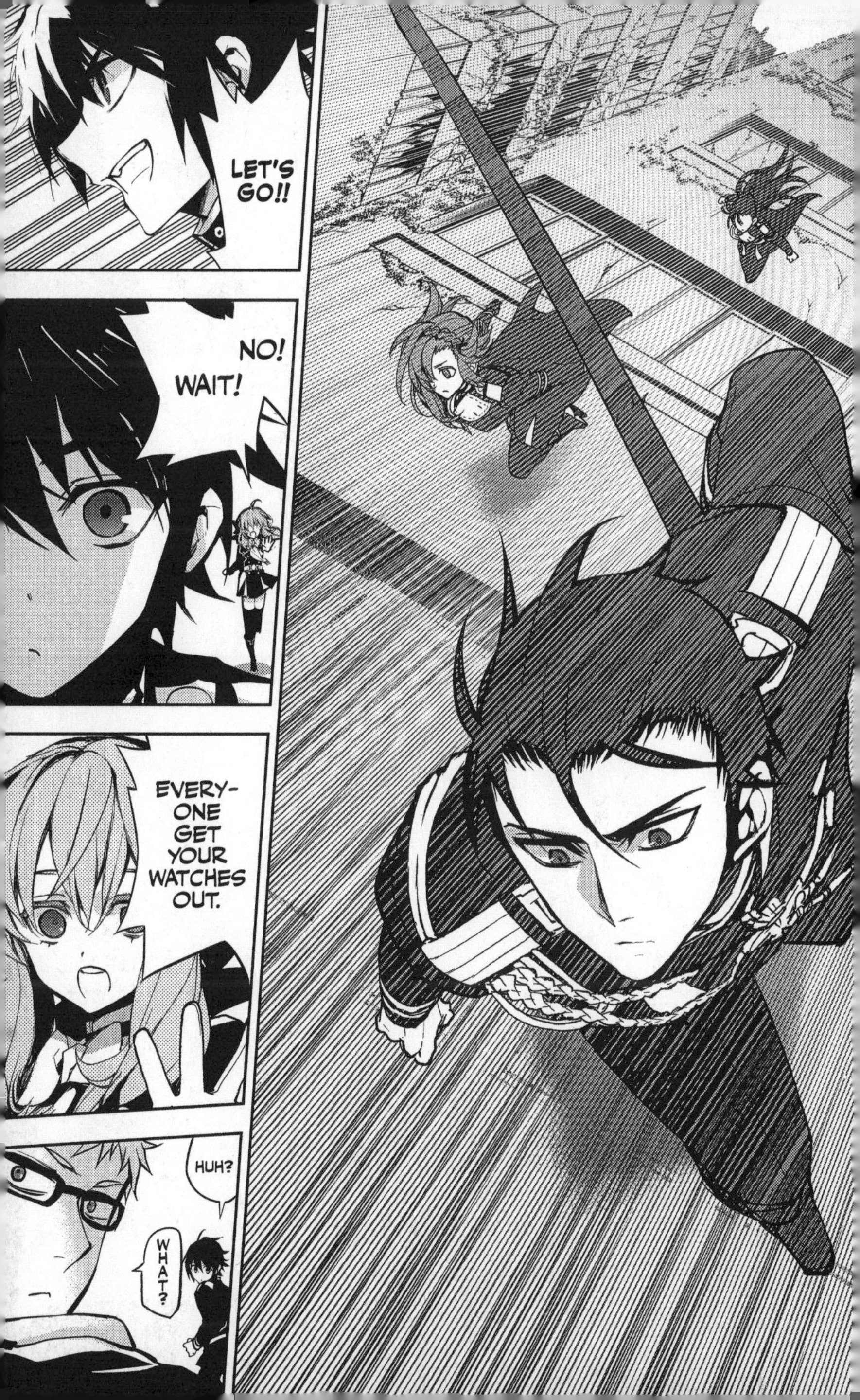
LET'S GO!!
NO! WAIT!
EVERY-ONE GET YOUR WATCHES OUT.
HUH?
WHAT?

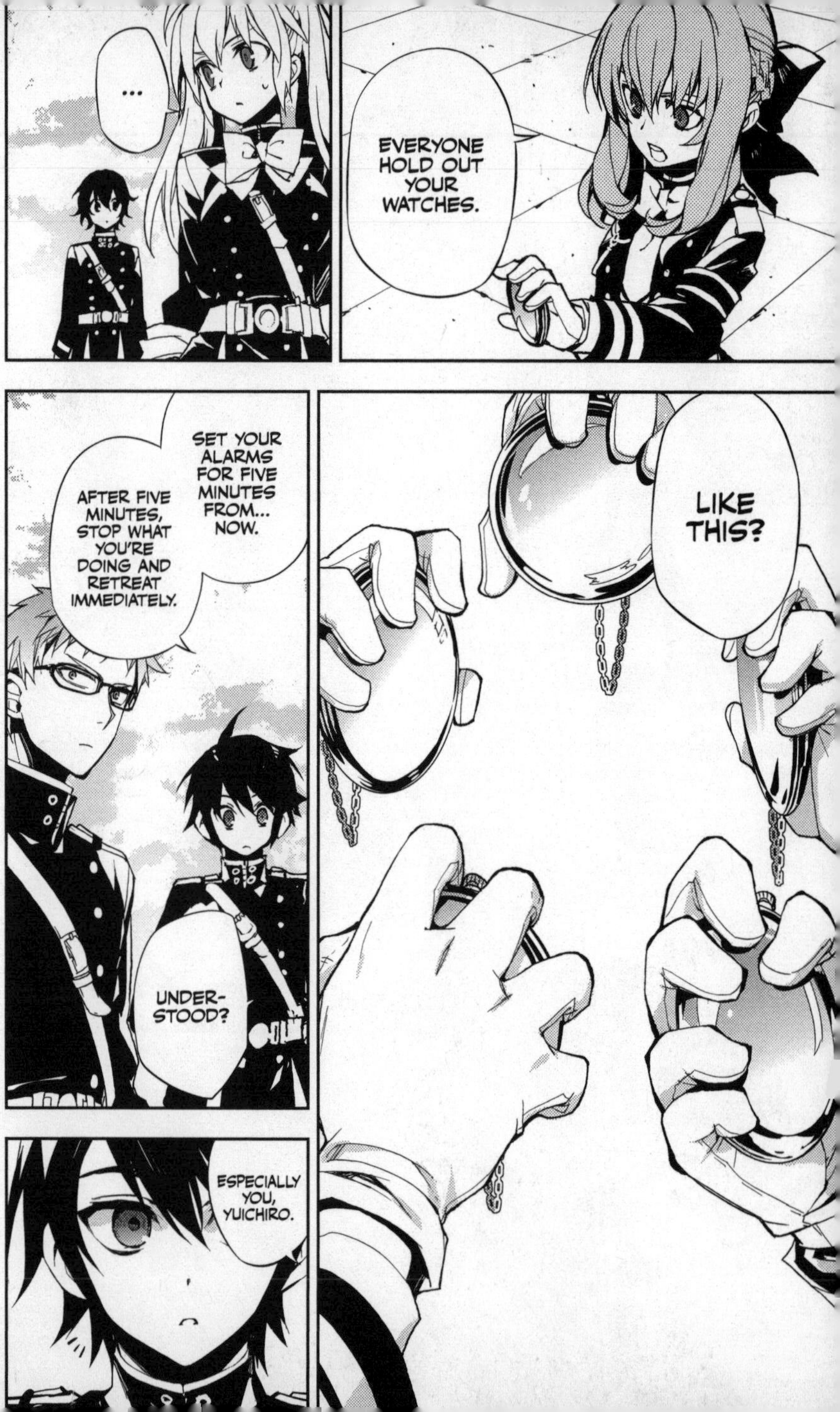
EVERYONE HOLD OUT YOUR WATCHES.
...
LIKE THIS?
SET YOUR ALARMS FOR FIVE MINUTES FROM... NOW.
AFTER FIVE MINUTES, STOP WHAT YOU'RE DOING AND RETREAT IMMEDIATELY.
UNDER-STOOD?
ESPECIALLY YOU, YUICHIRO.

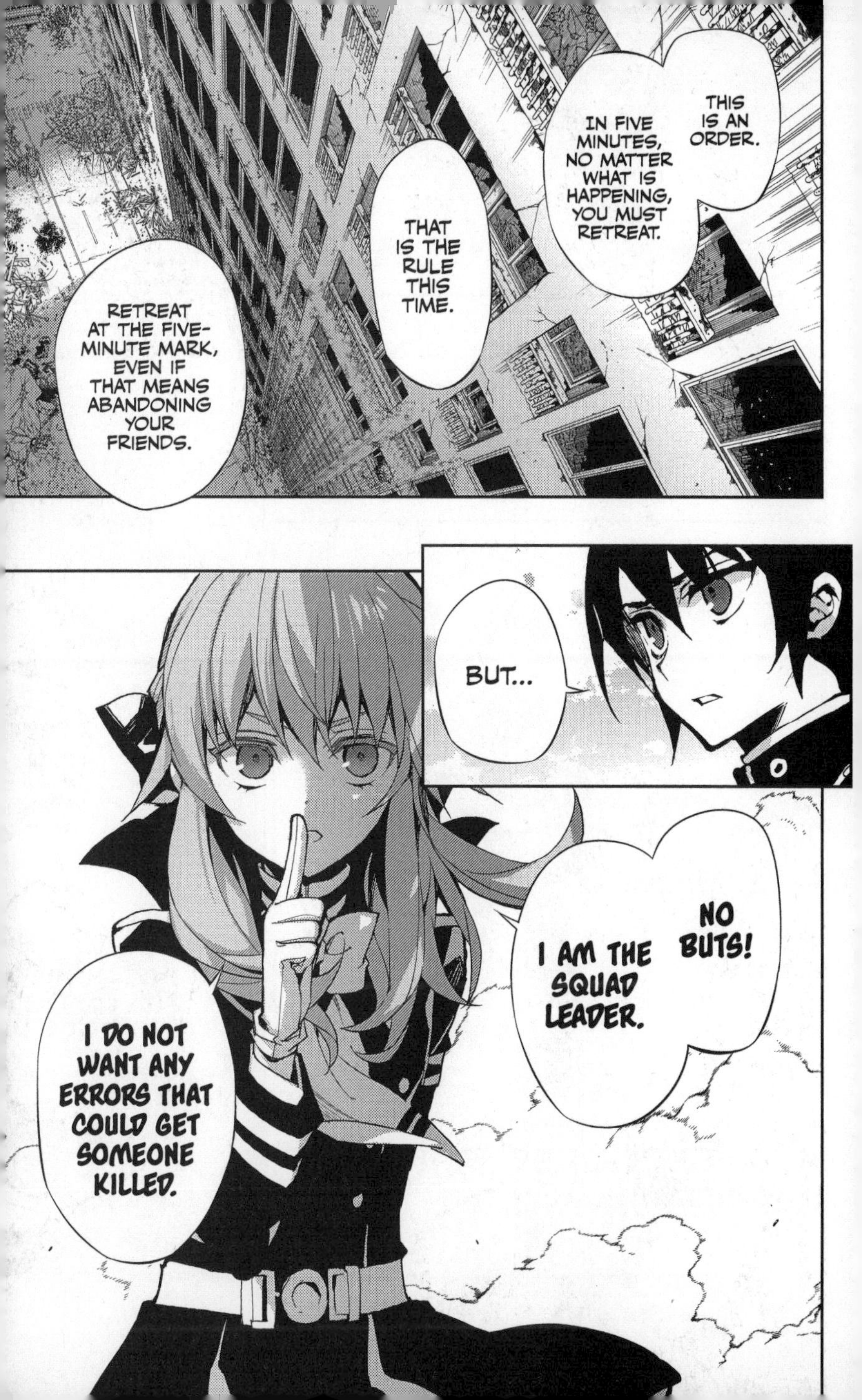
THIS IS AN ORDER.
IN FIVE MINUTES, NO MATTER WHAT IS HAPPENING, YOU MUST RETREAT.
THAT IS THE RULE THIS TIME.
RETREAT AT THE FIVE-MINUTE MARK, EVEN IF THAT MEANS ABANDONING YOUR FRIENDS.
BUT...
NO BUTS!
I AM THE SQUAD LEADER.
I DO NOT WANT ANY ERRORS THAT COULD GET SOMEONE KILLED.

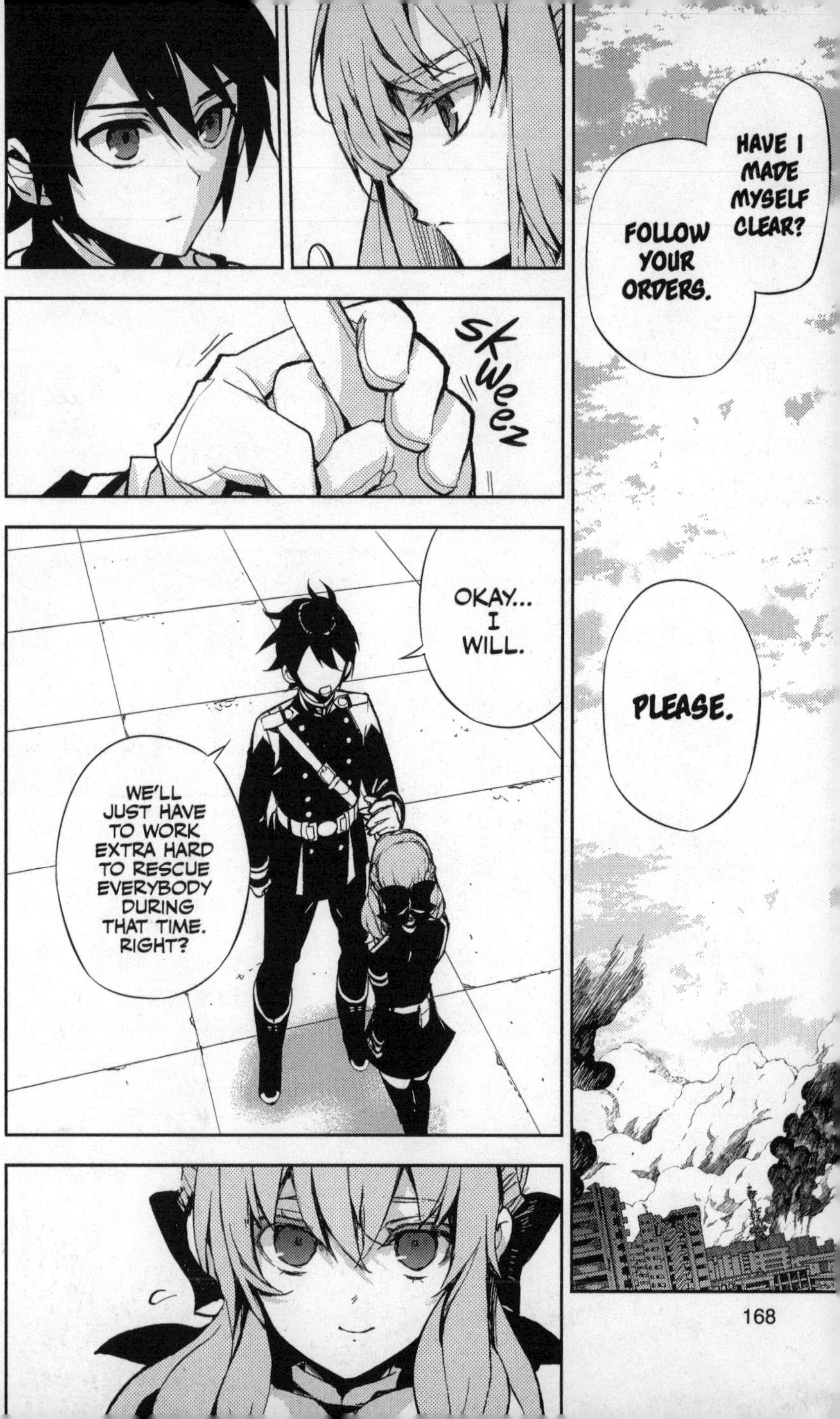
HAVE I MADE MYSELF CLEAR?
FOLLOW YOUR ORDERS.
PLEASE.
SKWEEN
OKAY... I WILL.
WE'LL JUST HAVE TO WORK EXTRA HARD TO RESCUE EVERYBODY DURING THAT TIME. RIGHT?

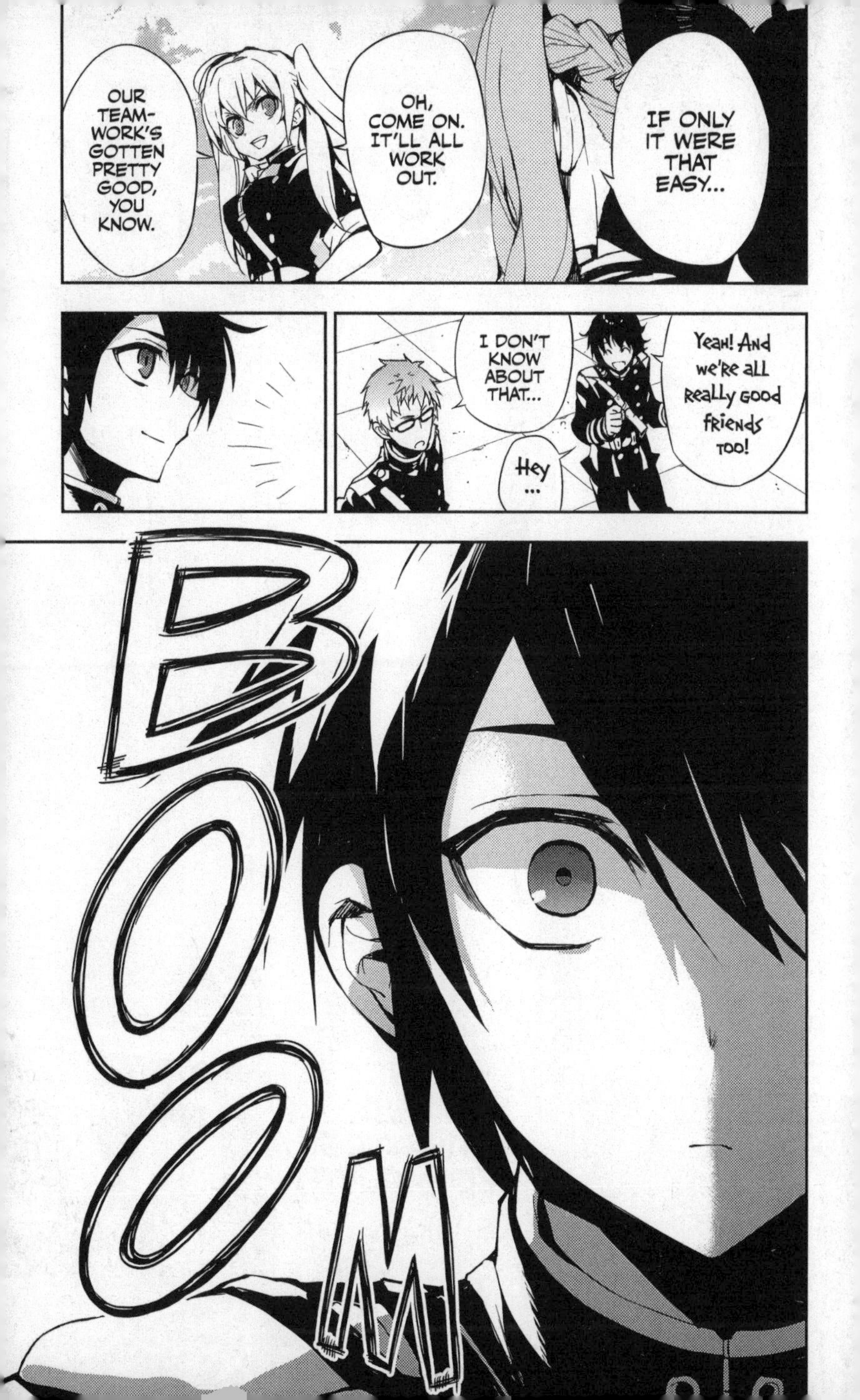
IF ONLY IT WERE THAT EASY...
OH, COME ON. IT'LL ALL WORK OUT.
OUR TEAM-WORK'S GOTTEN PRETTY GOOD, YOU KNOW.
Yeah! And we're all really good friends too!
I DON'T KNOW ABOUT THAT...
Hey ...
BOOM

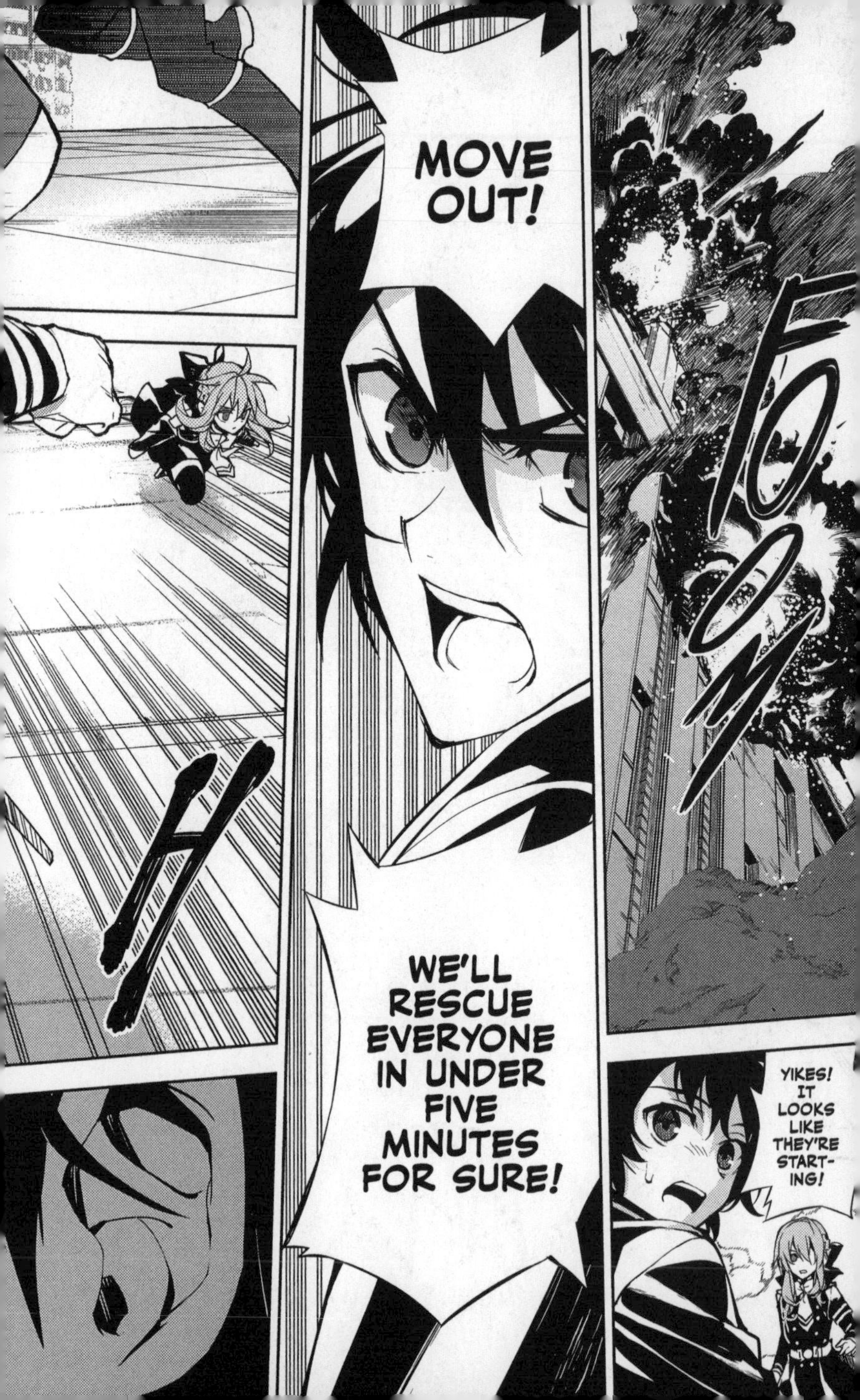
FOOM
YIKES! IT LOOKS LIKE THEY'RE START-ING!
MOVE OUT!
WE'LL RESCUE EVERYONE IN UNDER FIVE MINUTES FOR SURE!

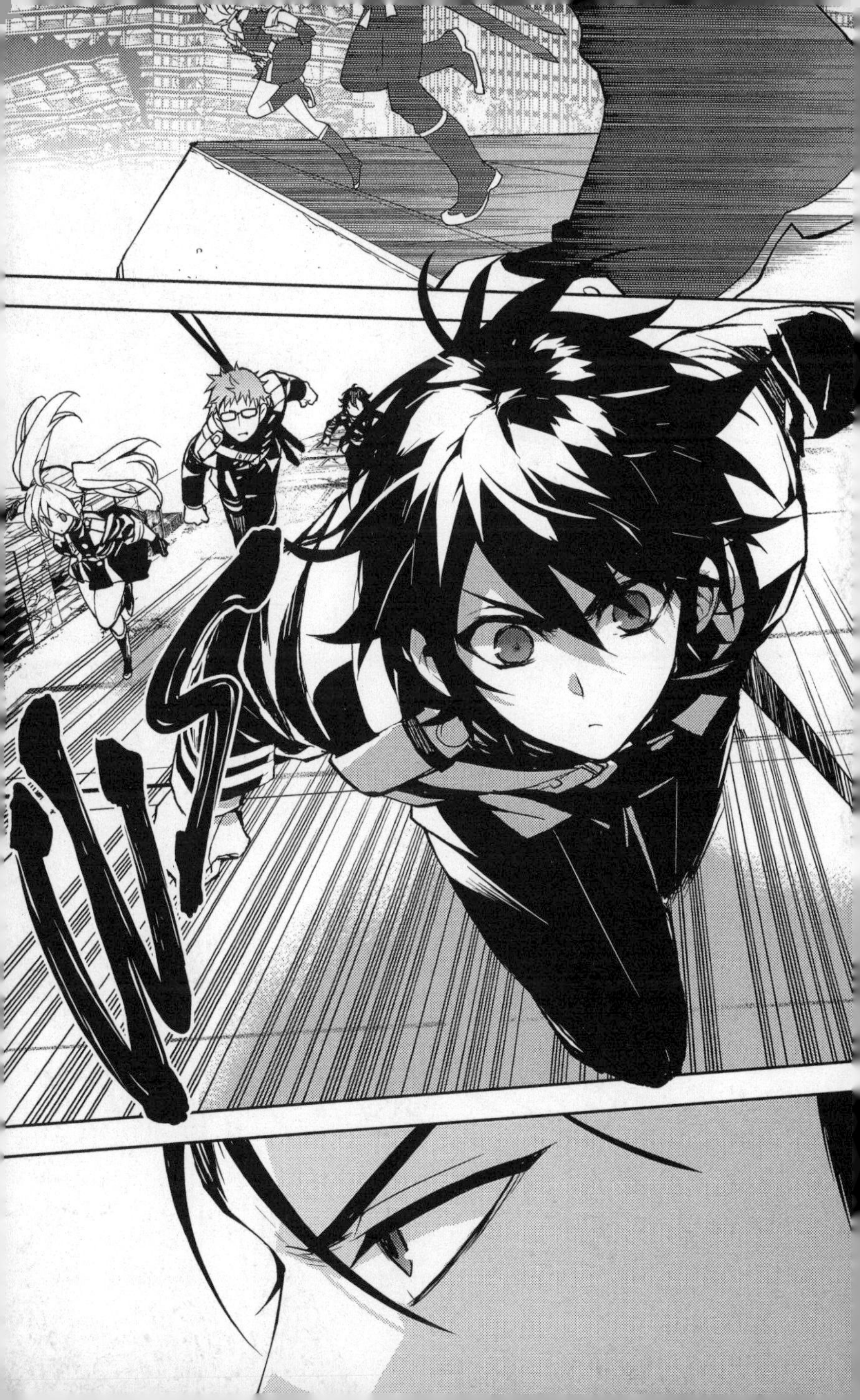

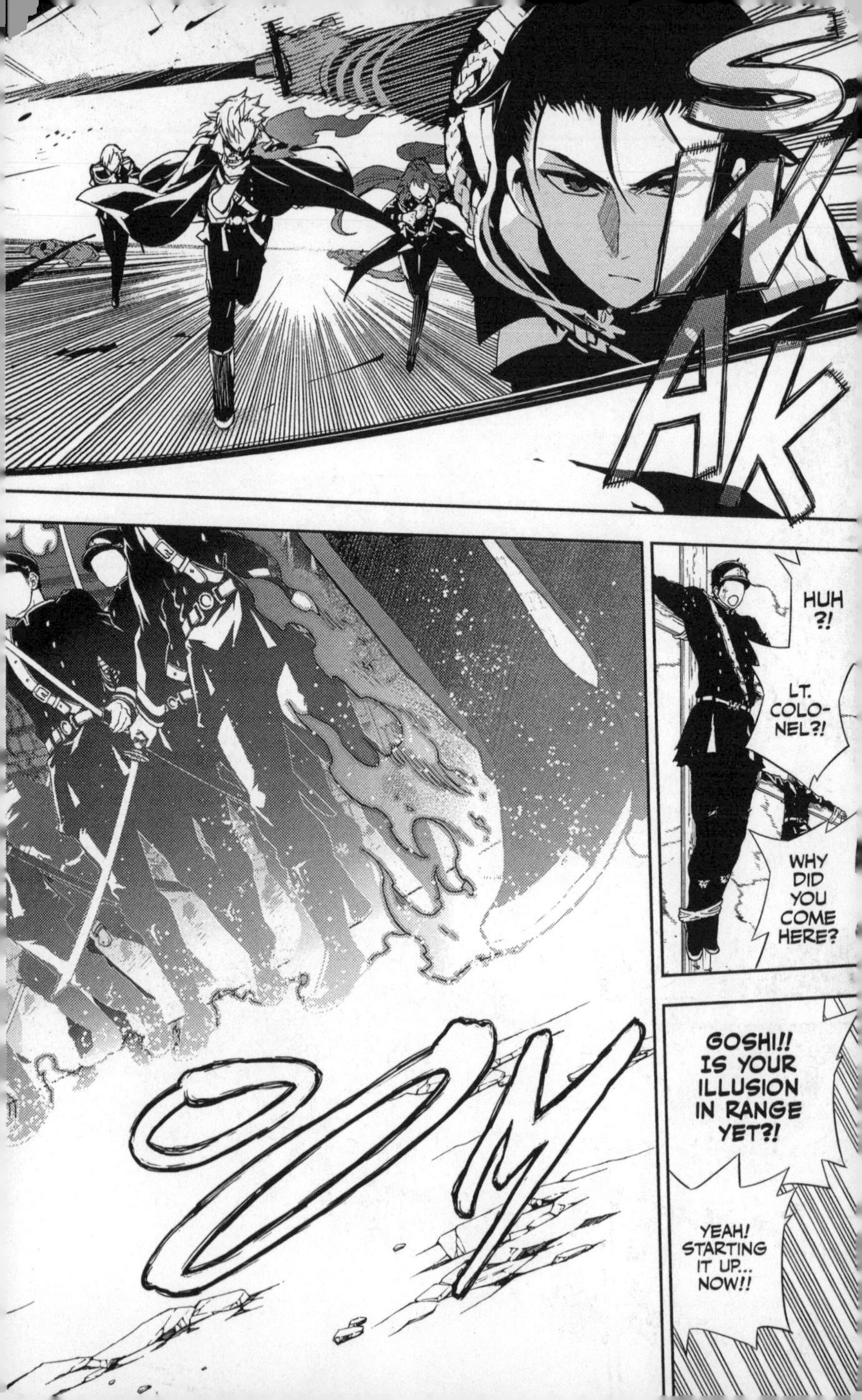
SWAK
HUH?!
LT. COLONEL?!
WHY DID YOU COME HERE?
GOSHI!! IS YOUR ILLUSION IN RANGE YET?!
YEAH! STARTING IT UP... NOW!!

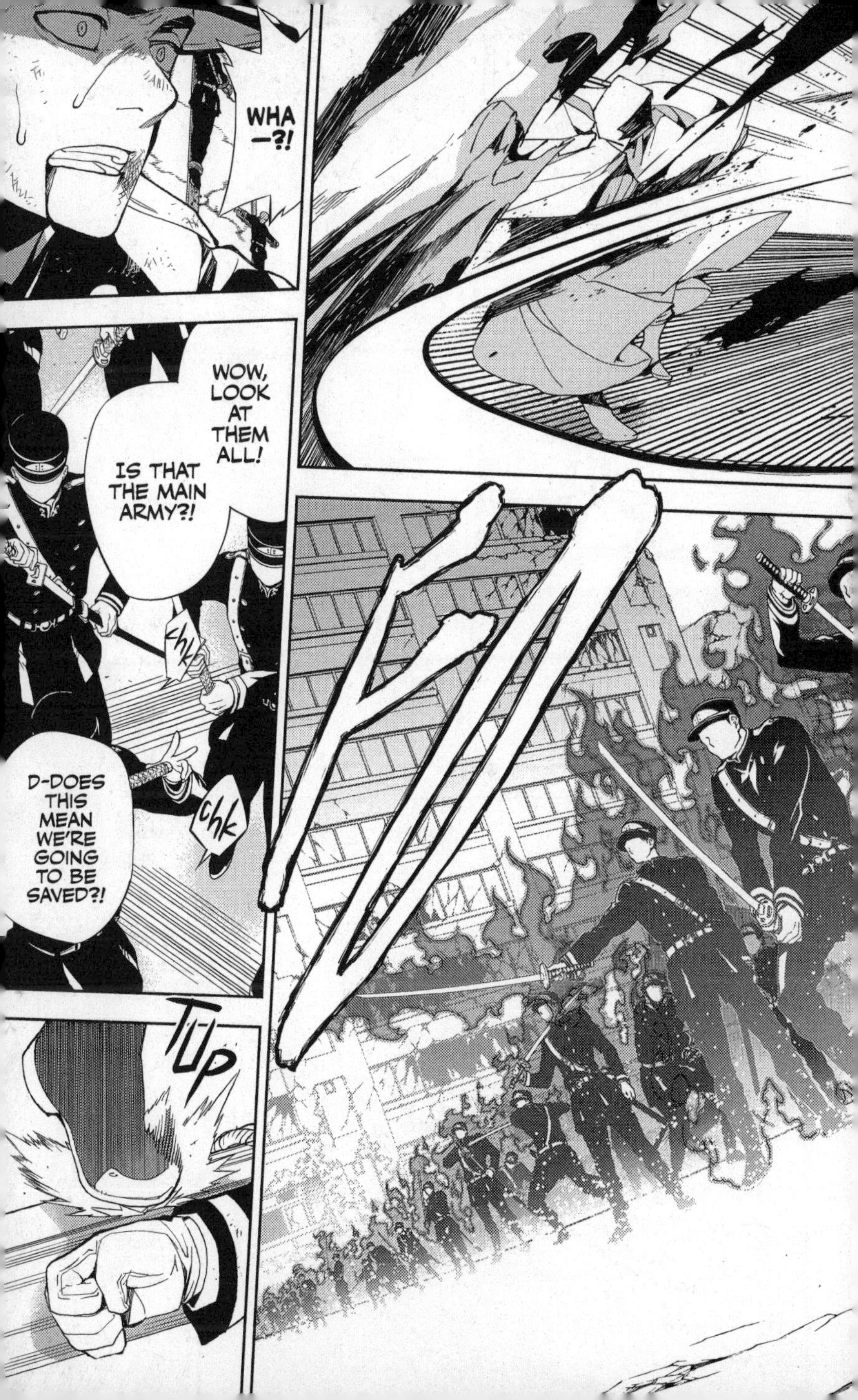

WHA—?!
WOW, LOOK AT THEM ALL!
IS THAT THE MAIN ARMY?!
chk
chk
D-DOES THIS MEAN WE'RE GOING TO BE SAVED?!
TUP

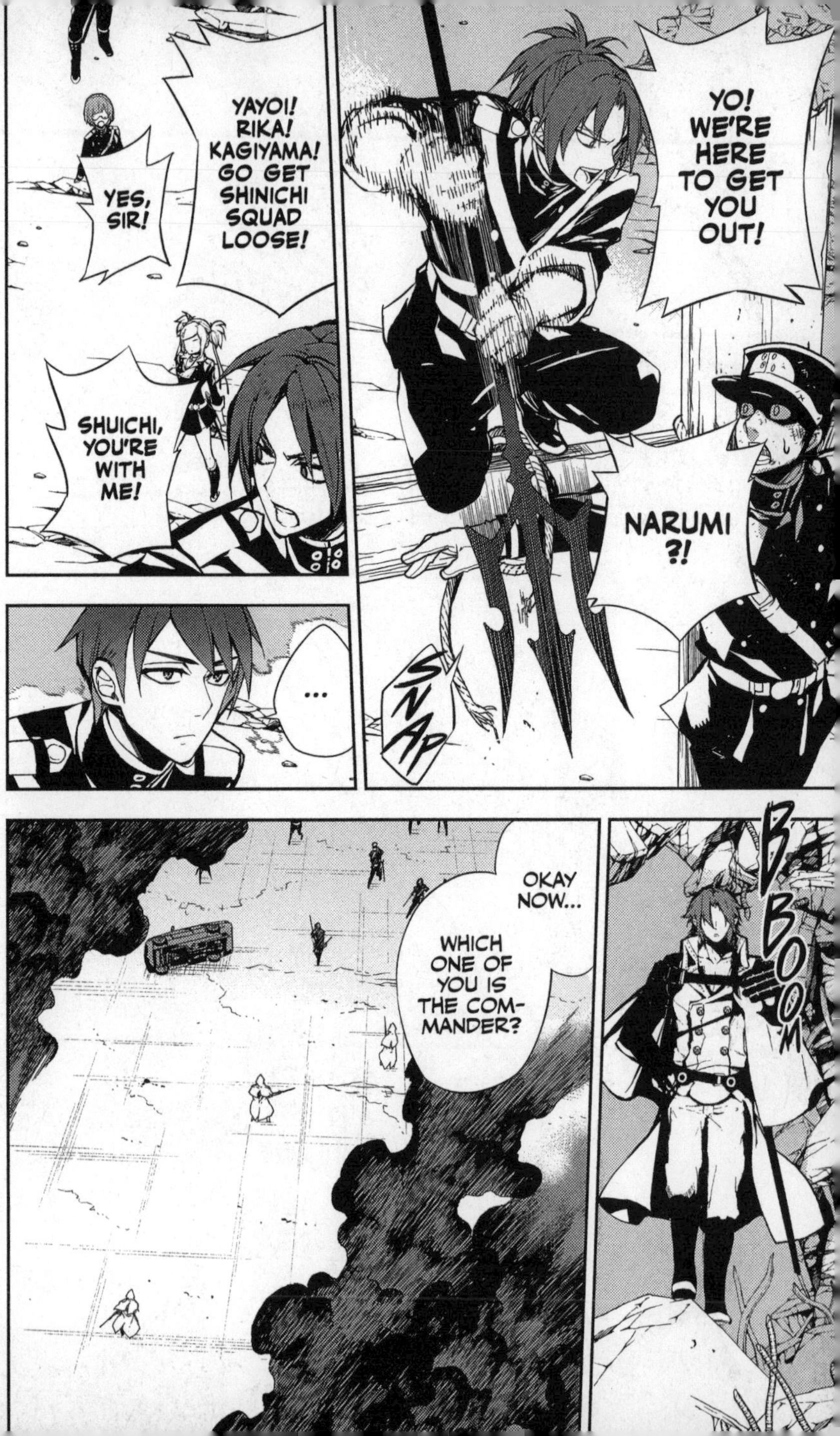

YO! WE'RE HERE TO GET YOU OUT!
NARUMI ?!
SNAP
YAYOI! RIKA! KAGIYAMA! GO GET SHINICHI SQUAD LOOSE!
YES, SIR!
SHUICHI, YOU'RE WITH ME!
...
B-BOOM
OKAY NOW...
WHICH ONE OF YOU IS THE COMMANDER?

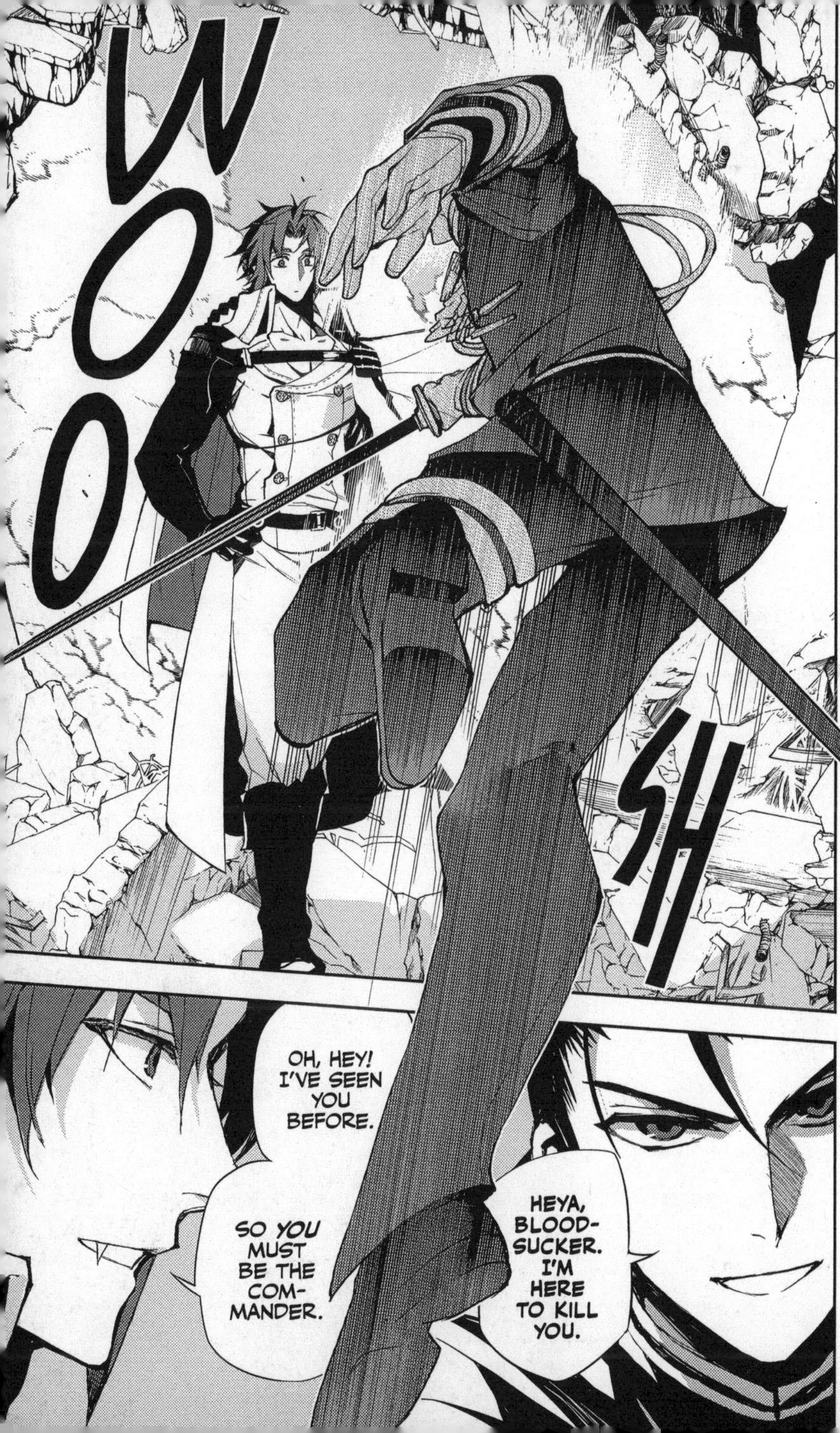
WOOO
SH
HEYA, BLOOD-SUCKER. I'M HERE TO KILL YOU.
OH, HEY! I'VE SEEN YOU BEFORE.
SO *YOU* MUST BE THE COM-MANDER.

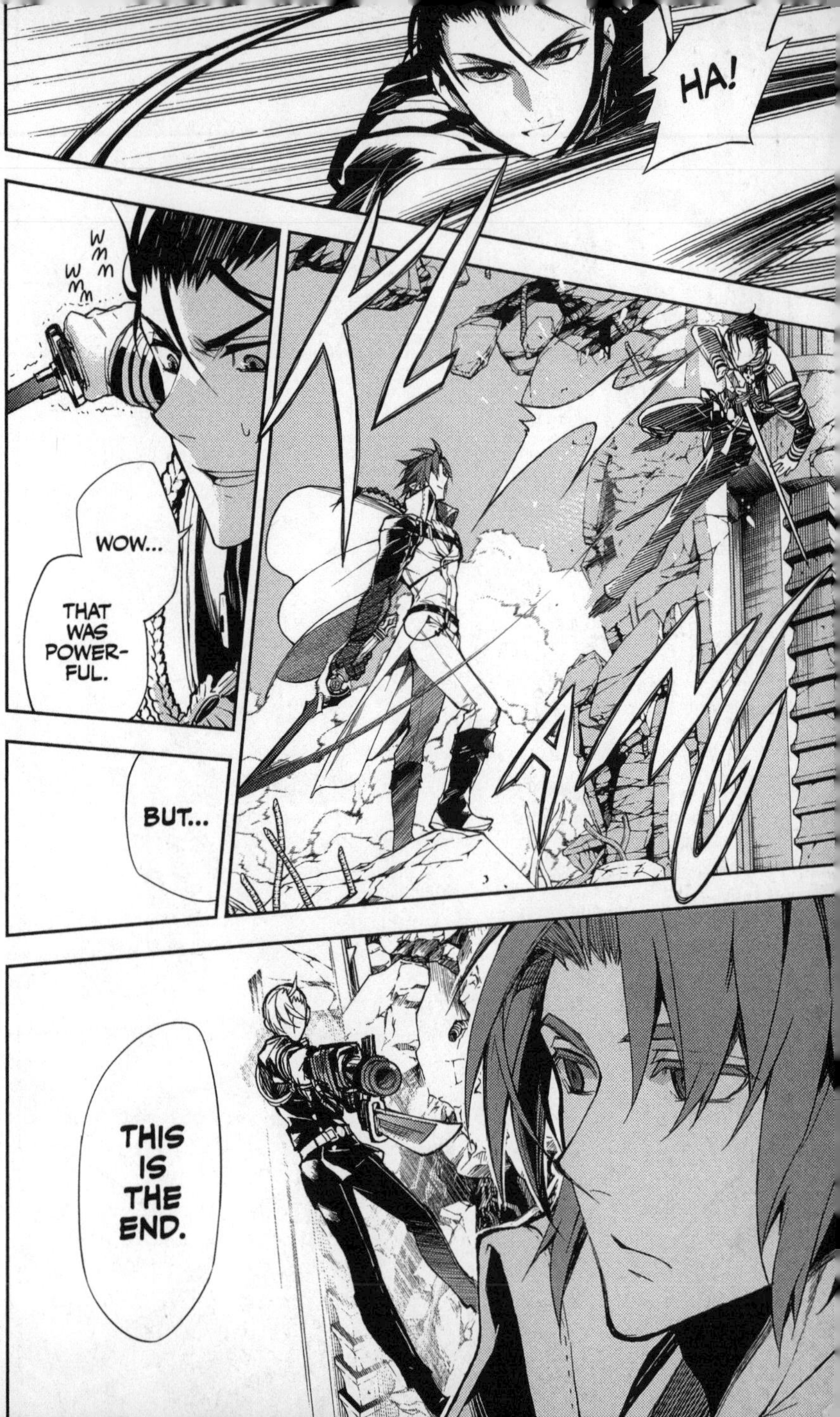
HA!
KLANG
WMMM WMMM
WOW...
THAT WAS POWERFUL.
BUT...
THIS IS THE END.

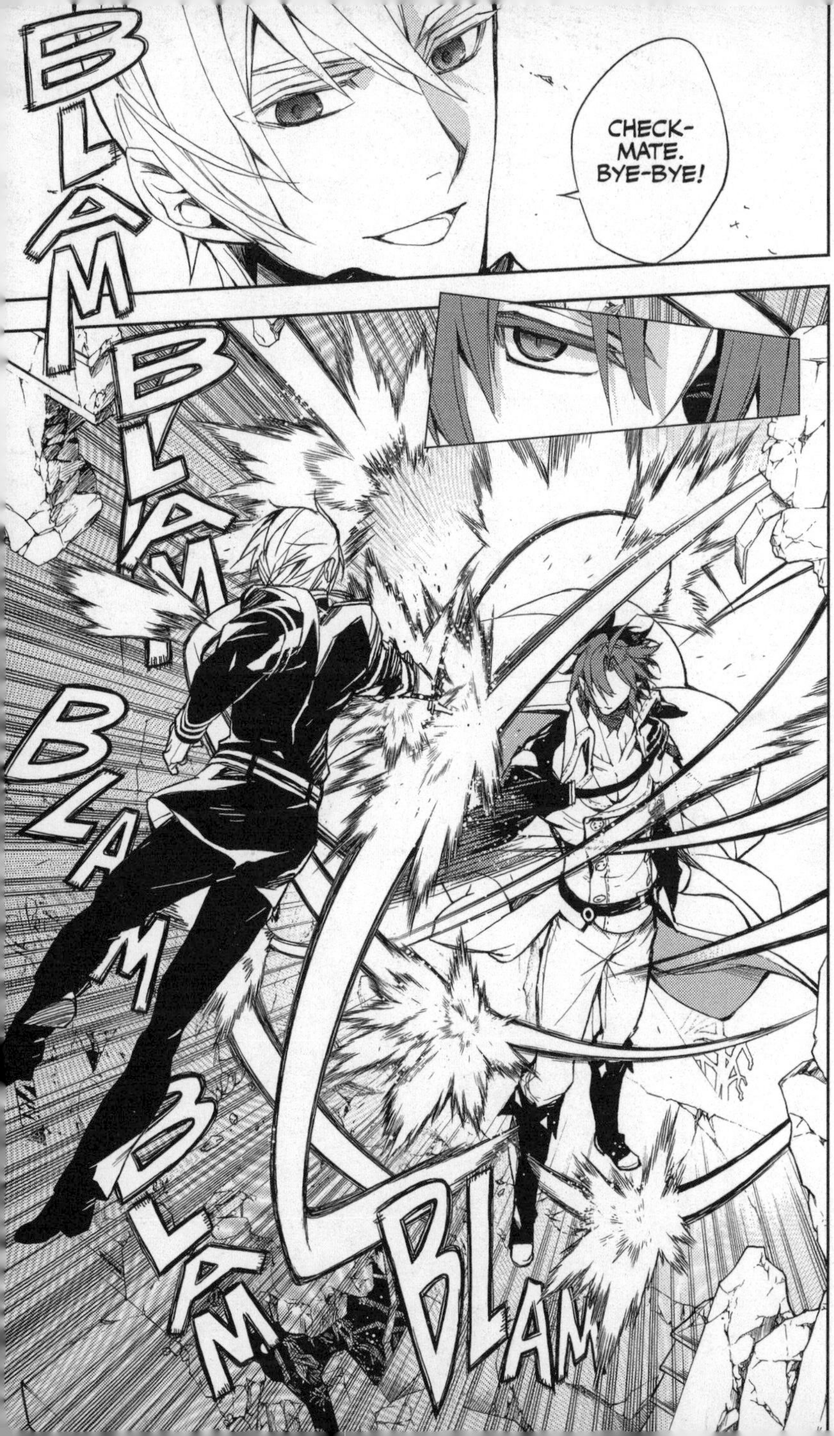
CHECK-MATE. BYE-BYE!
BLAM
BLAM
BLAM
BLAM
BLAM

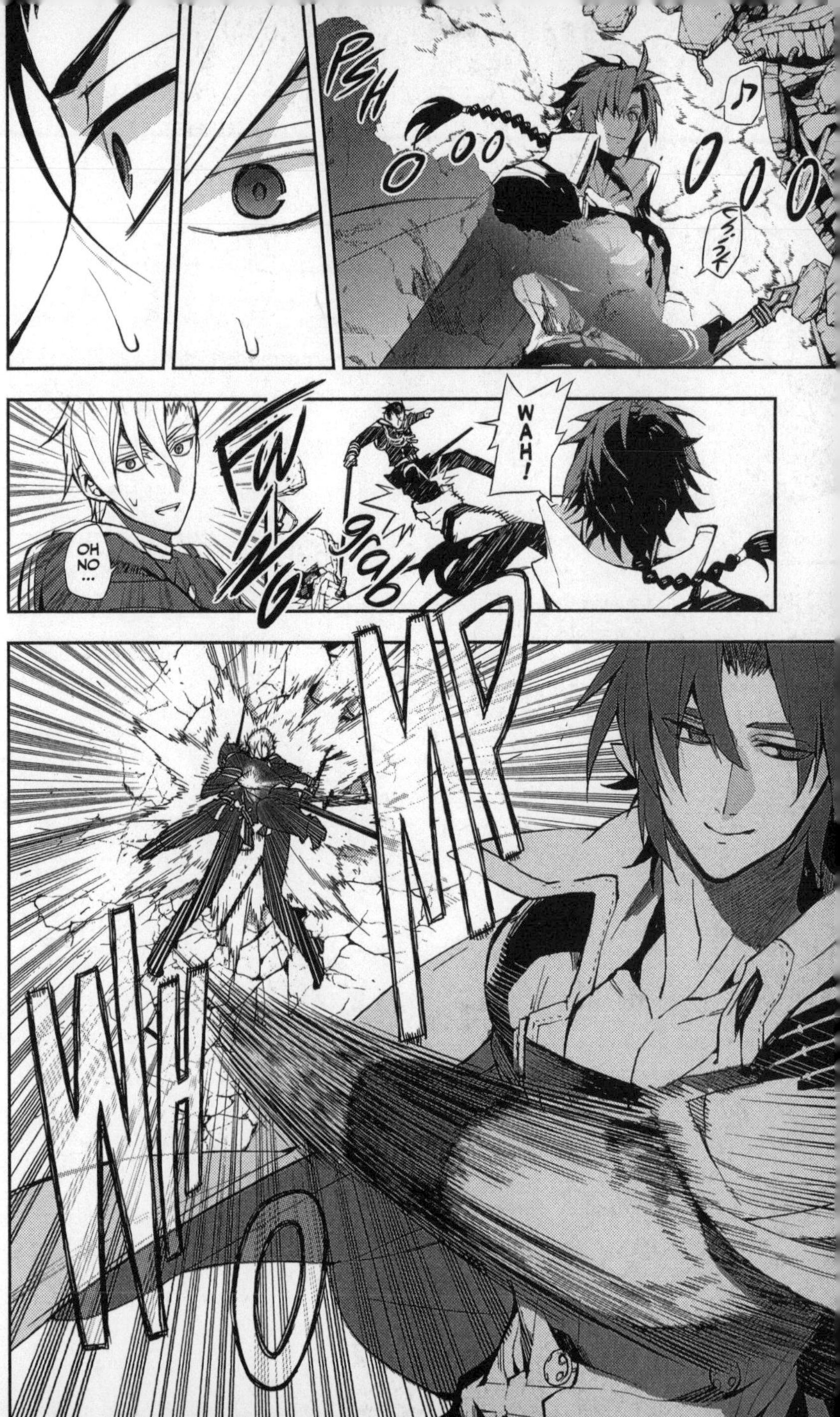

♪
chink
PSHOOOOOOO
WAH!
grab
FWANG
OH NO ...
WHOMP

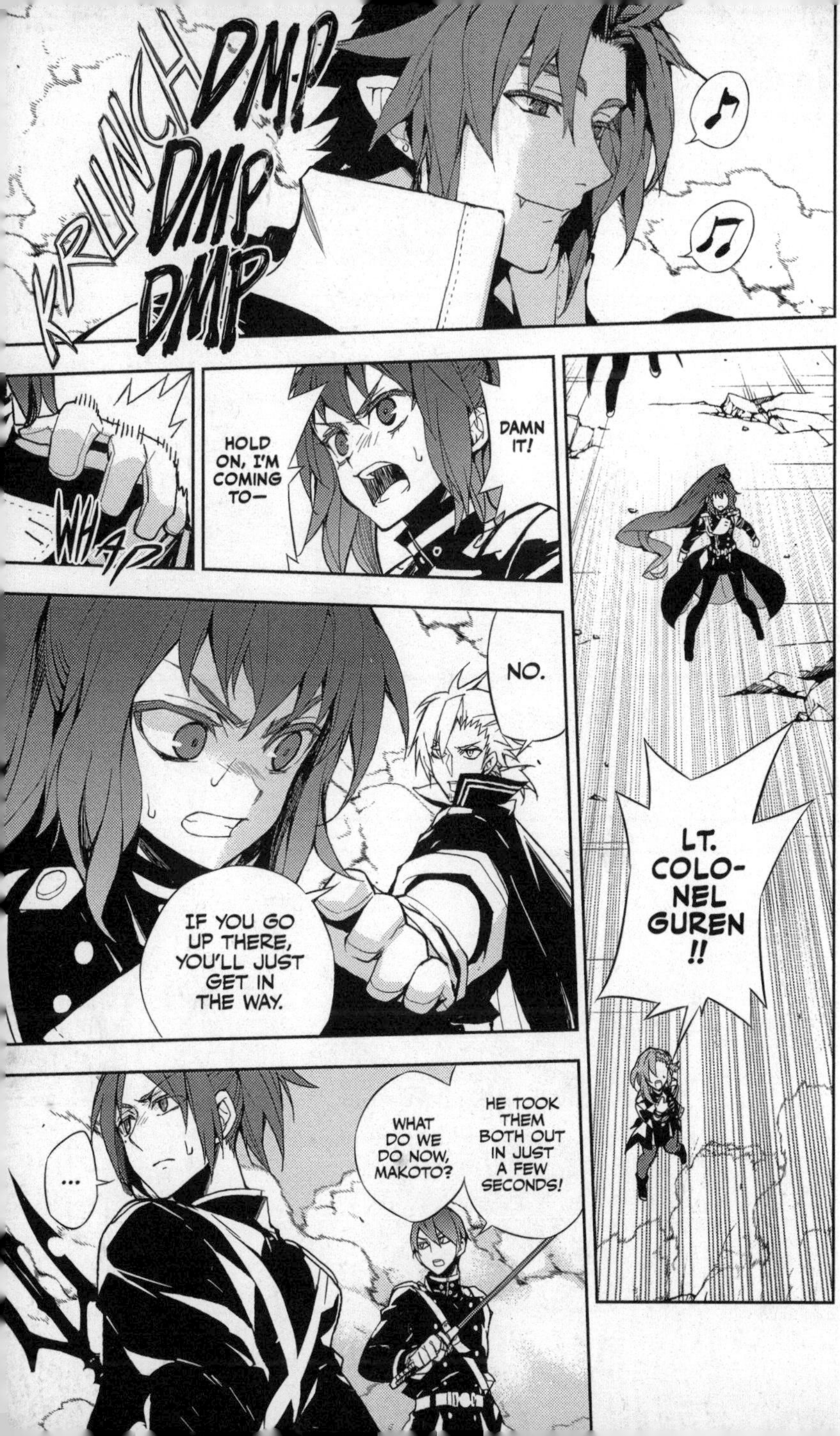

♪
♫
DMP DMP DMP
KRUNCH
LT. COLONEL GUREN!!
DAMN IT!
HOLD ON, I'M COMING TO—
WHAP
NO.
IF YOU GO UP THERE, YOU'LL JUST GET IN THE WAY.
HE TOOK THEM BOTH OUT IN JUST A FEW SECONDS!
WHAT DO WE DO NOW, MAKOTO?
...

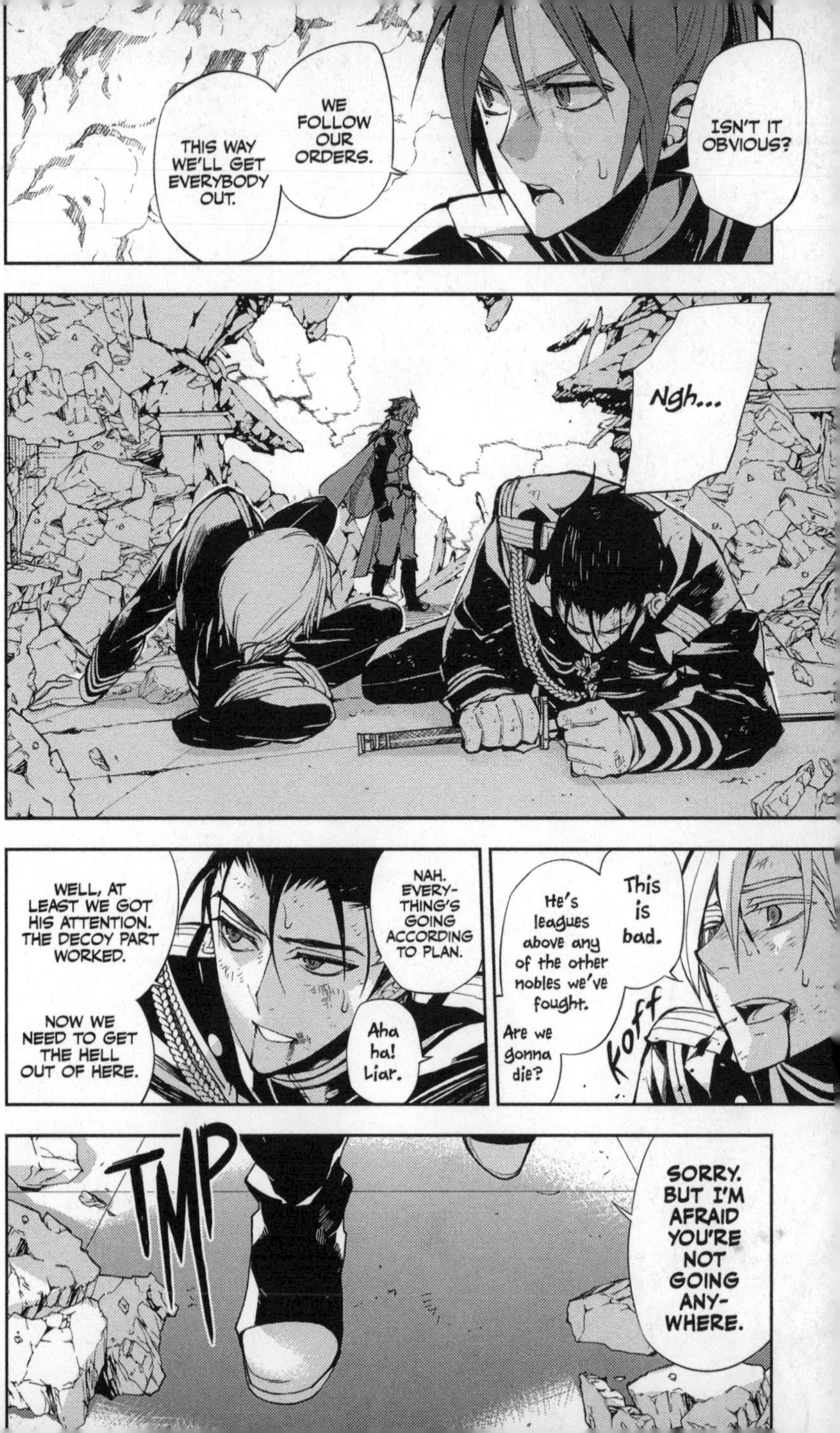
ISN'T IT OBVIOUS?
WE FOLLOW OUR ORDERS.
THIS WAY WE'LL GET EVERYBODY OUT.
Ngh...
This is bad.
He's leagues above any of the other nobles we've fought.
Are we gonna die?
koff
NAH. EVERY-THING'S GOING ACCORDING TO PLAN.
Aha ha! Liar.
WELL, AT LEAST WE GOT HIS ATTENTION. THE DECOY PART WORKED.
NOW WE NEED TO GET THE HELL OUT OF HERE.
TMP
SORRY. BUT I'M AFRAID YOU'RE NOT GOING ANY-WHERE.

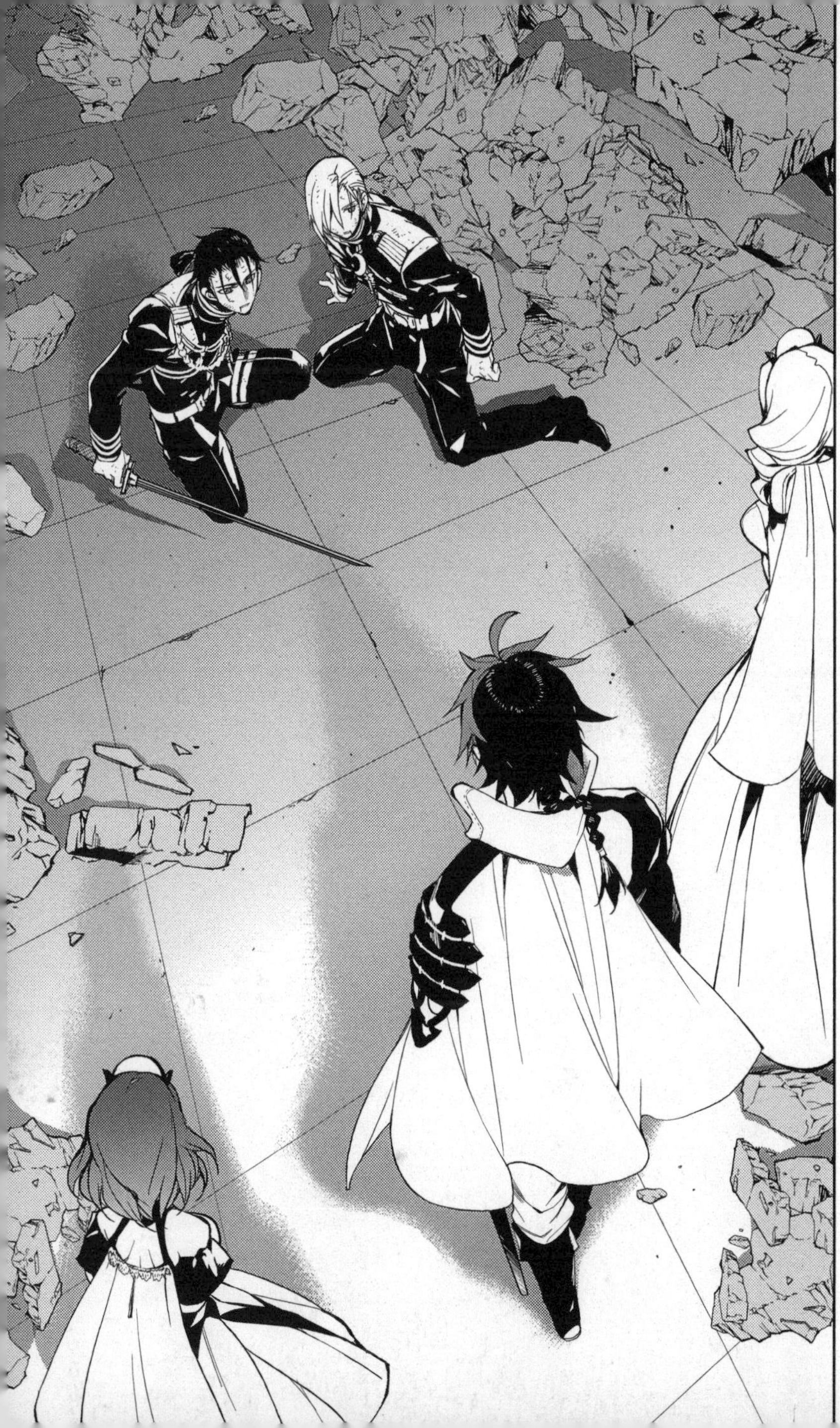

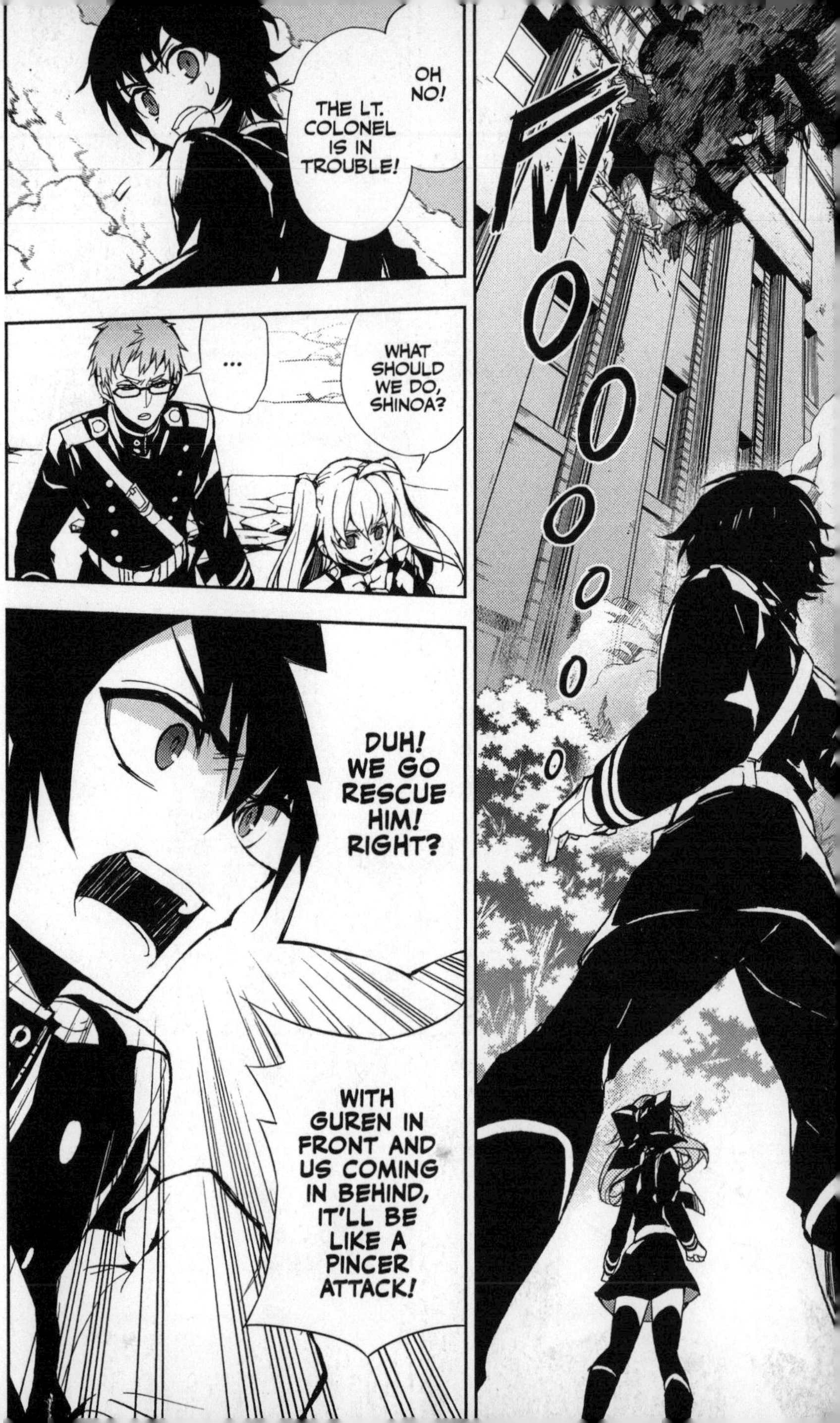
FWOOOOOO
OH NO!
THE LT. COLONEL IS IN TROUBLE!
WHAT SHOULD WE DO, SHINOA?
...
DUH! WE GO RESCUE HIM! RIGHT?
WITH GUREN IN FRONT AND US COMING IN BEHIND, IT'LL BE LIKE A PINCER ATTACK!

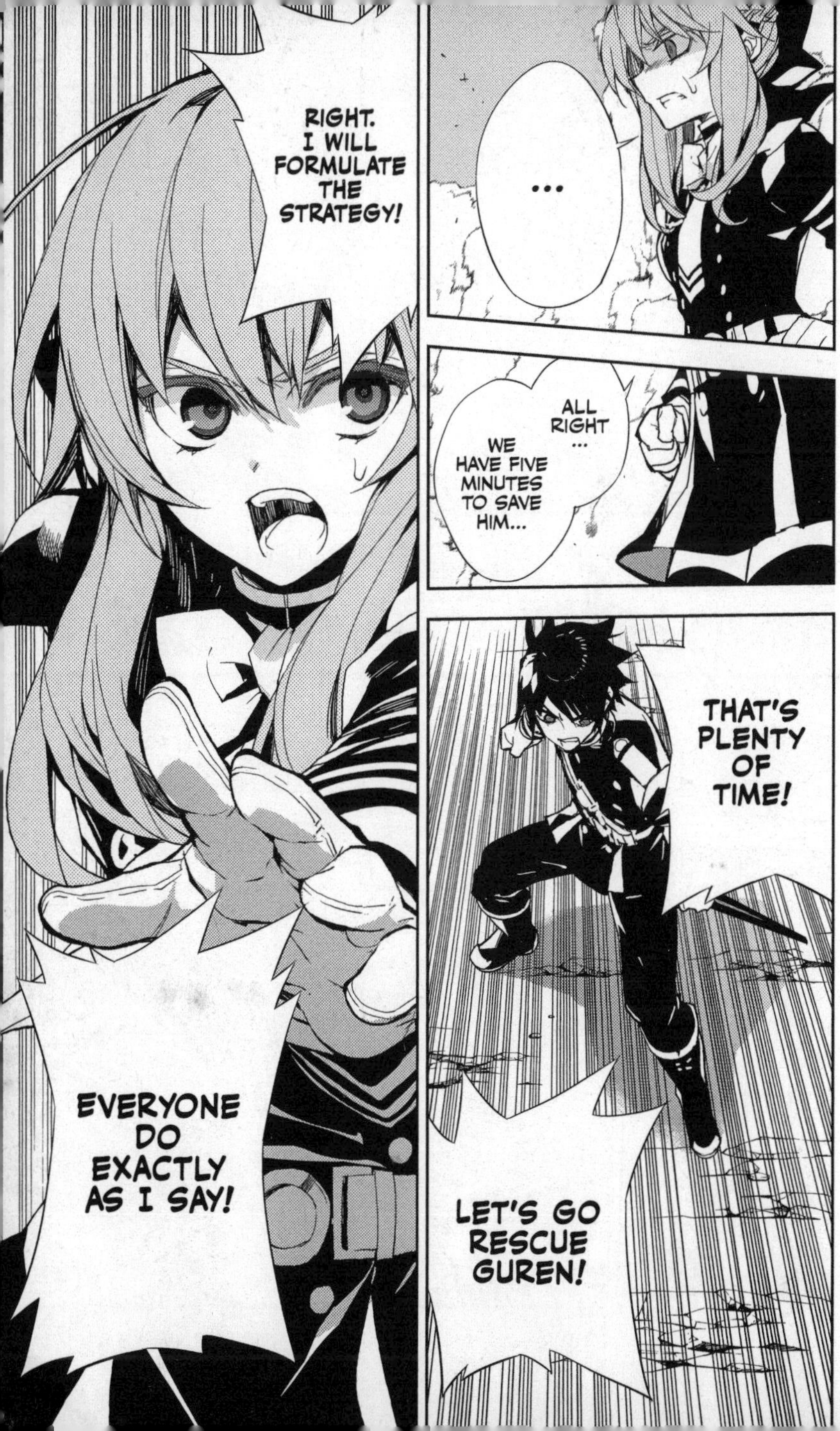
...
ALL RIGHT ... WE HAVE FIVE MINUTES TO SAVE HIM...
THAT'S PLENTY OF TIME!
LET'S GO RESCUE GUREN!
RIGHT. I WILL FORMULATE THE STRATEGY!
EVERYONE DO EXACTLY AS I SAY!

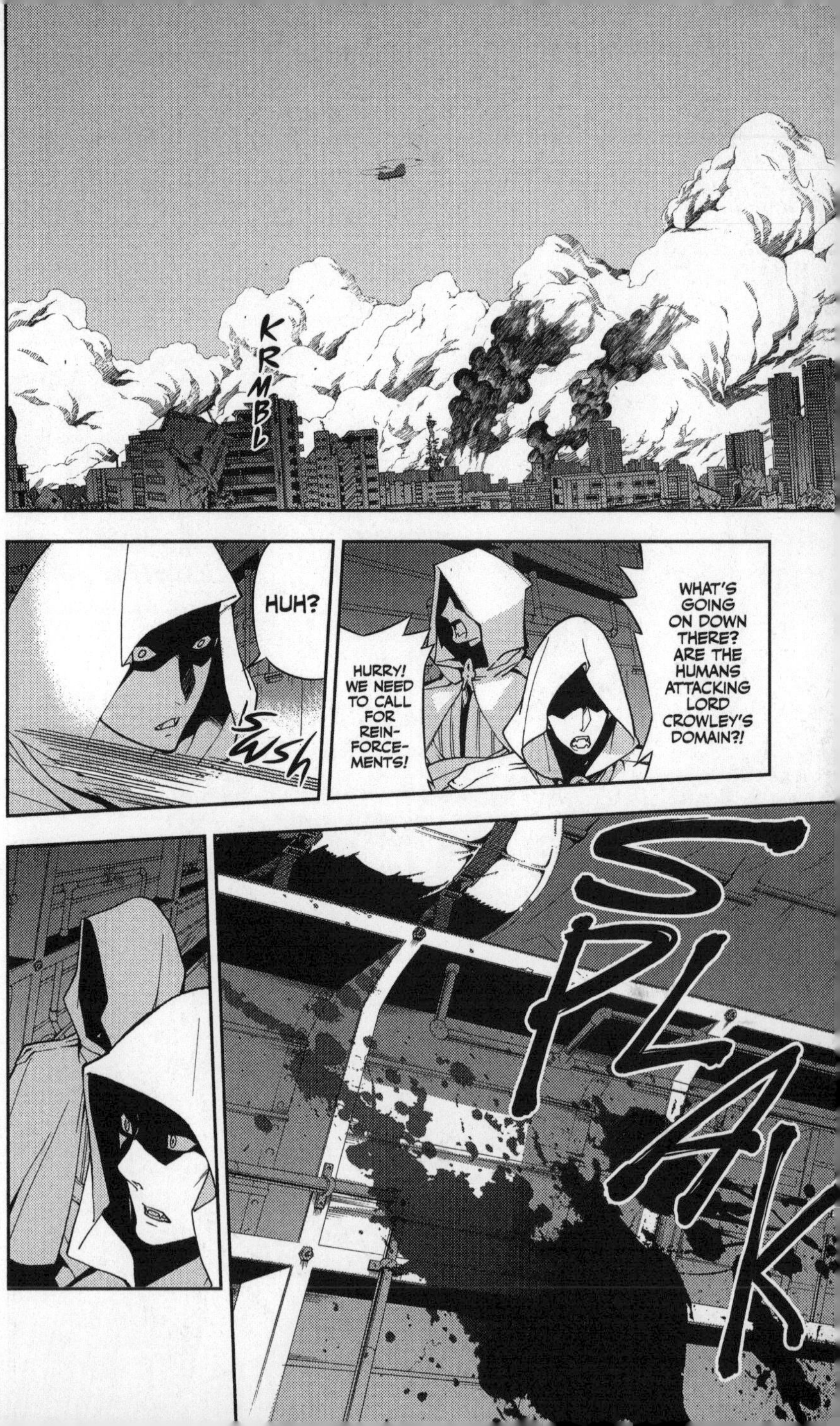
KRMBL
WHAT'S GOING ON DOWN THERE? ARE THE HUMANS ATTACKING LORD CROWLEY'S DOMAIN?!
HURRY! WE NEED TO CALL FOR REIN-FORCE-MENTS!
HUH?
SWSH
SPLAK

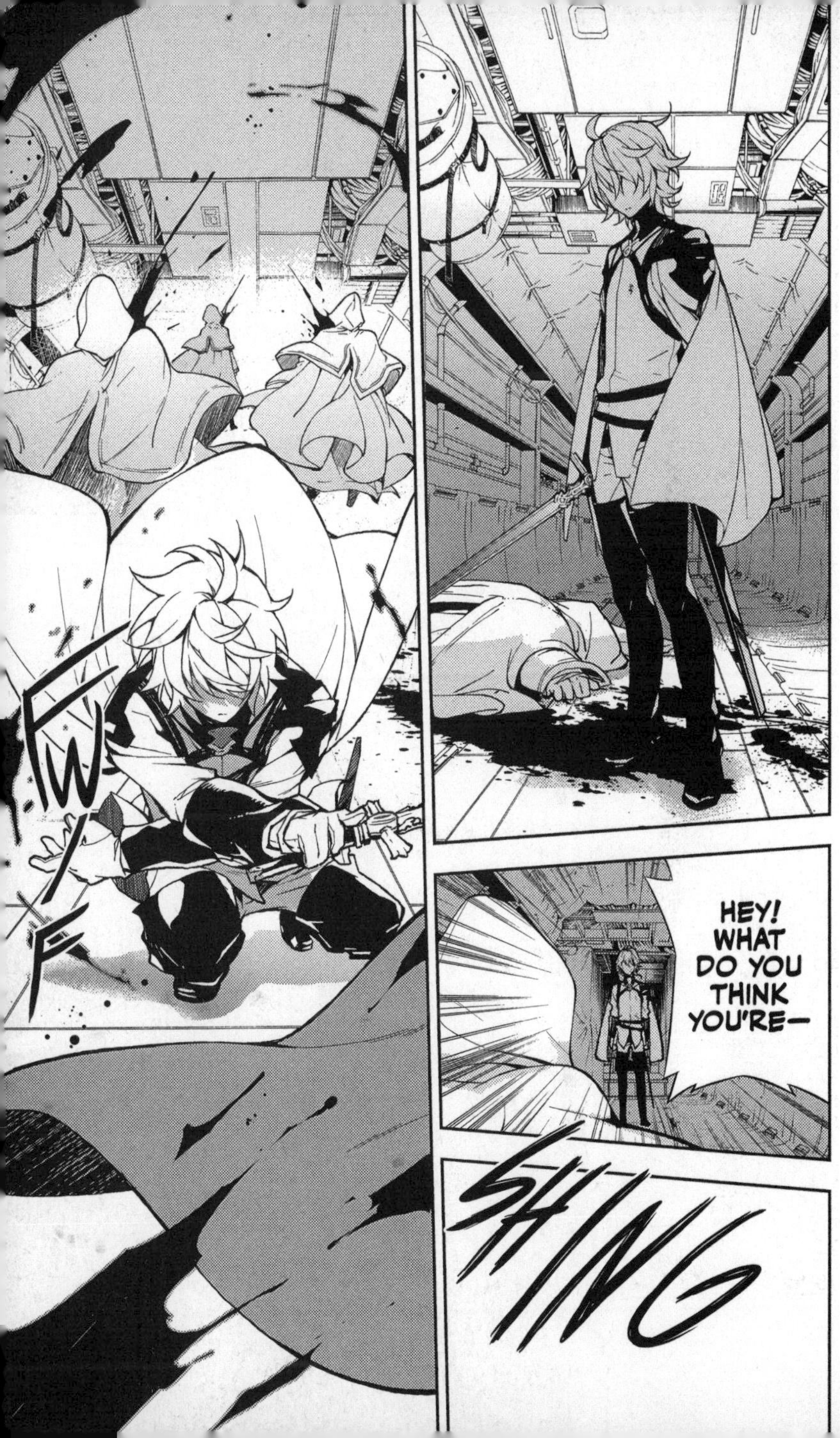
HEY! WHAT DO YOU THINK YOU'RE—
SHING
FWIFF

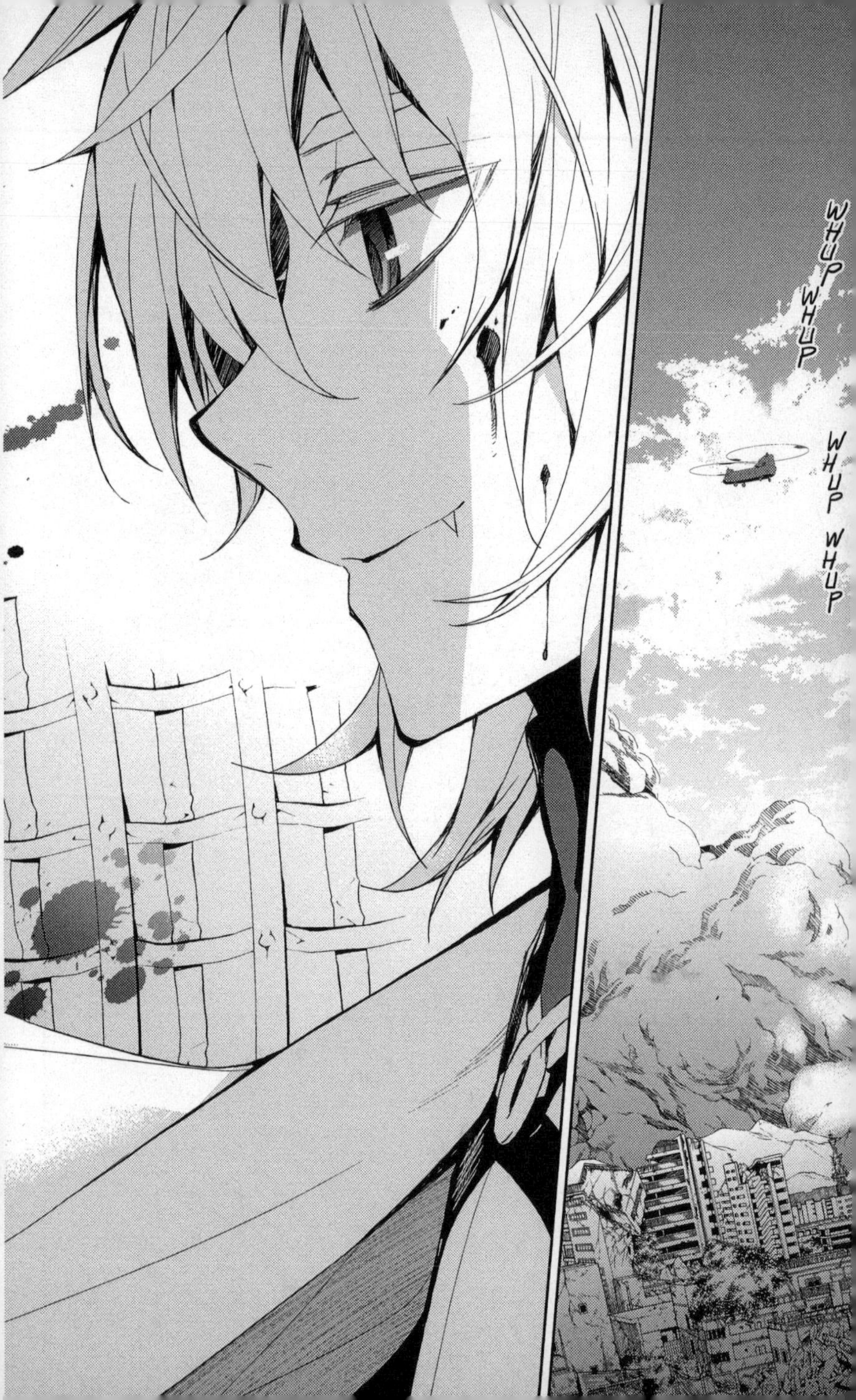
WHUP WHUP
WHUP WHUP WHUP

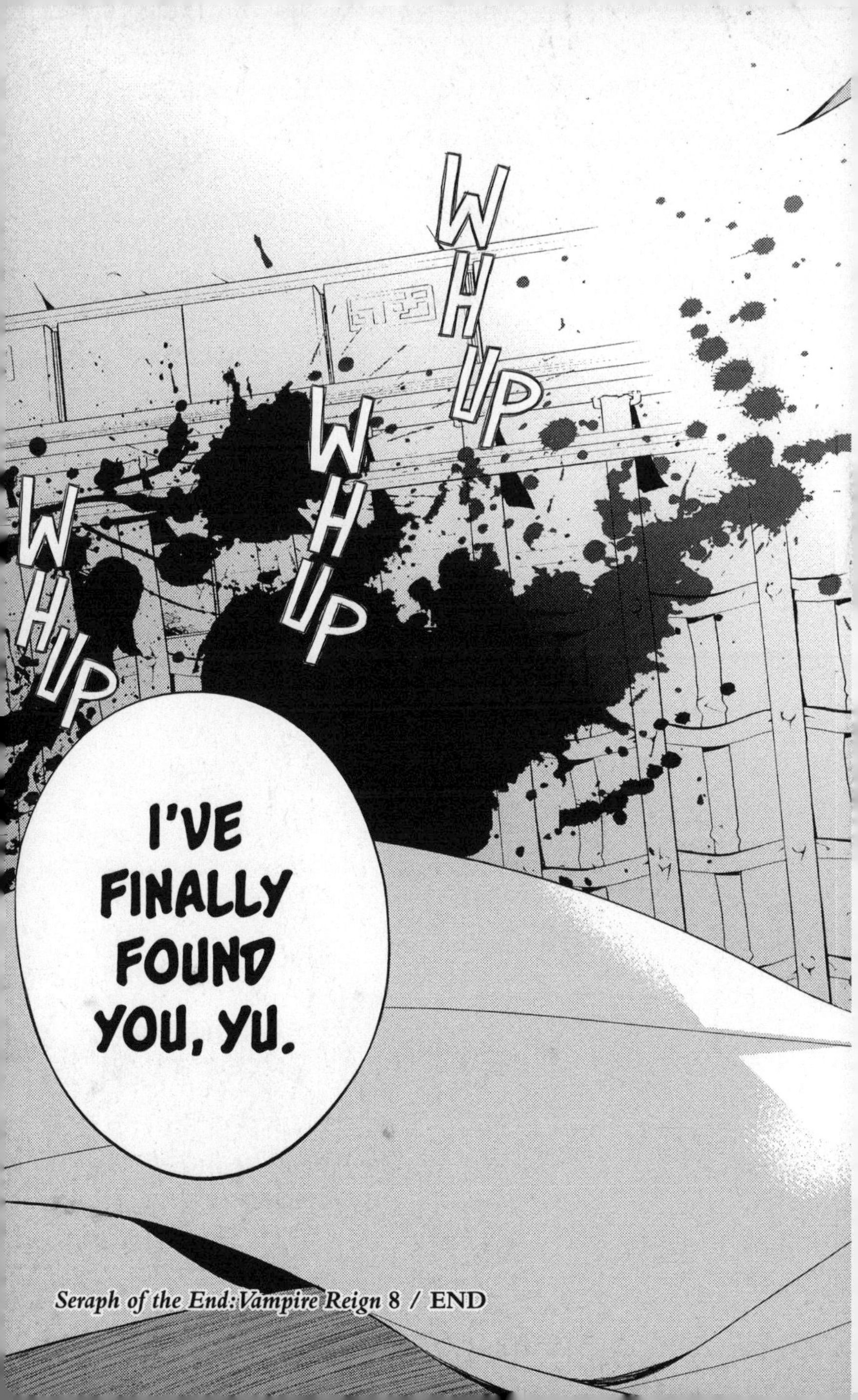
WHUP
WHUP
WHUP
I'VE FINALLY FOUND YOU, YU.

Seraph of the End: Vampire Reign 8 / END

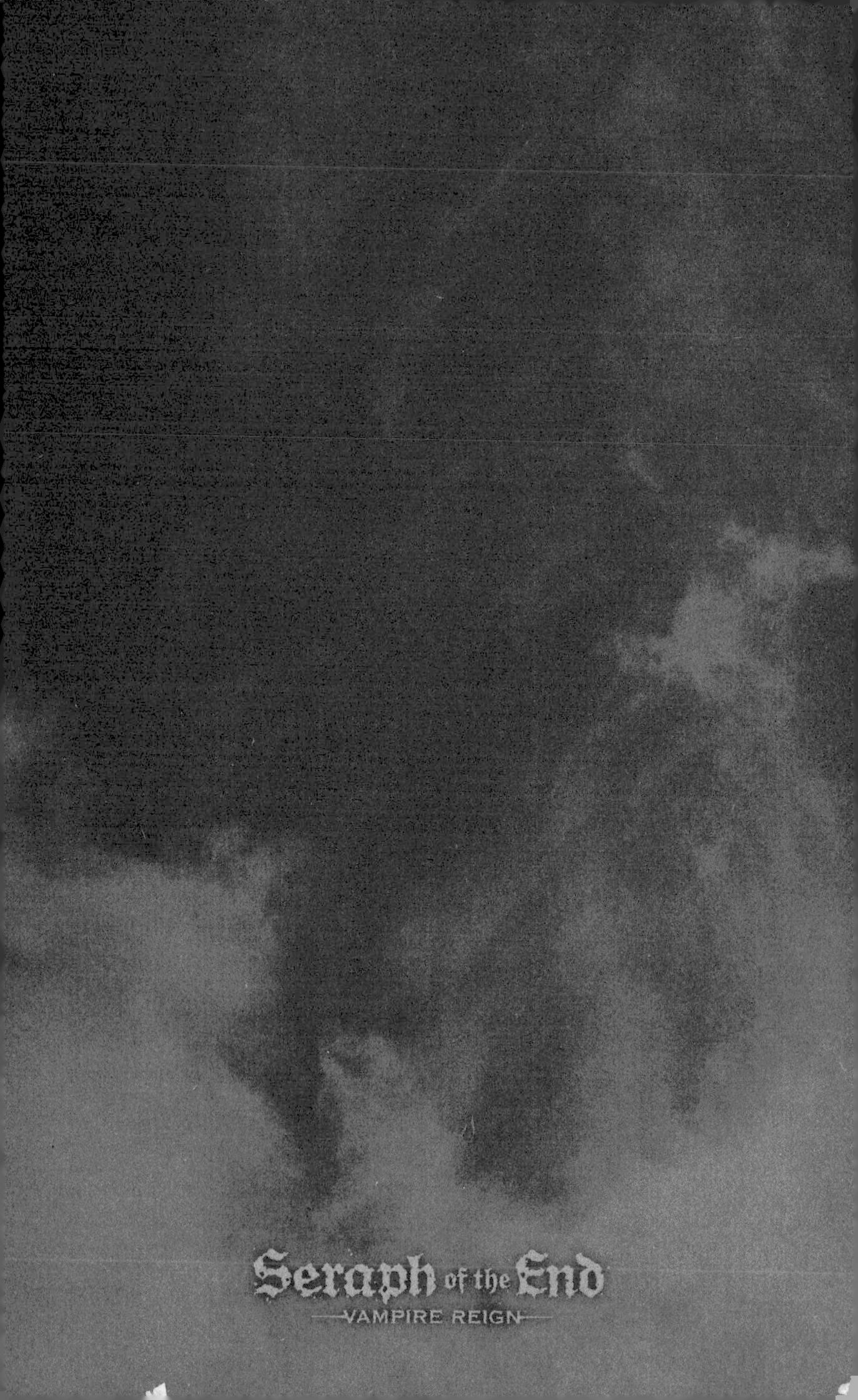
Seraph of the End
VAMPIRE REIGN

Guren Ichinose is supposed to be the *hero* who saved the world.
So why is he a lowly Lieutenant Colonel?

SHINYA: "WELL...THAT'S OBVIOUSLY BECAUSE HE HAS A BAD ATTITUDE."

GUREN: "SAY WHAT?"

GOSHI: "HE LOOKS LIKE A THUG TOO."

GUREN: "UH, JUST SO YOU TWO KNOW, I DON'T HAVE THE TIME TO LISTEN TO YOUR INSULTS—"

SHINYA: "YOU KNOW, I HEARD THE REAL REASON IS THAT THE HIGHER UPS FOUND OUT ABOUT YOUR PANTY-THIEVING DAYS."

GOSHI: "WHAT, SERIOUSLY?! DAMMIT! HOW COULD YOU GO OFF AND DO SOMETHING THAT FUN WITHOUT ME?! TAKE ME ALONG NEXT TIME!"

GUREN: "GO HOME. BOTH OF YOU. JUST...GO HOME."

GOSHI: "SO ANYWAYS...WHAT IS YOUR RANK AGAIN?"

GUREN: "HMM?"

GOSHI: "YOUR RANK. WHAT IS IT?"

GUREN: "JUST LOOK AT MY INSIGNIA. YOU KNOW WHAT IT MEANS."

GOSHI: "C'MON, MAN. JUST SAY IT. 'KAY?"

GUREN: "*SIGH* LIEU—"

GOSHI: "HA HA! I'M A COLONEL! I OUTRANK YOU!"

SHINYA: "HA HA! I'M A MAJOR GENERAL! I OUTRANK YOU TOO!"

GUREN: "AND YOUR POINT IS...?"

GOSHI: "YOU NEED TO SHOW US MORE RESPECT."

SHINYA: "I THINK I WANT SOME COFFEE. GO AND GET ME SOME COFFEE. THAT'S AN ORDER."

GUREN: "DO YOU BOTH HAVE A DEATH WISH?"

The truth of the matter is that Guren's rank isn't going to get any higher. Without him, the Japanese Imperial Demon Army would not have survived the apocalypse eight years ago. But since the centuries-old relationship between the the Hiragi Main Family and the Ichinose Junior Branch is so poor, his career won't advance any further. His junior branch heritage is holding him back.

SAYURI HANAYORI

Sayuri is one of the heroines in the novel series. She was even on the cover of one of the volumes! She is 24 years old in the manga and is the same age as Guren. Before the fall, she came to Shibuya as Guren's retainer. She was super uptight about keeping her master safe in a world ruled by the overbearing Hiragi.

The Hanayori family is an old, famous lineage devoted to serving the Ichinose family.

In the novels, I'm writing her as a happy 16-year-old earnestly in love. In the manga she has grown into a capable teacher for Yuichiro and the others. However, she still has a crush on Guren and acts girlish around him.

She is a really good cook. When Mr. Yamamoto did the first designs for her, he gave her a big chest. And so, I ended up writing her as having a big chest. Now that I think about it, she's the epitome of the perfect maiden. Unfortunately, in the novels, she has to contend with Shinoa's older sister...and Mahiru is a monster of a heroine. Will her love for Guren ever bear fruit?

GOSHI: "DUDE, WHY GO AFTER STUPID OLD GUREN IN THE FIRST PLACE WHEN YOU'VE GOT ME AROUND?"

SAYURI: "YOU SAID THE SAME THING TO YUKI YESTERDAY."

GOSHI: "UHH...WELL, ER, YEEEAH, BUT I MEAN, NO PRETTY GIRL COULD EVER GO WRONG STICKING WITH ME OVER GUREN. I DON'T HAVE THAT WHOLE DUMB 'GOTTA SAVE THE WORLD' HANG-UP HE HAS."

SAYURI: "..."

GOSHI: "PLUS, I'M NOT MANIPULATED BY MY SCARY, DEMON-POSSESSED EX-GIRLFRIEND."

SAYURI: "..."

GOSHI: "SERIOUSLY, WHAT GUY LETS THEIR FIRST LOVE DRAG THEM AROUND BY THE NOSE LIKE THAT? IT'S PATHETIC. THE WAY SHE HAS HIM DANCING TO HER EVERY WHIM MEANS HE'S GOTTA BE A VIRGIN. LIKE...FOR REAL. IN FACT, I THINK I'M GONNA CALL HIM 'CHERRY BOY' FROM NOW ON—"

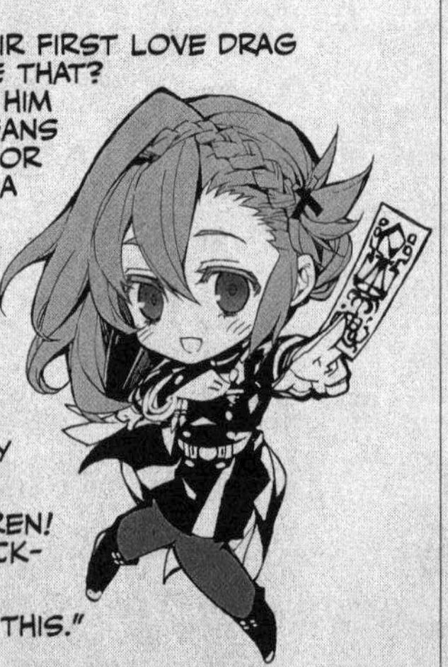

GUREN: "GOSHI! WHAT'RE YOU DOING HERE? YOU DON'T GET INTRODUCED THIS VOLUME. QUIT CRASHING EVERYBODY ELSE'S INTRODUCTIONS!"

GOSHI: "AHA! THERE YOU ARE! HI, CHERRY BOY!"

SAYURI: "EEP!! LIEUTENANT COLONEL GUREN! I, UM, I ACTUALLY THINK THAT NICKNAME IS KINDA CUTE—"

GUREN: "YOU SHUT UP AND STAY OUT OF THIS."

They've been adventuring together since before the fall of humanity. Guren's whole team are best friends with each other. Can't you tell?

SHIGURE YUKIMI

Just like Sayuri, Shigure is one of Guren's retainers. She's part of the Yukimi Family, another old and famous house that has served the Ichinose family for generations.

Sayuri calls her "Yuki."

Both she and Sayuri were trained from a very young age to serve Guren and, like Sayuri, she is incredibly fond of her master. If anyone insults Guren, she will try her best to kill them on the spot.

Born into a family that specializes in hidden weapons, she tends to integrate them with her spells. This is included in the manga timeline where Cursed Gear now exists.

She fought alongside Guren to preserve the Japanese Imperial Demon Army during the tumultuous period after the apocalypse. Since she is a retainer of the maligned Ichinose Junior Branch, she is also stuck with a low rank.

GOSHI: "IF YOU BECOME MY RETAINER, I'LL SEE TO IT THAT YOU'RE PROMOTED RIGHT AWAY!"

SHIGURE: "NOT INTERESTED."

GOSHI: "YEAH, BUT IF YOU GET PROMOTED—"

SHIGURE: "I AM NEITHER INTERESTED IN PROMOTIONS NOR YOU."

GOSHI: "OKAY, THEN WHAT ABOUT GUREN?"

SHIGURE: "LIEUTENANT COLONEL GUREN?!"

GOSHI: "MAN, GUREN'S RETAINERS DOTE ON HIM WAY TOO MUCH."

SHINYA: "DON'T WORRY. I'M HARSH ENOUGH ON HIM TO MAKE UP FOR ALL THAT DOTING. NOW THEN. GUREN?"

GUREN: "..."

SHINYA: "WHERE'S MY COFFEE?"

GUREN: "GET LOST. ALL OF YOU. NOW."

AFTERWORD

HELLO. I'M TAKAYA KAGAMI, AUTHOR AND SCRIPT WRITER FOR THIS SERIES.

VOLUME 8 OF THE MANGA IS GETTING RELEASED IN JAPAN IN THE MIDDLE OF QUITE A BIT OF CELEBRATION, REALLY. SEE, A DAY OR SO AGO THE FIFTH VOLUME OF *SERAPH OF THE END: GUREN ICHINOSE'S CATASTROPHE AT 16* (WHICH I AM WRITING FOR KODANSHA JAPAN'S LIGHT NOVEL LINE) WENT ON SALE. TODAY, THIS MANGA (BOXED TOGETHER WITH THE DRAMA CD, THE SCRIPT FOR WHICH I ALSO WROTE) GOES ON SALE. AND TOMORROW, THE ANIME STARTS AIRING ON TV!

SEE? LOTS OF CELEBRATORY THINGS GOING ON.

THE MAIN CHARACTERS ARE STARTING TO REALLY IMPACT EACH OTHER IN THE STORY.

YU, MIKA AND SHINOA HAVE NOW BEEN INTRODUCED IN THE NOVELS.

GUREN, SHINYA, GOSHI, MITO, SHIGURE, SAYURI, KURETO AND OTHERS ARE MAKING THEIR MARKS ON THE MANGA.

TRYING TO WRITE THE PAST AND THE PRESENT OF THE SAME STORY AT THE SAME TIME IN TWO DIFFERENT FORMS OF MEDIA FOR TWO DIFFERENT COMPANIES REQUIRES A BACK-BREAKING AMOUNT OF RECORD-KEEPING AND INFO MANAGEMENT. BUT THAT JUST MAKES IT ALL THE MORE WORTHWHILE TO WRITE! AT LEAST THAT IS WHAT I WROTE IN THE AFTERWORD OF THE NOVEL THAT WENT ON SALE YESTERDAY...

GEEZ! HAVING TO WRITE TWO AFTERWORDS IN A ROW DOESN'T LEAVE ME WITH ANYTHING RECENT TO TALK ABOUT!

SO I GUESS I'LL TALK ABOUT THE DRAMA CD.

IT CONTAINS A BRAND NEW STORY THAT I WROTE MYSELF!

WHAT HAPPENED WHEN MIKA WENT TO FERID'S MANSION TO OFFER THE VAMPIRE HIS BLOOD? WHAT WAS EVERYDAY LIFE LIKE FOR THE ORPHANS IN THE VAMPIRE CAPITAL? WHAT NEW AND ENTERTAINING WAYS DOES SHINYA COME UP WITH TO MAKE GUREN'S LIFE MORE DIFFICULT? I WROTE ABOUT ALL THAT AND MORE!

THE REGULAR EDITION OF THE MANGA HAS GUREN ON THE COVER.

THE LIMITED EDITION WITH THE DRAMA CD HAS MIKA AND YU ON THE COVER.

TRUE CONNOISSEURS WILL COLLECT ALL OF THEM SO YOU SHOULD DO IT TOO! AT LEAST THAT'S WHAT MY EDITOR SAYS.

RIGHT, EDITOR?

"RIGHT! WE HOPE THAT YOU WILL ENJOY THE HIDDEN STORIES BROUGHT TO LIFE BY FAMOUS VOICE ACTORS! AND, OF COURSE, AFTER THAT COMES—!!"

EXACTLY! THE ANIME IS STARTING!

IT'S KINDA TURNING INTO A REALLY BIG THING AND IT HAS BEEN A LOT OF WORK.

A LOT MORE VOICE ACTORS HAVE BEEN ANNOUNCED AND THERE ARE STILL MORE TO COME! HERE ARE THE ONES WHO HAVE BEEN ANNOUNCED SO FAR!

YUICHIRO HYAKUYA:	MIYU IRINO
MIKAELA HYAKUYA:	KENSHO ONO
GUREN ICHINOSE:	YUICHI NAKAMURA
FERID BATHORY:	TAKAHIRO SAKURAI
SHINOA HIRAGI:	SAORI HAYAMI
YOICHI SAOTOME:	NOBUHIKO OKAMOTO
SHIHO KIMIZUKI:	KAITO ISHIKAWA
MITSUBA SANGU:	YUKA IGUCHI
KRUL TEPES:	AOI YUKI
KURETO HIRAGI:	TOMOAKI MAENO
SHINYA HIRAGI:	TATSUHISA SUZUKI
CROWLEY EUSFORD:	KENICHI SUZUMURA
SAYURI HANAYORI:	ATSUMI TANEZAKI
SHIGURE YUKIMI:	YUI ISHIKAWA
NORITO GOSHI:	DAISUKE ONO
MITO JUJO:	YUU SHIMAMURA
ASURAMARU:	HIBIKU YAMAMURA
LACUS WELT:	TAKUMA NAGATSUKA
RENÉ SIMM:	YUICHIRO UMEHARA

AMAZING! LOOK AT THEM ALL!

I'M KINDA BURIED UNDER A TON OF DEADLINES, BUT I'M GOING TO KEEP TRYING MY BEST! I HOPE FOR YOUR CONTINUED SUPPORT!

—TAKAYA KAGAMI

A brilliant sketch of Yuichiro by the author!

TAKAYA KAGAMI is a prolific light novelist whose works include the action and fantasy series *The Legend of the Legendary Heroes*, which has been adapted into manga, anime and a video game. His previous series, *A Dark Rabbit Has Seven Lives*, also spawned a manga and anime series.

❝ Volume 8 is here! Since I needed to do a comment for the version of this volume that comes with the Drama CD too, here's my second comment!★ To those of you who haven't bought the version with the Drama CD yet—what are you waiting for? I wrote an original script for this! Plus the cover has Yu and Mika on it. So pick up both versions to enjoy Yu, Mika and Guren all together! ❞

★This version only available in Japan.

YAMATO YAMAMOTO, born 1983, is an artist and illustrator whose works include the *Kure-nai* manga and the light novels *Kure-nai*, *9S -Nine S-* and *Denpa Teki na Kanojo*. Both *Denpa Teki na Kanojo* and *Kure-nai* have been adapted into anime.

❝ It's been really busy lately with both the anime and the Drama CD coming out. Volume 5 of the novels just came out, and there was also a short one-shot bonus story in *Weekly Shonen Jump*. Check them out if you're interested. I hope you like them. ❞

DAISUKE FURUYA previously assisted Yamato Yamamoto with storyboards for *Kure-nai*.

Seraph of the End
—VAMPIRE REIGN—

VOLUME 8
SHONEN JUMP ADVANCED MANGA EDITION

STORY BY **TAKAYA KAGAMI**

ART BY **YAMATO YAMAMOTO**

STORYBOARDS BY **DAISUKE FURUYA**

TRANSLATION **Adrienne Beck**

TOUCH-UP ART & LETTERING **Sabrina Heep**

DESIGN **Shawn Carrico**

WEEKLY SHONEN JUMP EDITORS **Hope Donovan, Marlene First**

GRAPHIC NOVEL EDITOR **Marlene First**

Printed in the U.S.A.

Published by VIZ Media, LLC
P.O. Box 77010
San Francisco, CA 94107

10 9 8 7 6 5 4 3 2 1
First printing, March 2016

www.viz.com   www.shonenjump.com

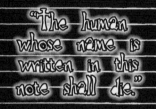

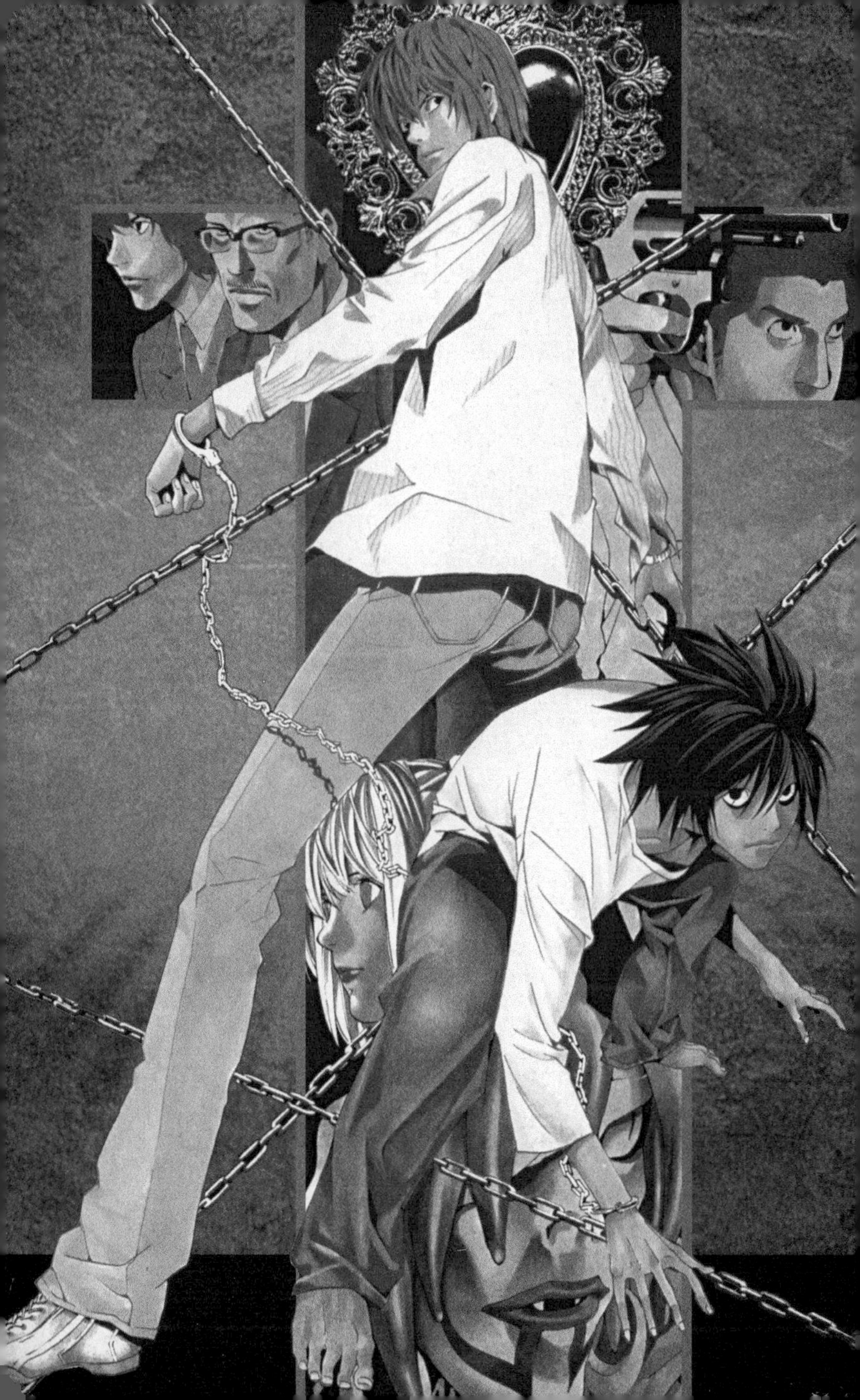

YOU'RE READING THE
WRONG WAY!

SERAPH OF THE END reads from right to left, starting in the upper-right corner. Japanese is read from right to left, meaning that action, sound effects, and word-balloon order are completely reversed from English order.

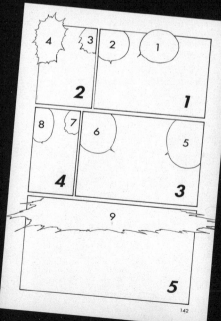